THE CELL BLOCK PRESENTS....

SOSA

THE PRICE OF POWER (BOOK ONE)

Published by: The Cell Block™

The Cell Block
P.O. Box 1025
Rancho Cordova, CA 95741

Website: thecellblock.net
Facebook/thecellblockofficial
Instagram: @mikeenemigo
Corrlinks: info@thecellblock.net

SOSA: THE PRICE OF POWER
Copyright ©2023, by Lou Garden Price, Sr.

Cover Design: Mike Enemigo

Send comments, reviews, interview and business inquiries
to: info@thecellblock.net

For those who truly count: my sister Leana ("Prissy"), Chad, Selena, "LC" (LeAndre Christine), Lay'Anna, and *Scarface* fans worldwide.

Wherever death may surprise us,
Let it be welcome,
Provided that this, our battle cry,
May have reached some receptive ear,
And another hand may be extended,
To wield our weapons.

– Che Guevara

TABLE OF CONTENTS

CHAPTER ONE

La Hacienda de Sosa
Cochabamba, Bolivia
September 11, 1984, 8:30 a.m.

"Tony Montana is dead," came the hollowed-out-tree-sounding voice of Benny The Skull over his satellite telephone to his boss, Alejandro César Dalmacci Sosa.

Sosa replaced the red-colored receiver of his highly-secretive "eleven line" and turned his attentions back to his still-panting, perspiration-drenched, supermodel wife. They were making love inside of their palatial master bedroom, atop shimmering gold silk sheets on an ultra-king-sized bed (measuring 14'×14'). Sosa delicately spread her out before him, kissing her full, beautiful lips, touching her velvety soft, slick, warm skin. Their passion for one another, their love and attraction, was evident by the way their breathing became as audible as the sounds of their mingled sighs and moans.

The love they were making was ravenous, hungry, intense, and wild, an uninhibited feast of love, flesh and sex.

Once it was over, her body limp, he held his Bolivian dream in his arms, stroking her long black tresses, kissing her and whispering his love for her until she fell asleep, purring like a panther cub. Sleep, however, eluded her husband – the 35-year-old boss of *La Corporación Mafia Cruzena*. He got up, showered, dressed into a charcoal-black sweatsuit, and walked out onto his bedroom balcony.

Deep in thought, his dark eyes scanned outward across the brightly-illuminated grounds of the mega-opulent Andean mountaintop fortress. His conscience repeatedly flashed and highlighted the hit he had ordered on the infamous U.S. crime boss Tony Montana.

"*Caracortada es muerto,*" Sosa whispered in Spanish. Then, adding in English, "Scarface is dead."

As the wee hours of the morning dragged on, like a freight ship losing steam, he paused to observe more than fifteen macaws suddenly land around the balcony just seconds after he had walked out there. Some of them perched atop the enormous cage in the corner to his left, others chose to stand clumsily on the balcony floor. *They must have been spooked in order to move around like this in the dark hours,* Sosa thought as he pulled open the door of the cage for the nervous birds. He leaned forward with both hands on the balcony railing, stopping to listen to the nocturnal sounds of the deep green forests that surrounded the fortress in the near distance. The shrill screams of a spider monkey high up in a tree served as a warning to others in its troop that there was a strange scent in the air that all of them needed to be concerned about. Perhaps it was a stealthy jaguar, a giant anaconda, or some other carnivore out hunting for a meal.

The first warning came from the spider monkey, followed by others in the troop. But then their screams became infectious and it escalated with various other animal species in the area. And, just like that, the entire forest came alive – as if in some strange way all the mountain creatures were aware that their lives depended on their loud calls and hysterics for survival.

Animals looking out for other animals, Sosa quietly acknowledged as the noise settled down.

Threat averted, thought Sosa.

Even though it was only 3:50 a.m., the wee hours of the morning, Sosa began his rigorous morning workout with warm-ups. At 35 years old, he was in better physical shape than some professional boxers. He started out with 1,000 jumping jacks to warm up. He performed five sets of those with 200 repetitions of each and no more than twenty seconds of rest between each set. Next, he moved into the more challenging U.S. Navy Seal-style exercises, beginning with the classic *standing 8-count,* better known as *burpies.*

During these maneuvers he realized that he felt genuine remorse for having Tony killed. Not only had Tony made a couple of hundred million for himself over the last few years but he had also generated close to a billion dollars for Sosa's organization – *La Corporación Mafia Cruzena.* No amount of sex with Yesenia, or physical training, could suppress the remorse he felt that he had killed a friend. But these would probably help to relieve the mental pressures of his other concerns ...

"Orlando Gutiérrez is still alive," he whispered the name and a sickly feeling threatened to derail his thought processes.

When he had completed ten sets of 25 burpies, he re-entered the 16th-century Roman Palace-style bedroom, kissed Yesenia's bare buttocks, and then boarded the elevator en route to the full-sized sports complex located in the underground level of the six-plex palace. Once there, he spent an hour sparring with members of his private army (Buro, Ivan, Lucho, Felipé, Edgar, Raquel, Coca, and many others were already down there). Maximum-level physical combat training was a daily requirement for Sosa's people (e.g., hitmen, soldiers, smugglers, pilots, et cetera). He led by example and took only Sundays off.

To complete the workout, Sosa dove into the outdoor swimming pool and swam ten laps. When he climbed out of the pool, he was met by his six huge Presa Canarios. He spoke to the dogs like one would to a group of ordinary men, while four heavily-armed soldiers stood nearby. One of the dogs, a 160-pound beast named *"Noses,"* had recently picked a fight with a young, adult male jaguar that had crept into the compound to prey on one of Sosa's ranch animals to eat. (Sosa owned vicuñas, llamas, chickens, horses, ducks, pigs, beef and dairy cattle, goats, sheep, and thousands of Andean bird species. The birds had naturally selected the fortress as their home/safe haven and since childhood Sosa had a deep affection toward birds so he encouraged them to stay by feeding them and building for them a number of elaborate zoo-like aviaries.)

Sosa and many of his other men and women had a lot of respect for Noses and the other Presa Canarios because all of them were proven killers. They had been born in Spain, pure-bred straight out of the Spanish Queen's kennels. Sosa had spent over $20,000 on each of them and their training. Without question he had gotten his money's worth.

Sosa re-entered the massive six-plex (or sextet) from the front entrance after briefly conversing with some of his armed men and women. As he walked up the walkway of the newly-constructed mountain fortress, he had to pause and appreciate the majestic beauty of it. His multi-talented wife of six years, Yesenia Dulce (or "Yessi" as she was affectionately called), was responsible for the architecture and design of the one-of-a-kind masterpiece that stood before him. She had dubbed it "the Pentagon" because of how it was built. Each of the six gargantuan "forts" was an individual mansion – the first one was occupied by the Sosas and their housekeeping staff. The other five mansions were occupied by Sosa's top men, their own housekeeping staff, and others.

It was much easier to refer to the palatial structure as a *six-plex,* each of them sharing one massive foundation, connected by beautiful 3rd-story steel, marble, stone, concrete and glass bridgeways. And deep in the mountainous earth below, they were connected even more intimately with a maze of underground tunnels and other well-protected secrets and mysteries. The six-plex structures were situated in

4

a circular sextetonal formation with the Sosa mansion facing what was considered to be the front of the estate, symbolizing his power position inside of *La Corporación Mafia Cruzena.*

"A sextet has *six* sides," Sosa had told his wife during the early construction stages when she had first nicknamed it "the Pentagon." "A pentagon has *five* sides." (He'd indicated by holding up five fingers.)

"So what?" she retorted. "It's my design. If I call it *'the Square'* then it's still a sextet. If I call it *'the Octagon'* it'll still be a sextet. I call it what I want."

He'd chuckled and held up his hands in a *"Don't shoot"* gesture. "Okay, okay. I back off. *'The Pentagon'* it is."

From an aerial view the sextet appeared to be one awesome home, an out-of-this-world mountaintop palace with six identical structures. It reminded one of some Disney-World-like fairytales where the castle floated somewhere high above the clouds, accessible only by a magic carpet or some other sort of sorcery or witchcraft.

In the "eye," or the center, of the units' "backyard" area – aside from the exquisite bush and flower gardens – there was an enormous Olympic-sized swimming pool with a 30-foot waterfall built by Italian masters. In the swimming pool's interior were 12-inch by 12-inch blue and white checkered tiles, also built by masters and designed by Yesenia who had an obvious love affair with marble designs. The palace floors, bedrooms, stairways, hallways, and bathrooms were all full of it. Wherever marble floors could not be seen, there were tons of gleaming granite in its place.

To describe one of the sextet's individual mansions was to describe them all because they were each identical. Architectural design work and home plans were second nature to Yesenia. When Sosa had given her the green light to build the fortress, she had met with her team of masters to create the plan. She had chosen to forgo a conventional Spanish villa or mansion. Sosa had given her an unlimited budget on absolute reconstruction of the main house and all other outbuildings on top of and around the mountain he owned. Yesenia had razed the previous structures and replaced them with her own architectural phenomenon – the Pentagon.

"All the truly great men throughout history built *something* to symbolize who they were," Yesenia had told him as the construction had gotten underway, "who they wanted others to know them for and also who their families were. You are *Alejandro César Dalmacci Sosa.* César is a name of greatness, of power, of strength, immortality, and wealth. This palace, this mountaintop fortress, will showcase your wealth and complement your closest men."

Sosa had men closer to him than brothers who had grown up with him and were each extremely important figures in the organization. It made sense that each man had his own place, his own private castle, his own sense of meaning, power and wealth …

Alejandro César Dalmacci Sosa,
Nancho Sebastián Lugo Toro,
Tatico Arturo Lugo Toro,
Javier Roberto Lugo Toro,
Vicenté León Romero Toro, and
Rafael Peluché Porras Amayo.

Six *La Corporación* figures, six homes, one ultimate boss: Sosa. Thus, it was Yesenia who had urged her husband to "give" his closest men their own homes. Prior to "the Pentagon," Sosa's men had lived with him in the Sosa mansion.

"Reward them for their loyalty," Yesenia had advised him. "They'll never *ask* you to give them their own castles. You're like a *Zeus, Ra,* or some other mythical god to them. They know that they are your subordinates but they are still *men.* Allow them to feel such awesome power. Then … *push* them to choose wives who will fill up their castles with kids.

With your high political connections, it would be simple to find for them fifteen- or sixteen-year-old virgins who would love to marry them."

Yesenia's wish for the "virgins" would be put on hold but not their Andean mountaintop fortress and all of its outer buildings. After eighteen months, countless tons of building supplies, machinery, imported labor forces and over $200M, here it was.

When entering from where Sosa was currently standing out front, there were stylish, all-white, glazed steps that led to a veranda with enormous Barcelona Castle double-entry front doors. Having consulted with Sosa and his men on security concerns, Yesenia had focused on creating a fashionable but impenetrable fortress of bullet- and bomb-proof glass, walls, doors and roofing. Every security angle was thought through carefully, including "panic rooms," vaults, underground bunkers, escape routes/tunnels, and emergency equipment.

Sosa walked through the electronically-controlled front doors and into the grand foyer. From there, one could see the magnificent view of the outdoor ("backyard") pool area through the large pocket sliding-glass doors far across/through the living room. It was amazing how big, airy, and spacious each room was. A beautiful black-and-red Spanish marble and stone fireplace with built-in shelves graced the right wall of the living room. To the left was a wall-mounted 42-inch television screen. Far opposite of the television wall (near the living room exit) there was an arched opening situated next to an all-purpose walk-in wet bar. Before walking out of the living room, Sosa stopped to remove a cold jar of orange juice from the bar's refrigerator.

Beyond the arched opening was an oversized family room with a state-of-the-art home entertainment center and another fireplace (this one was made from white and charcoal-black stones which sparkled underneath the light). Across the room, to the far left, large pocket sliders offered access to the sizeable covered lanai and outdoor kitchen area.

The houses each had a total of five floors, four of which were above-ground. Sosa used the east-wing elevator to return to Yesenia, who was now wide awake, conducting a conference call with her business partners at her new company, *Dulce Fashion & Design Co.* The spacious 4th-floor master suite included a private corner office for her business activities. Just inside the entrance to their huge bedroom there was a step-down sitting area which gave one or both of them the perfect spot for resting or relaxing away from anyone else in the house. Sosa undressed there prior to heading to the shower.

The luxurious master bath featured an oversized tub as the focal point of the room but even more noteworthy was the his-and-her toilets and the 24-carat bidet in a private stall for Yesenia's personal hygienic use. There was also another fireplace made of black and gold marble and stone. Next to it were two large walk-in closets and, last, his-and-her dressing areas, which completed the outstanding bathroom design.

Sosa loved the relaxing stream of the six shower heads (one to the left, one to the right, one hit his back, the other his front, the fifth came from the ceiling and the last from the shower floor). Yesenia joined him there and washed him herself, kissing and massaging him all over.

"*Dios mio,*" she said, seeing how large and swollen his manhood became as she soaped it with both of her hands. "What a *man* you are ..."

She knew how much a warrior like him needed servicing after a workout. Not only that but the things he'd done to her with his tongue last night deserved reciprocating. To complete her hand services, she took him inside her mouth and sword-swallowed him while she drove him wild with her hands and fingers in the most intimate of ways. What a sweet, wicked, innocent imp she appeared to be, Sosa thought as his knees buckled and he slid down to the soft black rubber mat on the shower floor, out of breath, as she milked him to pleasurable emptiness.

"Come, my love." She helped him up and put him to bed, completely nude. She covered him up and massaged him to drowsiness. "I'll get your suit ready and set the clock for one hour and fifteen minutes. Sleep, *Papi.*"

Eighty minutes later he was coming out of his closet dressed in an all-white custom-made silk Armani suit, gray shirt, black tie, and alligator shoes, also by Armani. He knew Yesenia had been busy laying out the groundwork for her company, so she could always be found in her office; that's exactly where she was, donning one of his shirts, on the telephone, speaking Italian with an Italian silk/fabric manufacturer.

Sosa mouthed the words, "*I'll be in my study,*" to her and exited.

There were 4,000 feet of living space on each of the four above-ground level floors. The top floor (or 4th floor) was the master suite, or *penthouse* suite. Beneath it, on the 3rd floor, was "the nursery" for their one-year-old son, Juan Carlos Sevilla Sosa, aka "JC" or "Juanito." There were four bedrooms that had been as lavishly furnished as all the others but contained double beds for the household staff: the cook, the nanny, Yesenia's personal assistant, and the housekeepers.

Each of the houses featured two elevators and a grand staircase. The grand staircase could not reach the basement level but the elevators could. Sosa used the east-wing elevator to descend down into the immense underground level. The basement, as it was most commonly referred to, featured the full-sized sports complex where he'd worked out earlier. It contained a basketball and racquetball court, a professional boxing ring, a weight-lifting court, a punching bag and speed bag, four wall-mounted large-screen televisions, a refreshment center and sitting area, a massage and therapy room, a heated swimming pool, Jacuzzi, and an endless inventory of sports and fighting equipment.

Walking out of the gym's double doors, down to the left, was the fully-stocked bar and media-game-home-theatre center. Further down to the right were the walk-in refrigerator-freezer units. Across the left from there was a soundproofed shooting range and arsenal. There were two other rooms at the west-wing end of the basement. To the left was the money room and vault with a German-made, highly-sophisticated, voice and fingerprint recognition system. And, last, to the right was an oversized office/library stylishly furnished to give it the comfortable look and feel of a study or den. This was the room where Sosa and his men planned most of the organization's strategies.

The study was as unique as it was highly secretive. It was one of several rooms that employees and guests were strictly forbidden to ever enter, under *any* circumstances. It took three keys to open its 500-pound reinforced steel doors. Sosa walked in and sat down at the huge presidential desk. To the right of where he sat was a row of mahogany bookshelves. To the ordinary human eye that's all it looked like: *book-lined shelves*. However, a black hardcover book that sat high on the fourth shelf, entitled *Plato's Phaedo,* was actually a lever that, when pulled, caused the "bookshelves" to push inwards. This was real-life *James Bond* versus *Get Smart* stuff.

Inside of the room, behind the book-lined wall, was a large enclosure with soft floor cushions. In the ceiling above were the mouths of two huge laundry door shafts such as the kind seen in large hotels. In case of an emergency (e.g., military, police, guerilla attack, shelling, fire, earthquake, etc.), the shafts were to be used for shelter and escape. The cushions were directly beneath the shafts to break the fall of those who may be jumping or sliding through them. Under the cushions, inside of the floor itself, was a trapdoor. Once opened, there was a concrete staircase which the escapees could walk down into and negotiate their escape through the five-foot-high, four-foot-wide tunnel systems running from the sextet and up through one of several "manholes" camouflaged around the mountain. Sosa and Yesenia were both fairly confident that a ground attack was highly unlikely due to the thousands of land and river mines that had been set up around their mountain fortress. The way their house had been built, if bombed or shelled from the air, they felt that they would have ample time for escape. Sosa's private army members were a highly-alert, well-paid, ruthless group of violent soldiers who had received superior training by some of the most sophisticated and notoriously deadly organizations on the planet: the Israeli Mossad, U.S. Navy SEALs, FARC, and the feared former Nazi Gestapo Klaus Barbie.

Sosa and his people were not worried. The same way Sosa spent money on his businesses and over-the-top, opulent lifestyle, he spent on weapons and a private army that knew how to use them. The Pentagon was literally a fortress eons ahead of its time. From its pile foundation (to keep it from sinking) to its massively thick, 30-feet-high, concrete and steel walls that surrounded it, to the bullet-proof/bomb-proof sextet itself. Sosa's home security arsenal was war-ready:

Anti-Air:
8	2x37mm Type 65s
20	2x20mm Derlikon K20s
24	HN-5 MANPAD surface-to-air missiles

Machine Guns:
300	M60s
300	FN MAG 60-20s
150	SIG MG 710-3s
200	Type 56 LMGs

Grenade Launchers:
150   Type 87 35mms
150   MM-1s
150   M79s
150   M203s

Shotguns:
300   Remington 870 and Remington 11-87s

Sniper Rifles:
100   Dragunov SVDs
100   Mauser mod. 86SRs
100   Steyer SSG 69 PIs

Assault Rifles:
100   5.56mms
100   Galil ARs
100   M4 AIs
100   Steyer Aug AIs
100   SA-80s
100   7.62mms
100   FN-FALs
100   SIG 542s
100   M-16 AIs

And more. Much, much, more. *La Corporación Mafia Cruzena*'s close alliance with former Gestapo Klaus Barbie made Sosa not only a buyer of weapons but also a dealer. Tanks, reconnaissance vehicles, armored personnel carriers, mortars, artillery, transport aircraft, and all of the additional equipment he had on hand was too lengthy to list. And that's not even mentioning his fleet of attack helicopters and a ready and able group of elite pilots who were expertly trained in air combat and logistical engineering. All were more than prepared to confront *any* threat to the mountain where Sosa was king.

No, they were not worried.

A few minutes after Sosa had sat down to ponder his next move, his closest men came walking through the door.

CHAPTER TWO

The Montana Estate
Coral Gables, Florida
September 7, 1984

Immediately following the epic fight she'd had with her husband, Tony, Elvira was ushered into a yellow taxicab by Manny Ray, despite her vociferous protests for him to leave her be. Manny, who was Tony's underboss, ignored her incessant ranting and calmly directed the taxi driver to take them to their mansion in Coral Gables.

"I don't need you, that bastard spick friend of yours – I don't need any of you!" she raged on between monster snorts of cocaine.

"But you need that cocaine," Manny spat back at her as she rubbed her already red, irritated nose. "*Look at you!* You prove him right, what Tony says. You *are* a junkie. No man wants a woman who's dead, doesn't wash, that smells. You put on perfume, make-up, brush the hair, but no shower."

"Screw you!" she yelled, slapping his face. "I do not smell!"

He laughed at her, rubbing the sting of the slap away as the cab driver observed them through the rearview mirror.

Manny shook his head, pitying her. "You are a has-been, hand-me-down, used-up, *former* supermodel with nothing left in you. A broken, empty shell of what was *once* a woman. Now, you are cold, dead, scornful, and full of flies

14

that are laying eggs in you. *That's* why you cannot get pregnant – maggots swarm your junkie vagina and devour the sperm. Think about it. What *Latina* you know that can't produce at least *four* babies in *three* years? You can't. That's what we're best known for. Making *muchachos*, and you can't give Tony even one. At *twenty-five*, man. You are cold and dead inside. A shame ..."

She stayed silent. Those chilling words burst something open deep down inside of her. Not being able to bear children brought on a pain different though as equally agonizing as losing a child. It was a pain that struck the heart and the very *womb* of a woman that only another woman could ever fully understand. After Manny's last words ... she'd been vitiated. The *viragos* was gone. She sat, as if in catatonia, staring out the window, looking but not seeing.

$$$$$

Upon their arrival at the Montana Estate, Manny immediately filled Chi Chi in about the restaurant incident.

"So what, they always fight," Chi Chi shrugged as they stood in the grand foyer of the mansion with several other henchmen. "Where's Tony? We got that thing to take care of."

"The thing in the Keys?" Manny half-heartedly asked as he picked up the foyer telephone and dialed a number. "The shipment?"

"The *shipment?*" Chi Chi frowned. "Nah, man. The South Beach thing with those crazy white girls with the pick-up truck."

"Oh! I can't ... Hello? Hey, Gina." Manny watched Chi Chi's face. "I'm on my way, baby."

"*Gina Montana?!*" Chi Chi exclaimed, an incredulous look on his face. "You still messing with her? Are you fuckin' crazy or what? You know how Tony is about her, bro."

15

"You worry too much, *chico*," Manny waved him off. "I gotta go … Oh yeah, before I forget. Elvira said she's leaving Tony. Again. She sounded serious. But the boss said let her go."

"All right," Chi Chi nodded, more concerned about Manny. "Be careful, Manolo. You're playing with fire."

$$$$$

Upstairs, Elvira wandered about aimlessly, smoking a joint, snorting cocaine, drinking scotch, chain-smoking cigarettes and plotting her next move. Feeling nauseous from the drugs and the booze, she ran into her bathroom and retched several times but could not vomit. She chewed on *Tums* to try to settle her stomach and then went back into her bedroom, feeling terrible.

She was still reeling from the public humiliation and disrespect Tony had unleashed upon her at the restaurant. They'd had more fights than Jake LaMotta during the three years of their being married, but never had Tony displayed such an open hatred and contempt for her. His words, and Manny's for that matter, had crushed her hard and cut her deep down to the gristle. She felt as if she'd been thrown into a meat grinder, reduced to sawdust, and burnt to ashes. Even in her highly inebriated state of mind, she could recall Tony's ruthless tirade verbatim:

Tony: Is this it? Is that what's it's all about, Manny? Eating, drinking, snorting, fucking? Then what? You're fifty and you got a bag for a belly and tits with hair on 'em and your liver's got spots and you're looking like these rich fuckin' mummies in here? Is that what it's all about?

Manny: It's not so bad, Tony, could be worse …

16

Tony: ... Is that what I worked for? With these hands? Is that what I killed for? For this? (Turning his gaze stonily on Elvira) *A junkie??? I gotta junkie for a wife? Who never eats nothing, who wakes up with a Quaalude, who sleeps all day with black shades on, who won't fuck me 'cause she's in a coma?*

Manny: Tony, you're drunk.

Tony: ... Is this how it ends? And I thought I was a winner. Forget it, man, I can't even have a freaking kid with her. Her womb is so polluted, I can't even have a fucking little baby!

Elvira: (reacting, threw her plate of food on him) *You sonofabitch! You fuck! How dare you talk to me like that! You call yourself a man!? What makes you so better than me? What do you do? Deal drugs? Kill people? Oh, that's just wonderful, Tony – a real contribution to human history. You want a kid? What kind of father do you think you'd make, Tony? What kind of stories are you going to tell the kid before he goes to sleep at night? You going to drive him to school in the mornings, Tony? You really think you're still going to be alive by the time he goes to school, Tony? You're dreaming, Tony, you're dreaming!*

Tony: Sit down before I kill you.

Elvira: You think of yourself as a husband, too, Tony. But did you ever stay home without having six of your goons around all the time? I have Nick the Pig as a friend! What kind of life is that, Tony? What kind of life is that? Oh, Tony don't you see what we've become? We're losers, honey, we're not winners, we're losers ...

Tony: (softly) *Go on, get a cab home, you're stoned.*

Elvira: No, I'm not stoned, Tony. You're stoned. You're so stoned you don't even know it.

Tony: All right, I'm stoned. Manny.

Manny: (reaching for her arm) *Come on, baby.*

Elvira: (resisting) *No, no, you stay right there, Manny, I'm not going home with anybody. I'm going home alone …* (staring at Tony) *I'm leaving you. I don't need this shit anymore.*

Tony: Let her go! … Another Quaalude and she'll love me again in the morning.

If I hate who I have become, she was thinking now, *surely everybody else will.* She undressed and stood nude in front of the floor-to-ceiling bathroom mirrors. Still bombed out of her mind, she stared at the woman in the mirror. She was so thin that her body resembled an all-white, hollowed-out shell of a giant sea crab. A bag of bones. *Manny was right … I am an empty shell. I'm the walking face of death. The Grim Reaper.*

"So much for *Lesson Number Two: Never get high on your own supply,*" she said aloud as she took two more monster snorts of cocaine and laughed at her cold humor.

Wearing only a see-through Oscar de la Renta robe, she sat on the edge of her and Tony's bed and picked up the telephone. At first she'd forgotten who it was she'd wanted to call … then it came back to her. A Maryland number, the state where she'd been born: (310)547-3865 …

The deep voice of a man: "Hello?"

Hearing the voice made her inhale as a reflex. "Daddy."

There was a pause. "*Elvira?* Is that you, honey?"

She began to sob. "Why'd you do this to me?"

"Because ..." he began but stopped himself. "I love you, baby. Come home. I love you ... I need you."

She replaced the telephone receiver back into its cradle. She was contemplating suicide. She hated her life, herself, her husband, Choppy, Frank Lopez, her mother, her father ... everything. As she retrieved the solid nickel .25 caliber semi-automatic Phoenix Arms pistol Tony had given to her, profound bits and pieces of what she had experienced in her early years came flashing back through her mind like a videotape on fast-forward. As the horrible thoughts flashed, she stared at the shiny little gun until she noticed how bad her hands were shaking.

Returning to the mirror, she looked at herself and began to speak. "Look at you, Elvee ... you've come too far in twenty-five years for it to end by your own hand. You were born in hell. Your mother never loved you. Your father *married* you ... and he's a mass murderer. You can make it past this shit. *You can make it ... You can make it ... You can make it ...*"

She had no plan but she did have what she'd always had: her own mind. And when a woman set her mind to do something, there was no stopping her. Elvira took a quick shower to try to sober up and then she dressed in Jordache jeans and a Ralph Lauren pullover sweater. With her thoughts now collected, she telephoned a car service. The dispatcher estimated fifteen to twenty minutes before the car would arrive.

"Please be sure he knows I'm going far away up north," she warned the dispatcher. "And I tip well."

She packed up a Louis Vuitton carry-on suitcase with all of her most important paperwork and travel documents. She knew she would need a lot of cash but she also had the presence of mind to be careful. Tony had a floor safe inside of his walk-in closet which she knew the combination to. Inside of it, in 30 neat stacks of one-hundred-dollar bills, was

$300,000. She took all of it and placed it in the secret bottom compartment of the carry-on case.

She hesitated, paranoid that Tony or one of his goons would catch her. She was about to close the safe but held the door open mid-way. *He'll kill me over taking these safety deposit box keys,* she thought. But that was only the adrenaline pumping its confounding chemicals through her veins (along with the booze and narcotics). Her hands, however, were already moving, her mind locked in.

Screw it.

She raided the safe of the safety deposit box keys; each had an identifying tag on it to identify which bank the key belonged to. Elvira knew each bank by heart since Tony had entrusted her to rent each of the 40 safety deposit boxes. Last, she lifted from the safe a stack of yellow manila files that contained all of Tony's financial information and holdings.

"Oh, fuck," she whispered as she read several of the labels on the files: *Zurich; Caymans; Panama; U.S. Bonds; Property.* "I'm dead. I'm so dead."

Not even bothering to look inside of them, she stuffed everything inside of the carry-on's concealed bottom. She then filled the bag to bursting with underwear, clothing, cosmetics, and other personal effects. She lit up a cigarette and put on a stylish jacket. Pausing to gaze around at the opulent bedroom, she picked up the carry-on case and walked downstairs.

Chi Chi, Nick the Pig, and several other of Tony's heavily-armed men eyed her curiously as she walked past them. Suddenly, she stood still.

"You're not going to try to stop me?" She looked back at the men.

"The boss said to let you go," Chi Chi shrugged. "So, go."

She nodded slowly. "Why so many new faces?"

"Ah, you know Tony," Nick the Pig said. "Paranoia."

"What's in the bag, Elvira?" Chi Chi wanted to know. He stood up, chewing on a toothpick.

She faced him unblinkingly. "Panties, bras, make-up – and a gun."

Chi Chi stared at her, then at the bag.

Her heartbeat was in her own ears.

A horn was blowing loudly outside.

"Your boss said to let me go, Chi Chi," Elvira said in a forceful, demanding tone. "Not to try intimidating me nor to try to feel me up! If you want, we can stand right here and I'll tell him you're writing your own policy."

Chi Chi took the toothpick out of his mouth. "Bye, Elvira. Have a bad trip."

"Yeah, later. Or never."

$$$$$

She climbed into the plush backseat of the waiting black limousine. "They told you I wanted to go upstate?"

The chubby driver in the white button-up shirt nodded and drove off down the driveway. "Tank's filled and ready to go, ma'am. Where to upstate?"

She could not chance standing around at Miami International Airport. The moment Tony caught on that she had stolen a great deal of his cash and securities files, he would stop at nothing to come after her with everything he had.

"Do you know how to get to Orlando International Airport?" she asked him.

"Yeah. I know it very well."

"Take me to the front entrance of the Delta Airlines terminal." She leaned forward and gave him five one-hundred-dollar bills. "Please push it to the limit."

CHAPTER THREE

La Hacienda de Sosa
Cochabamba, Bolivia
September 11, 1984 9:00 a.m.

"Benny the Skull called." The 35-year-old Sosa eyed his men as he lit up a cigar with a solid-gold handmade Zippo-style lighter. His dark-brown, sinister eyes quickly checked the time on the standard wall Timex. "Aside from some wild Mexican bandits we used for the mission … no one died from our side. Did he call any of youse?"

"Yeah, he called." Nancho Sebastián "Chito" Lugo-Toro took one of the cigars from the desktop cigar case, fired it up, and sat nearest to the enormous black marble and granite presidential desk that Sosa sat behind, a king holding court with his top commanders. Nancho, the youngest of the three Toro brothers at 31, kept a cleanly-shaven head, a thin mustache, and he had a thing for expensive silk business suits with micro-pinstripes. Nodding his head over in his brother Tato's direction, Nancho said to Sosa, "Actually, Tatico got the call and got Javi and me on the internal intercom."

Tatico Arturo Lugo-Toro, age 33, was also a great dresser. He favored black clothing the most. Rarely ever did he wear a tie or the so-called "businessman button-up" shirts, due to his large muscular build, which had earned him the moniker "Black Hulk." Also, of the three Toro brothers, his skin was darkest, as brown as a coconut. Neither the Toro brothers nor

22

their cousin "Benny the Skull" (Vicenté León Romero-Toro) ever hesitated to acknowledge their African heritage, although each of them was born in Bolivia.

Tatico, or Tato, at first glance, was clearly a Black man in every sense of the term and (in comparison to the other Toros) blended in best with other Blacks. He was rough, battle-tested, and he had a deep, raspy voice. When he moved it was with the slow, cool, swagger of a grizzly bear looking for a challenge.

Javier Roberto Lugo-Toro, the eldest of the Toros, age 34, was meaner and bigger than all of the Toros. For brute fun, and to show off his immense power, he was known for wrestling and killing 1500-pound black bulls. At six feet, four inches tall and 265 pounds, he towered over Sosa, Nancho, Tato, and Benny. And while his brothers sported bald heads, Javier kept his hair long and slicked back in a ponytail.

In keeping with the strict rule of Sosa's upper echelon, all of his men dressed like businessmen because, on the surface, that was their legal occupation. Javier confidently thought that he was the one – out of everyone – who would win the "best-dressed" contest if ever there were to be one. Perhaps his confidence lay in the fact that women were drawn to him like bees to an open can of soda pop at a picnic.

"Benny the Skull, huh, boss?" Javier asked with gold teeth flashing to the far right of his eye-catching smile. (A few years back he had lost three teeth and suffered a broken jaw when a black bull's horn had pierced through his open mouth during a fight with the violent animal.) Javier sat down on the long black leather sectional against the entrance wall.

The group of men chuckled humorously.

Tato jokingly looked back at the entrance door as if Benny the Skull would suddenly come walking through it. "Why do we feel like he can actually hear that, even though he's still thousands of miles away?"

Every man in the room knew the answer to that question so no one replied to it. Benny's remarkable story reached back a very long time ago …

$$$$$

Muchos Años Antes

Vicenté León Romero-Toro, better known as Benny or Benito, was first cousin to Nancho, Javier and Tato. As children they had all grown up in extreme poverty down in the lowlands of Cochabamba. In 1956, when Benny was three years old, he'd lost his father, who'd been shot and killed over a gambling debt at a cock fight. A year later, in 1957, his mother had died of pancreatic cancer.

For three months Benny and his eleven-year-old sister, Juca Bélen Romero-Toro, had been living on the streets, in the fields, in abandoned railway cars, barns, buses – whatever they could find which, sadly, was much better than living in one of Bolivia's orphanages. After she'd been raped and beaten by a teenage trio of local bandits, Juca Bélen had taken her baby brother to their mother's sister's small home in Cochabamba.

Simona Mira Lugo-Toro, their aunt, had already been raising her own three sons at the time she'd welcomed Juca Bélen and Benito into her home. Those three sons were, of course, Javier, Tatico, and Nancho. Simona had been well aware of the many horror stories being reported about Bolivia's orphanage system (which is the main reason why Bolivian officials permit children to live with their incarcerated parents while they serve out their sentences). When Juca Bélen and Benito had appeared on her doorstep, she'd welcomed them in with no hesitation.

The house Simona Mira had back then was old and shabby, and even though they'd been poor, family was family. Simona Mira's husband had been killed during a basic training "live rounds" drill in the Bolivian Army, and his accidental death had devastated the Toro household. Simona Mira had learned very early on about the rape, so she had not been surprised when Juca Bélen had begun to show signs of being pregnant. Still, Simona Mira had counted on eleven-year-old Juca Bélen to help look out for the Toro boys while Simona Mira was away at work. Juca Bélen had been way beyond her years and had performed her part well. Subsequently, when she had barely been twelve years old, Juca Bélen had given birth to Catalina Lilli Romero Toro, aka La Gata Negra (The Black Cat).

Not far from where the Toros had lived, close to *Rio* Chaparé, was an affluential section of Cochabamba called *del Norte*. The Del Norte neighborhood was quiet, clean, and it boasted its wealth. They'd had paved roads, traffic lights, schools, restaurants, stores, nice cars, mansions, and more. Even the cats and dogs had looked healthier and much better-fed than Bolivia's impoverished. Simona Mira, who was a very good-looking petite woman, had landed a job at the Sosa Estate, the biggest and prettiest mansion in Del Norte. It did not matter in the least to Simona Mira that the Sosa name, for years, had been associated with shady *Mafioso* activities. Simona Mira had only been concerned with being able to feed, clothe, and house her own children as well as her deceased sister's children.

Don Haché Sosa had always said: *"I'll always trust the poor over the rich because the poor you helped are grateful to be out of poverty."* All of those he and Doña Rosalie had hired had been poor. Simona Mira had been checked out thoroughly prior to being hired. There had been days when Simona Mira had had no choice but to bring her children along to work with her. Alejandro Sosa's father (Silvestre Haché Chabán Sosa) had been a wealthy land baron and majority owner of Andes Sugar Corporation (or ASC), the world's fourth-largest sugar producer. Haché had not minded that Simona Mira had brought the kids along with her whenever she needed to do so. He liked kids.

For a man who was rumored to be the boss of the Bolivian Mafia, who was supposedly connected to the Russian, French and Italian Mafias, Haché sure had been kind to Simona Mira and her children back then. On the surface Haché had not *looked* like a dangerous man. (She had been too naïve to notice; after all, her business was housekeeping.)

For the first few months of working at the mansion, Don Haché had been making secret passes at Simona Mira, but she'd always politely declined while demurely swatting his hands away whenever they'd found their way up her short dress. The black-and-white maid uniform all of the maids had been required to wear had been so irresistible to Don Haché.

One day, as she'd been vacuuming out the upstairs bedrooms, Haché had *taken* what he'd wanted. She'd weakly fought him but he'd removed her panties and covered her mouth. She had been fearful of losing her job and being found out.

"Shh, *querida,*" he'd ordered her. "Don't I take care of you? You have my *word* … always."

They had made love with the vacuum cleaner on. Ever since then, up until Simona Mira's illness and death from pneumonia a decade later, Simona Mira had remained Haché's personal servant in more ways than one. She had also fallen in love with him.

Anabianca Rosalie Dalmacci Sosa – Haché's wife – had probably been even more lethal than Haché himself. She was the beloved daughter of the infamous (now deceased) Don Vittorio Dalmacci, the most powerful Mafia boss in Italy's history. All it would have taken from the mouth of the beautiful Anabianca Rosalie (originally from Firenze – now Florence – Italy) was one word and her powerful connections would rain all of hell down on anyone of her choosing.

Especially a peasant maid like Simona Mira and/or even her husband.

Fortunately, just like her husband, she'd come to love Simona's children. Rosalie, for some unknown reason, had been no longer able to produce another child after Alejandro, their only son. And, because of who they were (a powerful Mafia family), their son had been growing up sheltered, alone, and isolated.

"Those Toros are tough," Rosalie had told Haché one night before bed, about 25 years ago. "I want Alejandro together with them. I think those kids should stay here."

Her wish had been Haché's command.

The strangest part of the story had not been the Sosas' choice to introduce their son to the more hardened and cold side of life, nor Haché's lusty affair with their hottest maid. It had been *Benito*. He'd been the furthest thing from a tough kid who came from out of the southern lowlands of Cochabamba. Juca Bélen? Yes. The Toro brothers? Certainly. Benito had been very hard to figure out as a child. He'd been cursed with a very large head and well-pronounced forehead.

Because of the size of his head, other children had been merciless, calling him such hurtful names as *Monstro* (Monster), Frankenstein, *El Esquelético* (Skeletor, after the *He-Man* cartoon character) and, finally, *El Calavero* (The Skull). That was the name that had infuriated him the most, because it was the only name that had stuck.

In an astonishing turn of events, Sosa had emerged as Benny's fiercest protector. Sosa, who was four years older than Benny, had started telling other neighborhood kids that the Toros were his brothers. They all had said it, and even to the present day they said it. Haché had been impressed with the Toro boys but, later on, he'd even been more surprised to see and hear that his son had become the meanest and dirtiest street fighter out of the entire group. Javier had surely been the strongest, but Sosa had had an extremely high fighter's

I.Q. He beat his enemies with his *brain,* while Javier, for instance, beat them with his brute strength.

Sosa had not allowed anyone to get away with teasing his "little brother" Benny. The boys all had each other's backs, but Sosa was especially protective of Benny. Haché had been aware, because his goons had never let Sosa out of their sight during his early years with the Toros. Haché had known all along that his son had had the heart of a lion. His shell had needed assistance with cracking, and the Toros had helped with that. Rosalie had been concerned about Sosa, because he'd developed a strange obsession with birds. Haché had informed her that Sosa had not been the only one with the bird obsession. Benny had had that obsession too.

"Now I'm *really* worried," Rosalie had said. "Benny's a soft kid. Now the birds. Maybe he's gay. Maybe both boys are gay."

Haché had known better. Alejandro had been his father's son, and Haché Silvestre Chabán Sosa had descended from a long line of royal Spanish kings and conquerors. His mother had descended from a powerful line of Italian explorers and wine-making mobsters. There was no way in *hell* the younger Sosa could have turned out "fuhgaise." Once Sosa had been given the blessing of brotherhood with the Toros, he'd transformed. His true identity had come out. His true blood.

Sosa had been a ferocious hand-to-hand combat fighter. Haché had been proud that Sosa had excelled in his mixed martial arts training, and that he'd made a name for himself in the streets and jungles of Cochabamba. He'd dealt explosively and violently with dozens of boys from the slums over Benny being picked on. Sosa had picked up the nickname "Hachito" (meaning "Little Haché") because everyone had both feared and respected Don Haché.

During those days, Sosa had been constantly pushing and begging Benny to fight, to force others to respect him. However, Benny had been so afraid and shy back then that it was heartbreaking to witness. Knowing this, Haché had begun to include all the Toro boys in mixed martial arts training, in which Benny had eagerly taken part.

"From now on, no one in this household will attend Bolivian schools, which teach students in Spanish only," Haché had announced one day. "It's an English-speaking world, and Alejandro will one day run the businesses. If you boys are to work at his side, do good in school. Benny ... I know there's a beast asleep inside of your heart, boy. I see it in your training. Let me see it in the street."

Haché had had no idea of what would happen next.

When Sosa had been twelve years old, and while out of the sight of Haché and his goons, a much larger Bolivian teenager from El Chaparé had picked a fight with Sosa. Benny and Sosa had been on a forest trail, searching for one of Sosa's oldest macaws who had not been in the birdhouse for two days. The big fourteen-year-old had come up to Benny, who'd had another macaw perched on his shoulder (the female mate of the missing male), and grabbed the bird.

"Give her back!" Benny had whined, fearful of the bird's safety.

The teen had looked at Benny with contempt; he sneered as he took the bird by its head and pulled the head clean off at the neck. He'd laughed coldly at Benny, calling him "a retard," and then he had turned around to call Sosa a derogatory racist term due to Sosa's lighter Italian/Spaniard complexion and heritage.

Sosa had violated a fundamental rule of martial arts combat: never attack an enemy out of emotion. The fight had been Sosa's worst ever. His own anger had done him in, and it had almost ended his life. The larger boy had been a true street fighter himself, as was evident by the missing teeth, and scars on his face and head. The teen had grabbed the thinner and much smaller Sosa by the shirt and slammed his body into the dark soil of the forest. Sosa had thought the boy would kill him with the bone-crushing blows to the face he'd gotten pummeled with. Sosa had screamed at Benny to help him but Benny had run away!

If only Nancho, Javi, and Tato were around! Sosa had thought. The big teen had found his grip around Sosa's neck and he had squeezed and squeezed! As Sosa had thrashed around underneath the teen's heavier body weight, Sosa had begun to lose consciousness. He had thought that death was upon him. Darkness had enclosed his senses …

Then, slowly, in came the light …

Sosa had come to, his face bloodied and swollen from the beating. One eye was so injured that he had been unable to see through it. With his good eye he had watched Benny … as the big-headed eight-year-old kid had stood over the larger teenager. Benny had had tears in his eyes, sobbing loudly, as he had lifted the heavy lead pipe he'd found high over his head and brought it down hard … again and again on the screaming boy! Cracking sounds of bones could be heard… !

"Benito … Yeah, Benny …" Sosa had slowly dragged himself up onto his feet, still coughing and gagging, but lucid enough to realize that Benny had not left him to die. However, as joyful as it had been for Sosa to finally see Benny get violent … Sosa's boyish excitement had turned into sudden shock as Benny, in an uncontrollable dark rage, literally bashed in the skull of the teen boy. "Okay, Benny. *Benny, stop!!!*" This was something Sosa had never seen. "You'll kill him! *Stop!!*"

But it had been too late.

The bigger boy had already taken his last breath…

When the boys had run the half-mile or so home, Rosalie had screamed at the sight of the two bloody kids. Haché and his goons had quickly deduced that someone or something had died. Haché and his wife had pulled the boys into the bathroom and removed the boys' clothing.

"Okay, neither boy is shot or stabbed, Doña Rosalie. Go out and wait for me. Go!" Haché had turned to the boys and talked with them as he'd given them a bath. Once they had told him everything, he'd simply said, "Listen to me ... Tell Doña Rosalie and anyone else that you were attacked by wild pigs. That's it. *Never say nothing else!*"

Haché had sent two of his men to retrieve the body. "It's not far. About a half-mile down the Chaparé trail. Get that pipe!"

Later that night Haché had shown Sosa and all the Toro boys the larger teen's lifeless corpse. "Benito ... you did this for your *monito?*"

"I helped my *monito,*" Benny had said and then he'd suddenly begun to cry. The dead boy had frightened him. "I did bad."

"No, Benny," Haché had said. "No tears, *muchacho!* You did good!"

"Good?" Benny had looked at the boy's body, confused.

"You were brave, son," Haché had told him. "I'm proud of you. This was a very honorable and brave thing you did! You saved my son, your brother, Alejandro César. Now I owe you. All of you," [looking at Javier, Nancho, and Tato] "you call Alejandro your brother ... so that makes you all my sons. Not to dishonor your fathers. Never forget that youse are Lugo-Toros."

"I saved my *monito,*" Benny had smiled, proud of himself. "I did good."

"Yeah, you did." Haché had ordered his men to chop the body up and feed it to the hogs. "Benny, Javi, Tato, and Nancho ... you all don't know it yet, but one day, Alejandro is going to be a very rich and powerful man, and he'll need loyal men around him. I believe those men will be all of you." It was Don Haché's prediction as well as his blessing.

And Don Haché had been correct.

Once Benny had gotten that first taste of blood, it had soaked deep down inside of him. He had seen early on in life how simple it was to end a problem: with murder. All it took was one swing of a pipe, his hands, a knife, or a bullet to bend a man to his will. From that day on Benny and his cousins had received the best that Haché could give them in careful training, coaching, and education.

Needless to say, no one ever called him "The Skull" anymore. At least not to his face, because the beast inside of him had been awakened.

$$$$$

Hoy

Sosa and the Toro brothers drank coffee and ate Bolivian *empañadas* and *salteñas* as they kept their eyes on the 27-inch television that sat atop a stylish oak table to the left of Sosa's desk. They had all the latest cable and satellite television connections. While they conversed, Nancho used the remote control to switch back and forth between *CNN* and UK-based *BBC News Channel* to see if he could catch the current news coverage of the Tony Montana murder.

"That's it, Nanchito," Sosa pointed at something he'd seen.

"Un-mute it, *chico*," Javi told his brother.

Nancho pressed the "MUTE" button on the television remote control.

"And after this short commercial break," a blond female news anchor was saying, "we will bring you live breaking news coverage from the massacre at the Miami, Florida, estate of suspected drug kingpin Tony 'Scarface' Montana. Please stay tuned."

CHAPTER FOUR

Astoria Hospital
Queens, New York
September 8, 1984

Elvira purchased a one-way, first-class ticket from Orlando International Airport to JFK International Airport at 10 a.m. the following morning. During the 2½-hour flight, she fell into a deep, dreamless sleep, exhausted by the miasma of toxic emotions from the previous evening. As her luck would have it, however, no sooner than a snap of the fingers, it seemed, a cute stewardess in a blue uniform with a red tie was standing in the aisle next to her seat, informing her that the plane had landed.

She groggily stood up onto her feet and used the shoulder strap of her Louis Vuitton carry-on case to haul the bag off of the plane. Seconds after she stepped out onto the enclosed disembarkment ramp, she was suddenly overcome by a brain-buzzing, knee-buckling wave of nausea and dizziness. She could feel a numbing sensation covering her face, and a cold, clammy sweat spread out all over her body. It felt particularly sticky in her armpits and in between her private areas.

"Help me ..." Her voice was a weak cry.

Airport security noticed rather quickly that she was having a medical dilemma, and they were at her side within moments.

"Ma'am? Are you okay?" A brown-haired, armed airport security officer kneeled down as he helped her to sit with her back against the wall of the carpeted ramp. He noticed that she was as white as a ghost. Sensing something grave was going on with her, he called for emergency assistance on his walkie-talkie. "I have a female passenger down, in and out of consciousness, inside of Delta Flight 39's disembarkment tunnel. Emergency, I repeat: Emergency. Over."

"Emergency transport en route," a woman's voice cackled back over the radio. "Stand by. Over."

Within two minutes a two-man medic team arrived on a motorized cart. Moments after the first two medics had arrived, two more came to assist. Throngs of passengers stood around to watch. Elvira was moaning as a medic shined a flashlight into her eyes, and that was the last thing she remembered …

$$$$$

She regained consciousness as she was being pushed into a hospital room. She looked down at her feet and saw her carry-on bag between her legs. On her face was an oxygen mask and on her left arm was an intravenous needle attached to a long transparent tube and a bag of clear fluids. She observed the NYFD medics having a conversation with a light-skinned, freckle-faced nurse who had shoulder-length reddish-brown hair, dazzling green eyes, an attractive figure, and a Caribbean accent. She was apparently some type of ethnic mixture – probably from an exotic faraway place. She was truly a pleasure to look at. Her eyes were slanted which suggested that she was part Oriental, most likely from the Far East of Asia.

"She's lucid. Are you watching me, gurl?" the exotic beauty said, grabbing Elvira's hands. "What's your name?"

At that moment Elvira vomited violently into the oxygen mask. She snatched the mask off of her face, nearly suffocating, groaning loudly from nausea and misery. The nurse put on rubber gloves and had the medics call in some other nurses and interns to assist. The pink-and-yellow-colored vomit continued to gush and spew out the contents of her stomach until all that was left was a few dry retches.

"Oh, my God, help me!" Elvira sobbed in anguish as an unbearable migraine attacked her. "*I have migraines!*"

"One of you contact Dr. Coles," the exotic beauty ordered one of the three nurses. "We have to stabilize her. Inform him that she's having a severe migraine attack, accompanied by nausea and vomiting. I smell alcohol; she also has something else in her. If I had to guess – cocaine. Requesting immediate *Demerol* and *Phenergan* injections, and we should admit her for observation. I see classic symptoms of overdose."

One nurse left the room as the others undressed Elvira. Working in the room together, the three women cleaned up the vomit, soaped her up thoroughly, rinsed her off, toweled her dry, and dressed her in a white hospital gown. The exotic-looking nurse, with Elvira's approval, opened up the carry-on case and removed fresh underwear. She also removed Elvira's wallet in order to identify her.

Minutes later the medication orders came and the nurse who brought them injected them through the IV tube while Elvira was being dressed.

"Elvira Montana?" The nurse looked at Elvira, who nodded in acknowledgement at hearing her name. "I'm a nurse, Rachel Janine Lee. Nina Lee [indicating] as my name tag says. You'll be asleep from those meds in about ten minutes. The Phenergan will abate your nausea. The Demerol will help your migraine. Are you insured?"

"Take the American Express," Elvira sighed, still in pain. She felt so defeated. Tears rolled down her face. "Nina ... ?"

"Hm?"

"I don't have anyone here to look out for me ..." Elvira looked up at the nurse pleadingly. "Stay close to me, okay?"

Nurse Nina paused to look down at Elvira for several seconds.

"I'm a *person*," Elvira whispered. "I know I'm just another doper to you ... but I'm a friggin' person. Just ... watch over me. Stay ..."

"You're in good hands, sweetie," the nurse said, gently stroking Elvira's hair back out of her eyes. "Are you allergic to any medicines or foods?"

Elvira slowly answered, "No."

"Are you pregnant?"

She opened her bloodshot eyes to say, "If I was pregnant, I wouldn't be here ... I wouldn't be a *'junkie wife.'*"

Nina felt compassion for Elvira. "You ... I've never met anyone as sad as you, baby gurl. But every woman I've seen with tears like yours either lost someone they loved, or a man was behind it. Which is it?"

"*Men* ..." she murmured as she reached for her bag and pulled it underneath the covers with her "Me... everybody I ever had did me dirty. I never had a fair chance. Not one time ..."

Nina stood by until Elvira went to sleep.

She fell asleep with her ears ringing to the distant sound of Tony's voice: *Is this it? Is that what it's all about, Manny?*

Then Manny: ... *maggots swarm your junkie vagina and devour the sperm.*

$$$$$

She awoke to the touch of Nina Lee checking her vital signs. "Hey, sleeping beauty, turns out that you *are* pregnant," the ethnic beauty blurted.

Elvira sat up against the pillows, stunned for several moments before she could say anything. "*Whaaat?* Pregnant? *Me?* [thumb-pointing at herself] *Elvira Montana?*"

"I know your name. Yeah, *you* [pointing in good humor back at Elvira]," Nina told her patient, showing Elvira her emergency room folder. "This is your file ... your blood labs came back with several concerns the doctor will discuss with you. One of them is that you are *definitely* pregnant."

Elvira pushed the carry-on over to her right side and sat frozen as an African-American woman entered the room with a tray of food and drinks. Although she was looking shell-shocked from the baby news, she was also famished. The room was suddenly permeated with the warm aroma of hot soup and sandwiches.

She started eating almost immediately. There were two grilled cheese sandwiches, chicken noodle soup, French fries, apple juice, and milk. Nina excused herself from the room, promising to return soon.

Ten minutes later, a doctor entered the room wearing silver, wire-rimmed glasses, blue scrubs, a white lab coat, and Nike cross-trainers that were tied so tightly it looked like the blood could not circulate. He was a gray-haired man in his fifties and he was a straight-to-the-point type of person, which Elvira learned from his first few words:

"Do you *want* to die, Elvira Montana?" he asked her bluntly. "Do you have a death wish?"

She put down the empty carton of milk and looked up at him. "No ... why – ?"

"I would also ask the child growing inside of you, but I can't," he continued. "I'm assuming she or he wants to live. *You're killing your child.* Every cigarette, every snort of coke, every Quaalude. Your baby is dying ... and so are you."

Elvira was crying. "I didn't know I was pregnant."

Nina came back into the room and stood on the opposite side of the bed from where the doctor stood.

"You young women," he sighed in exasperation. "Twenty-five years old … parties are fun but how do you have fun when fun is *suicide*? Self-murder? *You're killing you!*"

His booming voice made her jump.

"You don't know what I've been through!!" Elvira screamed back at him. "Until you've walked in my shoes, don't judge me!! I never had a fair chance, man!!"

"Your blood labs scare me," he told her in a softer tone. "You're pregnant, … you use drugs and alcohol. You're here, hospitalized, not because of the baby, but because of the drugs. You overdosed."

"*Overdosed?*" she said more than asked.

"You went completely pale-white at the airport," Nina informed her. "You're fortunate that there's medics at the airports. Your heart rate was like a rabbit's. Your blood pressure was *alarmingly* high. Exact words from the medics was '*It was like she'd died for a minute.*' You also have antibodies for hepatitis A."

"I have antibodies *and* hepatitis?" she frowned. "How'd I catch those?"

"No, no, no, you misunderstand." Dr. Coles held up his hand. "*Antibodies* are proteins produced in the blood as an immune response to a specific antigen. In your case, your body's immune system fended off the antigen found in hepatitis. *Hepatitis* is a disease of the liver. How, when, or where you were exposed to it I guess we'll never know. But your body killed it. Having antibodies for it, in other words, is a positive thing because you have an immune system that is strong."

"Okay," she nodded, understanding.

"The concern we now have is your drug and alcohol addictions," he continued. "You don't have to be a slave to them … no matter what you have been through in life. I've seen people get better … I'm a recovering alcoholic … almost lost my license to practice. Been sober for nineteen years, eight months, and one day exactly. I've counseled Vietnam War vets, Korean War vets, and Holocaust survivors. I've seen them get clean and stay clean."

Tears were streaming down her rosy cheeks like small rivers. "Last night it got so bad that I thought about suicide."

Dr. Coles and Nina exchanged glances. They had a duty to listen and take action if necessary.

"There's a more grotesque reality beneath the picture you see here," she said, touching her hand to her chest area. "I'm really like a caricature of a beautiful woman ... the one I once was. Now I'm skinny, ugly ... a *junkie.*"

"Is this your first pregnancy?" Nina asked her softly.

"Yeah ... well, not really." Elvira eyed the doctor and nurse closely. "I was molested as a child and impregnated at twelve years old."

Nina's mouth dropped open.

"The man who did it ..." She trailed off, catching her audience off guard. "He had a friend who was a horse veterinarian ... I'd been drugged, I'd bled for days, but all the while he'd still have sex with me."

"At twelve years old?" Nina Lee stated with a sorrowful expression of incredulity on her face. "And he continued as you still hemorrhaged?"

Elvira nodded and brushed her hands back through her blond hair. "It shames me to admit it, but that isn't even the worst part."

"What's the worst part?" Nina inquired. "What can be worse than that? Who the person was?"

She hesitated. "Maybe another time ... Needless to say, I never had the baby. They aborted it and discarded it into the horse feces on the barn floor."

Nina and Dr. Coles could not have been more astonished by Elvira's horror story. Dr. Coles took a deep breath, obviously very moved by this beautiful young woman's revelations, and he wondered what he should do. As experienced as the two trauma unit professionals were, it was difficult for anything to shock them. 1984 New York City was definitely one of the country's bloodiest places to live. Gunshots, stabbings, bludgeoning, decapitations, mutilations, burnings, suicides, poisonings, torture victims, et cetera, et cetera, they all came to Astoria Hospital and Trauma Unit. 1984 New York City was the real deal, like Afghanistan and Vietnam; 2,600 murders were the yearly average. Living in New York was like winning or losing in Las Vegas. There was excitement one day and misery the next. *New York's a great place to visit but you gotta be careful crossing the street.*

Dr. Coles and Nina Lee had seen and heard all the stories, seen all the blood, and they'd even lived through two emergency room shootouts between rival gang members. A year ago there had been a hostage situation and police stand-off involving a lone gunman who'd subsequently been shot and killed by an NYPD-ESU sniper. Many people had come in living … but plenty had ended up with a sheet pulled up over their dead bodies.

The decedent(s) – if adults – were stored like cattle carcasses, absent the meat-hooks, on stainless-steel carts or steel shelves in the refrigerated morgue located down in the basement level. On the other hand, the small children or babies were lovingly wrapped in dry paper and placed into Tupperware-type food storage containers and kept in a separate section of the morgue. Oftentimes, it would be Nina's job to place toe tags on the adults and children aged six and up. However, when it came to the babies, she'd put ankle bands on them, because their toes were sometimes too small. Pink tags would identify the girls, blue tags would identify the boys.

"They train us not to attach ourselves to patients," Nina said as she held onto Elvira's hand. "They teach us that it

40

would get in the way of our jobs ... It's an odious and impossible demand for so many reasons. Like yours. I feel compassion and sorrow for you. And I'm a woman; how *can't* I? We're not Nazis or religious terrorists with mass homicide on our itineraries. We help save lives, mon! I love it when I witness manual CPR be successful ... seeing kids leave here smiling ... and the hearing of the tiny voice of a newborn cry its first breath at birth, mon. I am who I am because of stories like yours."

"The '*non-attachment*' rule is a tad bit oxymoronic," Dr. Coles agreed, standing with his hands in his lab coat pockets. "Ours is a profession thought of as the paradigm of all professions. What you've said here to us highlights a whole new dark side of man I never even knew existed. But look. You need help. You do have a chance. Addiction *can* be defeated. But you have to *want* it, Mrs. Montana. No one can force you but we only hope good health for you and your baby. I'm assuming you want a baby? You wish to keep it?"

Elvira put her hands on her stomach and looked at the doctor. "I'd *kill* for this baby."

The doctor pursed his lips for a moment and a smile spread across his face. "How about just living for this baby first? The only killing you do is to the addiction. What kind of insurance coverage do you have?"

"I can afford it."

"Is the party over or what?" He wondered how serious she was. "Because you *need* intense in-patient treatment and counseling. If you're serious, then I'll refer you to the Aspen Clinic up in Rockland County – a town called Nyack – near Palisades Mall."

"There never was a 'party' for me, Doc," she told him. "No fun. Just escape. I'm serious. I was recently scolded that I lack the *womanhood* ... that I don't have the ability to have a child. You don't know what it's like hearing a man – *men* – degrade you as I was degraded. I'm keeping this baby. Call it what you want. I am more determined than you'll ever know, Doctor."

"Okay." He began writing.

"This Aspen Clinic," she went on. "It's not some *One Flew Over the Cuckoo's Nest* place, like the movie, I hope?"

"God, no!" He chuckled over some loud clamoring outside of the room. "You mean the Jack Nicholson movie?"

"Yeah."

He laughed and explained to her where he was referring her to. "We'd never send you to a crazy house. New York certainly has its bad places ... such as *Bellevue Hospital, Phoenix House,* or *Kings County Hospital.* We're sending you to the best there is. It's private, ritzy, and better than *The Betty Ford Clinic.* Aspen Clinics have four sites in the country. They cater primarily to the rich and famous. You'll see entertainment and sports stars. The Nyack site is their newest. Very beautiful, gated-off community. Very quiet. No press allowed. No cameras or recorders. They have many amenities: massage, hot tubs, aromatherapy, saunas, tennis courts, swimming pools, and a well-educated and experienced staff. It looks like college dorm buildings but they're actually condos. It may sound like a five-star vacation getaway but they have quite the reputation for success up there. Now, if you want something less expensive ..."

"I said I can pay for it," she repeated. "What I can't afford is *not* to go. This baby changes my entire calculus. That and my health. Hepatitis, high blood pressure ... what's next? A heart attack?"

"I've seen drugs do worse than heart attacks," Nina mentioned. "To women your age and younger."

"It's very real to you now, Mrs. Montana," Dr. Coles said as he continued to write. "It's despicable what you went through as a child, and I suspect those tragedies and abuses have everything to do with this hospitalization. Those alcohol and narcotics decisions have *diseased* you. Addiction is a disease. Let's get you treated for those underlying, unaddressed issues of abuse and give you a chance to live a full life. [Looking at Nina] Admit her to a private room. I've ordered more tests to be certain that all is okay with the baby. I'll also fax John Crispuso, the director at Aspen, your referral and financial information …"

"American Express," she told him.

"Are you sure?" Dr. Coles frowned. "They charge interest and they require the entire amount owed to be paid in the next billing month."

"It also builds great credit ratings," Elvira returned. "I can handle it. Trust me."

"Fine." He firmly shook her hand, looking her in the eyes and found determination there. "Get the tests done and take the medications I've prescribed. Nina will explain those to you."

"I'm dying for a cigarette, and I have to pee," Elvira said, grimacing uncomfortably as she looked at Nina. "The alcohol and coke I can kick. I've gone weeks without coke … Alcohol is not so deep an addiction that I can't do without it. The cigarettes I've never tried to kick. It's driving me nuts even talking about it. I'm sort of afraid."

Elvira went to the bathroom, which was only a few feet away from her bed. Nina helped her up. A few minutes later Elvira returned to the bed and lay down.

"I meant to ask you something." Elvira looked at her. "You are the cutest thing, I swear. What are you mixed with?"

"You mean *who* am I mixed with." She smiled as she covered Elvira up with an extra blanket to ward off the cold. "I'm half-Jamaican and half-Chinese. My dad is from Savanna La-Mar, Jamaica. Picture Bob Marley … his light-brown skin. My dad could pass for Bob's twin, almost. The green eyes are my dad's. My mom is from Urumqi, China. A city along the Tien Shan south of the Mongolia border."

"Tien Shan …" Elvira wondered what it was.

"Those are mountains," Nina answered with a light chuckle. "Nobody knows Urumqi or the Tien Shan mountains."

"I don't have anybody, Nina." Elvira sounded serious, a lonely tone in her voice. "You've been very kind to me."

"I'm kind even to the worst kind." Nina patted Elvira's hand. "You'll be okay."

Elvira nodded her head. "I'm going to need good people around me ... I want you to stay in contact with me. Will you do that?"

The way she sounded – almost like a small lost child – compelled Nina to sit down in the chair on the left side of the bed. "You have a lot going on with you, Mrs. Montana. For instance, the comments you made about wanting to commit suicide ... it put us on alert. That's why I haven't left you alone. And won't."

"I'm not going to kill myself."

"I know," Nina replied. "I have no problem staying in contact with you, but you have to get stable. Get treatment. I know a few of the staff where you're going."

"I like you." Elvira's voice broke with emotion. "You ..."

"I like you, too," Nina smiled warmly. "Are you going to fall apart on me?"

Elvira propped herself up on her left elbow and faced Nina. "No. Falling apart would be convenient, and convenient and I have never been friends. I've made all the wrong moves. With all I have on my plate, this baby ... it's time to make all the *right* moves. Plus ..."

"Plus what?"

Elvira laughed cynically. "Even if death came my way right now, it would probably keep on walking by because my life is so bad that even death wants nothing to do with me."

"So doomy and gloomy," Nina waved her off. "Be positive. You have a baby on the way. Think life. Health. Great lungs. Strong heart. Ten fingers and ten toes."

Another nurse, a young male nurse, entered the room to assist with Elvira's transfer to a private room upstairs. She was wheeled off on her bed and taken onto an elevator by Nina and Nurse Monroe. Nina got her settled into the new room and made sure that she was administered all of her new medications.

Elvira fell asleep with Nina at her side. There was something about Elvira that drew Nina her way. Something that was both frightening and intriguing at the same time. Something her father had warned her about once suddenly came to mind.

You're like this Angel of Life, he'd said to her. *You will make a very special nurse, because you have a need to help others. To help heal the sick and to mend broken limbs. But remember … there are a lot of people out there whose illnesses are too dark and too ugly to heal. Those are the ones who are too broken to be fixed.*

She wondered if her father's voice in her head was a portent of something to come. An augury of some sort.

An omen.

CHAPTER FIVE

La Hacienda de Sosa
Cochabamba, Bolivia
September 11, 1984 – 10 a.m.

A raven-haired, female *BBC* news correspondent with a crisp British accent was reporting live from the front entrance of the Montana Estate in Coral Gables, Florida. She was gripping a black microphone (the white *BBC* letters emblazoned across their red background) as she stood outside of the main entrance of the mansion's black security gates.

While the rain poured, she described the jaw-dropping events as follows:

"… law enforcement personnel will not permit anyone to enter the Montana property at this time except for crime scene investigators. Again, we are reporting live from the ritzy and glamorous Coconut Grove section of Coral Gables, where some of America's biggest sports and movie superstars live, such as New York Yankees owner George 'The Boss' Steinbrenner, Sean Connery, Diana Ross, Pete Rose, Al Pacino, and Tina Turner.

"What you are seeing directly behind us, through those fancy black security gates, is the front entrance of the Montana Estate. Crime scene tape cordons off the entire property. We have been informed by detectives that one of the largest massacres in Florida's modern history has occurred

inside and outside of the main house. We have also been told by detectives, and I quote, 'It looks like a war zone in there,' unquote.

"There appears to be some confusion among law enforcement regarding the correct body count due to conflicting reports by different on-scene agencies investigating the crime scene. One source tells us there are nineteen dead, another source reports twenty-four. One thing they are all clear about is that there are no survivors. However, witnesses have informed the police that they observed a gang of men, of Latino and African-American descent, fleeing the scene on foot. This was a bloody firefight to the finish ... One neighbor could not believe that what she'd heard was real gunfire because, she said, 'It's Coconut Grove, for crying out loud!' She'd mistaken it for fireworks and never thought to call police.

"A police captain who has spent twenty-seven years on the force told us that the death scene here reminded him of the Vietnam War and the Khmer Rouge. He positively confirmed that Antonio 'Tony' 'Scarface' Montana is among the dead, found face-down in a shallow indoor pool. Mr. Montana, if you recall, recently made headlines due to his arrest on federal money-laundering charges in which he'd posted a record-setting five-million-dollar cash bail – a move that had caught the attention of international media.

"Authorities believe that Mr. Montana was the country's leading supplier of cocaine, heroin, weapons, and marijuana, earning him the nickname 'Scarface' after the infamous Chicago mobster. No children are among the dead but police have confirmed that one woman – not believed to be Mrs. Elvira Montana – is among the dead, but has yet to be identified. We will have more on this story tonight at –"

"That beautiful, blond wife of his is out there somewhere," Sosa stated thoughtfully.

"*Widow*, you mean," Nancho corrected him as he drained the last swallow of coffee in his mug. "*La viuda.*"

"I met her once ... on a yacht off the Florida coast," Sosa mentioned. "She stood out from a hundred others on that big yacht."

"Let it go, *jefe*," Nancho told him. "You're insane to even fantasize of her after hitting her husband."

Tato had a scowl on his face as he rasped out, "Did we hit Tony for the *chocha* ... or the New York thing with our brother Alberto?"

"You know better than to ask that," Sosa angrily shot back, an ugly twist coming over his expression.

"*Señor* ..." Tato looked at his boss. "Her name has come up before and you have the same look on your face each time. That's all. I may *look* dumb," Tato mumbled.

Sosa left it at that.

On the television screen a *CNN* news helicopter hovered above the Montana Estate, shooting live footage of what was going on inside of the property. The coroner's office personnel had already carried out the bodies of the dead and put them into black body bags. Each of them were laid side-by-side in a line along the driveway, sort of like a "Brady Bunch mother" would in counting out the kids' bag lunches prior to a road trip.

Nancho, habitually palming and rubbing his clean-shaven head, argued with Javier over how many dead bodies there were on the ground directly in front of the multi-million-dollar mansion. The two brothers even got up close to the 27-inch screen to count out loud each body bag, thrusting their fingers at the TV, excitedly emphasizing what they both swore was the precise body count.

"You heard that British news hag, Chito! What have you been smoking, *hombre*?" Javier argued with his younger brother. "She clearly said nineteen to twenty-four, *hermano*!

Clean out your big ears. There's twenty body bags –"
pointing, indicating, " – lined up on the street."

"Imbecile," Nancho returned the insults. "There are
twenty-two," counting again.

Sosa, pouring himself a shot of whiskey, sighed as they
argued.

"And that's not even a *street*, you big idiot," Nancho said,
using his thumb to demonstrate what he meant. "That's dead
Tony's driveway. Now I understand why you lose so much at
the craps table. You roll *one* die but it looks like *two* to you."

Sosa had had enough. He pulled out a snub-nosed .44
Bulldog from his desk and pointed it at the TV. "Turn it off
… before I *shoot* it off. If youse are through acting like *chicas*,
we can go back to being professionals in an important
meeting."

Tato lightly chuckled.

Nancho turned off the television. "The hell you laughing
at?"

"Murders like this are so messy." Sosa looked at his men.

"Alberto …" Tato stated in his deep, raspy voice. "Is
Benny bringing his body home?"

Sosa saw the pain in Tato's eyes. "Tony killed him in
Manhattan. His body is in the world's largest mass grave …
New York's dirty little secret. Potter's Field on Hart Island.
Alberto, our brother, is in a mass grave."

"Potter's Field." Tato looked bothered by Sosa's
statement.

"What's that?" Javier inquired.

Sosa explained everything he knew about Hart Island,
sometimes referred to as *Hart's Island*, which is a small
island in New York City at the western end of Long Island
Sound. It is approximately a mile long and a quarter of a mile
wide, and it is located to the northeast of City Island in the
Pelham Islands group. The island is the easternmost part of
the borough of the Bronx. Historically, it had been used as a

Union Civil War prison camp, a lunatic asylum, a tuberculosis sanatorium, potter's field – a mass grave, most unmarked, for the poor, unclaimed, stillborn, etc. – and it was also once a boys' reformatory.

"*Señor.*" Tato stood up, tears threatening to fall from his eyes. "Our brethren needs to be brought *home* to be buried with full honors. I'll go myself to claim him – with or without your permission."

Sosa walked up to Tato, staring into his dark eyes and brown face. "You're challenging my authority … Tato?"

"I'll accept the twenty lashes, *Señor.*" Tato held his bald head down as the tears dropped. Then he looked back up at Sosa. "With pride. *Señor.*"

Sosa nodded, reaching out to wipe away Tato's tears. Sosa kissed Tato's forehead, running his hands along his cheeks. "I know you would, Tato … I know."

Sosa gently slapped Tato's left cheek and he returned to his seat. "There's no need for you to go. My cousin, General Cucombre, has sent La Gata Negra to intercept the body."

"Catalina." Javier perked up. "Our cousin. That's welcome news, Tatico. Alberto will be home, Tatico, don't worry, *hermano.*"

Nancho switched the subject. "Boss … are you second-guessing the Montana hit?"

"Murder is permanent, Chito," Sosa quickly replied, tossing back the shot of whiskey he'd poured minutes ago. He bit into a doughnut he'd lifted from a plastic platter near the pot of hot coffee sitting on his desk. "Too permanent to do-over, even if I did second-guess it. How many prisons are in Bolivia?"

Nancho frowned. "Fifty-three maybe?"

"Fifty-something," Sosa agreed, planting his elbows on the desktop as he ate the doughnut. "*Sea lo que sea.* [Whatever it may be.] San Pedro, Palmasola, and all the others are full of murderers who second-guessed the murder they committed. Tony … we all got to know and like. He made our thing – *La Corporación* – over a billion dollars. It's not in the genes of this machine we run to second-guess things. It was a good killing. *Un paso acertado.*"

"We have to make up for the loss of that revenue," Tato said, a profound tone in his raspy voice.

"The gang leader on the run for killing the cop in Los Angeles," Sosa suggested. "The *African-American-Nicaraguan*. Maybe he can be useful."

"He's being hunted and they know he's in Bolivia," Nancho quipped. "*Él es inútil.* [He's useless.] *Nos echará el mal de ojo a nosotros.* He'll put a jinx on us, boss. I'm having trouble trusting any involvement with him."

"He's a major gang leader with both *Nicaraguan* and *American* connections," Sosa stated, clearly set on whatever it was he was thinking. "He's a gateway as far as I'm concerned. We help him, he helps us."

"Hmph." Nancho stood up, grabbed a doughnut, and faced Sosa. "I know how important Nicaragua is to us … it's our most important transit hub to the western U.S. But we know many people in Nicaragua. Are you worried about their political situation?"

"Our interests are my priority," Sosa assured him. "That fucking Tony was one hell of a convenience to our bottom line. That MS-13 leader had power … something like four hundred members buying cocaine from his crew."

"Whose coke was he buying?" Javier asked curiously.

"Colombian," Sosa answered. He also noted, "The coke, however, came from Bolivia."

"Those Colombians, *hombre*," Nancho grumbled. "We supply eighty percent of their shipments for ten K and they move it into Honduras via Panama and make two to three times as much."

"It's time we say screw the Colombians and go in," Javier stated.

"The MS-13," Sosa told them. "He's key to the Gang Plan I've been talking about. See, those other MS-13's he has under him rely on his Central American connections to get the *yayo* back to L.A. He's asked for our help for that reason, I think. He feels he can benefit us and us him. I know he can move many kilos in L.A."

"You mean his four hundred contacts can," Javier clarified.

Sosa nodded as his men thought about it.

"We'll talk with him – at least." Javier said it to Nancho and Tato.

"Whatever you say." Tato shrugged, his mind still on Alberto.

"At least we'll talk to him," Nancho agreed. "He's down on the Chaparé, no? The river."

"*Sí*, as we think of what to do with him," Sosa said, leaning back in his seat. "Tony gave me his word … and broke it. He crossed a line, and he had to pay. Once you break your word, you are no good to me anymore. Your life is useless to me, to the air you take from the earth. Tony proudly boasted about how all he had in this world was his word and his balls, and he didn't break them for anybody. To my face and to my eyes he breathed those words … and I warned him not to fuck me." He glared at them menacingly. "That's exactly what he did." Pausing to contain his anger. "So … I took his breath. He didn't need it. If you lie, you no longer need to breathe. That's it."

Moments passed in silent agreement.

"Permission to speak, *Señor*." Tato sat on the sofa, legs open, hands on his knees.

"Tato." Sosa nodded his way.

"Tony came from Cuban slums," Tato slowly explained, speaking with his hands to express passionate meaning. "You made no error in selecting him. When we last saw Tony here – for the closed-door meeting on the United Nations hit – he was clearly *using* the *yayo*. He was a paranoid cokehead and we made him a very rich man. This man forgot all about who he was and where he came from. American culture, coke, the booze, the *gringa chocha*, the flash and the cash buried him, not us. He forgot Mariel, Cuba ... the twenty-five thousand *Bandidos* who escaped Castro. He became American, and Americans cannot be trusted. Not on such a high level as having one of them assisting us on so important a hit. We put trust in Tony due to his ethnicity and character. Boss ... it does not matter whether he was ethnically Cuban, Japanese, Haitian, Mexican, or Russian ... once you are *Americanized*, you no longer have your balls or your word. It's impossible because of the so-called *American Way*. Their veins flow with lies, their hearts beat with betrayal. Capitalism is a fatal culture and ideal that has men and women of *all* nationalities and races flushing their faiths down the toilet. We must remain ruthless and cold in our dealings with them, for we are the very descendants of the men, women, and children they ultimately betrayed: the American Indian and African. Your *Gang Plan*, even though the MS-13 leader we allowed to camp on our lands down along Rio Chaparé is ethnically African-American-Nicaraguan, we cannot trust him. It's *impossible*."

Sosa carefully thought through Tato's wise reasoning. "*Impossible* is a strong word, *mi sangrito*."

"Sixty-five percent of what we do in *La Corporación* is with people we don't trust," Javier pointed out. "I'm with Tatico's skepticism but, if done carefully, the Gang Plan is ... it can be gargantuan."

Tato stood up now, one hand in his right pants pocket. "Maybe so. I'm a skeptic because, to me, gangs are fractured units of weak people who can't be strong alone. Americans are weak. Making them rich makes them even weaker. Things *will go wrong* – arrests, shootings, et cetera – and an overwhelming majority will *sing*. Betrayal runs rampant in all areas of American society: politics, groups, religions, organizations, prisons, and especially gangs. Those idiots are nothing like us; they wear colors and jackets with their gang names on them. Easy to spot. Tattoos that say '*I sell dope*' on their necks. I hate to say it – because I have African in *me* – but the African-American is the *worst*! They are not yet able to trust *themselves*, let alone *each other*. I know Houston, New Orleans, New York, California, Chicago. I see them beat their women, I hear them call each other despicable, despicable racist names the white slave hunters used. *Any man on earth who would call me that word* – whether in hate or for fun – *would betray me*. Most African-Americans use it to greet each other or refer affections to each other! Boss ... [pausing] if you feel *strongly* about this Gang Plan, I advise you to consider using Bolivians, mainly *La Corporación* or its friends, to infiltrate American cities and gangs. Choose carefully those Bolivians with deep roots here. Loyal to us and our country. *Beneath them*, use only the most organized criminal organizations, such as the Italian Mafia, the Russians, and Asians. Then, consider only the most organized Latino gangs: Mexicanos, Hondurans, Nicaraguans, Guatemalans, Colombianos, Boriquas, El Salvadorians, Peruvians, Panamanians. But only *men*. Not kids. Grown men who won't crack under pressure. Thirty years old and over who are leaders."

"Okay, Tato," Sosa said, looking at the time. "Let's address this at another time. Right now we must touch on a more immediate worry."

"I was waiting for that," Nancho stated. "The human rights journalist. Our friend [with sarcastic cynicism], *Doctor Orlando Gutiérrez*."

Sosa grimaced at the very mention of the name. "Tony messed up so bad. If only he would have let Alberto bomb the car in front of the United Nations building as he was instructed, Gutiérrez would be dead and our problem solved.

Now, the UN security found the bomb. *That's* all over the news. Gutiérrez is more motivated than ever now. Prior to that UN speech, they'd told him about the bomb. He spoke with such fury that he received a standing ovation for two minutes, before the UN General Assembly. He used *my* name, the names of our Andes Sugar partners, General Cucombre, Ariel Bleyer, and, probably worst of all, he tied us directly to the infamous 'Cocaine Coup.' The Garcia Meza presidency!"

"The CIA helped us with that," Tato reminded Sosa. "Anyway – now what?"

"Gutiérrez must die," Sosa stated simply. "He's making multiple TV appearances in the U.S., such as *60 Minutes, Good Morning America, Geraldo Rivera, Phil Donohue,* and *Barbara Walters.* After that he's scheduled appearances in the UK, France, India, and Japan. Clearly what he's doing to pressure the U.S. is to go public in front of countries that are politically allied with the U.S." He removed a VHS tape from his desk drawer. "I want to show youse this tape." Placing it into the VCR, he pressed the PLAY button. "Watch and listen very closely. Your skin will crawl with embarrassment and anger at what this *chivato* is saying."

The video began to play.

CHAPTER SIX

Astoria Hospital
Queens, New York
September 9, 1984

A million and one things raced through Elvira's mind.

She was restless and fiending badly for a cigarette. *A drink and a Quaalude would be nice too,* she thought as she lay back on the hospital bed, bored to death. *The pills I can do without. The alcohol I don't need. But a cigarette ... God, that craving is more powerful than anything.*

She "questioned" herself:

Will I love my baby? Yes.

Will I get high? No.

Will I smoke cigarettes? No answer. Then: *Yes.*

Will I complete rehab? Yes.

The questionnaire stopped suddenly when she noticed an old African-American man walk by her open door. "Hey, mister!"

Hearing her, he stopped and came into her room, pushing a cart that carried cleaning supplies on it. In a Deep South accent he said, "Yes, ma'am?"

"I need a favor." She spoke furtively, in a hushed tone. She looked at his nametag. "Rufus Jones."

"I'm just the janitor," he informed her. "I'll go get the nurse." He pronounced *"nurse"* with a southern-sounding *"nuss."*

"I'm not having medical trouble!" she snapped, raising her voice slightly. "I need cigarettes. If you'll fetch me a carton of Marlboro Lights, I'll pay you a hundred dollars."

He hesitated a bit before answering. "I'd have to leave the hospital and come back havin' to do some explanations. Don't much like doin' explanations."

"Two hundred then," she offered. "I feel like a prison inmate."

"Three hunned dolla," he countered. "Fifty up front."

She opened her wallet and gave him a fifty-dollar bill. He left in a hurry, and she lay back to await his return. She used the remote control to flip through the channels on the wall-mounted RCA television. Nothing good was on at 2 p.m. except *Days of Our Lives*, talk shows, and reruns of *M.A.S.H.*

Her busy mind went back to thinking.

Maybe it would be best to file for a divorce and ... maybe at least ... consider an abortion? But as soon as the thought came, she dismissed it wholeheartedly. *I can't even believe I thought that.*

She knew that she'd never do anything to hurt a child. Especially not after what she had experienced as a child herself. She mentally berated that voice of evil inside of her head and scolded it repeatedly. *I will never hurt my baby ... I won't drink, I won't touch drugs, and I'll do my best to stop smoking cigarettes.*

In her heart and soul she knew for a fact that she could shake the so-called "party drugs" of the '80s. The coke, the Quaaludes, the Black Beauties, the Pink Panthers (mescaline), the Mary Jane, and, least of all, the booze. She knew she would struggle, but those things weren't "calling her" right now. The cigarettes were. Like many people in the world, she was a slave to the most addictive drug on the planet: *nicotine*. The other substances, she knew that she could kick them ... but only with the help of rehab.

I must check into Aspen. There's really no other way. I'll have to give Tony back the safety deposit box keys, the bank files, the bonds ... all of it. She suddenly felt like she had stolen millions from the Gambino crime family and they had an army of rogue cops and Mafia killers searching the world for her to kill her. *Oh, man ... what'd I do? Tony's going to kill me if I don't give him back what I took. I can't see him face to face. Not while I'm pregnant. He's too crazy. I have to stay away from him. I'll keep a million dollars, buy a small house, have the baby and then [maybe] I'll tell him about the kid. Right now, no. He can't find out. Not with all that mess going on ... the killings, the gangsters, his court case.*

She thought of Tony's legal problems ... *The court case may actually be a bright spot. Hopefully he'll get locked away, and then perhaps my having this baby will turn him into a real man. A father. A true CEO of Montana Realty Company. For now ... no Miami for me. No Tony. The bastard just told me that my womb was too polluted to bear him a child. I'll be damned if I allow the stress of that man, or that life, to cause me a miscarriage. You can do this, Elvira.*

A part of her wanted to pick up the telephone to contact Tony, but it would be better to settle in at Aspen first. Then she would call him and tell him to expect a UPS package containing all of what she had taken, minus a million dollars. She planned to state only that she was separating from him and that would be it. He'd have back his precious money, and she and her baby would be safe. She did not want to be vindictive, but Tony did not deserve to have a baby. Perhaps one day, but certainly not now.

What if I were to tell him I'm pregnant? she pondered as she flipped the channel to *All in the Family. He'd have the stupidest expression on his Turkish-looking face.*

Love. She loved Tony, but what did *she* really know about love? She'd thought that she had loved Frank Lopez, the man

Tony had overthrown about three years ago. The man she'd betrayed for Tony. The man Tony had killed and dethroned as drug kingpin. *Love.* As a child, there had been a man who had taught her all about love. He'd taught her that love was something you *take.* Not taking as in stealing, but taking as in blood-sucking another's *soul.* For her, love was something twisted and warped. The love she had for Tony was the same as the love Tony had for her. The kind that hurts and haunts the soul. Theirs was not the kind of love found in a Danielle Steel novel. Their love was one that was caught up in the glass box of purgatory. Lost in translation. If Stephen King or Alfred Hitchcock had made a movie about it, it would probably be entitled *A Graveyard Love.*

Elvira knew that she was no better than Tony was. She was abundantly aware of who the man was that she had married. It was no mistake on her part to marry Tony just a few months after he had executed Frank. It was this haunting fact that came back to her mind again and again over the course of their marriage. She would often stare at herself in the mirror and think, *God, what must Tony and his henchmen think of me? And Ernie! He was Frank's bodyguard! Manny, Chi-Chi, Nick the Pig ... they all know that I know that Tony killed Frank. They must think that I'm a disloyal, shameless, and treacherous woman. That I'm with Tony for the money.* The way she saw it, the marriage was doomed way before the church bells stopped ringing. Probably because of all the things that were – *deliberately* – left unsaid. The air around them was never "cleared." Everyone was left to *wonder.*

In Tony's deranged way of thinking, even as he would be exerting himself away between her legs, he was likely saying to himself, *This no-good evil witch will probably set me up to be killed by Gaspar Gomez or the Diaz Brothers ... and then she'll go bang one of them!* She knew exactly how he thought and since they had never "put it all out on the table" it was surely thoughts like these that separated and festered constantly inside of him, poisoning their union.

For her part, she never once thought *any* of what Tony had thought. Those ghosts were his and his alone. She was the ultimate forbidden fruit – and, in a way, Tony had committed as despicable an act as King David had committed in *2nd Samuel 11:14-17*: Tony had slain Frank Lopez similarly to how David had slain Uriah the Hittite. King David had lusted for Bathsheba and killed to have her as his own. In like fashion, Tony had killed Frank for the same ultimate prize. Once Tony had gotten a taste of Elvira's sweet blond bomb … he had married her.

Men are so stupid, she said to herself as she thought back on it, while waiting for the janitor to return with her smokes. *One look. One touch. One taste. One smell of a beautiful woman, and even the most powerful men in the world will kill for it. Queen of Egypt, Cleopatra, did it to Julius Caesar. Norma Jean Mortenson, better known as Marilyn Monroe, did it to John F. Kennedy. And now, Elvira does it to Frank and Tony. Stupid, stupid men. I may have loved Tony a little. Maybe. Maybe I'm unable to love. I'm obviously disloyal. Frank was killed, and not once did I cry. I packed my bags and screwed Tony that same night he came to pick me up. I'm not a good woman. For chrissakes if you think about it … "Elvira's" first four letters spell "Evil" when unscrambled. I've inherited the evil spirit of my mother, I guess.*

She yawned tiredly. A poem had been itching at her to write down while she felt inspired to do so. Before she forgot the words that were in her head, she grabbed a pen and started writing. Ironically, to match her dark mood, the pen was red.

She began writing, *Red … symbolizing the key to life, which exists as the key to reproduction …* She scribbled out those words and balled up the sheet of paper. Then she wrote out the poem:

Graveyard Love

Two enemies in love, shades of red rain,
For the hate of it or for the pain?
Givenchy dresses and blood diamonds, life is never sane.
My dreams are filled with Daddy's muffled screams,
Sounds of betrayal, death tastes a bitter vein.
Inhaling Anthrax, my spirit exhumed from the dirt,
A very small world, cocaine spilled on my skirt.
'Til death do us part, I've killed you in my sleep,
Blue-eyed cats, black and white dove,
Bittersweet red blood of my dear graveyard love.

By Elvira Montana

Not even taking the time to reread it, she put it on the table and rolled over onto her side just as the janitor returned with her cigarettes.

"What a slowpoke, man," she said to him. "The food here is way beneath my standards. It's like they shop on a budget."

"You tip well." He smiled pleasantly at her as he received the rest of the cash she had promised. "Anything I can do, you just holler for old Rufus Jones."

"I don't know when I'll be leaving," she told him as she opened one of the ten packs of cigarettes he bought for her. "But I'll need steak and lobster dinners. You can get me one tonight. I need a real breakfast too, like … bacon, sausage, cheese eggs, home fried potatoes, and croissants. Do you know *Au Bon Pain* bakery?"

"Sure do," he nodded his answer. "One of New York's Famous."

"Bring me a few boxes of their best," she ordered. "Muffins, sweet danishes, bagels. Load me up real well and I'll pay you well. Take care of me while I'm here and I'll take care of you. Deal?"

She handed him a thousand dollars. "Thank you, ma'am. Sho nuff, I'll care for you!"

"Okay, get going, old-timer," she said.

Once he was gone she hurried into the bathroom, lit up one of the cigarettes and smoked it. Guilty feelings cascaded through her as she did so, but as far as she was concerned, it was the lesser evil versus all the greater evils that she was battling against.

When she returned to her bed, Nina Lee was there, helping another assistant change Elvira's bed linens.

"You were smoking." Nina's tone was scolding and accusatory as she checked Elvira's vitals a few moments later. The assistant dropped the bed linens in a laundry cart and exited the room.

"I'm guilty, but don't get the FBI involved," Elvira replied once the thermometer was removed from her mouth. "I'm having withdrawals already. It's the lesser of evils for me, okay?"

"No, it's not *okay*." The exotic Chinese-Jamaican nurse had a stern look on her face. "Smoking leads to premature babies with extremely low birth weight; it can cause devastating health effects for your unborn. Retardation, cerebral palsy, what the hell, mon! With all you've been doing to yourself, you're risking miscarriage … you'll turn your kid into a cripple. Imagine him or her in a wheelchair, mon, unable to play with other kids or a pet dog. Unable to feed or wipe his or herself. Five hundred thousand in specialized medical care each year. Why go through the bloodclot pregnancy if all you're going to do is destroy your frickin' baby? Do you know what that will make you? A child-killer."

"I …" She trailed off, out of excuses.

"I've seen enough dead babies, mon," Nina Lee angrily continued. "I've also heard enough vain justifications from would-be mothers like you. I'm *horrified* for that baby. I'm tired of seeing dead babies, and you know what? I won't be surprised if I had to put a toe tag on you, too, like I do to hundreds each year. Because I know that if you can hurt your own baby, you'll hurt your own self! So, it's your bed, honey … bleed in it."

Nina turned and departed from the room, irate. For a long time after the nurse had retreated, Elvira brooded over all that had been said. Nina's admonitions reverberated in Elvira's ears like thunder echoing in the Grand Canyon.

CHAPTER SEVEN

La Hacienda de Sosa
Cochabamba, Bolivia
September 11, 1984, 11:05 a.m.

Sosa stood only a few feet away from the two-tiered wooden television stand as the videotape began to play the exact same interview that Sosa had played for Tony Montana nearly two weeks ago. Sosa turned up the volume.

Gutiérrez: More than 10,000 of our people are being tortured and held without trial. In the past two years, another 6,000 have simply disappeared. And your government – what does it do? It sells my government tanks, planes, guns, but not a word – not a whisper – about human rights!

Interviewer: I've heard whispers, Doctor Gutiérrez, about the financial support your government receives from the drug industry in Bolivia.

Gutiérrez: The irony, of course, is that this money – which is in the billions, Jim – is coming from your country. You are the major purchaser of our national product – which, of course, is cocaine.

Interviewer: So what you are saying, Doctor Gutiérrez, is the United States government is spending millions of dollars to eliminate the flow of drugs into our streets and at the same time is doing business with the very same government that floods those streets with cocaine … that's a bit like robbing Peter to pay Paul, isn't it?

Gutiérrez: Let me show you some of the other characters in the comedy, Jim. My organization just recently traced a purchase by this man [Gutiérrez holds up a photograph – he inserts the face on the TV screen; dour, ruthless] … *here he is, the charming face belongs to General Cucombre, the Defense Minister of my country. Two months ago he bought a twelve-million-dollar villa on Lake Lucerne in Switzerland. Now, if he's supposed to be the Bolivian Defense Minister what's he doing living in Switzerland? Guarding the cash register?* [Laughter. Gutiérrez holds up another photograph before continuing.]

This is Alejandro Sosa. Interesting character. A billionaire landowner and corporate exec with a majority stake in the fourth-largest sugar company in the world – Andes Sugar Corporation – and a list of other Fortune 500 companies. I'd say he's probably the richest man in Bolivia. A lot of people – thousands – love him but there's multiple layers of bad skin around him we are just learning about. Educated in England. Good family. The business brain and drug overlord of an empire stretching across the Andes. Not your ordinary drug dealer.

Interviewer: What are you suggesting we do about this, Doctor?

Gutiérrez: The United States government has to stop supporting these fascist gangsters who are running my country, that is what your country has to do. You have to set a strong example by calling for the observation of fundamental human rights. You Americans have no idea how important your country is as a symbol and a bastion of those rights ...

There was a long moment of silence after Sosa switched off the videotape, each man alone in his thoughts.

"The U.S. is an ally to Bolivia, right, boss?" Nancho wondered.

Sosa inhaled deeply and tried to explain. "We're *'friendly.'* We eat at the table together and shake hands. They trade with Bolivia; import-export ... There are some substantial agreements they have with Bolivia regarding eradication of coca trees, military training – things like that. The U.S. provides aid packages for our government in exchange for our country's cooperation. There's a U.S. Embassy in La Paz ..." Sosa trailed off.

"*Hermano,*" Tato cracked a smile Nancho's way. "You have to put in your resignation with Sosa before those *gringo* bastards in D.C. send you an invitation to the White House."

Chuckles rippled across the room.

"We don't impose our criminal will on our Bolivian neighbors the way the *Gambinos* do in New York, or how these *Shining Path* and *FARC-EP* plagues do in South America." Sosa spoke with obvious disgust for the guerrilla factions in the region. "Admittedly, we cross paths with them, and – by necessity only – we must associate with them. But they conduct themselves like heathen savages. We are *businessmen* and sanction murder when it's absolutely necessary. Not indiscriminately. Wholesale. We do it under the radar, with finesse. *Artisanship.*"

"*Artigiano,*" Javier said the word in *Italiano*, a language they all knew.

"*Si,*" Sosa pointed his way. "We're *kind* about it, *respectful.* Not wild cowboys and savage wolves like our associates Pablo Escobar, Gonzalo Rodriguez Gacha and La

Viuda Negra, among many others we use to traffic our product around the world."

"After what the Medellín Cartel did last April, no *narcotraficante* south of the U.S. border is safe," Nancho commented. "They assassinated Colombian Minister of Justice Rodrigo Lara."

"*Exactamente,*" Sosa concurred, "which prompted Colombian President Belisario Betancur to announce on national TV, '*We are now extraditing Colombians to the United States.*' The very words that paralyzed the Medellín Cartel with fear. Who's first on the list? That big-mouth cokehead Carlos Lehder Rivas. See? We cannot do that! Sure, we must respect Pablo and Gonzalo for taking it to their government but their war arose from fear of being extradited. *Muchachos,* if we have extraditable warrants, then it is simply time to leave Bolivia."

"They should have taken notes from us," Tato stated smartly. "When we staged a successful coup and purchased the presidency, we had our own man running the show. General Garcia Meza."

"Well, he was certainly one of ours, and still is, even though his own blatant conduct got him forced out in '81," Sosa stated in disdain to his men. "But, yes, Garcia Meza was our purchase, but we were also provided with serious political power from Washington. Anyway, the point I was making is that we must conduct ourselves like businessmen and maintain strong alliances with our friends and family in military and government. We can't '*kill to terrorize*' or else our own countrymen will turn on us and betray us. We can't return to the 1980 military junta, the infamous '*Cocaine Coup.*' The world now knows about us, what we're capable of. As for this Gutiérrez and the human rights crap ... Bolivia no longer has a dictator! Meza is out! What the *hell* is he going on about? These *lies!*" Sosa boomed, fuming.

"Easy, boss." Nancho held up a calming hand, gesturing him to tone it down. "We'll silence Gutiérrez."

"Boss is right ... I thought the same thing while watching the interview," Javier stated. "Gutiérrez said that *ten thousand* Bolivians are being held without trial and being tortured. Bolivian prisons can barely hold eight thousand so where'd he get that figure? He's lying; this must be a revenge crusade. The *six thousand* he said had disappeared ... *that* could be credible. Garcia Meza, Luis Arce Gomez, General Cucombre, Ariel Bleyer, and Hugo Banzer killed large masses of demonstrators, many were buried in mass graves, and others were tied to irons and sunk out in the Pacific."

"Don't forget Klaus Barbie," Tato reminded him.

"That Nazi pig," Sosa scowled. "But he has the mind and mastery of Hitler. With Klaus came the strategies of war, torture techniques, training, weapons, men. Gutiérrez's speeches and interviews are political, and his numbers are exaggerated to bolster his story. We – *La Corporación* – stay out of politics but this *chivato* sewer rat has been publicly aligning our photographs with Bolivia's generals and other public figures. We have to move fast to stop the bleeding. There are lawmakers in U.S. Congress such as John Kerry, Joe Biden, et cetera, who are growing distrustful of the Bolivian government ... and they threaten to end military and economic aid if certain '*austerity measures*' are not complied with ... such as coca eradication and a crackdown on *narcotraficantes*. That means *La Corporación*. You, me, everyone we employ. Gutiérrez is our biggest threat. He's not only exposing us, but he's exposing our people in the Bolivian government who protect us and shield us from prosecution. You saw the pictures he put up. The U.S. – if they lose confidence in General Cucombre to implement the *security* aspect of the '*austerity plan*,' then we lose the *key* to our future. Cucombre may be forced out ... the U.S.

exchanges *billions* with our country, *hombre*. Find and kill Gutiérrez ... and then we can breathe again."

The telephone on Sosa's desk rang shrilly.

"We don't need this heat," Javier said angrily to his younger brothers as Sosa handled the telephone call. "Not when the demand for *cocaine* is skyrocketing worldwide. We have shipments going out to five continents, sixty countries; the U.S. being the biggest. If we don't silence Gutiérrez ... it'll all domino."

Sosa slammed down the telephone and stared at his men. "Good news. We have eyes on Gutiérrez."

"Yeah!" Nancho was on his feet with Tato and Javier hugging each other excitedly.

"Don't celebrate yet," Sosa warned them.

"You want his head or his balls, *jefe*?" Tato inquired.

"Neither," Sosa stood up and joined his men in a circle. "That was Cucombre on the phone. Mobilize two elite kill units. Our best men only. There will be no room for mistakes. Get ready for anything. Two helicopters, two airplanes, ten men. I'm waiting for specifics on that *chivato*."

The men turned to leave.

"Tato." Sosa stopped them. "*Chicos.*"

"Something else, boss?" Tato asked slowly.

"La Gata Negra is on her way back," Sosa nodded, his lips taut with emotion.

Tato held his breath. "Yeah?"

"She has Alberto with her."

Javier, Nancho, and Tato all had tears in their eyes saddened for the loss of their fallen comrade.

"That Catalina ..." Tato grabbed Sosa's shoulder, grateful. "She's sure turning out to be something. *¡Vamanos, muchachos!*"

They left Sosa alone in the study.

CHAPTER EIGHT

The Aspen Clinic
Nyack, New York
September 11, 1984

All the waters of the world cannot wash the blood off of my husband's hands, Elvira quietly reflected as she was being driven up I-87 North, also known as the New York State Thruway. *But there is a piece of me that yearns for him ... I also have dark secret fantasies I know I can never again relive. I hate my father but when I think of all the things he used to do to me, I feel both alive and dead. I am so screwed up ...*

When she was initially checked into the Aspen Clinic, she almost immediately wanted to call a taxicab and flee. But, to her surprise, the Aspen staff were very kind and persuasive to her as were the few celebrity residents she quickly recognized from television and several magazines. It became obvious that there were some residents there who had developed the serial habit of suddenly "appearing" in the intake section of the administration building to get a peek at the new person being admitted.

"Don't mind them, Mrs. Montana, they're just looking for their favorite movie star or rock star to come in," Nurse Cynthia Redding explained. "They just being nosey so they can gossip or see if they know you. Aspen gets all the troubled celebrities. Millionaires, billionaires, business and music moguls, sports stars, Hollywood types, and even plain old rich kids. As for those gossips, I have trouble getting them to come down here to take baby aspirin. [Reading from Elvira's file] Elvira Montana. Are you a celebrity?"

"I have enough problems." Elvira, looking aloof, shook her head no. "I was a pretty well-known model at one point but models are not celebrities ... except to girls or boys who aspire to be models. Nobody cares when our looks fade. Wouldn't you know if I were a celebrity?"

"I'm no Robin Leach or Barbara Walters. What would I know?" She stared at Elvira for a moment. "You're cute enough. Blond, skinny ... whiter than a Norwegian. That's two-thirds of Hollywood right there, baby! Ha! Ha! We've had Richard Pryor, Farrah Fawcett, Mick Jagger, Ozzie Osbourne, Natalie Wood, and many others."

Elvira was impressed. Those were all names that she knew very well. "My gosh, Natalie Wood was an actress I looked up to. I remember her death like yesterday. November 29th, 1981. They say she died of drowning off the coast of Catalina Island, California. I was so sad at hearing about that. I was very suspicious about the death."

"Yeah," the nurse sighed. "Shame. She was one of the few big stars to open up this site. Accident my butt. Anyway, let's learn from her. The consequences of drinking and drugging is nothing but doom and gloom. For the persons doing the consuming, for the people who love them, and for the community. These behaviors have an infinite ripple effect, Montana. Everybody pays. We all pay the cost of what we've lost. Society pays. Stop, Elvira. Learn about your behaviors, baby. Stop. Live healthy. Help your baby live healthy."

When Cynthia had completed asking Elvira a list of mental and medical-related questions, Elvira was escorted out of the administration building and into one of the separate buildings. Each of the units on the massive suburban property held four condominiums. Cynthia left her with one of the male counselors – Brett McNichols. Elvira had to avert her eyes from his, because he was inadvertently causing her temperature to rise. *He is so hot*, she was thinking, as the 30-ish brown-haired man shook her hand and led her into her new temporary home.

"Oh my gosh!" she whispered upon entering. "It's beautiful."

The condominium looked more like a luxury vacation home in St. Kitts than it did a rehabilitation residence. Each room was spacious, well-lit, immaculately furnished in Italian and Scandinavian styles, a fireplace in the living room and another in the master bedroom. The master bathroom was what finally made up her mind to really stay – it was just too cozy and much too comfortable of a "getaway" to turn away from. The bedroom had a huge walk-in closet with ample shelf room. The kitchen was a contemporary gourmet style. Every room, including the kitchen and bath, had low-noise ceiling fans, and central air-conditioning and heat. There was a back porch with a polished oak deck, barbeque pit, and Jacuzzi. From where she stood she could see the community swimming pool with an enclosed fenced area surrounding it.

Brett McNichols sat with her at the kitchen table and took the time to explain what the program was all about. He answered all of her questions and told her what Aspen expected out of her.

"It's a really laid-back place," he informed her. "It's all life-based and community-based. You'll have to sit through two orientation classes, watch a videotape in each. We'll give you copies to watch alone in your home if you need them. You'll follow a curriculum specifically designed to fit your needs. There's one-on-ones and group therapy meetings. Your minimum stay is twenty-eight days. Those stays can be pretty intense. All staff have already reviewed your case. You're pregnant, withdrawing from Quaaludes, cocaine, alcohol, marijuana, and cigarettes. Do I have it right?"

"If you only knew," she replied wistfully. "Ashamed to admit it ... but yeah. The cigarettes are what I struggle most with. I feel helpless to fight that addiction. The others, I ... desire them and if they were here, I'd be tempted to use them."

"We can help you," he promised. "Nicotine is the most powerful and most addictive substance on the planet. Tobacco companies hire the world's best scientists to create even more addictive chemicals to mix into their products to get us even more addicted. Trust me, I understand. I smoke. But I'm down from a pack-a-day to three-a-day."

"How do you do it?"

"I light up one smoke and put it out three times." He smiled as he said it. "It's three cigarettes but I'm smoking nine times per day. Not everyone can cold turkey such a strong addiction. Do what's possible for Elvira to do. Develop your own discipline. There is no one way to do it."

"Makes sense."

"You have every incentive to try," he reminded her by pointing to her belly. "There are such profound ramifications for your child if you smoke during pregnancy. Remember cigarettes contain poison. Poison kills. If it affects you it will affect your fetus. Almara Quijano – one of our addiction counselors – she works almost exclusively with pregnant and nursing mothers. You're the only one we have here at the moment so you'll be seeing a lot of her. She'll replace your nicotine cravings with junk foods. She's going to feed you and feed you and feed you. Let's hope it takes your mind off smoking for the sake of your baby."

"Almara is her name?"

"We all call her Ally or Almara," he replied and paused to see if he forgot anything. "You're a female so only a female counselor and female nurse will have keys to your residence. They are in and out frequently. I'm pretty sure that Ally will be your assigned counselor. She lives in Brooklyn. Since she hates the long drives home, she stays in staff's quarters. How old are you?"

"Twenty-five."

"She's thirty, I believe," he told her. "She's such an old soul; wise beyond her years and so very tough. At 3 p.m. each day we have what's called a 'Daily Residential' meeting. It's mandatory. That's where the residents air out whatever's on your minds, submit grievances, ask questions, get answers, and so on."

"How many people are here?"

"Um, nineteen women." He stopped to think for a minute. "Thirty men. This Aspen can house up to sixty-six people, but you'll never see everybody at once, because it's all divided into smaller groups. We stay at full staff, so no one is overloaded with cases. There are other locations for Aspen Clinics, too. This one opened in 1981, so it's the newest."

Brett excused himself a few minutes later.

She took the time to unpack her Louis Vuitton carry-on suitcase and realized that she needed to go shopping. She wrote out a list of what she needed and hoped the staff would allow her to go.

She showered and dressed in a skin-tight designer jogging suit and beach-style flip-flops. She applied make-up and put on her diamond jewelry, including her wedding ring. She slowly inspected the condo room-by-room and noticed the cameras. The only place the cameras were not present were the bathroom and walk-in closet.

"So, my closet is my dressing room," she said aloud to herself. "And cameras will watch me while I sleep. Great, I'm in Attica."

"Three hundred grand cash," she murmured minutes later as she placed the carry-on into the closet. "And millions in bearer bonds. Where will I hide all of it?"

Her previous thoughts had returned: … rogue cops and Mafia killers …

For the time being she would have to leave her valuables in the closet. But then she thought, They have keys to the place. She made up her mind right then. I'll carry the bag around with me. At least until I can get to a bank.

At three o'clock, Brett escorted her into a very large room. "This is the atrium. Most of the group meetings are held up on the stage here. Remember, it's the one thing you cannot miss."

The room was enormous. It looked like an oversized movie theater, filled with rows of cushioned seats. The stage was long and wide; chairs were placed in a circular formation. Then she saw it. The huge movie screen partially obstructed by long burgundy curtains.

Elvira, with shades on, lips pouted, gazed around disinterestedly at the dozen or so men and women already seated on the straight-backed, cushioned, wooden chairs. More people continued to file into the atrium from three separate entrances. Now that she had had a good look around, it sort of reminded her of a Broadway theater. What irony, she thought. Hollywood's best actors are real-life addicts being treated in a theater. A young woman seated nearby informed her that movies were shown in the atrium once a day starting at 6 p.m.

"They're usually great movies, too," the blond woman commented. "Hi, I'm Megan Riley. I love your hair."

"Elvira," she said dryly. "I need to go shopping and stop at a bank. Whom do I speak to?"

"Really?" the petite girl said, smiling. "I'm here to address two problems. Alcoholism and sex addiction. I drink and cruise bars wearing the sexiest dresses. Red, white, or black, it all depends on my mood. Then I hunt … for the well-endowed. Get what I'm saying?"

Elvira looked at the girl's sweet, innocent face. "Are you some kind of friggin' nutcase or what?"

The woman shrugged. "Whatever, you stuck-up spitwad."

This chick is a psycho, Elvira thought as she walked away.

"You must be Elvira Montana," a very cute, round-faced Puerto Rican woman stated as she extended her hand in greeting. "I'm Almara Daniela Belarios Quijano."

First there was the mega-hot Chinese-Jamaican nurse at Astoria Hospital, whose beauty surely had men worshipping her, and now there was this Spanish goddess, Almara. She had one of those deep, throaty voices, but hers exuded a sassiness and sexiness that was a perfect fit for her personality. Her shiny black pixie-cut hair, her glossy brown eyes, and every other physical characteristic she had, it all sort of just blended together naturally with who she was. She was not a petite woman, like the psycho Elvira had just run away from, but, height-wise, she was about the average. Her curvy figure was what a bikini model would die to have, but Almara moved about as if no one had ever told her about the beauty she had, the body of some mystical goddess from an erotic Cathryn Fox novel.

Almara was born and raised in Brooklyn, New York, in a section called Williamsburg. She did not hesitate to tell Elvira who she was and that she would be honored to be her counselor. Elvira took to her instantly. Almara burst at the seams with energy and enthusiasm. Her down-to-earth style and presence was motivating. She had the "gift of gab" and a way about her that drew people to her. She spoke with that classic Brooklyn (Nuyorican) Rosie Perez accent, and she used a straightforward cynicism that had that natural Lenny Bruce appeal to it. But hers was not comedy; it was real and sad. She was loud, but very profound in all she said and did.

"So you'll be my counselor?" Elvira wanted to know for sure.

"You want me to be, then no," Almara said. "But if you need me to be, then yeah."

"I need you to be."

"Wish granted."

"Thank you," Elvira stated sincerely. "I need you to help me get to a bank. It's urgent. Also, I came with very little so I need to shop for clothes and personal things. Last, I'm new to New York, and I'll be staying so I'll need to order a car and stop to speak to a real estate agent."

"Sounds like a full day," Almara told her. "Plus, your circumstances will permit me to take you. Be ready at 7 a.m."

"I'd appreciate that."

Ally lightly touched Elvira's shoulder. "Let's get you introduced to everybody."

The group meeting began.

CHAPTER NINE

The Department of Defense
La Paz, Bolivia
September 14, 1984

One of the benefits of having eyes and ears in multi-international government is having easy access to an enemy's telephone calls, credit card and bank transactions, computer activity, and even his or her flight plan.

Juan Gabriel Benino Cucombre (aka "Nino"), the Minister of Defense for Bolivia, completely understood the gravity of the Dr. Gutiérrez dilemma and he was doing everything in his power to assist Sosa (General Cucombre's cousin) in "stopping the bleeding." That is, in locating, then assassinating Gutiérrez.

While Dr. Gutiérrez was not the only person in Bolivia being surveilled by the government, he was listed as a "moderately radical threat to the peace and stability" of Bolivia and thereby warranted an official investigation by the Department of Defense (or "DOD"). Cucombre did not trust every DOD official, but there were a handful of *La Corporación* members he'd strategically installed in the DOD who were very reliable and would not let him down. One of those members was Catalina Lilli Romero-Toro, aka *La Gata Negra* (i.e., The Black Cat).

The 24-year-old Catalina was mistress to General Cucombre, who was head-over-heels in love with her. She was the daughter of Juca Bélen Romero-Toro (Benny the Skull's elder sister). Catalina lacked the breathtaking curvaceousness of her mother and aunt (the late Simona Mira Lugo-Toro). Catalina had inherited little from the women in her bloodline, except for their beauty and black hair. Catalina was what men would call a "hairy" woman; her tall, slender body was covered by a light coat of fine black peach fuzz. Her brown eyes were piercing; *wise* was the word for them. Her full eyebrows made her look younger than she really was. Her lips were full, pouty, and they seemed to draw attention to the rest of her oval face. The way she walked, with the sassy bounce of her long, black, lustrous tresses, reminded one of a runway model.

If her personality had to be compared to anyone in her family, it would have to be Benny, because of how quiet and mysterious she was. Catalina Lilli was smart, curious, articulate; she worked hard, and she always left a profound impression on those she came into contact with. Perhaps it was because very few women in Bolivia sat where she sat, which was up close and personal (very personal) with the country's most powerful general.

The sleek and sexy Catalina knocked twice on General Cucombre's office door prior to entering. He was on the telephone, but he waved her in anyway. She closed and locked the door behind her before sitting on one of the two large brown cushioned leather chairs in front of his presidential desk. He had one eye on her as he spoke to the President of Bolivia. He watched her white-stockinged legs cross … and then uncross. She spread wide her knees and he saw between the creamy whites of her thighs … *the softest place on earth.*

"Something critically important just came up, *Señor Presidente*," he told the President. "I'll call you back."

"General," she greeted him with a mischievous grin on her face. "I have something good for you."

"I can see it." He took off his uniform jacket. "And ... I can also *smell* it."

"*From there?!*" she giggled, opening wider.

"Orange blossoms," he told her, sniffing the air.

That made her laugh.

"Why are you doing this to me? You'll put me on heart pills."

"You ordered me to grow the hair back on," she said, pointing. "It's trying to follow orders."

"Why's it so ... *pink* like that?"

She blushed. "Arousal."

"And it's moist."

"Thinking of you made me touch it."

He walked over to her. "You just ruined a good work day."

He got on his knees before her and put his hands all the way under her buttocks before she palmed his forehead, stopping him from going in for a taste of paradise.

"*¡Espérate!*" she said emphatically. "I said I had something good for you."

"But *this* is good," he complained, slapping her hands away.

"Better," she promised as his balding head disappeared under her black dress, kissing her creamy thighs.

"Nothing in the world is better to a man than the taste of *chocha*," he said before digging in.

"I ... *oh!*" she moaned as she did a weak job of wiggling away. "We have emergency information on the journalist!" she managed to blurt out.

He froze and sat back on his knees to stare up at her. "*¿Gutiérrez?* Dr. Orlando Gutiérrez, the squealing pig?"

She nodded.

"Well ..." He stood up, wiping her off of his face. "Right now that *is* better. But only for now."

He snatched the file she held in her hand and wagged a finger in her face. "You have been a very bad girl, you know that? Later, I will be spanking you."

"You're right," she agreed, standing up. "I *do* need a spanking. But I did very good, right? And I also brought Alberto back home to be properly buried."

"*Sí* ... *Sí* ... Let me read ..."

$$$$$

Años Antes ...

Catalina was well-informed about the humble beginnings of her relatives, the Toros. The Toros' lasting association with the Sosas was a question no longer even asked and Catalina was too young to even wonder about it anyway. In the beginning, nobody had wanted to reveal to Catalina that she was a product of rape when Juca Bélen had been eleven years old. However, hiding it from her would only mean that they *were* feeling shame. There was nothing for anyone to feel ashamed about. An eleven-year-old had been gang-raped. Benny had told Catalina when she'd been twelve about the rape, and he had promised her that he would find out who did it and avenge Juca's honor.

Years later, neither Simona Mira nor Juca Bélen could fathom why Catalina had elected to forgo college in Spain or Italy and, instead, enlist in the Bolivian Army. Uncle Benny, Sosa, and her cousins, the Toros, had all known why. Catalina had fallen in love with Sosa's cousin, General Cucombre, when he was 49 years old, and she was only 17. Benny was the one who had told his sister, Juca Bélen, about the affair.

"*Don Benino Cucombre??!*" Juca had exclaimed. "He's an old man compared to her!"

Benny had thought it through carefully. "*Piensalo, hermana. Piensalo.* [Think about it, Sis. Think.] What do you want from her? To give it up to a *no-good*? That's what most seventeen-year-olds do. So what he's forty-nine? He's the most powerful general in Bolivia, behind Garcia Meza. He's a respected diplomat all over the world. He's very rich, educated, and he's one of us. Cousin to Don Haché and the Sosas. Our Cata ... give her some credit."

"But he's married," Juca had lamented.

"That's even better," Benny had shrugged. "She's even smarter. He'll make her rich and give great gifts of guilt to *Doña* Cucombre for the privilege of allowing him one small snack. Cata will use her wit to establish a career in the military. He's a fool for that kid."

"You mean use her *chocha, hermano,*" Juca had said with some disgust.

Benny had looked at his sister. "What woman *doesn't* use the *chocha* somewhere along the line? All of you do. God knows it – that's why he made youse with one. And, look, Nino has an old hag for a wife, who's never given him kids. He'd never divorce her ... she at least has to allow the man some kids. He won't abuse our Cata. There're strict laws we have in our *cosa.* And Catalina is not foolish. He's been charming her for a while. He asked her to stay and promised her his full support. And, also, she's not pregnant."

"*No?*"

"No."

"She could be killed, Benito," she had said worriedly. "It's the army."

"*Nino's* army," Benny had calmed her. "It'll all be career-building for her. Army Intelligence is the main goal for her. Remember, Nino is first cousin to the Sosa family. Nino, Garcia Meza, Arce Gomez, Hugo Banzer, Ariel Bleyer ... we own *all* of them."

Juca Bélen and Simona Mira had been reassured about Catalina's welfare, and they did not get in her way. They'd had to trust Benny that she'd be safe. And he had been right

… Catalina was more than just good looks – she was much more, and not all of what had come to her came easily …

In Bolivia, the army was organized into ten territorial divisions. Each of them, with the exception of *Viacha*, occupied a region generally corresponding to the administrative departments, with some of them overlapping. Due to the influence General Cucombre had over her career at that time – 1978 – the then eighteen-year-old Catalina was initially sent to one of the army's six military regions (i.e., *regiones militares* – or RMs for short).

She was stationed at RM-4, in Sucre, which covered the departments of Cochabamba and northern Chuquisaca. She was assigned to the 7th Division Army, BMP-272, and graduated Basic Training (BCT) on her own merit, not Cucombre's. Of course, the senior officers and army personnel at BMP-272 had known who she was and they'd all given Cucombre the respect he'd earned and *"kept their hands off the goods."*

For two years she'd been a Bolivian Military Police officer with the 7th Division, until an instance of terror had come to shatter the peace she had known there. It was in the summer of 1980 when she'd heard the women's locker room door slam open, the growling voices of men ordering a thrashing female to keep quiet. Catalina, who had only been wrapped in a towel at the time, had grabbed her service revolver and tiptoed quietly into a nearby mop closet. The woman was being slapped and beaten for trying desperately to escape and yell for help. To Catalina's horror, the gang rape had taken place on the linoleum floor directly in front of the mop closet. The door had had an old rusty louver-type ventilation cover on it which had enabled Catalina to witness each man take a turn with the eighteen-year-old cadet.

Catalina had wanted to stop the brutal sexual assault, but she had thought better of it. The men had not only been armed, but they'd also been senior officers that she had known and respected. If she had come out of that closet there had existed the extreme likelihood that they would have killed Catalina and the cadet (to cover up the crime). Catalina had not been just another MP. She had been the *girlfriend* of one of the most feared generals in Bolivia's history.

Catalina had waited as spiders and other insects had crawled over her in the dark closet. Hours later, she had come out smelling like a filthy mildewed mop. She'd showered, dressed, and placed a telephone call to Cucombre that same night, and she'd told him everything she had witnessed. An hour later, Catalina had been picked up and taken to the Sosa estate, where she'd fallen asleep. That following morning General Cucombre had arrived with a packet of photographs he'd wanted her to look at.

"There's a total of sixteen officers in the 7th Division," Cucombre had said as he laid out all sixteen of the photographs on Sosa's desk in the study of the old mansion. "I want you to pick out the bastards who raped that cadet. The *United States Armed Forces* may permit their female soldiers to be raped and sexually harassed without recourse. Not Bolivia. *Not me!!*" he had boomed.

She had not hesitated in picking out the five rapists. "Those are the five dogs that did it. I'm sure of it."

The following evening one of Sosa's henchmen, Diego, had escorted her to an abandoned meat-packing plant on the outskirts of Cochabamba's business district.

"Diego, right?" she'd asked the driver of the new black Dodge van.

"Yeah."

"They got them?" she'd asked.

"Yeah."

"That the only word you know?" she'd joked.

"No."

They'd pulled up alongside two other dark delivery vans parked outside of the meat-packing plant's rear loading docks. They'd entered the facility sometime after midnight. There, she had almost immediately, upon entering, heard the agonizing screams of men being tortured. When she had physically laid eyes upon them, she'd thought she had been seeing things. Benny had come up to her holding a white full-body *Tyvex* suit, the kind worn by HAZMAT and CDC workers while cleaning up toxic waste or handling deadly viruses inside of a laboratory or hospital.

"There's a lot of blood," Benny had warned her. "But first … you can turn around and leave if you want. They're going to die in here tonight. But if you stay … it's your big night – if you want it."

She looked at him with slitted eyes. "You mean I'll be brought in. I'll be *Mafiosa. En la pandilla.*"

Benny had frowned at her. "*Never* use that word again. This is a *business*, not a gang. Are you in or not?"

"I want in."

She'd put on the Tyvex suit and was led into the heart of the old facility where, before her very eyes, she'd seen four men hanging – suspended, completely nude – from chains that were bolted onto sliding steel conveyor belt beams high above. *This is a scene straight out of a Stephen King or Alfred Hitchcock movie,* she had thought. The beams and chains had apparently once been used to transport the heavy carcasses of cattle, horses, pigs, vicuñas, and llamas to and fro across the facility.

"*La Gata Negra* (The Black Cat)," General Cucombre warmly greeted her, hugging her. "Here they are. Before we finish them off, *mi amor*, let's be one hundred percent sure that these are the rapists."

She'd closely observed the four severely beaten and bloodied men. They hung from the chains like chandeliers. Each man had had two giant rusted meat hooks thrusted into the soft tissue areas of their backs. She had looked at Nancho, Tato, Javier, Benny and Rafa and knew instantly where most of the blood had come from. These men were experts at inflicting physical pain and violence upon an enemy. The blood of the rapists had been noticeable on the Tyvex suits each man wore.

Catalina Lilli Romero-Toro had realized that she'd been brought to the slaughterhouse for what was to be the very last stage of a very lengthy torture-killing.

"Are you kidding me, Niñito?" she'd scoffed at her older paramour. "They're already half-dead ... on *meathooks*. '*One hundred percent*' or not, they're dying. What – if one is wrong you'll *free* him?"

"No." Cucombre had shrugged. "Stop breaking my balls, *mijita*. I was only checking."

"They're beaten and swollen," she'd told him. "I don't know. But there's one missing. There were *five* I picked out in the photos."

Benny, indicating with a thumb over his shoulder, had said, "The fifth guy's in the van, dead. He was so scared he had a heart attack ... or choked on something."

"Yeah. Right." She'd looked around at the men she had known and loved all her life, then at the rapists. "What do you want me to do?"

"It's your show, *mi sobrina* [my niece]." Benny had handed her a jagged-edged hunting knife, the kind Sylvester Stallone had in *Rambo*. "Three killings is the *La Corporación* minimum for those chosen to be brought in. Members are chosen mostly due to their skill and experience ... and they're ordered to go out and kill enemies of *La Corporación* to prove their loyalty. Since you lack that skill – *for now* – the three required targets have been delivered to you."

She'd stared at the big knife. "Why a knife? Why not a gun?"

Nancho had laughed in her face. "*Mi prima*, everybody with a brain knows that even the most cowardly *bandido* on the street can shoot a gun. Your first kill is for your lifetime marriage to *La Corporación Mafia Cruzena*. Make it personal. Look each man in the eyes, so you always remember ... don't you ever try to betray *La Corporación*, or else this will be you. Always remember the blood, *mi prima*. If you screw up there's nothing anyone here can do for you. Remember the blood."

Once she'd gotten past the nerves, she had conjured up the brutal images and sounds of the teen cadet the men had savagely raped and beaten. She'd then placed the sharp knife firmly against the throat of 2nd Lieutenant Pedro Monroig and froze while staring him in the eyes, listening to him beg for mercy.

Benny and Cucombre stood at her sides.

"*Mi sobrina* ..." Benny had whispered. "Make believe his neck is a piece of lamb. Cut hard and deep. He'll never rape a young girl again."

Catalina had sliced Lieutenant Monroig's throat from left to right and she'd stood there to watch the blood spurt and flow until he'd stopped screaming and lost consciousness. She'd stood there ... staring, frozen.

"He's gone, *mijita* ..." the general had whispered. "Gone. Keep going. It gets easier to snatch souls after the first one."

The next Bolivian Army officer she'd killed was 1st Lieutenant Colonel Marco Ramirez. General Cucombre had been correct: the second kill had been easier. "*A murderer is a murderer whether you kill one man or even a hundred men*," Cucombre had whispered. Marco Ramirez had been the one Catalina had seen anally sodomizing the cadet. The last officer she'd been ordered to kill was 2nd Lieutenant Hector Villareal. As he had squirmed and choked on his blood, without even being told, she'd taken the knife to the throat of the last man – Captain Herber Velasquez. She had calmly placed the sharp tip of the blade to the jugular vein area and shoved it up and in, causing the blood to squirt and splash several rivulets onto her uncovered face and Tyvex suit.

"Ha, ha! That's why there's the hood section of the suit you should have put on," Nancho had laughed and had given her a handkerchief to wipe the blood off with.

Shortly after that bloody night, her induction into *La Corporación* was made official at an *El Concejo* ("The Council") ceremony. Subsequent to the ceremony she had made the choice to remain in the military (with a little urging from General Cucombre).

She had entered into the *School of Command and Staff* within the RM-4 and, upon graduating, she had entered into the RM-6 (in Santa Cruz) army aviation company and the highly coveted *Bolivian Condores School of Special Forces*, where she had learned to fly and gained expert knowledge in weaponry and bomb-making. Upon graduating, she had been elevated first to sergeant and later to lieutenant. Soon after that she had been appointed by General Cucombre to fill in a vacancy at the Department of Defense's Special Intelligence Division.

She had accepted the post not only because it had been an important one for a woman to have but because she had been in love with General Cucombre for some time. She had known that the relationship was not "right" but it did not feel wrong either. And, as time had passed, General Cucombre – dour, bulldog face and all – had worn on her despite the 32-year age difference between them. He had explained to her that his wife had never given him any children and had promised Catalina that if she would bear for him one or more children that he would leave for her and their child(ren) the bulk of his riches upon his demise.

"They'll be labeled illegitimate," she had worried. "*Bastards*. You're married and famous. What will people think?"

"I will give them my name," he had promised her. "They'll be wealthy. No one will care."

"I have to work until you die?" she had asked him. "What about if I want to stay home for them ... and for you? Don't you think I'd need my own money? My own *security*?"

"Ah." He had gotten it. "The day you give birth to our first child, you'll have a bank account for ten million dollars. And a Will shall be made and kept at a Catalonia, Spain, law firm for you and the children."

She had agreed to those terms.

$$$$$

Hoy

General Cucombre studied the contents of the file and looked at Catalina. "Catalina Lilli Romero-Toro, this bastard, Gutiérrez, is going to Argentina? Is it confirmed?"

Catalina nodded. "I checked it out personally. I suggest we get a chopper fired up right now and put Sosa on notice immediately."

"We have one last shot at this guy." Cucombre sat behind his desk and began writing furiously.

"*¿Qué estás haciendo?* [What are you doing?]" she asked him as she stood up.

"Preparing a coded letter for Sosa," he answered over the sound of his pencil furiously writing out the letter. "It'll take me a few minutes, and then I'll need you to type it. Call for a courier and have my private chopper ready to go up to the Pentagon."

She hurried to do as he ordered.

CHAPTER TEN

The Aspen Clinic
Nyack, New York
September 12, 1984

"The two best serial killers in the world are?" Almara was asking the large group of residents from the atrium stage in an early morning meeting at the Aspen Clinic.

"Mother Nature and addiction," a slender, older White male, billionaire NFL team owner answered the question.

"Very good, Mr. Kessel, I see you have stayed away from the telephone long enough to learn a thing or two about why you're here," she said, smiling to take some of the bite out of her admonition. *"There is no better serial killer than Mother Nature.* Throughout history she has racked up more casualties than all other murderers combined. She's most efficient and there's nothing man can do to stop her devastation."

"You mean like the Great Flood," Mr. Kessel chimed in. "That wasn't Mother Nature. That was God himself."

"I believe in God," Almara said to them. "But for the sake of those who do not ... God's name is Mother Nature."

"Okay ..." Mr. Kessel conceded.

"Anyway, trust me. I know what everyone here is going through," she continued, turning her gaze onto Elvira. "Elvira Montana is new here. So, let me once again testify as a witness against that other serial killer called addiction ...

Elvira, would you please step up here on the stage and sit in this chair?"

Elvira left her atrium seat and did as she was asked. She sat down in an orange-colored armchair across from where Almara was already seated in an identical chair.

"*I am a recovering alcoholic.*" Ally ran a hand back over the left side of her pixie-cut hair. "Just because I have a job and I look clean means nothing. I am in recovery. My last drink was ten years ago *to the day.* September 12, 1974. This is a big, big milestone for people like us. Anyways, we'd been drinking all the cheap stuff – *800, Private Stock, Malt Duck, Mad Dog 20/20*, and maybe a few beers. You know the kind ... *Corona, Guinness Stout, Heineken*, and that Dominican beer *Presidente*. Me and my friends. I was a straight-A student from Williamsburg housing projects in Brooklyn. I was a good girl, so my parents thought, just graduating from high school and about to attend Columbia University on a track and field scholarship. We were out that evening celebrating our graduation as if we'd won the New York lottery. Me and three girlfriends were all chillin' in my old *Buick-Oldsmobile.* I call it that because half of it was Buick, the other half was Oldsmobile. It had different color doors, different color hood – pieced together from the auto graveyard. It looked like a checkerboard."

There was a ripple of laughter but tears were beginning to pool up in her eyes. She was being serious.

"We were coming from this popular nightclub in the Bronx called *The Fever*," she explained, struggling to contain the emotion as she was revealing her tragic story. "It was very late, so the traffic was not that bad. I drove around the Bronx looking for some weed. First, we went up to Elliot Avenue and the Grand Concourse; then on up to Marion and Bedford Avenues, but we couldn't find weed. Finally, we ended up finding some up on Story Avenue. We smoked it, and, at around 3 a.m., I got onto the Bronx River Parkway South, right there at the Gun Hill Road on-ramp. As soon as I drove onto the parkway I saw the construction cones, the orange pylon things that caution drivers to slow down. There was a long row of them, about a hundred yards worth. I also saw the yellow caution lights and the construction workers."

Elvira was staring at the floor intently, avoiding eye contact because Almara was getting more emotional by the minute. She was doing her best to control her tears but she was losing the battle.

"I don't recall how fast I was going ..." She was now fully crying, her voice full of remorse. "I was speeding ... and ... and *I hit a man!* A construction worker! I hit him so hard that his body came into the car, through the windshield! I thought he was dead!" she screamed out her anguish.

"Oh my God ..." Elvira's heart went out to her. Elvira's tears were flowing, too. She reached out for Ally and pulled her up from her seat, embracing her. Other residents came up onto the stage and joined the embrace. Pain and remorse like what she was witnessing here was strange to Elvira. The story itself was not what was so moving; it was the pain and sorrow Elvira saw coming from this beautiful Latin woman. The guilt of what she had done was still ripping her to shreds inside, even after ten years.

"Did he die?" Elvira wanted to know.

"No." Almara shook her head and sniffled.

"Thank God," Elvira sounded relieved.

"I have a problem thanking God for what I did to that man and his family," Ally admitted through the tears. "I made him a cripple. He was mangled. They had to amputate his foot, remove what remained of his eye, he later developed gangrene and then they had to remove more of his leg. For me ... the judge killed me with mercy and kindness. He was lenient because I was a student with no arrest record, on my way to a prestigious university. He sentenced me as a 'Youthful Offender' so I'd have no record. He gave me five hundred hours of community service and ten years' probation. I went on to college where I studied psychology, substance abuse, and addiction. I graduated with a double bachelor's degree in those subjects and I've been working with Aspen for seven years. I accepted a transfer to this site when it opened in 1981."

"The man who you hit," Elvira stated curiously. "Did he – did you apologize?"

"I tried," Almara answered, drying her eyes with a Kleenex someone had given to her. "Through my attorney, but he refused to see me."

The story drew Elvira closer to Almara because now the two women, it seemed, were even. They were both beautiful women with ugly flaws in their past.

$$\$\$\$\$\$$

September 13, 1984

As promised, Almara and Brett escorted Elvira to the Bank of New York in Nyack where she rented a large safety deposit box, and opened up a checking and savings account. They spent the day shopping at various stores in the state's biggest mall, *The Palisades Mall*. She spent so much cash that she had to have most of her purchases delivered to Aspen.

Fortunately, inside of the mall was a well-known real estate franchise office. She took full advantage of the thirty minutes she was able to spend in a meeting with the agent she spoke to. She left with a stack of several books she would later examine to see if she would be interested in buying or leasing a home in the region.

The last stop she made was at a Chevrolet car dealership, where she placed an order for a fully-loaded luxury van.

"You mean like the one on the showroom floor there?" an Italian man asked in a deep New York accent.

Elvira turned in the cushioned swivel chair she was sitting in and nodded. *"Exactly* like that one but I'd like it to be all-black with a sharp gold detail. I also want leather seats, two telephones, a television; you know, turn it into a luxury office. Everything that's in an office, I want in that van. Surprise me."

She left a deposit of $30,000, cash.

Later that evening, Almara helped Elvira cook a steak and lobster dinner which they ate together. All of the groceries were put away after the delivery van came and dropped off all of Elvira's things. Almara was using a washcloth dipped in sudsy dishwater to wipe off the store items when she noticed Elvira laughing.

"What's so funny?" Almara was smiling as she wiped off a gallon of milk. "That I'm wiping off the groceries?"

"Uh-huh."

"The dishwater is clean and it has a cap of bleach in it," Almara stated in an admonishing tone of voice. "The bleach, of course, kills germs and bacteria. Everything in the store has been touched by other people. People who pee, doodoo, wipe themselves, dig in their butts, noses, they change Pampers, sneeze or cough into their hands, handle dirty money, open door handles, clean toilets, masturbate, and many fail to wash their hands. You're talking bacteria, viruses, germs of all kinds that spread. You never learned, coming up at home, to do that? To alleviate the virus before it becomes a disease?"

"Like addiction."

"Exactamente."

"It's a lot of items."

"You bought a thousand dollars' worth of groceries."

"The cupboards were empty."

Elvira helped her complete the job.

After her shower, Nurse Samantha Rogers came in to administer Elvira her medications and to check and record her vitals.

"How's the withdrawals?" the nurse inquired.

"Bothersome," Elvira answered. "I'm anxious, a little shaky but it's manageable. It's the cigarettes that I'll kill for."

"You're doing a swell job," the nurse commented as she calmly took notes. "You're scheduled for a sonogram tomorrow. It's on-site, in the medical building. You'll bring her up, Ally?"

"No problem."

"All the pregnant women we keep an *especially* close eye on," Nurse Samantha said prior to her exit. "Okay ladies. Next check is at 2 a.m. so don't get creeped out that we're going to be checking you every four hours."

Samantha said "good night" and left the condo.

"There's some notes in your file that stood out to me," Almara stated as she sat down in a comfortable armchair next to the nightstand. "Very, very disturbing things which you alluded to in front of Dr. Coles and Nina Lee at the hospital. Something about you being sexually assaulted and impregnated at the age of twelve."

"Dr. Coles and the Black China Doll," Elvira muttered. "Do you know her? The Chinese-Jamaican girl?"

"I've picked up clients from there before," was all she said about Nina Lee. "Tell me about the molestation."

"I don't know, Ally." Elvira kicked off her sneakers and looked at her feet. "I need my hands and feet done. I look like Mary Lou Retton down there and a coal miner up here [indicating her hands]."

"I see," Almara realized as she inspected a stack of newspapers and magazines Elvira had bought from a magazine stand at the mall. An article on the front page of the *USA Today* stood out to her. "Hey, Elvira?" Almara said slowly.

"If you really want to know, I'll tell you," Elvira relented with a sigh. "I've never revealed – I have never told the details about it. The Vietnam War was less grisly."

"No, Elvira," Almara slowly stood up and sat next to Elvira on the bed. "I didn't mean that. You should see this."

"See what?"

"Your husband is in the *USA Today*."

"He's in many papers." Elvira looked disinterested, aloof. "I couldn't care less about his legal woes. I have my own issues."

"He's been killed, Elvira," Almara said in a solemn voice. "He's dead."

Elvira stared at the paper, stunned.

CHAPTER ELEVEN

La Hacienda de Sosa
Cochabamba, Bolivia
September 14, 1984

"*Dulce Designs* … you're talking big-scale fashion designer stuff," Sosa said, staring firmly into the eyes of his wife as they sat across from each other on the balcony of their master bedroom. He was slowly thumbing through the drawings Yesenia Dulce had made in the stacks of 14"x17" bristle pads sitting on top of the large, round, frosted-glass table between them. "Like *Nina Ricci, Ralph Lauren, Yves Saint Laurent, Dior, Gucci, Vuitton, Givenchy* … Global."

She followed his eyes, gauging his reaction. "Yeah."

He had known all about her passion and drive for drawing, architectural designs, modeling and high fashion but what he was seeing in front of him, on the bristle pads, he had not noticed before. He was amazed.

"Yesenia, you'll have to forgive me," he stated, scratching his temple. "I knew you were a creative artist … the oil paintings, the architecture/home plans, the Miss Bolivia 1983 trophy, and the numerous beauty contest trophies and plaques in your personal gallery-room … But, *mi amor*, you've never shown *these* to me. You are part of the blame."

"What did you think I did with them, write the Pope?" she joked without a smile. "I draw things."

Sosa sat back in his seat. "Like in the garden … in the center pool, out back."

"*Sí*. I draw things."

He pointed at a page that displayed a beautiful open-shouldered wedding gown. "Staring at the rose bushes, you'd draw this party dress."

"Maybe," she responded with a nod. "That's a wedding dress. I may have been sitting or standing anywhere, doing anything. Some of the things I've drawn for fashion were when I was twelve, eleven. I started a long time ago. I still agree with some of what I drew when I was twelve. I like some of my earliest drawings."

"Like what?"

Now she smiled. "Like the wedding dress."

"This one?" He pointed at it.

"That one, yes. It is a *re-design* of a *Dior* gown."

He spent all of two minutes looking at the dress and thinking.

She waited patiently.

"You have your own accounts in Bolivia, Colombia, the U.S.," he reminded her. "BBVA in Spain. At least a million in each bank, no? Plus the credit cards?"

"Nowhere near what I need to finance a global company," she frowned. "I need a hundred million to take us out onto the international stage."

He stood up and walked over to where one of his macaws stood perched on top of its cage. He reached a finger up toward it and the bird nipped at it playfully and squawked loudly. He reached into his pocket and pulled out a shelled peanut which he gave to the green and yellow macaw. The beautiful bird took the nut and carried it back into the huge cage, where he cracked it open and ate it.

"A hundred million," he repeated as he looked out at the vast mountaintop property, idly wondering where the other macaws that frequented this particular cage had flown off to. "And you're sure you know what you're doing?"

"I know it's a fortune," she acknowledged. "But you also know that I know what I'm doing."

"Yes ... I guess I do." He sat back down, swatting at a fly that came too close to his tall glass of iced coca and lemon tea. "I have a greater concern. It's not that I don't trust your business acumen. On the contrary. You're a prodigy. A *King Midas*, if you will. The company, *Imperio*, is doing well. The organization ... it's been very prosperous. I gave you the green light on building the Pentagon because ... the money is literally too big to do anything legal within the global markets."

"It's not laundered, you mean."

"*Exacto*," he nodded, inhaled, and exhaled deeply. "So, it's not trust, Yessi. If you wanted I'd let you burn it and barbeque dinner for us with it all winter. The American and European cokeheads have been generous. However, we cannot just go around the world dropping money and not expect to arouse suspicion. Particularly in the U.S., France, the UK, and Spain. Laundering takes time, sophistication, and intelligence."

"Don't you think I know that, Alejandro?" she countered.

"Well ..." he began but paused. "You never proposed so big a number to me before. I know you've been buying properties and a few other things but this is ... *substantial*."

She smiled at him. "Okay. Don't pretend that you have been keeping track of each thing I've been doing. Tell me what '*properties*' and '*other things*' have I purchased?"

Several other macaws appeared suddenly, landing on top of the cage and around the balcony, curiously eyeing Sosa.

"An office building and warehouse in La Paz," he answered smugly, tossing a pile of peanuts to the birds.

"What else?"

"You got me," he admitted, his eyes on a smaller, female macaw. "Forgive me, *mamita*. Explain to me your business plans."

She pushed a black leather-jacketed book across the table to him. The white sticker label on it read *BUSINESS PLAN*. "That's what *this* is."

He looked at it as if it were a black mamba. "You know what I want to hear."

"I have no plans to get us into trouble with any tax authorities," she began. "Not here, the U.S., Europe, or elsewhere. Nearly every dollar of the hundred mil I need is itemized in my Business Plan. I've been working on *Dulce Designs* for two years. I have not been acting like the spoiled lazy White wives you read about in American magazines and spending money on vain things. I did lease the warehouse and offices in La Paz. But that's only the start; *Dulce* will need something much more prestigious. I have taken advantage of my perfect credit and I've secured several substantial loans worth the amounts we'll need to cover the start-up costs for our South and Central American locations."

He had begun reading the Business Plan. "La Paz, Santa Cruz, Cochabamba, Oruro, Sucre, Beni, Viacha, Potosí, and Tarija."

"We must begin with Bolivia," she stated. "A Bolivian-based company whose factories will supply the entire South American and Caribbean markets with our products."

"Clothing," he said as he read.

"For men, women, and children," she said. "Women's dresses, shoes, pocketbooks, scarves, undies, hats, gloves, jewelry, perfume, skin care products, oils, lotions, et cetera."

"In one word: *everything*," he said.

"The same for children, and men," she nodded. "Our campaign focus will be on high fashion but we won't forget the lower-income families. Those who can't afford high fashion prices."

"You have baby diapers?" he chuckled lightly.

"We have to do anything and everything to target mothers, the women," Yesenia pointed out. "I have designed cloth *and* disposable diapers. Not only that but I've designed sizes for the skinny, the curvy, the petite, the plus-sized and even for the obese. We have to be sensitive to what *every* woman needs. It starts with them."

"So ... the La Paz building will be ... ?"

"Our training facility," she explained. "It'll begin there. It *has* begun there. But it's not a little retail shop or La Paz boutique. It's a titanic fashion and design corporation. Its every design is to be a global enterprise."

He kept reading and, for a while, she was quiet. She even took a bathroom break.

"I had to come to you," she was saying after she returned from the bathroom. "My credit is, or will be, overextended on loans for the Latin American locations. A New York location is mandatory. That's the snag right now. Once we secure the New York location we can use it for collateral on more loans. I have a location in mind and it will cost eight million dollars to acquire. That's one-quarter of the money I have been promised from loans."

He sat back in his seat. "So, you don't actually have the money yet?"

"No," she shook her head. "I've only applied. I haven't yet signed. I had to have this meeting with you first. This way I'd know how far to go."

He finished reading the Business Plan.

"Look, *Papi*." She reached out and put a reassuring hand on his. "I know everything I do has to 'look' clean. That hundred mil will be the magic wand behind *Dulce Designs* that will put us out front like *Jordache, Calvin Klein, Gucci, Yves Saint Laurent, Ralph Lauren, Chanel, Louis Vuitton,* and all the others."

"You'll be the magic wand behind the company's success," Sosa stated confidently. "The loan money, and money you already had in your accounts, is what you're using to pay for what you've already been doing." It was a question that sounded more like a statement.

"Correct, but the loan money I have not received yet," she clarified. "You're asking if I'm using visible/legit money *over* the table. Yes, I am."

"The hundred mil ..." he trailed off. "It's *all* under the table, according to what you wrote in the Business Plan."

"That's also correct," she clearly stated. "The same way you establish drug connections in Europe, U.S., Australia, Africa ... you leave no paper trail. There's similar dirt to be done within *Dulce*. You've read the Plan. *Univision, Telemundo, Caracol, Globo, CBS, NBC, ABC,* other television, cable, and movie executives, *Marie Claire, Cosmopolitan, GQ, Sports Illustrated, Ebony, Essence, Elle, Jet; New York Times, USA Today, Los Angeles Times;* all the big international news and TV media. We'll bribe all of them. Did Victoria Principal, Christie Brinkley, Farrah Fawcett, and Grace Jones become brand names on looks alone? They made power moves."

"Do you find Grace Jones beautiful?" Sosa inquired. "Be honest."

"Well?" She had to hesitate. "Conventionally, no. I don't think anyone does. However, she has created her own category of beauty. She made me stop and say '*Wow, what a woman!*' She's wild. Tall. Different from what mainstream media has brainwashed us with. Because of *Cosmo, Sports Illustrated, People* and other magazines – and big network media – being a blonde, white, sick-looking anorexic-bulimic Barbie in make-up is fashionable. With Grace I think America saw her as a newly discovered animal. An odd-looking monkey of some sort; unlike anything ever seen. Regardless of those racist attitudes, she showed the world that being

Black and different is beautiful. Oh, my God, imagine how she must be in bed. Without a doubt it was her *chocha* that got her the opportunity, not her face. Never underestimate the *chocha*."

Sosa chuckled and said, "I never have."

"Many, many bribes must be made," Yesenia went on. "And all of them must be made under the table. I know I have Rafa as my head of security, but I need negotiation specialists to bribe who I tell them to bribe and muscle those who need to be muscled. You know I can't do those things *and* run the company."

Now she was speaking a language that Sosa could understand. "Muscle."

"I won't allow them to tell me no," she stated. "It's as simple as that. I won't let you down. Rising to the top is the only option. In three years' time *Dulce* will employ twenty-six thousand employees worldwide. Ten thousand of those will be in Latin America, the U.S., and Canada. We'll gross two hundred fifty million dollars in sales in four years. We'll be at the top whenever a conversation about fashion and design/cosmetics and models are being discussed."

A female macaw suddenly flew across the balcony and landed clumsily on the table. She stared at Yesenia and then at Sosa. He tossed a peanut on the table and she picked it up with her beak. She cracked it open and ate it before flying back over to her cage.

Yesenia watched Sosa carefully. "What is it with you and these birds? Not just the macaws in and around the house but all over these mountains?"

Sosa smiled and shrugged. "I grew up with some of them. They live for a very long time. That female and male there [pointing] are twenty-five years old. Most of the macaws that we – *the Toros and I* – have we grew up with, in the forests. Some are forty, fifty-something. Their children and grandchildren trust us. They love us."

Sosa was speaking modestly. He had a fond relationship with a large number of birds in the forests that surrounded the Pentagon. Some boys and girls had cats and dogs as children. Sosa had had those, too. He'd also been fortunate enough to have horses, llamas, vicuñas, a bull and other types of animals. His father had never bought him a bird, although they were common in many Latin American households. His mother, however, could not stand the noises birds made. As a child Sosa loved birds. He was not lying when he told Yesenia that the dozens of macaws that lived in and around the Pentagon were adult birds that he had grown up knowing. Actually, he had raised them in his own aviary. When he'd been given the mountaintop estate by Haché, Sosa had brought the birds with him. They still had their own birdhouses but the birds also had cages in and around the Pentagon's backyard, and balconies which they would frequent.

"What about the others?" Yesenia questioned him. "Out in the jungles. You grew up with them, too?"

"We'll talk about them another time," he waved her off. "Let's finish one thing at a time. You were telling me about your economic projections for *Dulce*."

"I won't make trouble with the money," she promised. "It won't be used to buy traceable things such as cars, houses, properties, et cetera."

"Okay, you got the money," he informed her as he saw the helicopter come into view. He stood up. "You'll also get the muscle. Fill Rafa in, let him read your Plan, then lock it away."

She thanked him by kissing him deeply.

He lightly smacked her buttocks. "That's Nino's helicopter; go on inside."

$$$$$

Sosa shook the hand of the *La Corporación* courier Benny the Skull had escorted into the residence. The courier, a young Bolivian man who worked for Cucombre, handed a sealed manila envelope to Sosa.

"Benito." Sosa opened the envelope. "Get Pablo here a whiskey or anything he needs. Then send him on his way."

"That's okay, Mr. Sosa," Pablo politely refused.

Sosa turned to stare at the brown-skinned courier. "People are starving in Bolivia. It is ungracious not to accept food and drinks when you are a guest in my house. Eat. Drink. Relax."

Pablo nodded and apologized. "I'm just ..."

Sosa had already walked off.

"Are you stupid or crazy?" Benny whispered harshly into Pablo's face. "You just disrespected one of the most important men on the earth."

In his basement study, Sosa studied the coded letter and put a call through to the Department of Defense, using General Cucombre's eleven line. When Cucombre answered, all Sosa said was, "A party for Jose is the least we can do."

"Thank you," Cucombre said, ending the call.

Sosa used the in-house intercom. "Benito, send the boy home. I need everyone in the basement study for an emergency meeting."

A few minutes later Benny was the first to enter the study. Sosa immediately gave him the coded letter. Benny read it aloud:

We really need to get together soon for a good poker game, friend. It's been weeks since we sat down for dinner. How are you and the wife doing? I need you two to do something fun for Jose's birthday such as invite him up to the Pentagon to practice his shooting skills.

Why don't you visit him? He turns twelve next month. We'll call you later tonight. Be prepared for the vacation! Invite Yesenia and the boys. Buenos Aires has legal gambling! At least so I've heard. Afternoon traffic there is horrendous. Tomorrow I'll make reservations.

Anyway, be sure you kiss the baby and hug Yesenia for me and let her know I bought the silk and cotton materials she asked for so I didn't forget. Tell her I may be getting old but I'm sharper than ever! Talk to you tonight. NC.

Benny had a mean scowl on his face as he deciphered the code. "The intel is in the second paragraph."

Nancho, Javier, and Tato came in.

"We got something on the journalist," Sosa told them.

"We noticed the chopper," Nancho stated. "Let's have it, Benito."

They all huddled around the desk, reading the letter.

Benny explained it as he wrote it out. "It's an Israeli *Mossad*-style code. Second paragraph, starting with sentence two, the first word in each sentence."

He wrote the words out like so:

He
We'll
Be
Invite
Buenos Aires
At
Afternoon
Tomorrow

Sosa explained the message more clearly. "Interpreted, it means *He [Gutiérrez] will be in Buenos Aires at afternoon tomorrow.*"

Nancho cracked his knuckles and spoke forcefully. "*Señor,* everything you'd ordered to be done is done. The elite kill unit, the helicopter, and two Antonovs. All are ready for the mission."

"Round up the kill unit," Sosa ordered. "Nancho, you get on the radio and do that. Javi and Tato, make the call to fire up the transport chopper for the trip to our Santa Cruz airstrip. Time is not on our side. Have the second chopper on standby." This was no drill; stomachs flip-flopped with anticipation.

Minutes later a team of men – and one woman – entered the room. Sosa had laid out several maps of South America across the long conference table. He looked up to assess the kill unit. He walked up to the dark-haired young woman and stared into her face.

"*La Gata Negra,*" he acknowledged her respectfully. "Did you stop in to visit your dear mother, Juca Belén?"

"I will before we depart on this mission, *Señor,*" Catalina promised.

"You don't have to go," Sosa told her. "It'll be dangerous."

"I *want* to," she stated in defiance. "Where my family is involved so I am also. With all due respect, *Señor*, stop treating me like a little girl … please."

The men in the room all laughed.

Sosa scratched his head and looked around the table at his people: Benny the Skull, Tato, Nancho, Javier, Rafa, Felipé Borca, his cousin Edgar Zerboni, Diego "Buro" Cortez, Lucho Pantoja, Nono "Bushwacker" Carbajal, Victor José Nava, Ivan Manuel Rendón, and, of course, Catalina Lilli Romero-Toro, *alias La Gata Negra* (The Black Cat).

"We have two jets ready to go." Sosa stood at the center half of the table pointing at the maps while the unit gathered around. "One plane will make a 'legitimate' flight into Buenos Aires. It'll be the lead flight out in case the combat plane and/or unit gets into some trouble. It just so happens that Buenos Aires' *Farmer's Supply Company*, or *FSC*, is where we purchase about a fourth of our equipment and supplies from for Andes Sugar. Our planes are familiar with the Bolivian and Argentine aeronautics authorities, you know the country flight codes. Take with you the usual supply list. You'll be expected. They will meet you at the *Aerolineas Argentinas International Airport* and load the plane up there. Gata Negra, Benny, Tato, Nancho, Buro, Bushwacker, and Lucho – the combat plane. You'll go in under the radar, as if fifteen tons of merch were being smuggled in during the cover of night. We prefer a kidnapping so we can make the media and authorities think that it was *The Shining Path* guerrillas or the work of some other Argentine criminal organization. Felipé, Edgar, Victor, Ivan, and Javier, *you'll* go in to 'shop' for the supplies. Your true role, of course, is *support*. You'll arrive at the airport ahead of the strike unit. Benny will be at the command."

"What about me, boss?" Rafa wondered. "I want this mission."

Sosa looked at Yesenia's top bodyguard and paused. "There's a greater need for you here. The *Señora* has some big things going on and ... her security is vulnerable without you there. Okay?"

"*Señor.*" Rafa did not sound happy but he was obedient to Sosa. Internally, however, he was seething at being excluded.

Sosa glanced over at Benny the Skull. "Benito."

"The landing light," Benny said, looking at Javier. "The support team can leave now but first let us coordinate the plan for the landing lights. Javi."

Javier was already aware of it. "As soon as we land, we'll make it to the strip. I have a question, though. There're two strips we have there which we use for loads shipped to Europe and Australia. The one just southeast of Buenos Aires between *Lomas de Zamora* and *La Plata* ... and the one near the *Mar de Plata* shipping port."

Benny pointed to the map. "The dry riverbed – Lomas de Zamora and La Plata. We'll land there. I'm glad you asked."

"Give us ten minutes' notice," Javi said. "We'll pour oil and gas along the edges of the riverbed landing strip. That's your landing light."

As they usually did, prior to embarking upon dangerous missions, the men all hugged. Some even prayed. Moments later Javier, Ivan, Victor, Edgar, and Felipé exited the office. Nancho made a radio call to Sosa's security office.

"Fire up another helicopter for us," Nancho radioed out to one of Sosa's private army aircraft pilots. "*Cambio.*"

"Ten-four," the reply came back. "*Cambio y afuera.*"

"The flight plan." Benny turned his attention to the maps before him. "Tato, I'll need you here [indicating]. The routes we must take are tricky."

Tato nodded, understanding. Using a red-tipped sharp-point felt pen, he drew lines on the map. "Tricky isn't the word. *Treacherous* is closer to the truth ... The Mar del Plata port and the Lomas de Zamora locations were not tailored for flights from any of our Bolivian narco ops; but, instead, were created for our Chilean operations. The Chilean merch are packaged in six places."

"Chuquicamata, Monte Patria, La Calera, Linares, Copiapo and Rancagua." Benny pointed to each town. Tato circled them and drew lines across the treacherous mountain region stretching eastwards to Argentina. "That merch is airlifted to our transit hub in Cerro Ojos del Salado, Chile. Those planes get into the Mar del Plata and La Plata airstrips via this Chilean Andes route. If we had our eyes shut, we could navigate our way through Cerro Ojos, which is seven thousand feet above sea level ... descend lower over the mountains in San Fernando del Valle de Catamarca, Frias, Jesus Maria, Rafaela, south to Pergamino, Junin and on eastwards to those airstrips of ours."

Tato drew out the flight plan coordinates since he knew the most favorable flight path. They could not just beeline their way into Argentina due to the prolific radar capability the country had. In fact, it was a monumental challenge for Sosa's planes to leave Cochabamba due to the hundreds of miles of Bolivian airspace necessary to cozen through safely, without radar detection. Oruro, Potosi, Sucre, and Tarija were the Bolivian cities in between the Pentagon and the northern Argentina-Bolivia border.

"See here?" Tato was saying. "To save time, since this is a nighttime flight, we'd have to fly at least at sixty-five hundred feet to avoid crashing into the mountains ... even that's too high. There's a valley *here* [indicating] but I know it well. At the end there's a colossal crag that extends about two thousand feet across, twenty-five hundred feet above sea level so we can ascend four thousand feet from here to here – thirty-point-three miles. The An-26 is my favorite plane and I know Bolivia's northern mountain ridges better than anyone."

Sosa passed Tato a cold glass of iced coca tea which he drank down eagerly.

"Once we fly to Portachello and pass the rock crags it gets safer," Tato said as he drew on the map. He was studying two old maps they had used previously to compare them with the maps he was drawing up plans for now. "From these old maps ... we know these paths. After Portachello we stay at four thousand feet around the northeastern and southeastern ridges of the Cordillera Oriental Mountain range. Once we cross the border there are lowlands all throughout eastern Argentina. There's a military base *here* [indicating] that we must avoid by one hundred miles. We take *this* path [indicating] to San Ramón de la Nueva Orán, over these rainforests, Rio Bermejo; Gran Chaco is all of *this* [indicating an expansive area] ... Anatuya has very low hills at twenty-five hundred feet ... Reconquista, we stay steady ... In Vera, steady for thirteen miles and then we drop lower along the Paraná River to Santa Fe, Paraná City, here, to two thousand feet. Gualeguaychu, Dolores, Zarate has zero hills and mountains through this path [indicating]. We stay steady at two thousand feet as we teeter around the outskirts of Buenos Aires, over Rio de la Plata, into La Plata, and finally into our landing zone. The support team will have it lit for us."

"We're ready." Benny studied the new map and then compared it with the old maps they had used before on this very same flight path. "Wait ... since it's a night flight and I'm helping to pilot ... we have to go over it once more. The coordinates, everything. Sosa, you need to call up whatever friends we have in the military, police, and underworld and promise payment for us to get through in case we get spotted on radar."

Sosa got General Cucombre on the SAT-phone.

Tato looked at the standard wall clock. "We're losing precious time, *primo*."

Benny nodded in acknowledgement. "I know ... but I'd rather lose time than crash. Those are old maps. I didn't realize until a few minutes ago how dangerous this route was. Surely, you remember it."

"That's why I'm comfortable with it." Tato sounded nonchalant. "I need you comfortable too so let's do it."

The tension in the war room tripled.

CHAPTER TWELVE

The Aspen Clinic
Nyack, New York
September 13, 1984

There it all was, as clear as day. Almara sat closer to Elvira in full support of this tragedy. This girl's life is a mess and just when she makes a move to fix her problems, here comes more heartbreak. Man, life is so unfair, the Puerto Rican counselor was thinking. But little did Almara know ... the saga had just begun. There was no one, in any of the Aspen sites, who was as screwed up as Elvira was. Sure, there was something mysterious about her as there was with every new person Almara met. But there was also something vulnerable and likeable about Elvira that Almara wanted to get to know and even defend. What Almara could not yet see was that there was also something ominous looming within this woman. The darkness that had been cocooning Elvira all of her life was starting to unveil itself and there was no butterfly at the end of the metamorphosis. There was only evil, corruption, destruction, great loss, sadness and death.

"This can't be true," Elvira whispered after she'd read the article. "The paper says it happened on the night of the tenth or the wee hours of the morning on the eleventh."

"You said the restaurant fight was ... ?"

"That was on the night of the seventh," Elvira filled in where Almara had trailed off. "I know because of my plane ticket stub. And my hospital papers – I was admitted on the eighth. I stayed there for three whole days, which would make it the eleventh. I've been here for two days … today is the thirteenth."

It all added up.

She took her time to reread the two-page spread in the center of the *USA Today's* "Nation" section, pages 4A and 5A. The headline read, *Drug Kingpin Known as 'Scarface' Murdered in his Miami Mansion.* Elvira was shocked as she read the report. She scowled at the photo layout of the mansion's interior, exterior, and there was even an aerial photo of the entire property. The authorities had apparently released substantial details and facts of the massacre because *USA Today* had published a diagram that depicted the location of those who had been killed there.

"It was an all-out war," Almara murmured, reading along with Elvira. Almara pointed to a separate diagram. "A 'crime family' tree. At least you're not on that, huh?"

Elvira looked at it closely. "I have no idea who most of them are. These here, I know them because they lived with us in our Coral Gables mansion. My God, it says Manny was murdered in his Coconut Grove estate! I didn't even know Manny had his own place. [Reading further] They suspect Tony of killing Manny?! There's no way! They were too close!"

"Who's the pretty girl?"

"That's Gina Montana," Elvira answered. "Tony's baby sister. Chi Chi, Nick the Pig, Ernie, Gina, Manny, Tony … all wiped out. This is unbelievable."

Almara saw that Elvira was shocked.

"Let me tell you something," Almara said. "I'm from the Williamsburg projects. I can't pretend that I know what you're going through but I do know what losing a loved one is like. My younger brother was shot and killed in my projects. He was selling weed to buy diapers and baby formula for a baby later tested not to be his. The mother was this really cute fifteen-year-old from Queens who looked like an angel. She was nothing but a liar. So he died thinking that that kid was his. My family and I were so angry ..."

Elvira was listening intently but her mind was numb.

"Anyway," Almara sighed. "My brother, Ricky, he probably would have still been dealing. He was small-time but, still, let's be honest. He was in the streets, that fifteen-year-old was a product Ricky picked up from off the streets. We – meaning my family and I – came to terms with it. He was killed doing wrong. Doing crime. We love our loved ones no matter what they do. But I can't compare my brother's facts with your facts. Let's be practical. You're the wife of no ordinary dealer. One of the most infamous criminals in the country. Your situation is alien to me."

Elvira sensed that there was something more to what Almara was saying.

"This is different from anything Aspen has experienced." Almara shrugged her right shoulder.

Elvira had stopped crying. "Maybe they won't know."

"It's a two-page spread in the *USA Today*," she emphasized firmly and clearly. "I'm only saying it to prepare you for what they'll be gossiping about."

"Can I be expelled from Aspen?" Her voice was laced with concern.

Almara thought about that. "It'll certainly be discussed at the staff meeting tomorrow with the director, John Crispuso. It would disturb me terribly if they threw you out. You've only just begun treatment for a very ruthless and unforgiving disease. Residents read national newspapers. The story about your husband won't go away because of all the other issues on the subject of drugs written by *USA Today*: escalating crime in Miami and other major U.S. cities, the so-called 'cocaine boom,' the War on Drugs declared by the President, and the so-called 'Cuban Crime Wave.' They've found a new face for America's problems: Tony Montana."

"But he's dead."

"That's true," Almara agreed, sitting up and looking at the article again. "However ... the buzzards come around only after the dearly has departed."

"You said you'd be disturbed if I were to be thrown out," Elvira spoke after a long silence. "Look at me. Tell me what you mean?"

Almara turned around. "Yeah. I'd be disturbed."

"How disturbed?"

Almara thought about some of what she'd read about Tony Montana ... Kingpin Posts Record $5,000,000 Cash Bail ... ; Montana Assets Estimated at $36M; Feds Seize Record Shipment of Cocaine Off Florida Coast (estimated street value of $100M; believed to be Montana's).

"Well." Almara put the newspaper down. "You're pregnant, underweight, and in need of treatment. Throwing you out in your delicate condition would be tantamount to cruelty and abuse. It's just unfathomable that a prestigious organization like this one would do something so despicable over ..." She could not find the words.

"Controversy. You mean controversy."

"Which they are used to." Almara raised her voice. "We're a house that was built off of those who've been down on their luck. Who've been to and from some very dark places."

"Those who are rich and have been down on their luck," Elvira criticized. "But still rich."

"You're right about that." Almara paused. "I'll argue to the supervisory staff that you won't be a distraction. That we're not new to controversy and that you pose no risk or threat to anyone. That we conferred for hours about your background, about this, and I'm satisfied that you've been truthful."

"I've made up my mind to rehab," Elvira murmured tiredly. "But I'm starting to think that even my attempt to save my child's life is futile. I can't win. Not for one moment in my life have I won once! Not even once!" She sounded distraught.

"According to our talk at the mall ..." Almara hesitated, looking down at her. "If you did not get away when you did ... you would have been massacred along with the rest of them. So, you can win. You would have been dead. Your baby, too."

"Maybe."

"What?!" Almara exclaimed, incredulous. "There's twenty-plus dead at that estate! You ... whoever was involved was killed. There was only one survivor."

"Survivor?" Elvira's eyebrows furrowed with the question.

"Yeah. A tiger," Almara stated. "What in God's name were youse doing with a tiger?"

Elvira tried to explain. "Tony always said that I reminded him of a tiger. Even in bed. We never made love. We fought, sucked, choked, tore, bit and scratched at each other. Like enemies. There was love ... but the lust was hotter than the lava in the earth."

Elvira got up and went to the bathroom. She came out wearing white panties and a tight nylon tank top. She had obviously taken a few minutes to shower because her hair was wet and her skin was moist. She got into bed and noticed that Almara was asleep.

"I want to stay here, Ally," she assured her.

"I know."

"But I have to fly down to Miami tomorrow," Elvira told her. "I have to send them off right. It's a must I do that."

Almara was fully awake at hearing that. "Elvira ... you think that's wise? It might be dangerous."

Elvira laughed cynically. "What was dangerous for Tony is not dangerous for me. I'm a nobody in his underground world."

"They also killed Gina," Almara reminded Elvira. "Was she a nobody too?"

"Wrong place, wrong time," Elvira said. "It's strange to hear that she was even there because I rarely see her there. I see her in Miami Beach, in the downtown area of the city, clubs, and at her beauty salon. Nobody would have wanted her dead ... except something very, very evil."

"Or someone," Almara added. "I come from a place where murder is a joke. They do it for 'props.' This Tony Montana ... this thing is beyond murder. Massacres, Mafias, hundred-million-dollar seizures, my goodness. [Sighing] I'll meet with John Crispuso, our director, and Psychologist Supervisor Rob Manfred in the morning. When you leave treatment ... you should not leave alone."

Elvira studied Almara's face for clues. "What's that mean?"

"I want to come with you," Almara said. "You'll need me to keep you honest."

"Honest?" Elvira smiled. "You mean sober."

"That, too," Almara confirmed.

Elvira thought it over quietly. "Like an on-the-road rehab."

"Montana." Almara stroked her hair. "More than anything what you need in your life right now is a rock underneath you. I'm willing."

Elvira mulled it over some more. "What if they say no? What if they won't let you leave or me return?"

"Like I said. You need a rock," Almara repeated. "Many rocks would be nice but start with me. I'll stand up for you, Elvira."

"I'd appreciate that," Elvira stated from her heart. "But I'd feel so bad if you lost your job."

Almara stayed quiet. "I'd feel helpless then."

"I could hire you." Elvira carefully framed her words. "Truth is I could use a person like you. Specifics I can't give but I'm certainly able to pay and pay very well – for a very long time. It'll be a roller-coaster but … let me know how that meeting goes."

"Will you be all right?"

Elvira nodded, yawning. "Thank you, Ally."

Almara exited the condo wondering what tomorrow would bring. Elvira closed her eyes and tiredly thought if life would ever stop hurting her.

CHAPTER THIRTEEN

La Hacienda de Sosa
The Gutiérrez Mission
September 14, 1984

At nightfall the powerful new $4-million Russian-made An-26 Antonov was roaring through the skies along the eastern Andes, en route to the clandestine riverbed/airstrip located on the outskirts of Buenos Aires, Argentina.

Tatico Arturo Lugo-Toro, arguably the best low-flying smuggler in the world, piloted the Russian jet like the gutsy ace he was born to be. Benito sat in the cockpit to Tato's right, with Nancho seated behind Tato, as co-pilots. Benny and Nancho kept their eyes on the map, the navigation system, and the sophisticated control panels. They assisted Tato in every manner and made aviation notes on the flight path map all throughout the first leg of their journey.

"Benny … you hear that?" Nancho looked at his cousin. "*Escucha, primo*" (Listen, cousin).

All three men wore headsets equipped with microphones through which they communicated with each other. Nancho was busy on the high-powered radio scanner listening to the garbled radio transmissions it was intercepting from the airwaves.

"*¡Maldito!*" Benny cursed and tapped Tato on his left arm. "I heard it! One hundred miles ahead there's a hurricane. There's no way around it because they say it's five hundred miles wide and it's packing winds over one hundred miles per hour. No one said there would be a hurricane in our path."

The three men in the cockpit were stone-faced after news of the dangerous weather had fully sunk in. They each looked at one another.

"*¿Qué se pasa, muchachos?* [Whatcha say, boys?]" Tato solemnly asked.

Nancho was first to answer. "I'd rather face the hurricane than fail the boss. We must get to B.A. to silence the demon in that rat's mind."

"What do *you* say, Tato?" Benny looked at him.

Feeling the build-up of adrenaline Tato nodded. "What Nancho said." He put a stick of gum into his mouth. "You're the Commander here, Benito."

"All right then, let's do it." Benny tightened his seatbelt. "Listen close. Once we're on the storm's outskirts, you climb us up to thirty-three thousand feet! That should put us above the rains but that won't guarantee us an escape from the winds."

Nancho got up out of his seat and went back to check on the others. Catalina, Buro, Bushwacker, and Lucho were all seat-belted in, cat-napping, in the rear cargo area of the plane. Nancho was glad that they looked relaxed because he had the feeling inside of his chest that death was looming around the corner.

$$$$$

Muchos Años Antes

Twenty-five-year-old Rafael Peluché Porras Amayo, alias "Rafa," was as close to Sosa as the Toro men. The only thing different about the green-eyed, bald-headed, muscle-bound Rafa was the story of how he had come to know Sosa and the Toros …

In 1972, when Rafa was thirteen years old, and back when Sosa had been handed over control of *La Corporación* by his father (Haché), Sosa had traveled to Nauta, Peru. Nauta was a small farming town that sat about 50 miles south of Iquitos, a fast-growing, bustling city situated along the Rio Marañon. Sosa had met with a group of ruthless Shining Path guerrillas who had, at that time, controlled critical swaths of western and northern lands which *La Corporación* had not only coveted for their coca plant production potential but also for their prime drug smuggling routes going into and out of neighboring Colombia to the north.

Don Haché and many other Bolivian and Peruvian druglords had utterly despised the Shining Path, who had historically been a worse plague to Bolivian drug smugglers than FARC-EP guerrillas had been to Sosa's drug associates in Colombia and Ecuador. Namely, the Cali Cartel bosses in Colombia (e.g., Jonathan Almanza-Orejuela, Gilberto Rodriguez-Orejuela, and Jose Santa Cruz-Londono) and the Medellín Cartel bosses (Pablo Escobar, Gonzalo Rodriguez Gacha, the Ochoas, and Carlos Lehder Rivas).

When Sosa had inherited Haché's position in the empire, *La Corporación Mafia Cruzena* had relied heavily on moving their merch on the ground through Peru, Ecuador, and Colombia. They only had a few small Cessnas back then and even fewer airstrips. It was not always ideal to fly merchandise out of Bolivia, via Peru and into Ecuador or Colombia during the late '60s and early '70s due to Haché's lack of a viable working political relationship with the government powers of those said countries during that time period.

The Shining Path problem was one that Haché had lived with for a long time. The guerrillas had been charging Haché's smugglers exorbitant *"people's revolutionary taxes"* for each kilo of cocaine paste being carried through the Nauta,

Peru, route. Sosa had inherited the Shining Path problem just like he'd inherited everything else.

In the beginning Sosa had been able to grit his teeth and bear the shame of dealing with the Shining Path because the Colombians were literally buying 200-300 kilos of cocaine paste a day from Sosa's drughouses in Puerto Francisco de Orellana, a city close to the Ecuador-Colombia border. In the early '70s Sosa had cemented a number of close associations with over 100 major druglords from Bolivia, Peru, Ecuador, Colombia, Venezuela, Panama, Costa Rica, Nicaragua, Honduras, El Salvador, Guatemala, Belize, and Mexico. In each country he had used to traffic his merch through, there had always been one or more authority figures waiting for payment. Whether the police, the military, town mayor or the guerrillas, someone always had to be paid. In Peru, the city of Nauta had been a critical transit hub for *La Corporación* merch. Sosa had kept the police and military paid off but the greedy Shining Path had demanded $1000 per kilo. Their prices amounted to extortion and when Sosa had taken over, he had vowed to renegotiate a lesser price with the guerrillas.

"*Jefe,*" Benny had told Sosa after hearing of this plan, "the only way to get the guerrilla to accept a lesser tax is to force it."

"That's why I want you and the boys to build up an army," Sosa had ordered. "It's time we change things."

During his 1972 visit to the Shining Path's camp on Rio Marañon, Sosa had been able to successfully negotiate a new deal with SPG which had included SPG security for all Bolivian merchandise belonging to *La Corporación* coming out of Bolivia, going into Peru, that was bound for Sosa's Puerto de Francisco Orellana drughouses and two new drughouses along the Ecuador-Colombia border in Tulcán, and the port city of San Lorenzo.

Shining Path Commander Cespédes Villanueva had been well aware of the vast amounts of money *La Corporación* was worth. He had actually checked and learned a whole lot about *Imperio, Inc.*, their thriving conglomerate. *Imperio* (meaning "Empire" in English) was the *legitimate* business owned by Sosa and his business partners. On the other hand, *La Corporación Mafia Cruzena* was their highly secretive underworld society no one outside of *La Corporación* knew much about. Villanueva, however, had found out enough. For one, he had unearthed the details regarding *Imperio's* assets. Namely Andes Sugar Corporation, of which Sosa was now majority stockholder. That particular company was the world's fourth-largest sugar manufacturer. Then there were the astonishing land assets – acres rumored to be in the millions – owned by Sosa and his top-level associates. In Villanueva's mind that single fact could mean only one thing: unlimited land equals unlimited coca crops.

With that graphic in mind, Villanueva had made his exorbitant demands clear to the then 23-year-old cocaine lord. Even at that age Sosa had cool eyes of cunning and a twisted, knowing smile.

"Those days with Don Haché and one thousand a kilo is outdated," the big curly-haired commander had said during the meeting held inside of his tent. Tato, Javier, Nancho and Benny had accompanied Sosa. Villanueva had provided Sosa with a handwritten list of demands. "We want roads, bridges, stop lights, and a hospital. We want houses – one hundred ranches – with electricity, hot water, animals … pigs, chickens, goats, roosters, llamas, horses, vicuñas, sheep, and cattle. Build three schools, a large grocery store, fifty trucks, twenty cars, clean water, and a railroad."

"Clean water," Sosa had commented with a poker face. "That would, at the very least, require drilling. Maybe digging trenches to divert water from the river and treat it. The railroad track is not going to happen. Not by us it's not."

"Why?" the commander had asked.

"It's unduly burdensome," Sosa had shrugged and explained. "It'll take Andes Sugar Corporation years of court battle to do it. The government will turn it into something political and put a spotlight on all of us. You and me. ASC are *visitors* with the Peruvian government; we can't cause a proxy war with them. You want us to build your people a living community, some infrastructure, and necessities, we can get the permits for that. I'll even promise a hundred men and women of your choosing labor jobs for the new ASC property in Iquitos and a hundred more for help with your demands."

"Ah," he scowled. "The women only need to take care of the house, lay on their backs, have babies, and cook our meals."

Sosa thought of Yesenia and Catalina and feigned a laugh. "Sure, Commander. Everything else on this list is doable. We have done the same for many of our people in Bolivia. If you want I'll hire the law firm of your choice to fight for a railway but ... a railway is a major, major government project. You can't win."

"Why, then, are you willing to pay for a law person to fight?" Villanueva had questioned Sosa as they sat smoking cigars and sharing a bottle of whiskey in the sophisticated tent.

"*Señor* Villanueva," Sosa had held his hands up in a "I surrender peacefully" type of manner. "I want this deal done. If it gives you peace of mind to sleep at night, then fine. I want you as my business partners. The arms and munitions, the million dollars in cash each month, all these items we can do. How about I compensate for the railway in another way? I have three attack helicopters ... *or* an additional five hundred k per month."

"*Señor* Sosa," the commander had leaned forward and extended his hand. "The helicopters *and* the five hundred k and we have a deal."

Sosa had slowly pulled out his shoulder-holstered .45 semi-automatic and sat it down gently on the table. "Commander Cespédes Villanueva ... Now you are taking advantage of my kindness and willingness to do something good for you and your people. You must think that because of the manicure and business suit that I'm a coward? If that is true, then pick up my gun and shoot me with it."

"You have me wrong, Mr. Sosa." He looked startled.

"Pick up the gun, Mr. Villanueva," Sosa had said with a calm look. "Or, choose the deal fairly."

"I have no pilots anyway." Villanueva had strained out a laugh to break the tension. "The five hundred k, Mr. Sosa. That will do fine."

The meeting had ended. As Sosa had exited the cabin with Nancho, Benny, Tato, and Javier, Nancho had indicated to Sosa with his head swinging to their left. Sosa had hesitated and looked over at a small shack made out of wood, brick, and cement. It had obviously been the guerrilla's makeshift prison. The *La Corporación* men had kept on walking toward their helicopter until they'd heard something that caused them all to pause.

"*Señor* Sosa! *Señor* Sosa!" It had been the voice of a young boy. "I kept hearing that you would come! You know me! Please help me, *Señor* Sosa!"

The building had no windows that they could see into but they'd stopped to listen to the boy. A Shining Path guard who had been observing had put his hands on his M-16 and walked toward them.

"How do you know me, boy?" Sosa had yelled back.

"I worked on your fishing boat!" the boy had said. "I ran for your father – Don Haché – and your mother, Doña Rosalie."

The guard with the gun had waved the men on with it. Sosa ignored the guard and looked at his men.

"You're the boy who painted for Diego?" Sosa had called back to him. *"¿Rafael Amayo?"*

"¡Sí, Señor! ¡Sí!" the boy had yelled, excited to have been remembered.

"Why's he here, in *Peru*?" Nancho had asked Sosa.

"I think they moved here," Javier had answered.

"The guerrilla are going to put me on trial and execute me, Mr. Sosa!" the boy had told him. "They killed my whole family!"

"Go," the guerrilla guard had ordered them. "That boy will be executed. He's a murderer and a horse thief. Go. Leave. Now!"

"You can wait." Javier had hovered over the guard.

"You must *leave*," the guard had said back.

"Or what?" Javier had knocked the guard's hat off.

"Hey!" the guard picked up his hat. "You leave now!"

Sosa and his men had walked away and re-entered the commander's tent, ignoring the soldier.

"Mr. Sosa." The commander and a few of his top men had been busy counting the $1.5-million advance Sosa had left behind for them. "Did you forget something?"

"I want that boy out there," Sosa had demanded. "Give me the boy and I'll deliver the three helicopters."

The commander had thrown back a shot of whiskey and slammed the glass down on the floor, breaking it. "That boy is a thief and a killer."

"And he's a friend of Don Haché's and Doña Rosalie," Sosa had responded. "Plus he's Boliviano."

"He knifed to death three of my men and for months before that he had been stealing our horses and selling them in Iquitos. We had to storm his father's ranch … too bad what happened there. Why do *you* want him? Simply because he's *Boliviano*?"

Sosa had chuckled. "The question here is will it serve your interests better with the helicopters or by killing the boy?

Also, it will hurt the boy more to let him live. His family paid for your dead *soldados*."

"You're right," the commander had said with a sigh. "Those choppers are worth more than the life of a horse thief. He'll live sufferably knowing that it was his actions that got his family killed. I just hope that I don't regret it later."

Sosa had first met Rafa face-to-face as he'd stood there being unchained by a guerrilla guard. Rafa had been only thirteen; his ribs had been visible through his skin because he'd been severely underfed, beaten, and abused. Rafa had been made to lie in his own urine and feces so the stench of him had been overwhelming. They'd flown the boy to a Cochabamba hospital to treat a list of afflictions which had included malnutrition, lice, crabs, influenza, boils, rat and insect bites (likely from the parasite-carrying tse-tse flies of the Amazon), infections, diarrhea, and tuberculosis.

It had taken some time but Rafa had rebounded and healed. He had come to live with Sosa on the mountaintop estate Haché had given him. On Rafa's 17th birthday, in 1976, Sosa had sat Rafa down to talk.

"When you had come here four years ago, we could have had this talk," Sosa had told him. "Anyone who went through what you went through … is wise beyond their years. You have known all along that you could have left us. You are not my servant or slave, you owe me nothing. But you stayed."

"Excuse me, Don Sosa," Rafa had interjected. "You are wrong, sir. I *am* your servant. You purchased my freedom and my life. I'll never leave you or Benny, Nancho, Javier, and Tatico. I'll never break my loyalty. You want me in the coca fields, I'll be your best picker. You want me to kill, I'll kill. But I won't leave you, *Señor*."

Sosa had seen the tears in Rafa's eyes." Okay, *hijo*. The first thing you must do is stop thinking there's even the slightest chance that I'd ever order you to leave. Also, stop eating like tomorrow won't come. No one will take your food. You carry food in your pockets."

A sheepish look had been on Rafa's handsome face. He'd removed the bread from his pockets and put it into the trash can that had been near Sosa's desk.

Sosa had chuckled. "You're lucky you're seventeen and all muscle or else you'd be a big fat cow. No ... you're here, we all love you, you're my family. Keep up the solid work you've been doing and you'll be brought in."

"*Brought in?*" he had said excitedly. "It'll be an honor!"

"You'd like that?"

"Of course, Don Sosa," Rafa had nodded.

"Don't be asleep when the day comes," Sosa had warned him. "Because the time *will* come ... you'll be required to kill enemies of *La Corporación*. Surely you remember the Shining Path guerrillas."

At the mention of the name an icy, profound expression of hate had washed over Rafa's face. "The Peru Shining Path."

Sosa had cleared his throat. "When Commander Villanueva told me about your family being murdered, I had it in the back of my mind that you'd one day want revenge. I knew how skillful you were with knives. Now that I've seen you grow in size, and increase in skill and knowledge ... do you want revenge?"

With tears of anger Rafa had stood up. "Don Sosa. They *raped* my mother and *cut off* her breasts. They *raped* my eight-year-old sister and *slit* her throat. They nearly raped me until they realized I was a boy. I ran for my life and watched from up a tree as my father and brother were stripped naked, beaten savagely, and hung from the front entrance beam of the horse stables and *castrated* ... I ate snakes, snails, bird eggs, and insects. I ate whatever I could find or trap, to survive until they caught me ... It would be an honor and a pleasure to go back up there and slaughter those animals. You only have to tell me when, Don Sosa."

"I'm sending you to Angola, then to Israel for training," Sosa had informed the young man. "All of us have trained abroad. You'll train with Klaus Barbie, an old Nazi war criminal. He specializes in killing, maiming, and torturing. He's gotten them all to talk – *KGB, MI6, CIA, PLO, Mossad* ... it doesn't matter. He teaches people how *not* to talk."

"I don't need to be taught how not to talk," Rafa had stated defiantly.

"Ha ha!" Sosa had laughed at the remark. "Every man has a breaking point. None of us know it until we face it. Klaus will take you to yours. Once you get there you'll face it and he'll teach you how to push past it and gracefully accept *death* and *pain*. Those two things – separate or together – have made even the best trained soldiers and agents turn into crying pigs. Rats. We've all been there, among other places. You'll return here on weekends. After six months with Klaus Barbie you'll go on to Hebrew University in Israel. While studying there you'll train with our associate Aaron Goldberg. He's an ex-Mossad agent who trains Jewish extremists, former U.S. military personnel, and Israeli commandos in bomb-making, military intelligence, aviation, and weapons development. Once you're done there you'll live here, train with my private army, and you'll earn six figures on my payroll. By that time we will be ready to take the Shining Path to war."

It was not until 1979, when Rafa was twenty years old, that Sosa had made good on his promise. It had been a massacre. Sosa and his men had fictitiously staged an enormous shipment of cocaine and munitions to be sent to Puerto Francisco de Orellano, Ecuador, in the jungles near Rio Napo. There, along the Rio Napo, Sosa and his private army of 950 men and women had ambushed and slaughtered 125 Shining Path guerrillas.

Sosa himself had been there on the front lines with Rafa, Tato, Nancho, Benny the Skull, Javier, Diego, Lucho, Felipé, Edgar, Bushwacker, Victor, Ivan, and many others. They'd had houses and camps under surveillance during the massive ambush. Upon one radio call from Sosa, the surveillance teams murdered many of the Shining Path while they were sleeping.

"Everyone with them dies," Sosa had ordered his death squads. "Mother, father, sisters, nephews, kids – *to the dog.* Burn their houses, barns, cars, *everything.* Leave nothing with breath that can come up to us in ten years wanting revenge."

In a matter of days *La Corporación* had wiped northern Peru and central Bolivia clean of their Shining Path infestation. Rafa had been given the vengeance Sosa had promised him. Rafa had been able to kill Commander Villanueva himself with his favorite weapon: a jagged-edged hunting knife. Rafa had stopped counting his kills after 75 because he did not want to be thought of as a psychopath.

"I don't mind being called a killer," Rafa had later said over the great pile of burning bodies. "But don't call me a psychopath. Psychopaths keep count and they don't *feel.* Me, I have honor in following Don Sosa's orders ... but I'm not proud to have slain a child and its mother. It just needed to be done. I had little pleasure in it ... I'm just a soldier."

Sosa had looked at him, thinking, *A soldier who finds pleasure in killing with a knife.*

$$$$$

Hoy

"I wanted badly to go on that mission, *jefe*," Rafa told Sosa after the men and La Gata Negra had departed the Pentagon for Argentina. "I mean no disrespect, *Señor*, but I feel like you when she drags you to the clothing stores and shoppes in

Sucre and Santa Cruz. I have to watch little girls at the dance studios giggle at me."

Sosa suppressed a laugh. "It's more to it than that."

"Don't think I don't know." Rafa poured Sosa and himself a shot of tequila from Sosa's living room bar. "I think danger is around every corner for her and your son, Juan Carlos. I check bathrooms, dressing rooms, and we even pass out hundred-dollar bills to people so she could have the restaurant all to herself. So, yeah, you know I know there's more to my rude humor. It's an honor to protect your family, *Señor*. I see our brothers go and I guess I feel like I have it easy. I need some action."

"Down, boy," Sosa chided him as if he was talking to one of his high-priced Presa Canarios. "Be careful what you wish for. You'll be getting plenty of action soon, I promise you. For now the *Señora* is about to push full steam ahead on *Dulce Designs*."

"I know," Rafa nodded. "She's been obsessed with it."

"She needs big projects," Sosa said, indicating the house. "You see how the Pentagon came out. Have you ever looked at a magazine, a catalog, or commercial and seen those long-leggy supermodels with the bright silvery eyes, full pink lips, long hair … looking like the candy in the window you want to taste but you can't get to it because the store is closed?"

"*Sí,*" Rafa acknowledged lustfully. "Like the Brazilians and the rich *chicas* in Catalonia and Madrid. Those Catalonians – *oowee!* – they were made strictly for emperors and kings."

"*Exactamente,*" Sosa concurred with a wry grin of his own. "For men like *us*. You're about to get a front row seat to the world's biggest fashion shows because of Yesenia Dulce. You'll have a backstage pass to the most legitimate and expensive form of prostitution on earth: *modeling*. Shows, parties, celebrities, millionaires, billionaires, and so on. All that sweet *chocha* you're about to be around ... *¡Dios mio!* You okay with that?"

Rafa nodded eagerly. "Sure, boss."

"Maybe you'll collect more *concubinas* to live with you and sunbathe on the rooftop to drive the *soldados* crazy?" Sosa nudged him playfully. "How many you have up there?"

"Just three," Rafa answered. "Three good choices. No more will be coming here. What I meet on the road in my own time I'll leave on the road."

"*Muy bien.*" Sosa walked off with Rafa. "Be my eyes and ears over there for potential female recruits. *La Corporación* can use them if you can turn them into killers. Models are opportunists; it's sex they're selling. If they'll sell sex, they'll sell their souls to us for the right price. We need hitters and spies for our international high-end associates – you know ... for any future problems."

"We have our own women ready for that," Rafa pointed out.

"True," Sosa replied as they walked through the kitchen where three of Sosa's female staff were cooking dinner. "Smells delicious, Carmen. What are we having?"

The plump, pleasant-looking cook smiled. "Thank you. Tonight is Argentinean four-inch steaks fried with chimichurri sauce, garlic, parsley, olive oil with red and black pepper."

Sosa walked on out of the kitchen and continued his conversation with Rafa in the den. "Our sister-brethren are not disposable. The outsiders are. The best they can do for us is to be pawns in our own chess games ... Let me switch the subject. You and I have to ready a hundred million dollars for Yesenia's access. Think of it as a 'petty cash' stash because she has vowed to spend it under the wood as bribe money. She won't haul it with her all at one time but five million dollars should be kept on the jet at all times and the jet has to be guarded. I suggest you find a way to hide cash in the jet where customs can't find it – like in the seats or the floor."

"That will be done," Rafa noted. "Is it true that we're getting new planes?"

"*Sí*, but we'll discuss that another time," Sosa confirmed. "The cash, wherever it is, must be under armed guard twenty-four/seven. It'll be your responsibility to record the transactions. I want to know how the money is being spent. You'll travel with a team of seven security. She'll need some muscle, where necessary, in getting a bribe completed. Such as with an advertising executive at *NBC* or *Sports Illustrated*. They *will* do what she wants. *¿Entendido?*"

"Or they'll be thrown off the roof."

"Authorities are *not* to be able to track this cash," Sosa continued. "It's to be used in the *strictest* of secrecy, to power-pump oxygen into the machine she's building. The entire thing – getting *Dulce Designs* to the Top 10 in fashion, cosmetics, et cetera – revolves around global advertising. She's asked for one hundred million dollars and she's got it. I'm putting the care and responsibility of this money on *you* and *you only*. No paper trail, no indictments. We cannot stand a blow like that anywhere."

"I hear your fear, Don Sosa," Rafa stated his awareness. "I'll make them my own. *Te lo juro* [I swear on it]. I will not let you down, boss."

"*Bien, hijo* (Okay, son)."

After having dinner with Yesenia and Juan Carlos, Sosa and Rafa went down into the basement money room/vault. They loaded $100 million onto a steel pushcart and pulled a sheet over it. Sosa pushed the cart into a far corner and wrote a note out on the counting table in big letters: *DO NOT TOUCH! FOR YESENIA ONLY!* the note read.

"A reminder to myself and others," Sosa told Rafa. Sosa picked up a large hardcover book and handed it to Rafa. "Itemize each dollar. Keep a neat log of every transaction."

They exited the vault and went back upstairs on one of the elevators.

"Shouldn't Benny be checking in on the SAT-phone, *jefe*?" Rafa asked while they were on the elevator.

Sosa, glancing at his presidential Rolex, idly nodded. "They'll page me first and then they'll call the SAT."

However, for the moment, neither man knew anything about the horrifying circumstances both aircraft were about to confront.

CHAPTER FOURTEEN

Elvira Montana
Nyack, New York
September 14, 1984

At 10 a.m. the next day Almara let herself back inside of Elvira's condo and called out her name. The Puerto Rican counselor heard water running in the kitchen. She told the young woman she was with to follow her. They both entered the kitchen but Elvira was not there. Almara abruptly stopped short and stared down at her shoes in disbelief. The kitchen floor was flooded with water that had overflowed from the kitchen sink. She knew instantly that something was wrong.

"Montana!" Almara turned off the running water and rushed through the house searching for Elvira. They found her crying, sitting on the bathroom floor with wads of Kleenex thrown all over the place. "Elvira!"

The bathroom was also flooded and Elvira was soaked. Almara turned off the running bath water and drained the tub.

"Nina Lee!" Elvira sobbed, her tears were flowing as she recognized the exotic nurse.

"Come on, baby; *up.*" The Black China doll reached down and helped Elvira up onto her feet. "I came to surprise you but then I heard the news."

Almara put a call out onto the intercom that an emergency clean-up crew was needed at the Montana condo. She then hurried back into the bathroom to assist Nina Lee, who had

135

come on a surprise visit to check up on Elvira's progress. Almara and Nina undressed the distraught, shivering cold young woman and put her into a hot shower to warm her up. They dried her off and dressed her in pajamas before tucking her back into bed. Nurse Rebecca Poler came in to help while a maintenance/HAZMAT team came in to clean up the mess.

An hour later only Nina and Almara were there in the bedroom with Elvira.

"What happened, Elvira?" Almara questioned her. "The water?"

"My tears," Elvira told them. "The water symbolizes my tears."

Nina glanced at Almara and took a deep breath.

"Elvira, I need you to talk to me," Almara urged. "Were you, or are you, thinking about hurting yourself?"

"No." Her answer was simple. "I already friggin' hurt! I want *one day* where I feel no pain! One friggin' day!"

"You're off the drugs and alcohol," Nina told her. "One week clean. We'd like to keep you off of psychotropic meds but you are clearly depressed."

Almara nodded, agreeing. "What you've suffered through as a child and now as an adult ... you're getting to grieve now. *Absent* the substances. This is how you deal with tragedies."

"I need your help," she said sadly. "I need both of your help ... I can't do this mess alone. No psych meds."

"We'll help," Nina promised. "What do you need?"

"Okay." Elvira reached for Nina's hand. "Ally. Get that Louis Vuitton carry-on."

Almara did as she was directed.

"Look inside of the bank envelope," Elvira ordered. "Don't empty it. Just look at what's there."

Almara and Nina looked inside the envelope at the stacks of money.

"That's a hundred grand," Elvira said, her voice low. "I already have more millions put away than I can count. I need both of you to work for me."

"You mean *permanently?*" Nina questioned her. "Elvira ..."

"Quit our jobs you mean?" Almara stated slowly.

"Yeah and yeah," Elvira nodded.

"You can't be serious." Nina sounded incredulous.

Almara was listening attentively. She was considering it.

"I wouldn't survive without youse with me." Elvira looked at each woman, reading their faces. "I'd relapse out there ... I know y'all just met me and think I'm nuts so, to show you I'm not crazy ... I'll pay each of you ten grand – right now – to *quit; effective immediately.*"

"Ten thousand dollars is a lot of money." Nina spoke up first. She smiled nervously, thinking of what she could do with money like that. "I'm not saying no ... but I'm skeptic. I have responsibilities for greater than ten grand. I believe you mean well ... but after Almara's call last night and what I see today, it is clear that you are suffering from PTSD. Maybe more."

Elvira chuckled lightly. "I wish one textbook term could define me and my problems, Black China Doll. Sure, I am all screwed up. I admit it. But I know what I'm doing. In a few minutes I'm going to pack up, call a taxi, and be gone. I have to bury my husband and all of his associates because no one else will. I met you two over this past week and you're all I can trust. There's only me, my baby, and money for incentive. All I can do is ... I'll tell you what. Make me *your* offer. You must be worried about job security right? Bills?"

Almara nodded. "Definitely."

Nina nodded. "Student loans, credit cards, car payments, helping my family. But, goodness ... to just up and leave?"

"Ten thousand now ..." Elvira handed each woman a stack of the cash. "And *twenty-five* thousand more in twenty-four hours when we fly via private charter jet to Miami. That gives you twenty-four hours to resign, handle your immediate affairs, and return here to me at 10 a.m. tomorrow. As my employees, your only client is *me*. Your only patient is *me*. Be my rehab counselor and nurse. Be my friends and my assistants. Get me healthy, *keep* me healthy. For that you each will make five thousand dollars, in cash, per month. Pay your own taxes. I'll set up a payroll account later with a million dollars in it – after I handle some tax issues of my own. How's that for starters?"

"Okay." Nina looked a lot more confident. "Count me in."

Almara had been waiting for the right opportunity to come her way. "I love this job but I can do without the politics that come with it."

Nina got up. "Will you be okay for twenty-four hours, boss?"

Elvira smiled. "Yeah. Both of you can go."

Before Almara left the room, she turned back to Elvira. "That meeting this morning …"

Elvira listened closely, curious as to how it all went. "What happened?"

"They decided to discharge you," Almara said, a frown on her face. "They made it a whole lot easier for me to accept your offer. For what it's worth, I fought for you and probably came close to being fired for insubordination."

Elvira feigned a smile. "*Screw them.* It's okay, Ally. I'm so tired of the world screwing me. I'm tired of men screwing me. All my life, Ally, it's been men who've had all the friggin' control of my life. No more. My luck is about to change."

Almara did not take what Elvira said as some angry rant. "How you figure?"

"I'm not betting on losers anymore," she swore as she sank deeper under the covers. "From now on I'm betting on winners only, baby. *Winners.* It's been a man's world too long. I'm putting my money on *women*. Beautiful, beautiful women who want to *win*!"

CHAPTER FIFTEEN

The Sosa Support Unit
Somewhere Over Argentina
September 14, 1984

"Black Crow to Red Scorpion, *cambio*," Ivan called over the radio from the support plane. He looked at Javier and Victor, who sat in the cockpit of the Antonov. "Black Crow to Red Scorpion, *cambio* (over)."

No response.

Felipé, Edgar, Victor, Ivan, and Javier had already been given permission by Argentinean authorities to divert the airplane east, around Hurricane Isabel, to Uruguay, to avoid disaster. They were flying legitimately, on business, as employers of Andes Sugar Corporation (ASC) so they readily modified their flight plan and accepted the command to reroute. The storm was a monster, a rarely seen 500-mile-wide behemoth moving slowly northwest through Argentina.

"Keep trying, *chico*," Javier ordered as strong winds and rain pelted the aircraft. "We gotta tell Red Scorpion to turn back. We'll have to handle the mission ourselves. Keep trying, *hombre!*"

Ivan continued to try but to no avail.

"Whoa!" Javier yelled as wind knocked the plane around like a roller-coaster ride. "Parachutes, just in case! Everybody put on parachutes! If the combat plane can't make it ... Gutiérrez still has to die!"

"Javier," Ivan looked at him. "Sosa wouldn't want us to –"

"*Ivan!!*" Javier roared at him. "What Sosa says goes! We have to assume that a low-flying smuggling jet cannot make it through this storm, *hombre*! Especially not at low altitudes. The mission is ours now, *hermano*. If we have to jump, we jump. Gutiérrez must die."

"*Señor*," Ivan nodded and indicated to the other team members standing at the cockpit door to prepare for the possible emergency jump. "Youse heard him! *¡Muevense!*"

Javier pushed the jet to a maximum speed of 600 miles per hour and he climbed the jet up to a height of 34,000 feet. Every now and then he'd adjust the aircraft's altitude depending on how violent the wind currents became. He watched Ivan put on his aviator's gear and parachute equipment. Javier took a few minutes to put on his own while Ivan controlled the aircraft.

"Contingency protocol is clear!" Javier told his crew. "If we have to jump, the last man out must remote detonate the C-4 bombs once you clear five seconds! Our backpacks have communication and other equipment we need for the mission, especially weapons! We'll need to regroup and locate immediate transportation to B.A.! Even if we have to steal or hijack a plane – or helicopter – we must get to B.A. by noon tomorrow! Got it?"

"*Señor!*" the crew chorused loudly.

"Where are we, Ivan?" Javier wanted to know. "If we jump we at least need to try to jump somewhere other than a volcano or a minefield!"

Ivan studied the control panel, made some notes on one of the maps and pointed at it. "Seventy-five miles northwest of Reconquista."

Javier looked at Ivan. "I hope God stays with us. Try Red Scorpion again. Keep trying."

$$$$$

At the same time, inside of the "Red Scorpion"/combat plane, Nancho had an idea as he returned to the cockpit with his brother Tatico and his cousin Benny the Skull. "Benito, Tatico. If Black Crow, the support plane, is in the sky, safe … and we contact them, we have two choices. One, tell them to carry out the mission or, two, they have to allow us, to *somehow* allow us, to catch up to them and maybe try to fly side by side with them to trick the radar into believing we're one plane. The air traffic authorities will be confused. Nine out of ten they're having a nightmare with commercial flights because of the storm."

Benny had sweat pouring down his face as he flew the jet through the turbulent weather. The cockpit was hot and humid and Benny was worried. He stayed silent as he piloted the aircraft. They were hearing what sounded like rocks pounding against the jet's exterior. They could not visually see them but apple-sized pieces of hail were coming down as they entered into the brim of the storm.

"*Oye*, we're in it!" Tato said excitedly. He spoke as if the storm was a person. "*I respect you, Baby. Be nice to us, okay?*" He paused and responded to Nancho. "Argentine AWACS systems are superior. Radar will detect the two flights. Anyway, we're going in as we already said. Stop worrying, Nanchito. Refill Tank One. Have everyone prepare for contingency. The radio waves are going nuts about the size of this thing. Everybody in full gear with back-up parachutes. Bring ours up here."

Nancho stood up but he was slammed backwards as the wind whacked the plane hard from the right side, forcing all three men to hold on tight. "*Maldito!*" Nancho growled.

"I'll call Black Crow, Nancho," Tato stated as he reached for the radio.

"Use the SAT-phone, *hombre*," Nancho yelled over the deafening sound of the hailstorm blasting against the body of the plane like missiles. "Stay off the radio. You know why … Even if we ascend to ride it out, we have no authorization code to fly over Argentina. But, if I'm right on this, I highly doubt they'll scramble warplanes to intercept us if we tell them we were knocked off course because of the storm. If we avoid sensitive airspace we'll get through. We're *one* plane, not an enemy fleet. They'll ask for identification … think of something."

Javier was quiet as he mulled over what Nancho had said. "He's right, Benito. It's easiest to create radio static in a storm like this. In the static we could claim to be a plane in distress. We can talk our way through and make them believe our communication system is failing. I'll make up a story, an identity, that I'm … Hugo Arenciba … from Calama, Chile. This is a personal aircraft …"

"Let's hope it works," Nancho told him. "Make it sound half good, half radio static. Claim you need to get to Bahia Blanca, Argentina. That you have the fuel to reach as far as Florida or Montevideo, Uruguay. They'll divert you and provide the path. They'll get us into Uruguay but they may order us to land in B.A. for questioning and inspection. If so, immediately agree to comply. We'll only disappear as planned anyway."

Nancho exited the cockpit. He had to hold onto the overhead rails to support himself from the violently escalating wind turbulence.

"Buro, Catalina Lilli, Bushwack!" Nancho yelled to the three crew members. "*¡Vamos! Ayúdame.*"

Even those three could no longer rest because of the terrible wind gusts and hailstorm bombardment on the Antonov. The three soldiers followed Nancho to a long row of blue, industrial plastic, 100-gallon barrels of jet fuel. Nancho hurriedly tied a rope around his waist and ordered the

143

others to do the same. They tied the ropes to the railings above for an added safety precaution against the brutal turbulence.

"The wind currents in this hurricane are knocking us around like a kite!" Nancho yelled over the loud tatter of the hail. "The rope will keep us from being thrown too far."

Nancho dropped to his knees and opened up the fuel cap. Most of Sosa's air fleet had been modified to carry extra barrels of fuel in their cargo areas. Nancho stuck a large clear tube down into one of the many barrels of jet fuel and the other end of the tube into his mouth. He immediately began to siphon the fuel by sucking it up hard into the tube. The reddish-colored fuel gushed upwards through the tube, filled his mouth, and splashed out onto his arm and down to the floor below.

"¡*Maldita!*" Nancho yelled, spitting the awful-tasting fuel from his mouth just as the turbulence slammed him about eight feet backwards. Buro and Catalina were thrown with him while Bushwacker was able to hold onto the Velcro straps that were hanging from the wall. Fortunately, the ropes that Nancho, Catalina, and Buro had tied around their waists had prevented them from being flung farther into the cargo hold. However, the jet fuel had continued to gush out all over the steel floor of the plane until – on his hands and knees – Bushwacker quickly retrieved the fast-spewing tube and bent it over at the end to stop the rush of the fuel. He crawled over to the hole in the floor and thrust the fuel tube down into it. Nancho got back onto his feet and stared at Catalina. "*This is what you wanted?!*"

"Not now, Nancho!" she snapped.

He glared at her. "We do this so the women in our family don't have to! You wanted adventure? *Danger?* Well, you got it now, baby. You might die tonight!"

Bushwacker managed to mop up the spilled fuel on the floor with some old towels. Buro opened up a large bag of sawdust and covered the remainder of the fuel as best as he could with it.

Once the refueling of Tank One was completed, they refueled Tank Two. Soon afterwards, Nancho was barking out orders for emergency jump preparations. "We must ready ourselves! If we have to jump, we'll jump! This is what we *might* have to do. The backpacks all have the necessary equipment! The radios are sealed in plastic so we don't lose contact! I'll be the last to jump because I'll be the one whose job it is to remote detonate the C-4 bombs aboard! Just remember the destination: *Aerolineas Argentinas*, at the *LAN Airlines* terminal, at noon tomorrow."

Nancho was about to brush past his cousin but he stopped and held her pretty face in his hands. "You all right?"

She nodded, tough as nails. "*¡Sí!* Have you ever been in a hurricane like this?"

Nancho thought about lying but not to a comrade. Catalina was with them, she was *La Corporación*, so she was a comrade. "Not one like this, *prima!* This one is a monster! It's a big, evil monster out to kill as many animals and people as it can! Get dressed!"

"Shouldn't we try to put the extra parachutes on those motorcycles?" Catalina pointed down the aisle to the black motorcycles parked in a line at the end of the cargo area.

"That's a good idea." Nancho knew that they'd need transportation. The least they could do was try to save the bikes. With everyone's help they were able to equip each of the motorcycles with a parachute.

"There we go," Catalina quipped, proud of herself afterwards.

"*¡Muchachos!*" Nancho yelled, a devilish grin on his face. "This is what we *live* for! What we train for! And if we must – what we'll *die* for! Our families are taken care of! *Whooooo!!!*"

Nancho's excitement was infectious to the men. Bushwacker, Buro, and Nancho all hugged each other and clutched each other's heads. Catalina observed the laughing men and thought to herself, *They're crazy. All of them are crazy.*

The four of them got dressed with their gear and parachutes. Nancho returned to the front …

In the cockpit Tato had struck gold.

"*That's Javi on the SAT-phone, mijo!*" Tato rasped excitedly. "Hello, Javi."

Nancho, Bushwacker, Buro, and Catalina whooped and hollered after hearing that the support plane was still airborne!

"*¡Ya! ¡Ya, hombre!* (Okay! Enough already!)" Tato shouted and held up his hand. "Red Scorpion here! Black Crow! *¡Hablame!*"

Even the SAT-phone had troubles. Tato was certain that he'd heard his older brother's voice when the SAT-phone had rung just a moment ago.

"Tatico! Tatico!" Now Javier's voice got clearer.

"*Hablame, hermano, sí, ¡sí!*" Tato shouted into the phone, tears in his eyes at hearing his brother's voice. "Youse are okay?"

A long, frustrating pause … then, " … okay! We're all okay! If youse can make it, we'll be at the rendezvous! If you think you can climb, you'll be much safer at thirty-five thousand feet! As long as you maintain altitude and communicate distress to the people below, I think you can fool them enough for them *not* to send up a fighter jet! We'll be landing in two hours. *¡Dos horas!* Do you *believe* – not *think* – you'll make it?!"

Tato looked at Benny. The sweating had stopped.

"Do we believe we'll make it?" Tato asked Benny.

"The hail's gone," was all Benny said.

"We're taking the butt-kicking of our lives!" Tato responded as he looked at his elite unit of killers. "We think that –"

"Oh, shit!" Javier shouted on the other end.

"*¡Javi!*" Tato shouted. "Javier!"

The line was dead.

"What's up?" La Gata Negra asked.

"*No sé* [I don't know]." Tato hung up the SAT-phone. "He ... I heard a yell. Then nothing."

They all eyed each other. Tato tried to call Javier's SAT-phone but there was no answer. They waited, with trepidation in their facial expressions, for Javier to call them but the call never came.

CHAPTER SIXTEEN

George Sheffield, Esq.
Miami, Florida
September 15, 1984

The three women were not kept waiting. A cute red-headed legal secretary ushered Elvira, Nina, and Almara directly into the office of famed attorney George Sheffield, Tony's former lawyer. He stood up from his grand mahogany desk to greet the well-dressed women with brief hugs and pecks on their cheeks.

"Elvira." He held both of her hands, looking her in the eyes with his most sincere expression of sympathy. "I'm very sorry for your tragic loss. Everyone has been talking about it, wondering if you were okay."

He closed the door and directed them into three comfortable, black cushioned chairs that were situated in front of his desk.

"You said 'everyone,'" Elvira stated, curious. She crossed her legs. "Whom are you referring to when you say 'everyone'?"

"Oh, you know,' he grinned, finishing off a bourbon he'd been nursing before their meeting. "The streets talk. [Shrugging and pouring himself another drink] Can I get you ladies a drink?"

"No, thank you," Elvira declined.

"Tony *did* leave a Will." Sheffield got right to it. He removed a folder from a locked file cabinet and handed it to Elvira. He sat back down. "You don't mind discussing any of this in front of your friends? [Nodding at them] Ladies. No offense."

"None taken," Nina smiled.

"Meet Ally and Nina," Elvira introduced them. "Don't mind them."

"He left you everything," Sheffield told her. "As you know, he had been owner of the building that housed Gina's Hair Salon and he'd leased to a number of other shop and boutique vendors there. That property he left to Gina but she's dead, too. The mother – Georgina Montana – has been trying to locate you. She's lost on what to do. She has no cash. I'd told her if she wanted me to liquidate the property, I'd need thirty to sixty days at least. She's desperate to sell. She needs money to bury her children. The least I could do was give her what I had on me, which was only about two grand."

Elvira thought it through. "Okay. Do you have her number?"

"Certainly." He went through his Rolodex and pulled the phone number out.

Elvira stood up and grabbed the receiver as Sheffield dialed the number.

"Hello?" came Georgina's accented English.

"Mama?" Elvira said. "Mama Montana?"

"Elvee?" She sounded uncertain. "Is that you?"

"It's me," Elvira answered. "I'm at Tony's lawyer's. I'll be paying for all of the burials. Don't worry."

Georgina breathed a sigh of relief. "Thank God."

"Don't do nothing," Elvira stated. "Have you already located where all their remains are?"

"*Sí*," Georgina replied. "Gordon's Funeral Home. The hospital sent them there. I guess when no one claims them, the funeral home cremates them and the city pays? I'm so happy you call. I'll call Gordon's and say not to cremate?"

"Right," Elvira responded. "I'll see you soon, at your house."

"That takes care of that." Sheffield sat back in his chair.

"These businesses." Elvira held up the paperwork. *"Montana Realty Corporation; Montana Supply Company; Montana Construction Company; Montana Clothing and Apparel Company,* and *Montana Trucking Company."*

"All owned by MRC, Montana Realty Corporation," Sheffield explained. "MRC began as his own little money laundering operation. As he got bigger, he bought up struggling businesses and muscled out their previous owners. If I were your lawyer, I'd advise you to liquidate every asset he had because Washington has been making examples out of Miami dopers."

"But I'm not a criminal," Elvira argued.

"Honey, you don't have to be!" Sheffield stood up and sat on the front edge of the desk with his arms crossed. "Reagan has sworn to bring a ring of fire around drug traffickers and put an end to the extreme spike in violence and drug-related crimes. That means drug money, laundering operations, banks, businesses, and so forth. The drug cartels have been hiding untold billions of dollars in American banks and businesses. And Washington – that is, the IRS, Department of Treasury – have put together a Federal Drug Taskforce and they are starting *in Miami.* You can claim your ignorance however much you like; it won't mean a dagburn thing to them. They'll freeze every asset you have, and even if you prevail in court, the businesses will fold and be rendered useless by all the months, or even years, of litigation they'll drag you through."

Elvira opened up her trusty Louis Vuitton carry-on case and gave Sheffield a $100,000 cash retainer. "Sell the businesses and all their assets, but I want it done through Montana Realty Corporation."

"It'll be a risk to retain even *one* company," Sheffield said as he locked the money away in a lockbox he kept inside of his bottom desk drawer. "Listen to me – as *your* lawyer now. Dissolve MRC and reregister it elsewhere. *Trust* me on this. Pablo Escobar, Carlos Lehder, Griselda Blanco, Gonzalo Rodriguez Gacha, the Mexican cartels, now this Alejandro Sosa and his Bolivian –"

"Wait," Elvira stopped him. "What about Alejandro Sosa?"

"According to some reports I've heard, he's on the radar of the U.S. Government," Sheffield told her. "Not a whole lot is known about him but it's suspected that he's the *head* of the mighty dragon. Was that who Tony was involved with?" He looked into her eyes.

Elvira shrugged. "I'd have no way of knowing that. Just thought the name sounded familiar."

He looked at her for a pausing moment before continuing. "Anyway, these heavy-hitting drug bosses are scrambling for cover; they're moving cash and assets out of the way of U.S. authorities as we speak. You do not want to have anything that can link you to Tony's shady businesses."

"I'll take your advice," she agreed with him. "Dissolve MRC. I'll reopen and reregister it in New York. Now [looking at another section of the Will] these accounts ... Spain, France, Italy, and Japan. I never knew anything about them."

"Your name is on each one – *jointly*," Sheffield said. "Produce the Will, Tony's death certificate, and your marriage license, along with your passport, and make your withdrawal. Of the four banks, there's about six million in total. Tony never lied to me in this office. He spoke very frankly. It was my understanding that he actually had serious trouble in finding places to stash his cash."

"What are you getting at, Sheffield?" Elvira asked.

"In the Will there's only the six million," Sheffield said, biting off the end of a cigar he was preparing to smoke. "Way I see it … [lighting the cigar] there's at least twenty, maybe even thirty times that stashed elsewhere. If you need my help looking for any of it …" He let the thought linger.

"Thanks for the offer." Of course Elvira knew *precisely* where the money was stashed at. "It's my understanding that he died over that money. They killed him for it. If there's any more money, he died with the only knowledge of its whereabouts. I wish I knew. You focus on the sale of those companies. Me [sighing] I'll focus on burying Tony. I'll be in touch, Sheffield."

Sheffield nodded, escorting the three women to the door. "Once again, I'm sorry for your loss, Elvira."

Elvira let Nina and Almara walk out first. Once they were out of earshot, Elvira turned back to Sheffield and looked him in the eye. "You know, Sheffield, I could have retained any other high-powered lawyer. F. Lee Bailey, Johnnie Cochran, maybe even Alan Dershowitz. But I chose you. Familiarity, I guess."

"I like you, too, Mrs. Montana," he smiled.

"I just sort of got the feeling that something else was at play here when you spoke about money Tony *may have* stashed somewhere other than these four foreign bank accounts."

"Oh, Mrs. Montana, you musta been reading me wrong." He gave her his best schoolboy smile. "Nothing else is at play."

"*Gaspar Gomez*," she said. "*Lugo; Nacho Contreras; the Diaz Brothers …*"

He took a deep breath. "What about them?"

"I know who's who in Miami." She gave him a cold stare. "Just because I'm a woman, you think I'm less of a threat than those clients of yours?"

"*Elvira …*"

"*George*," she threw back at him. "*The streets talk; Escobar, Lehder, Blanco, Gacha, Sosa ... scrambling for cover; moving their cash and assets out of the way of the IRS, the Feds.* I hear well, Sheffield. I also caught you indirectly interrogating me about Tony's so-called motherlode of green. Don't play me for a fool, Sheffield. So, whichever one of your clients put you up to do some poking around on Tony's money, here's my advice: *End it.* There's *no money* outside of the Will. If my suspicions are wrong ..." She let the comment hang.

"Yeah?"

She stroked his shaved left chubby cheek. "Then I'm sorry. I came to you not only because Tony came to you but Frank Lopez did also. And I used to watch you come into the Babylon nightclub and the fine restaurants around town and meet with rich gangsters on one side of town and on the other side the governor, mayor, and judges. I won't be pushed around, Sheffield. We clear?"

He nodded and watched her walk off. He closed the door to his office, wondering what the hell had just happened. He picked up the telephone and dialed a number.

"Gaspar Gomez here," a man answered with a deeply accented English.

"She's in town," Sheffield said to him. "As you predicted. I persuaded her to sell the business. I advise you and the Diaz brothers to come into my office and help me come up with a number to give her that doesn't sound insanely low."

"Tony's money," Gaspar growled into the phone. "Where is it?"

"Maybe that's what Tony and his crew died trying to defend, I don't know." Sheffield emptied his ashtray into the small garbage can next to his desk. "She said that much herself. Besides ... she's obviously a tough cookie but she was never in the thick of things with Tony. He didn't trust anybody. He even had other lawyers. She came to collect what was in the Will and bury all of those stinking rotting corpses down at the morgue. The only money she'll walk away with is the six million in Tony's foreign accounts and what she'll receive from the Montana Realty Company fire sale."

Gaspar Gomez was silent for a moment. "Since she's in town I'll put eyes on her to see if we can find out more. If he died protecting the bulk of the cash, then it would be spent in our clubs, brothels, clothing stores, and our *yayo*. Money like what he had changes the economy. While I watch her locally, you put investigators on her to follow her internationally."

"Okay, Gaspar."

"Nacho Contreras is here," Gaspar said on a different note.

"Really." Sheffield turned in his large swivel chair to stare out the window at downtown Miami. "How's my friend, El Gordo, doing?"

"Sheffield," came El Gordo's voice over the phone.

"El Gordo."

"That wretched woman once dated a Frank Lopez underling named Choppy," Gordo said. "He was killed in prison under Frank's orders. Blondie became Frank's girl. Scarface comes from Cuba, works for Frank, and later Scarface establishes a connect with Alejandro Sosa. Frank's hit, Blondie becomes *Tony's* wife. After a few years, Tony's the country's top supplier, then he's hit. Massacred. What's that say to you about Blondie?"

After hearing that, Sheffield was at a loss for words.

CHAPTER SEVENTEEN

The Sosa Elite Kill Units
Buenos Aires, Argentina
September 15, 1984

Sosa had been informed about Hurricane Isabel by one of his two female horse veterinarians who had come directly to his house with the news.

"I'm sorry to bother you at this hour, Don Sosa," Sessi Maria de Dios said hurriedly. "But it's urgent."

"Come in out of the cold, Sessi Maria." Sosa had stepped aside to let her in. The house staff had been asleep and he had been in the kitchen eating a late evening meal. "What is it?"

"Well," she had begun, "you know how the animals get when a storm is coming. They get riled up. The birds are all packed into the buildings. The barn, all the stables, they're everywhere. Not just your regular macaws ... many, many others have come but you can look at them and tell. It's very strange."

"Tell what?"

"It's been on the radio all night," she had informed him. "They're saying the biggest hurricane Bolivia has ever seen will be here in thirty-six hours. I'm *very* fearful for the animals."

"Fear is good," he had reasoned. "Since you can't run, you use what you know to do what you do best. We won't lose even one chicken if you do that. Warn all the *rancheros*

155

to prepare, move all animals indoors by first rain. We cannot flood up here so that's not the worry. Go!"

Sosa had made a SAT-phone call to Bolivian Minister of the Interior Ariel Bleyer. "You know I don't watch too much television these days. How bad is the storm going to be?"

"*Devastating.*" Minister Bleyer had not sugar-coated it. "Possibly catastrophic. We're monitoring the destruction it's causing to Argentina. Nobody in Bolivian government or military is sleeping for the next three days. The President is thinking of announcing a curfew and a state of emergency even *before* the hurricane hits – something no Bolivian President has ever done."

Sosa was worried about his comrades and the Gutiérrez mission. After he had finished speaking to Minister Bleyer, he summoned Rafa and three of his private army sergeants to his kitchen to warn them about the hurricane's fast approach.

"We're already on high ground," Sosa told them. "And since we're on a rock we don't have to worry about mudslides. All the animals and equipment must be secured. Many birds feel safe in the stables and the barns. The supply houses and helicopter hangars must remain open for the meateater birds – the harpy eagles, vultures, et cetera. You may want to put a few dead pigs in there. The macaws won't allow them into the barn. The meat-eaters will smell the dead carcasses and be attracted to the shelter. Sergeant Pappy Meza, you take your men and double check all supplies: bottled water, batteries, candles, flashlights, non-perishable food items, the gas pumps for the generators, food for the animals … whatever is on those supply lists, our storage units must be packed. The hurricane will prevent us from going into the cities due to the state of emergency, the flooding and so forth."

"The Quechua tribe down at the bottom of the mountain, boss," Rafa reminded him.

"*Dios*, of course." Sosa thought it over for a moment. "Let Chief Roshapo know about the storm. They number about three hundred. Tell the Chief that his tribe and their animals have shelter here until the floods subside. If he refuses, remind him of the land mines – they *cannot* move up the mountain. They must be escorted by you but their exodus should start now."

"I'll go with them, boss," Rafa volunteered.

"*Me duele la cabeza*," (My head hurts) Sosa sighed.

Knowing his boss well, Rafa looked at him. "No one is invincible, *jefe*. Especially against an act of God ... which is what weather is. Those units you sent are the best on earth. Trust in that if nothing else. They're alive, boss."

Sosa looked at Rafa. "If you were out there ... what would you do?"

"You mean what are they thinking," Rafa said. "They're brave men. They're death junkies. They probably have on aviator's gear, backpacks, parachutes, and back-up parachutes, if the planes fail them. They'd be too ashamed to come back home without killing that *sapo*. They won't let you down, boss."

"*Vete ahora, muchacho.*" (Leave now, boy) Sosa gently slapped Rafa's face. "We have a storm to get ready for."

$$\$\$\$\$\$$

Javier brought the support plane to a complete stop and, minutes later, he was disembarking with the rest of his crew. They passed through customs without any problems and exited the LAN Airlines terminal in a rush.

Felipé, Edgar, Victor, and Ivan waited out front until Javier coasted up in an all-white Dodge passenger van he had rented from Hertz Rental Car.

"*Entonces,*" (Okay, then) Edgar began as Javier drove them out of the airport parking lot. "Where are we going?"

"Where you think, *hombre*," Javier gruffly stated as he maneuvered the van through the Buenos Aires late-night traffic. "I mean, I have to assume that our brothers will make it to the landing strip. That's where we're going after we make a stop at a gas station. We need to buy oil and gas so that we can light up the strip for them. That hurricane rain, *hombre*, [sighing and shaking his head] … it'll be messy but we have to try. No one saw it coming. We're warriors; we have to take the ugly with the pretty."

"That SAT-phone still dead?" Ivan asked Felipé, who was sitting in the back seat trying his best to fix it.

"No luck." Felipé looked pissed off.

At the gas station Javier put a call through to Sosa's SAT-phone.

"Javi." Sosa sounded relieved at hearing Javi's voice. "Everyone safe?"

"My unit is," Javi stated. "I don't know about the other."

"What happens now?" Sosa asked, putting his deep concern about the other plane to the side. "What's going on?"

"We made it through that hellish weather," Javier reported. "We were diverted … we're just about an hour or two behind schedule. We made brief contact with them via SAT-phone, but our aircraft was hit by lightning and the phone dropped … Now it's completely disabled. We thought we'd have to jump ship even on the diversion path to Uruguay. If the other unit is going to make it, they'll be in just before dawn. You should try to contact them while I'm on the line."

"How long ago was it since your contact with them?"

"About ninety minutes. Two hours tops."

"*Espera,* [wait]" Sosa told him as he called the combat plane's SAT-phone from his eleven line. There was a very bad connection but it was Tato who answered it. "Tato … *Tato!*"

"*¡Jefe!*" Tato's voice was distant, garbled.

As frustrating and stressful as it was, Sosa waited patiently for a clear moment in the static to break through the line. "Tato, I'm here … Tato … Tato."

"Boss, I think we're blind up here," Tato finally said clearly.

"Is everyone all right? Is the ship in distress?"

"Everyone's fine," Tato told him. "The ship has some exterior damage from the lightning strikes but it's holding. Javier? The others?" He was deeply worried.

"They're on the ground – safe," Sosa revealed to him, calming him. Sosa heard Tato tell his crew the news and a thunderous cheer could be heard in the background. "I have Javi on the other line. Stick to the plan. *Plan A*. They'll be there. What's your status?"

"We're caught in this storm," Tato informed him. "We're at thirty-five thousand feet … it's the wind that's more the problem now. Air traffic authorities have granted us permission to land in Buenos Aires but we've provided them fictitious information. We've been blown off course …"

"*No, chico!*" Sosa emphasized sharply. "You *cannot* land in B.A … .Are you lost?"

"*Sí.*"

"Use *them* to guide you into B.A.," Sosa instructed him. "Once you see the city you'll know where you have to go. The storm has passed through B.A. already so visibility should be clear."

"The airstrip/river bed will be washed out."

"Stop worrying, Tato," Sosa admonished him. "They'll be there momentarily and report back to me on that. I'll call you and tell you whether to divert to the other strip. We'd be better off stranding the plane than the mission. The ship is a phantom. It's untraceable."

"*Señor.*"

"Javi?" Sosa said into the SAT-phone.

"*Sí.*"

"Leave a radio with one of your men and post him at the payphone you're using," Sosa directed him carefully. "This way, if there's too much water at the river bed, call me and I'll have Tato divert to the other strip."

Javier hung up the phone, knowing he had to hurry.

$$$$$

Tato had not been exaggerating their plight. They'd been more than 30 miles off course prior to their first contact with a National Air Traffic Command Center who had spotted the plane on radar as it had flown over Santa Fe. After a few exchanges, Tato had been granted permission to land in Buenos Aires. But they were not out of the frying pan yet. Far from it.

Although the storm had passed over Buenos Aires, there were some smaller residual storm clouds left behind that blocked the plane's visibility. Sosa had called them back and informed Tato that the rendezvous strip was "safe enough" to use.

"What is 'safe enough'?" Benny sounded flight weary as he looked over at Tato. They had flown over B.A. and they were delighted to see that the city was remarkably clear. However, as they flew above it their visibility was being obstructed by an ominous pre-dawn fog. "Now we can't see anything," Benny scowled.

Tato knew that the way in which they just zoomed past the airport and over the city of Buenos Aires, every law enforcement agency – and military unit – available in the area would be investigating the low-flying Antonov. What the Antonov did was extremely high-risk and likely spooked the Argentinean authorities. Tato did his best the keep the air-traffic controllers at bay by telling them that the plane's landing gear had malfunctioned but it did not sound like they were buying it.

"The strip has to be very close." Benny sounded calm but Tato and Nancho could see the sweat streaming down his face again.

"It'd be great if we could *see* it!" Tato rasped out loudly and nervously. "The clouds are too low."

"Make up your mind; *fog* or *clouds*," Nancho said. "We're at twenty-five hundred feet."

"Fog, clouds, who cares?" Tato scowled. "They look alike from here."

Catalina stood in the doorway of the cockpit with Buro and Bushwacker.

"Isn't twenty-five hundred feet too low?" she asked nervously.

"Holy Father God, *hombre*! We're about to die!" Tato made the sign of the cross. "There's hills all around where we're flying! Pull up, Benny! Pull up!"

"If you and Nancho don't *shut your mouths* ... I'll shoot you both!" Benny growled at them. "That's low-hanging clouds *and* fog down there! Before I crash the plane, *please* help me spot the fires!"

"Screw you, Benny. You just need to go ahead and shoot me," Nancho snapped as he stared out the windows, straining his eyes in an attempt to see through the dense fog.

"I'm going lower," Benny announced as the plane descended. "Descending ..."

"*Coño*, man, just kill us all, Benny!" Tato was more angry than he'd ever been. "Nose-dive us down into the earth!"

Catalina covered her eyes. "Oh, God, *fifteen hundred feet!*"

"*Shut up!!! Shut the hell up!!*" Nancho turned on her and Tato.

"Who you think you're talking to?!" Tato jumped up out of his seat.

"*¡MIRA POR LA VENTANA!* [Look out the window!]" Buro pointed. "There! *Look!*"

Benny was already descending. "Going down ..."

"Is it fire? What if it's not fire?!" Catalina yelled at them. At that moment she vomited from the sheer terror of it all. "*Agghhh!* My God! He's gonna kill us!"

"Then we'll be dead." Benny stopped looking at the altitude gauge after 700 feet. He knew only that they had to land the plane or risk them being spotted by military helicopters or jets, and possibly being shot down.

The fog was so dense that Benny and the others were uncertain about where they were landing until the plane was 50 feet from the runway! Benny, with more shouting help from his cousins, landed the plane and brought it to a halt against some of the river's thick underbrush and muddy turf.

"Move out!" Benny yelled at his unit. "We need everyone on board fast!" He paused to look at his niece, Catalina. "Eat a mouthful of mints so your breath doesn't kill anyone."

The rear drop-door of the Antonov was opened and it hit the muddy ground with a heavy thud. Javier was first to leap up into the plane and hug Catalina, who was happy to see him.

"What a good trip, huh, *niña?*" Javier kissed her pretty face as she began to cry from the emotional relief. "Don't cry, *mamacita.* We're here, eh?"

Felipé, Edgar, and Victor also came up into the combat unit's plane and hugged their comrades. Catalina, Benny, Tato, Nancho, Diego "Buro" Cortez, and Bushwacker all greeted each other with tears in their eyes, strong embraces, and hard slaps on each other's backs.

"Ivan." Tato was first to notice. "Where's Ivan?"

"He stayed near the payphone so the boss could assist youse in the air," Javier said with his big, long arms over the shoulders of his two younger brothers, Tato and Nancho. His voice croaked with emotion as he spoke. "Everyone's still alive after that, eh?"

Catalina put a soothing hand on his chest and patted him. "All of you ... bandits and killers ... crying." But she was crying the hardest.

The men wiped their eyes and pretended like she was mistaken.

"We stick to plan." Javier cleared his throat. "First, we must pull the dirt-green camouflage netting over the plane. They may be looking for it. Get it armed for remote bombing just in case. Buro, you're designated to stay behind to guard it. Find a place from three hundred yards off to watch it. Refuel it first, inspect it for any damages as best as you can ... The sun will rise in a few minutes and the fog will be chased away. Felipé, Edgar, Victor, myself, and Ivan – when we pick him up – will head to *Farmer's Supply* and have the plane loaded. If the military or national police spot this thing, Buro ... *boom* it goes, understand? There's enough C-4 and napalm in it to blow the thing into outer space."

"*Señor,*" Buro nodded. "So maybe I'll see *some* action."

Javier's eyes stayed trained on Buro. "There's a dozen motorcycles here. You take one and hide it in case you need it to make it back to the airport. Stay in radio contact because ... if you have to blow the plane, they might just lock down the airports. Who knows? You combat units may have to hide out until we can get youse back home. If they make it back okay, then this plane is your ride home. [Turning to face Benny] We'll stay grounded, at the airport, until we hear from youse. The boss wants a kidnapping. If it's implausible or impossible, then a kill is a kill. But if we lose this plane, then ... you can't just walk Gutiérrez through LAN at gunpoint. Any questions?"

There were no questions.

"Let's move!"

CHAPTER EIGHTEEN

Elvira Montana
Miami, Florida
September 16, 1984

Lies circle the globe way before truth can take its first step,
Elvira murmured as she thought about her encounter with
Sheffield the day before.

"You say something, El?" Nina asked as she gave Elvira
a full-body massage in the living room area of the luxury
apartment they had rented at the Miami Hilton. Elvira lay out
on her back on a cushioned massage table, nude, as the
Chinese-Jamaican nurse rubbed warm, scented oil all over her
boss and kneaded it deeply into her skin.

"Just talking to myself." Elvira covered her exposed
pubes with the tiny white towel that kept falling off. "This
tiny thing won't stay!"

Nina put Elvira's right leg up onto her right shoulder and
gave it a deep massage up and down. Almara came into the
living room and laughed.

"What's so funny?" Elvira peered over at Almara.

Almara sat down on the large white leather sofa. "If I
could only film this moment ... it would look like a triple-X
lesbo scene. Her buttcrack is in full view and her – she needs
a bikini wax! Eww."

"Shut up," Nina laughed. "She's so crazy."

Elvira had to laugh at the humor also. "Wow, that would look so funny on film."

"It's 11:30 a.m.," Almara told them. "Mama Montana will be here any minute ... Also, I put out a full-page ad for the funerals and after-party at the Babylon nightclub. The manager gladly accepted the ten grand to ready the place on such short notice. He sends his condolences to you. I also paid off two other Miami clubs."

"All that done and it's only eleven-thirty," Elvira mentioned. "You girls are lifesavers ... I'll attend the funeral but I'm having some apprehension about attending the parties."

The telephone rang. Almara answered the sofa-side phone. "Montana residence ... Send her on up." Ally looked at Elvira. "Mama Montana will be up in a couple of minutes."

Elvira got up with Nina's help and went into the master bathroom to shower and get dressed. She came out to the living room and hugged the clearly distraught woman. The two just stood there for an extended period and sobbed in each other's arms. Nina looked at Almara, and Almara at Nina, and both women wept in silence at the deep sorrow they were witnessing.

"It's not as easy as I thought it would be," Nina whispered as she sat next to Almara.

"Hang in there, *chica*." Almara patted Nina's knee.

The day before, they had picked up Mama Montana and they'd all gone to Gordon's Funeral Home, where they'd been permitted to view the remains. Tony, Gina, Manny Ray, Chi Chi, Nick the Pig, Ernie, and several other fallen henchmen of Tony's. The stench of death and rotting flesh that had been refrigerated too long was still with each of the women. Elvira had given the undertaker her American Express card for the most stylish funeral possible, telling him that thousands would be attending.

"Money is not a problem," Elvira had told him. "I demand fancy. The man you're burying in there is *Scarface* ... Tony Montana. He changed American culture. Everyone in the game wants to do it like he did. Let's send him off right ... and all those who fell with him. Tony, Gina, Manny, and Chi Chi will all be laid to rest in the most expensive mausoleum we can find ... in a cemetery on a high hill facing south, toward Cuba. I want it to look like the U.S. President's funeral but I want Benzes and Bentleys; Moet and Dom."

"The type of mausoleum you speak of," the undertaker had clarified, "is all marble and runs upwards of two hundred fifty k."

"I wouldn't care if it was a *million* dollars," she'd stated. "That man earned it. And I'm carrying his child. His kid must one day know how important his or her father was. Do it. You need anything more, I'm staying in the Presidential Apartment Suite at the Miami Hilton."

Now, Elvira once again faced Mama Montana. They all sat around the living room, drinking coffee and having a light breakfast. Elvira explained to Mama who Nina and Almara were and why she'd hired them.

"That's a very noble thing for you," Mama complimented Elvira. "So ... they are professionals?"

"Yes, ma'am," Nina nodded. "I'm a licensed RN and Ally is a licensed psychologist."

"You're very serious about the baby," Mama observed. "Good."

"I am." Elvira gave a stern nod.

"I say to myself, now, that Castro was not so bad." Mama sounded angry. "Tony is gone. Gina is gone. My husband walked away long ago. I risked my life, and Gina's, to come here on a boat to have a better life. And look ... no one is left to bury me. My kids – it is common in this country for parents to bury their kids," she lamented.

"Mama, I'll look out for you," Elvira promised.

Mama shook her head no. "I can take care of myself."

"I know," Elvira returned. "I didn't mean that. The mausoleum I've ordered can hold up to ten tombs. It's bought and paid for so when it's time for us to go ... we'll be laid to rest there. So, don't worry. You'll own your place there; no one can take it."

Mama nodded slowly. "Okay. Thank you."

"I know you had a tumultuous relationship with Tony," Elvira spoke softly. "But me and you, we've been okay."

"You're okay," Mama repeated. "I like you. You're a beautiful and nice woman. You could have done better than with my ... Antonio."

That drew a smile from Nina and Almara.

"You'll be a grandmother to my son or daughter," Elvira told her. "I have no family for the baby to know. And I certainly can't teach it *Cubano* culture and history. I need you around me, Mama. So, come to New York with us and help prepare for the baby."

"*Grandmother,*" Mama repeated the word. The very thought of it seemed to strengthen her slouching shoulders. She looked a bit lit up about it. "I don't like this, the lavish and big. Wherever you live, I want my own small place."

Elvira was confused. "I'm building a home in New York. It'll be enormous. I want a mansion. I'll build for you a small house on the estate. It'll be yours, no one can take it. Not me, not anyone."

"Drug money," Mama frowned.

"Actually, no," Elvira started. "Well ... listen. *I'm* not a drug dealer. Tony was. However, Tony had been establishing himself in the business community because even he knew drugs were a dead end. Montana Realty Corporation was the mother company of several businesses of his. I'm selling them off and starting anew in New York. I've abandoned drinking and partying because I'm sick and tired of the hurt and pain. I'm taking the money and starting my life out new.

Right now I'm doing a lot of guessing but New York is no guess. The money – there's a lot of it and I'll invest it for your grandchild's future. That is, if the IRS even allows me to keep it."

"So they know of the money?" Mama asked her.

"Tony has six million in foreign banks," Elvira explained to her. "I'll be wiring that money to my account in New York along with other money I have access to, including the money coming from the fire sale of the Montana businesses. I'm reporting the money to the IRS and hope they'll allow me to keep it."

"Can you get into trouble?" Mama questioned her.

"I suppose so," Elvira shrugged. "But that's a chance I'll take for a new life. Generally, it's when you *fail* to report money that you get into trouble with the IRS. I'll be sitting with an attorney in New York, a tax attorney, to find out all of my options."

"So you *want* to pay taxes on the money," Mama said.

Elvira nodded her affirmation. "True."

"I come to New York," Mama finally agreed, realizing that Elvira was aiming to do something right with her life. Mama also appreciated the fact that Elvira had had the common sense to hire two professionals to assist her in her journey back to good health. And if Elvira was next to fall, Mama hoped it was not before Elvira had the baby. "I look out for you and the baby. My grandbaby."

$$$$$

Tony Montana and his fallen comrades were sent off on their final ride in an epic style fit for a king. People who had known Tony had come out and even those who did not know him had come out. The word on the street was that Tony "Scarface" Montana was being buried and that the entire city was invited to come salute him farewell and then come to several VIP after-parties later on that night.

The police had been aware of the full-page ad taken out in *The Miami Sun Times* and it pissed them off that someone would have the audacity to put out so much money to lay a thug to rest. To the authorities a thug was less than a dog, never realizing a dead man was a dead man no matter what he had done in his life. There are people who honor a criminal and people who choose not to. There are those who honor JFK even though he was a liar, an adulterer, and commander-in-chief of a military that murdered untold thousands of men, women, and children in Vietnam. America is a country which glorifies violence, thieves, rapists, and murderers, like Jesse James, and the more pioneering gangsters such as John Dillinger, Verne Miller, Al Capone, Lucky Luciano, Bugsy Siegel, Meyer Lansky, and so forth. Movies are being made about them just like movies will be made about the mobsters that will follow. The same hypocrites who hate them will be first to see their movies. Especially the cops.

"I don't give a damn what the police and feds think," Elvira told Sheffield after the doors of the white and black marble and granite mausoleum were shut and locked. "Do I say anything when a cop is shot or a President dies? They have their fancy circus parade and the rest of us who want to see something else on TV just change the channel. Well, this is my fancy circus parade."

"I was just mentioning it," Sheffield stated as he led her to her Mercedes stretch limousine.

On her way down the hill she recognized drug bosses she had become familiar with during her time with Frank Lopez and Tony Montana. There were literally thousands of people in the cemetery. Many of them were young Black and Latino youth who had come to say goodbye to their hero and true street legend, Scarface. Elvira had not realized, until now, the level of respect her husband had achieved here. Nina and

169

Almara were observing all they could and making their comments known.

"They must've really loved Tony," Nina was saying as they stood along the side of the white Mercedes. "At the church, now here, I see so many girls crying for him!"

"They *knew* him?" Almara asked Elvira.

"He built parks and pools for kids," Elvira stated, shrugging. "He gave away money and food to the poor. Bought bikes and toys – truckloads would be given out to kids all over the city. Yeah … he had their adoration. I was never out here on the street with him but he was very generous."

"My son did that, huh?" Mama stared at Elvira.

Elvira looked at Mama. "Guys like your son, Mama … all they want to do is hold onto a little piece of this big planet for as long as they can. Tony had a big heart. Look [pointing] all around. I know it got Gina killed but she *chose*, too. It's so sad … but he wanted everyone around him to be happy. Me … I don't think I have the capacity for happiness. That saddened him. He bit off so much …"

Gaspar Gomez, Nacho Contreras, the Diaz Brothers, and a line of others came by Elvira offering their condolences. Many of them had heard the news that Elvira was pregnant and rubbed on her belly. It stood as a symbol, something tangible and sacred of Tony's that the masses could touch and memorialize. Mourners gave cards and flowers to Elvira and Mama. If not flowers and cards, then kisses on their cheeks and/or their hands.

Sheffield ushered the women into the awaiting Mercedes and climbed in with them.

"There's a private group of investors looking to make a quick profit on a small line of businesses such as those MRC owns," Sheffield told her. "I had made a few calls and received three separate offers but they're low-ball offers."

"What's the highest offer?" Elvira perked up.

"Two million five," he threw at her.

She knew what the dirtbag shark was doing. "Let's get it done. And I hope you don't think I'll pay you commission off such a poor offer."

Sheffield frowned. "I kind of was wishing for five percent."

"Bring me a higher offer," she shot back. "I reread those quarterly accounting reports. The businesses are worth four times as much, and they're all making money. I'm not desperate, Sheffield. I merely took your advice to sell before an audit comes my way."

"I'll meet you at your hotel at 9 a.m. tomorrow," he told her, "if you're not comatose from the after-parties."

"No more parties for me, Shef."

"That's a pretty penny you spent on those funerals and the parties. I see you bought out *The Babylon*."

"Tony loved that place."

"I always thought you were a classy girl, Elvira. I mean that."

She stared at him. "That's funny. I always thought you were full of crap, Shef."

They both shared a laugh at the rude humor.

"I know you have a lot to do," he said before being dropped off. "After I deliver the check, and our business is done, you should meet with the Miami-Dade Police Homicide Division. They've been investigating this case. I mean, there's nothing you can really tell them but if I were you, I'd give them the *appearance* of cooperation."

"I'd planned on it."

"Great," he nodded. "We'll shoot straight over there after our business meeting is over."

She agreed as the limo driver stopped in front of Sheffield's house. After he got out of the car, she wrote down the address to his house.

"Okay," she called up to the driver. "Take me back to the Hilton."

CHAPTER NINETEEN

The Assassination of Gutiérrez
Buenos Aires, Argentina
September 15, 1984

Catalina, Benny, Tatico, Nancho, Bushwacker, Lucho, and Buro were roaring into the capital city of Argentina at 8:40 a.m. on all-black Ninja motorcycles. They looked like a motorcycle gang out enjoying a morning ride. However, that was light years away from the truth.

Not at all deceived by the time, Benny broke away from the seven-man formation, saying over the radio, "I'll see you at LAN."

Benny zoomed past the airport's east entrance and drove the sleek black Ninja back through the downtown area traffic.

About a mile or so away from the airport was one of the city's oldest high schools. The students were out in full force, some still arriving, many others just hanging around smoking cigarettes. There was a group of thuggish-looking teens leaning on a brick wall near the parking lot laughing it up with a few female students before the school bell rang.

Benny parked the bike next to the group of thugs who were eyeing him and the bike. Leaving the bike's motor running, he hopped off the bike and walked away. He knew the mischievous kids would steal the flashy new bike. Benny could care less what happened to it either way. Next, the highly-skilled assassin walked out onto a main thoroughfare and waved down a taxicab.

"Where to, sir?" the chubby Argentinian driver inquired after Benny climbed into the backseat.

"I'm not going anywhere," Benny said, producing a silenced Beretta 9mm. "You are." *Pfffttt! Pfffttt!*

Benny jumped out of the cab, opened the front door, and shoved the dead driver over onto the front passenger side. Benny drove off and, a short time later, he pulled into an alley. He dragged the dead body out of the front seat and into the backseat. When he got back inside of the cab Benny noticed the blood spatter on the driver's side window caused by the point-blank range head shots he had delivered.

The silent assassin, known as The Skull, located a wad of white fast food restaurant napkins the driver had stuffed beneath the armrest of the old, odd-blue Renault wagon/taxicab. In the cup-holder, on the dashboard, was a paper cup half-filled with iced tea. Benny removed the top and the straw, and thrust all of the napkins down into the cup. When they were soaked with the iced tea, he used them as a wet towel to wash away the blood spatter.

Prior to driving away, Benny picked up the cab driver's white straw Panama hat and revisited the backseat. Benny sat the chubby driver upwards and put on his seatbelt. As he tightened up the belt, the dead man farted. A first for Benny, who stepped back to avoid the smell.

"You've been eating beans, *hombre.*"

Benny reached back into the cab and pulled the Panama hat down over the dead man's eyes so it would appear as though he were asleep to passersby.

Lighting up a Salem menthol, Benny drove away ...

$$$$$

At 10 a.m. Catalina Lilli, Nancho, and Buro were already inside of the LAN terminal, awaiting the arrival of Dr. Gutiérrez's commercial flight. Nancho and Buro sat inside of a waiting area near the disembarkment ramp doors that Gutiérrez was expected to walk through. Catalina used the payphone next to an escalator. When she terminated the phone call, she sat down next to Nancho.

"His flight is en route," she informed him. "No significant weather troubles or delays. He's traveling with his wife, six- and seven-year-old kids, and two guests. There'll be a black rented passenger van with tinted windows."

Nancho looked into her piercing brown eyes. "You mean gunmen, not guests, gunmen."

"We'll just have to see about that, huh, *primo*?" she said cynically.

"They're probably ex-police or ex-military," Nancho surmised.

"You're half right," she responded. "One is Dominican-American, the other is ex-Bolivian Army. He's a plant by yours truly."

"You?" Nancho's eyes widened.

"Why not me?"

"Real sweet. So, *that's* why you're on this mission?"

"I *said* why I'm here," she said, her eyes on the disembarkment doors. "But I also need to make sure that the plant is terminated."

"Why?"

She sighed. "Welcome to *La Corporación*. The stakes can't get any higher than this."

$$$$$

Benny stopped at a red light a few blocks away as he searched for a place to dump the body. A slender Argentinian woman waved to him from the sidewalk, obviously thinking that he was a taxi driver with only one passenger. She rushed out into the center-left lane where Benny was stuck waiting at the red light. She reached for the left rear passenger compartment door but Benny used the power locks button to keep her from opening the door.

"That guy back there," Benny indicated with his right thumb. "He doesn't want to ride with anyone. Not even with a pretty lady like you. He said he's dead tired."

Benny shrugged with a *"What do you want me to do?"* expression on his face and drove away. A few minutes later he spotted a "DEAD END" street and parked at the end of it. The raggedy houses looked quiet enough. Chickens were being chased around by a small boy on one side of the street. A goat was tied to a tree like a dog on the opposite side. He got out of the car and opened up the right rear passenger compartment door where the dead passenger was seated. Benny undid the seat belt and dragged the man out onto a dirt patch on the ground.

"What's that you're doing!" an older Argentinian man yelled from the house where the goat was.
"Who – ?!"

Pffftt! Pffftt! Pffftt!

The assassin was back in the driver's seat before the man had even hit the grass, clutching the three holes in his chest.

Fifteen minutes later, Benny was in the airport taxicab line, posing as one of the many taxi drivers who were outside of the LAN Airlines terminal waiting for easy fares. He made radio contact with Tato, who Benny could see out in the parking lot from his position next to the taxicab.

"We know anything new?" Benny radioed. *"Cambio* (over)."

"Espera, cambio." It was Catalina. "Where are you?"
"Out front, *cambio.*"

Within a few minutes she was standing in front of the Coca-Cola machine. Just a few feet away Benny was leaning against the taxicab. He approached the beautiful young woman and acted as if he were trying to break a dollar for her so that she could buy a Coke. Catalina quickly explained the latest developments.

"It's almost eleven-twenty," Benny said, glancing at his watch. "Have Buro stay with you inside of the terminal so we'll have eyes on him at all times. Is there a vehicle waiting for him that we know of?"

"All we know is that it will be a black rented passenger van," she revealed. "It was pre-reserved and it has tinted windows."

"Doesn't sound like anything reserved or sent to him by the Argentinean government." Benny looked ahead at all the black vans double-parked alongside the taxicabs. "Maybe his visit isn't official. Was he sent by those people he has up in New York? Bolivia? Washington? What do we know about where he's going? What he's up to?"

She understood the frustration. "What do you want to do, *Tio* (Uncle)?"

"*Bomba* [Bomb]." He lit up a Salem. "Locate the van, *chica*. We'll plant enough C-4 in it to make it evaporate like steam, and open up the earth beneath it."

She left him standing there to carry out the order.

"Nancho, come on out, *cambio*," Benny ordered over the radio. "*Afuera, chico.*"

"Copy."

"Leave the bike, Tatico." Benny waved him over. "The key, too."

Tato sauntered over to Benny on foot, leaving the bike in the parking lot.

"La Gata Negra is searching for the *chivato*'s waiting black passenger van – it has tinted windows," Benny spoke as his eyes scanned the passing vehicles and parked vans. "If we find it, can you attach bombs to it?"

Tato indicated his backpack. "*'If'* is the only question, *primo.*"

Tato stalked off like a hungry beast looking for his next meal.

Catalina walked up the sidewalk, eyeing each black van she passed. Similar to the other reserved limos, vans, shuttle buses, and cars awaiting their paying passengers, there were several drivers who held up square paper tag boards with the names of their arriving passengers scribbled across them. Catalina tried not to look too hard at the tag boards because the drivers might remember her face later. She was about to call it quits when she observed one driver who held up a sign that she could barely read. It was not because his writing was illegible but because he had written the name with an ordinary *Bic* pen, with blue ink, instead of using a black marker. It was difficult to make out.

On closer inspection she saw the name clearly written across the white tag board: *Dr. Orlando Gutiérrez.*

La Gata Negra's stomach flip-flopped. Tato, who had kept his eyes on his cousin the entire time, noticed her head nod toward the Gutiérrez van. Tato wasted no time. He walked directly up to the driver and struck up a friendly conversation with him.

"Nice day, *Señor,*" Tato said, feeling as if he were speaking to the twin of Mexican actor-singer Vicenté Fernandez.

"*Sí,*" the driver smiled, fidgeting to the left to look around the hulk-sized Tato. "You're blocking my view. Will you – ?"

"How's *this* view?" Tato pulled up his shirt to let the man see the large caliber .45 semi-automatic in his waistbelt. "This is all you need to worry about. You have a wife?"

The man was so afraid that he was unable to give Tato a straight answer. "I-I-I ..."

"Be quiet." Tato grabbed the man's left hand. "Nice wedding band. You have kids?"

"T-t-two," he stuttered.

"You'll do as I say and you'll be home in an hour to hug them," Tato said calmly, deadly. "You make the wrong move I'll open up your chest. Now, *get in!*"

"*Vicenté Fernandez*" hurriedly got into his van.

"The driver's seat! *Move!*" Tato rasped harshly. "Drive!"

The driver's hands shook as he drove out into the parking lot. Moments later Tato directed him into a parking space approximately 100 yards away from the LAN terminal taxicab line.

The post-hurricane humidity had perspiration rolling off of Tato's bald head and face. They were parked alongside a brown and yellow station wagon at the end of the parking lot. Tato grabbed the man violently, put him into a headlock, and cut off his breathing. Once he was unconscious, Tato radioed Catalina. By the time she made it out to the parking lot Tato had the man undressed.

"He's not a very big man," Tato told her, holding up Vicenté Fernandez's black chauffeur's uniform. "They'll fit you a bit loose but … make it work, *mijita*."

Tato dragged the man out of the van and laid him down next to the station wagon. Tato then busted out the rear window and opened up the flip-down door of the station wagon. After stuffing him inside of the rear flatbed compartment of the old vehicle, Tato used a sharp knife to slit open the unconscious man's throat. Tato shut the door and returned to the van.

Catalina, remembering her bomb-making and weaponry teaching from the *Bolivian Condores School of Special Forces*, assisted Tato in rigging the van up with two C-4 bombs which they mounted beneath the front and rear passenger seats. One of the bombs would completely obliterate the van but Tato was well aware of the fallacies associated with remote-detonated devices. To be safe, he "doubled up." That was the trained thinking process of Sosa's *La Corporación Mafia Cruzena.*

Two Antonovs.

Two elite units.

The plan to kidnap versus two bombs. Dealer's choice. This one was a critical, touchstone mission. No room for failure.

"How do I look?" Catalina asked after she put on the chauffeur's uniform over her own clothes.

"Ready for anything, let's go," Tato said with mild urgency. "Get back over there and wait for the target. Hold up the sign with his name on it. If his security tries to I.D. you … we'll make the hit right there. If all goes well, pull into a gas station along the way, shoot the plant and the other security before they see us coming. If there's too many witnesses, the cops, or military authority around … just find a moment – *any* moment – to step away from the van."

"Just don't blow me up with them." She jumped into the driver's seat of the van.

"Don't say stupid things," Tato growled at her. "If that's your only worry, then you have none. Go!"

As an international norm, commercial flights were rarely ever on time. The one Gutiérrez was expected to be on was no different. It was 52 minutes late, arriving at the disembarkment gate at 12:52 p.m. Nancho spotted the dark curly-haired Dr. Gutiérrez first.

"I have eyes on him, *cambio*," Nancho said in a low voice over his radio.

"Copy," Benny replied and warned Catalina and Tato. "So much for no delays. Wake up, *muchachitos*."

Gutiérrez, a tall, slim man in his late forties, walking while holding the hand of his seven-year-old daughter, Penelopé. His beautiful wife, Gloria, was following him as she held the hand of their six-year-old son, Jason. The two security men walked ahead of the Gutiérrez family as Nancho and Buro observed their every move.

Buro went outside to join Lucho and Bushwacker, who were on motorcycles. Minutes later, Nancho came out and got into the taxicab Benny was driving. Tato sat inside of the hot-wired station wagon, keeping a close watch on Catalina as she spoke with the two security men.

"Improvise, *chiquita* ..." Tato whispered, gun in his right hand, the two detonators on the empty seat next to him. He spoke on the radio to the others. "*Mira*. She's speaking to the security. If she walks away far enough, right now, the C-4 would rip 'em all apart."

"Down, boy," Nancho slowly chided. "*Relájate, hombre.*"

The conversation made the Black Hulk, Tato, nervous. "They're going to make her. They're talking too long."

"Stay in the car ..." Benny slowly ordered. "I'm the Commander here, remember?"

Seconds later the tension eased when Catalina began loading the group's luggage into the van's rear storage space. Some of the luggage had to be placed into the seats where the children sat. Within a couple of minutes she was driving out of the airport's main entrance.

"Wish we knew what only she knows," Nancho commented as Benny tailed the van at a safe distance.

Benny remained alert. "*Armas listas* [Weapons ready]."

Checking his rearview and sideview mirrors, Tato radioed, "The police are tailing the bikes."

"We see 'em," Lucho returned.

The bikes all had Argentina license plates, thanks to the rapid thinking and preparation call by Sosa when he'd ordered up the two elite kill units. There was nothing to worry about there. However, Buro made the decision to "pop a wheelie" and veer off into a popular mall parking lot. That drew the attention of the police officers, who quickly followed him.

"You'll be okay, Buro?" Lucho asked him.

"Yeah," Buro replied. "I can handle these cocksuckers. I'll put them down ... and meet you back at the strip."

In the van, La Gata Negra told the Gutiérrez bodyguard, who was sitting shotgun across from her, not to smoke inside of the van. "I don't smoke ... and I don't think the kids smoke either. Put it out, please."

"First, don't order me around," Martín Casillas Vasquez demanded as he lit the cigarette anyway. "Second, you do smoke."

She followed his gaze to the cigarette butt-filled ashtray. "Well, not with kids in the car. And especially not at a gas station."

He looked forward as she drove slowly up into a Shell gas station and parked next to a pump. Martín, a Dominican-American, took one more drag from the cigarette and mashed it out into the ashtray. She stepped out of the van as one of the two station attendants asked her how much gas she wanted.

"Fill it." She stood next to the driver's side door, listening to the children play in the rear and she silently observed Benny, Tato, Lucho, and Bushwacker drive into the parking lot of a small restaurant next to the Shell station.

"I have an easy question for you," Martín said to her from where he had remained seated inside of the van. He held up a cigarette butt as the Gutiérrez couple and her own plant observed. "Why is it that I see no lipstick on these Marlboro cigarette butts but you wear lipstick on your pretty lips?"

"You're a very disrespectful man, Mr. Velasquez," she told him through the window. "If you need to know, I am one of four drivers that drive this particular van."

"All right." He then held up a black leather handbag. "What's this?"

"*Martín*," Dr. Gutiérrez spoke up, "we reserved a van and a driver, *and* we got a van and a driver. Leave the young lady to her job before she throws all of us out."

"With all due respect, Mr. Gutiérrez, allow me do mine," Martín stated with a profound look in his eyes. He then turned back to Catalina, showing her the black leather handbag. "Why do you carry around a bag with a man's shaving supplies, men's cologne, and … the identification documents of *Immanuel Colón?*"

"He must have left the bag by accident," she reasoned. "Manny is a co-worker and friend of mine."

"*Your* documents," Martín demanded. "Let us see them."

"Mr. Velasquez, *enough*," Gutiérrez ordered.

"You have no police authority over me, sir," she shot back indignantly. "In a few seconds you're going to be walking. If that means all of you, then so be it. I won't allow you to intimidate me. You'd better watch it."

"I'm telling you, Mr. and Mrs. Gutiérrez, something is not right here," Velasquez warned them, removing his sidearm.

"Whoa, Velasquez!" the Bolivian Army plant spoke up quickly. "Put that away! Stay with Gutiérrez. *I'll* check her I.D. and flag down a police officer."

Silas Ramirez Cruz, from Potosi, Bolivia, let himself out of the van and walked rapidly up to Catalina.

"*Señora*, if you'd please show me your papers we can …" Cruz was speaking loud enough for Velasquez to hear while at the same time she was steering them further and further away from the van. Silas, not knowing anything about the bombs, slowed her down by holding her arm.

"Listen, Cruz!" she hissed at him. "There are C-4 bombs inside – we have to *run!* When I run, *you* run!"

They almost immediately began to run toward the parking lot where the rest of her unit was waiting! The very second they took off, the side doors of the van opened. Tato turned on the first detonator, and then the second! The green light on each small, gray, tin box came on to indicate *"ARMED."* When the two were enough of a distance away from the van, Tato put his fingers on the two tiny, silver, up-and-down switches. The realization that there were explosives in the van must have hit Velasquez at the last second because he began to shout at the Gutiérrez family to get out of the van!

But it was too late ...

The first blast was so powerful that it nearly pulverized the van and its occupants! The explosion ripped it into small pieces of shrapnel and its forceful impact and heat caused a succession of other explosions to occur at the small gas pumps. The engine was sent into a 100-foot arch upwards and the tires went flying hundreds of yards in four different directions. The heat from the C-4 had turned the rest of the van into a molten pile of burning lava. Dr. Gutiérrez, his wife, and two children were dead, blown to pieces by the devastating bomb blast. The awesome 10,000-degree heat generated from the C-4 cooked their flesh so well that the bones could be pulled apart like a freshly baked turkey. The white-hot afterfires from the C-4 were so effective that even their bones and teeth were turned to ash. On the ground, close to the van, were blackened pieces of the Dominican-American security man Martín Casillas Velasquez.

Although they had been at a safe enough distance to survive the blasts, Catalina and Silas Ramirez Cruz were thrown to the ground from the violent supersonic shockwave produced by the bombs. They made it back onto their feet and to the station wagon where Tato was waiting.

Benny led the way back out into the slowing traffic. The thick black smoke and fire was now spewing up into the sky endlessly. As they drove away with the motorcycles close behind them, Benny noticed the enormous crater in the ground where the van had once been. The main building of the gas station had collapsed and the engine of the van had flown through the roof of a grocery store next door to the gas station.

$$$$$

During the flight back to Bolivia, there was one more thing that had to be done.

Ramirez Cruz lay awake on the floor of the Antonov with his head propped up against a backpack that belonged to Catalina, who sat on the wooden bench across from him. Bushwacker, Lucho, and Diego "Buro" Cortez were all asleep on the floor, exhausted after the mission.

"Hey, Ramirez Cruz, I need to get into that backpack!" Catalina told him over the roar of the screaming engines of the Antonov.

Cruz sat up and tossed the backpack to her. "I was not informed about the assassination of the journalist and his family. *Kids*. I thought it would only be a spy game, Cata."

"You are so innocent," Catalina reminded him as she removed a silenced black Walther PK .380 from her bag and leveled it squarely at his chest. "Innocent or not, you are a soldier and soldiers follow orders."

"Why – what are you doing?" His eyes widened. "I followed orders. I did everything you asked me to."

"And General Cucombre sincerely thanks you for your service." She sounded almost apologetic as she held the gun on him. *Pffftt! Pffftt!*

Bushwacker, Lucho, and Buro all pulled out guns and pointed them at Catalina, alarmed at the sudden sounds of muffled gunshots. They looked at Ramirez Cruz, then at her.

"Cucombre gave the orders," she told them as she put away her weapon.

"That's good," Bushwacker said. "Now, you have something to do for the rest of the ride. Cut him up. Head, hands, feet, *and* teeth. He definitely has dental records so take out each tooth. Cut off the skin of his fingers so no prints can be done. Destroy the face. Then dump him piece-by-piece every five miles."

"I need help," she said.

"That's your job, *nena*," Bushwacker said. "You and you only got those orders. We have another big job coming up in Europe. We need sleep."

She sighed and set out to do as she was told.

CHAPTER TWENTY

The Montana Home
Miami, Florida
September 17, 1984

She silently contemplated her dreadful, but unavoidable, return to the Montana Estate in Coconut Grove. It was going to be a horrifying death scene but she had to see the damage that had been done. That, however, would come later in the day.

First, as they'd previously discussed, Sheffield sat down with Elvira and a lawyer named Michael Scott Baker, who represented a prominent Miami/South Florida realty corporation. She signed off on the sale of MRC and all of its properties and assets in the living room area of her Hilton apartment.

Once the deal was completed, she met with local and federal investigators at Miami-Dade Police Department HQ regarding the massacre. The District Attorney, her assistant, and several federal investigators asked her a number of questions while she was in the presence of her attorney, George Sheffield. There was very little that she could give them and it was not like they were trying very hard to find who was responsible for ordering the hit on Tony anyway.

"When does the hurt end?" Elvira stared at the female District Attorney and the others. "The drama? Sure, I cared for my husband but he kept me deliberately ignorant to what he did. Probably so if there ever came a time cops came asking his wife questions, she couldn't say anything."

"Even about his own assassination?" the D.A. said.

"I guess so," she shrugged. "Let me ask. Even if you found a suspect and tied him to my husband's murder, you'd want me to testify … at a trial of *someone who's capable of a massacre??* These are drug wars. I'm a woman – a *pregnant* woman with no man to protect me."

"There's Witness Protection," D.A. Monica Seymour offered.

Elvira laughed in her face. "Let's see who you'd protect me from: Cuban Mafia, Italian Mafia, the Colombian cartels, the Mexican cartels, or maybe the Russians. Those people learn what *they* learn from being poor, broke; necessity, survival. Killing is what they do to live and feed their kids. You guys – cops, D.A.'s, Feds – *you* learn what you learn as a career choice. For a tiny paycheck and a plaque for 'employee of the month.' The Witness Protection guys are who? Pizza and Pepsi-ordering junkies with snub-nosed .38s? You have to be friggin' kidding me. The Colombians have high-powered military-grade machine guns and missiles that shoot down warplanes. *Rockets*, for crying out loud. No way, man. Not me."

"We're getting nowhere here," the D.A. said, looking around at the other authorities in the room. "I'm done with her if everyone else is."

"I'm sorry but it's just facts." Elvira stood up. "To even *think* you could compel me to *testify* for your side is what I'd have to call malignant narcissism. If I knew something, I couldn't tell you. It's just not who I am. But the men I've chosen … it's how they were. They told me nothing. Not Choppy, not Frank, and not Tony. I'm sorry."

Elvira was led out of the conference room. She heard a male's voice say, "*She's feeding us a line of dog poop.*"

$$$$$

The Montana Estate

Elvira laughed so hard that it hurt. Not because any of it was funny but because she could not imagine how utterly stupid somebody could be. "The art collection is still here!" she exclaimed.

The hitters had turned the mansion into a war zone, looting it for its many valuables: vases, artifacts, jewelry, cash, clothes, food, et cetera. Elvira, Nina, Almara, and Mama toured through the entire house with a large crew of movers and a group of contractors.

"Aside from the custom-made portraits we'd had created, I had to assist him with choosing art, among other decorations." She pointed at an enormous portrait of her and Tony on the dining room wall. "Those idiots who killed him looted the place pretty good and there's some substantive damage done from the firefight and ransacking. Here's how smart they were: they left untouched the most expensive items of all."

"The art," Nina indicated as they stood inside of the living room where there were a dozen pieces of rare art on display.

"Yes, the art," Elvira concurred and sighed. "They could have simply tucked them beneath their arms and that would have been that. You're looking at *millions* of dollars' worth of Italian art."

"All I know about art are the most famous pieces," Almara said as she walked around looking at the painting. "*Picasso, Leonardo da Vinci,* and *Dalí.*"

"Right there. That's da Vinci's *Annunciation.*" Elvira showed them the masterpiece above a white marble table." Next to it is Piero della Francesca's *Flagellation.* Across the room, from the left, is Titian's *Venus of Urbino.* Next to it is

Titian's *Sacred and Profane Love*. Another sexy one to look at is that one: Botticelli's *Venus*."

Nina stared at the *Venus of Urbino*. "Look at her. Wow."

"Okay guys," Elvira said to the movers. "Begin room by room. I want *every* item packed carefully and inventoried. The paintings excluded. Do not forget the basement level ... there's tons of stuff down there."

At first Elvira had had her doubts about the crew of eight movers being enough, but once they'd gotten started her doubts evaporated. She watched them get to work and they moved quite fast.

"Nina." Elvira turned to her. "We need armed security detail. The movers guesstimate that it'll take two eighteen-wheelers to haul all of this stuff up to New York. While I'm not overly concerned about the stuff, it does belong to me so I want the trucks escorted by security cars. The real concern are the paintings. The house and storage garage are filled with paintings – though most are not as valuable as the ones in the living room, they're expensive nonetheless. They must all be transferred via armored vehicle. Can you handle it?"

Nina nodded and replied, "I'll need a telephone."

Elvira escorted her to the kitchen and sat her down at a table near the side door of the mansion which led out to the driveway and attached storm roof.

"I'll give them a check when they arrive," Elvira told Nina. "We need them *now*. Yesterday. Two cars, one armored truck. Let's say a dozen men with heavy firepower. I don't want any .38-packing idiots here."

Elvira spoke with the contractors next.

"We dealt with your company before we moved in," she said to the foreman. "There's a lot of bullet damage and debris. The police marked the holes pretty good. I don't want patchwork. I need full renovation. I have to get this house ready for sale, so I want around-the-clock work done on it until it's all new again. Make your assessments, do your

189

surveys, print them up on a typewriter – not by hand – and show me photos of what needs to be done. Ally …"

Almara stood nearby. "I'm here."

They walked away to Elvira and Tony's bedroom.

"I can't stay here," Elvira told her. "I thought I could sleep here for a few days, but I can't. There's coke still here, pills, booze … and I'm itching for it."

Almara hugged her. "Good girl. Show me the stashes."

"They're overwhelming." Elvira pulled open a dresser drawer and reached way back into the drawer slot. She pulled out a small black teddy bear. "A few grams are inside of his belly."

It took some time to do but Elvira located and gave up all of the cocaine, Quaalude, and liquor stash spots. Almara flushed it all down the toilet inside of the master bedroom.

"You okay?" Almara quizzed her. "How do you feel?"

"Like I was running." Elvira sat down on the bed. "I'm sweaty. Do I stink?"

"Far from it, silly." Almara smiled and let her relax a while.

Nina came back to report her progress. "They're on their way. They said they'd be here at 4 p.m. Anything else while I'm on a roll?"

"Use my American Express to secure several storage units in New York," Elvira instructed. "What's that ritzy county south of Rockland County? It's also south of Nyack by –"

"Westchester County," Nina answered. "That's a pretty big county. Any town there in particular?"

"Scarsdale," Elvira said thoughtfully. "Reserve eight full-sized units. The paintings will need more secure safekeeping and care. I won't be seeking to sell them, so … I'll need to contact a curator to keep them until I settle in New York."

"You mean to contact a museum curator," Nina guessed. "I'll start with *The Museum of Art and History* in Manhattan."

"Smart girl," Elvira complimented her.

"Ally." Elvira looked at her. "There's a separate line in Tony's office. We own a white Rolls Royce and a gray Bentley. I don't want to keep them but I also don't want to leave them. Call a dealer about transporting them up to New York. I guess we could park them at ... where'll we live?" She realized her dilemma. "I'm homeless."

Ally grinned and shook her head. "Nina lived with her mom and dad. They're retired and travel a lot ... I have an apartment in Fort Greene, Brooklyn." She shrugged. "One bedroom."

None of them had it all figured out. Almara had no children and, prior to accepting employment with Elvira, she had spent a great majority of her time at Aspen. Almara had family members in New York but she had no one in mind who could offer them a decent housing situation. Nina was in the same position.

"We're homeless," Elvira repeated as she lay down on the bed. "I can still smell Tony."

Almara looked down at Elvira. *What a remarkable background she has,* Ally was thinking.

Nina returned to them. "*The New York Museum of Natural Art and History* has a curator there who will take the collection. He'll discuss fees, terms, and whatnot when the collection arrives ... Why the long faces?"

"We're homeless." Ally stood up. "And she smells Tony on the pillow."

Ally went to arrange the automobile transportation.

"I got it!" Elvira sat up. "Ally! Ally, c'mere!"

Ally came back into the bedroom. "What happened?"

"We'll live on a boat," Elvira beamed. "I'll buy the boat, actually a luxury yacht, and have it transported up to New York. Tony and I had one but it was a lease. It had several bedrooms, a living room, bathrooms, hot tubs, kitchen, and a staff. I'll make the call to the local super-yacht dealership where we'd leased the first one. I know the exact one to buy. I'll also arrange for where we should port it up there. The dealer will know luxury marinas and yacht clubs ..."

Elvira left them alone.

"She's going to spoil us," Nina whispered, sitting down on the bed next to her friend.

"Yes, she is," Almara agreed, glancing at her watch. "She's unlike all the millionaires and billionaires I've been around at the Aspen Clinic. Those people were so cheap that they'd squeeze a quarter 'til the eagle screamed."

"Not Elvee." Nina twisted a small lock of her hair and licked her pink lips. "On one hand she's a bit everywhere with it ... she sort of cares about life, then she kind of doesn't. She kind of cares about money, but then she doesn't. She's paid *eight* friggin' *thou* a night at the Hilton. Would you live in this house?"

"Does a rabbit crap in the woods?" Almara retorted. "I'd kind of feel funny that there was a massacre here but ... wow. Look at the love all those people came out to the church and burial to show him! Whites, Blacks, Chinese, Latinos. I saw it with my own eyes. That was *respect*. For a mobster."

Nina was silent for a moment. "Is it just me or do you feel like something's going to go wrong?"

"Like what? Something bad, you mean?"

Nina shrugged.

Almara touched her friend's hair, looking into her eyes. "Stop, Nina Lee. Don't start that."

Nina looked at Ally, sighing. "Nerves is all. Coming from all the death I've seen in the E.R. I guess. It's hard not to be haunted ..."

"I told you I had a way out, didn't I?"

Nina nodded at her friend. "You definitely said that."

Almara leaned in closer, kissing Nina's forehead. "Was I wrong?"

"No." Nina looked into the eyes of the cute Puerto Rican. "You said you'd take care of me."

"I meant it, too." Almara softly kissed the Black China Doll on her soft lips.

Nina pulled away. "No, Ally. Not yet and ... I'm not ready for all that. Especially not where she can see."

Nina walked away just as Elvira returned.

Elvira sat in a comfortable leather chair and wrote something down on a small notepad she'd been using. "These movers are far from slow. The armed security will be here by 4 p.m. I'll put the movers up at the Hilton for twenty-four hours before take-off to New York so they're well-rested. We'll all fly to New York, us three, and I'll meet with the curator. By that time the yacht will be delivered to Davenport Park in New Rochelle, New York. One of us must stay on the yacht and do a few things in town such as help me search for an experienced crew for the ship. Place an ad in *The New York Times*, make some phone calls. One of you must return here with me because I have things to do here. Almara, you come with me. Nina, you'll have your hands full in New York. You have to meet the trucks at the storage facility and facilitate the transfer of my things to the storage units."

"Let's itemize each move that needs to be made." Nina took the pen and pad from Elvira and wrote down a neat itinerary. Fifteen minutes later Nina had written down everything, making mention that it would be best to type up the notes afterwards. "They will need – I'll write down precise directions for them even though their company already instructed them ... The movers know how to get to New York but we may have to remind them that trucks are not allowed on New York parkways."

"That's exactly right," Almara agreed. "They're allowed on the expressways and thruways only. Good thinking, Black China Doll, although they should already know."

Nina concentrated on writing out the directions for the truck drivers and security personnel. Elvira led her into the study, where they typed up all of the notes.

"These are perfect, Nina," Elvira complimented her. "A nurse that can type. Whoever would've thought?"

Elvira then planned her next significant move:

Gathering and securing the cash fortune left behind by her late husband, Tony "Scarface" Montana.

CHAPTER TWENTY-ONE

La Hacienda de Sosa
Cochabamba, Bolivia
September 16, 1984

Due to the massive size and strength of the storm, both airplanes could not dare to enter southern Bolivia via Villazón, Tupiza, or San Pablo. Instead, the support plane was directed by the air traffic command in Santa Cruz to come in through Tarija, southeast of San Lorenzo, because the airports in La Paz and Santa Cruz were still on lockdown. The hurricane had already passed over Tarija but they had only suffered the outer eastern brim of the storm, which had hit them with minimal flooding and some wind damages.

Tarija had a total of nine airports; Bermejo Airport, Sanandita Airport, Sipuati Airport, La Vertiente Airport, El Condor Airport, El Escondido Airport, Capt. Oriel Lea Plaza Airport, Tcnl. Rafael Pabón Airport, and Yacuiba Airport. Javier had been instructed by Catalina Lilli to land at the Sanandita Airport in the Province of Gran Chaco.

"Why that one?" Javier had asked, distrustful.

"General Cucombre has men there, in the customs," she had answered. "I'm your *prima*, Javi. I won't steer you wrong."

Armed with that information, Javier had told the combat plane to land there also but Benny had chosen to do otherwise subsequent to a conversation he'd had earlier with his co-pilots.

"No one is supposed to know this plane is in the air, *chico*," Tato had radioed back. "We have something else in mind. See you at the Pentagon."

The radio waves had been alive with hundreds of reports regarding the storm. There was flooding, power outages, lightning strikes, downed trees and power lines, mudslides, and countless deaths in major swaths of the eastern and southwestern regions: Villazón, Tupiza, San Pablo, Cotagaita, Uyuni, Villa Martin, Potosi, Sucre, Challapata, Sabaya, Uncia, Huanuni, Oruro, Corocoro, Cochabamba, La Paz, Achacachi, Copacabana, and many other areas all throughout those lands. That would also include the Altiplano and Nevada Sajama salt flats and lowlands. There were streets being ripped up, houses and cars floating away, thousands of animals left stranded or drowned and, in some places, bandits were busy looting.

Benny knew that Sosa would not like it but what other choice was available? The plane had exterior damage from either the hailstorm or the lightning strikes and the tanks were running out of fuel. With the daylight still on their side, they entered Bolivia via the Gran Chaco lowland plains and headed home on a route they'd never used. Since the daylight was still with them, albeit darkened by the storm – and visibility was about 65 percent – they felt that they could do it. Especially over the lowlands.

"The boss will be pissed," Tato said, worried.

"I'll take the blame." Benny was sweating all over again. By this time the body odor of everyone on the flight was noticeable. "I smell like a wild animal," Benny grimaced after sniffing his armpits.

"We all do," Tato stated, sniffing his own armpits. "Remember, you take the blame. The boss will be pissed. He doesn't like mission jets landing up there."

"Stop talking, Tatico," Benny growled at him.

The plane looped through the lowlands east of Monteagudo, Lagunillas, Santa Cruz, Warnes, then west to Portachuelo, Buena Vista, until they reached Cochabamba.

$$$$$

Sosa picked up the intercom phone in his study and was informed by one of his private soldiers, "General Cucombre notified us that a helicopter is transporting the support craft crew to the Pentagon. The jet is in Sanandita."

"And?"

"We detect an incoming unknown aircraft on our radar," the soldier told him. "We've attempted to make radio contact but no response."

"How far off is it?"

"We estimate ten to twelve minutes from the high rate of speed it's doing," the soldier answered. "It's only one, *Señor*. Hold on, please ..."

Sosa was on his feet, his eyes on the television screen watching the news coverage about the gas station explosion in Buenos Aires. He wondered if that was the work of his assassins.

"*Señor*."

"Speak," Sosa said.

"We're getting a garbled transmission from the incoming," the soldier informed him. "It sounds like they're saying '*Red Scorpion ... low on fuel.*'"

Sosa's heart beat faster. "That's our combat plane! If they're coming to the Pentagon, then they're in trouble. Get two Spider Attack helicopters up in the air now! If that aircraft isn't the Antonov, I want it sent down into the forest in a million tiny pieces! *¿Está claro?* (Is that clear?)"

"*¡Si, Señor!*"

"*¡Rafa!*" Sosa barked over the intercom.

Rafa, despite being sexually engaged with one of his three "concubines" in his own bedroom, suddenly stopped in mid-stride upon hearing Sosa's voice. *"Esperate, niña;* wait a minute, *mamacita."* Reaching over to the nightstand on his right, still deeply imbedded inside of the woman, he hit the "speak" button. "Boss," Rafa panted.

"In ten minutes we either have Red Scorpion coming or an invader," Sosa spoke fast. "Get on the roof and ready those surface-to-air missiles just to be on the safe side."

Rafa jumped off of the dissatisfied Solangel and said, "I'm sorry, baby."

"When are you going to be your own boss?" she pouted.

"Watch your mouth," Rafa growled at the Bolivian sex kitten. "Or I'll break your face."

"You always say that."

"Well, this time I mean it." He hurriedly dressed in green army fatigues and black boots. "If the alarm sounds, you get the other girls and get to Sosa's to make your escape. Pack nothing. If you hear the alarm –"

"I heard you!"

Rafa grabbed two sidearms, an M-16, and he filled a bag with extra ammunition, magazines, grenades, and RPGs. Then he bolted from the room.

CHAPTER TWENTY-TWO

Elvira Montana
Davenport, New York
September 24, 1984

The curator at the New York Museum of Natural Art and History was more than happy to keep the Montana collection in its care ... for a price. The curator, Walter Clem Thurman, asked Elvira for permission to put the 12 original masterpieces on display through New Year's Day 1985 and she agreed but only after her insurance policy was updated and a contract was signed.

"So, if it's lost, stolen, or destroyed you're owed twelve million?" Nina asked as Almara maneuvered the brand-new black luxury van through the Davenport parking lot and parked it in their reserved space.

"Tax-free," Elvira responded as they exited the van.

"The museum will make more money displaying those pieces than what you would've paid for the care of them," Almara mentioned. She saw some school-aged neighborhood boys playing catch football nearby. "Boys! Y'all want to make five bucks?"

The three youngsters looked at the women cautiously. Seeing no threat, the oldest one came over. "*Each?*" he asked.

"No way, man." Almara shook her head. "There're only some light grocery bags. You think we're rich or something?"

The twelve-year-old pointed. "Rolls Royce, Bentley, Chevy van, and that super-yacht makes me think you have five bucks each for us, rich or not."

"Smartypants; get the bags," Almara commanded the three boys. "Y'all are what – Indian?"

"Everybody says that!" the youngest boy laughed as they grabbed the grocery bags out of the van. "We're born in America so we're American-Bangladeshi."

The three women followed the three boys out of the parking lot and out onto the boat docks. From the concrete breezeway, to the left, there were about a hundred yards of docked water vessels that were tied to piers and dock posts: sailboats, dinghys, fishing boats, yachts, and speedboats. To the right of the breezeway there were no dinghys or small vessels due to the larger size of the shipping wharf. At the end of the boardwalk, tied to the quay, was Elvira's new 200-foot super-yacht made by Riva of Italy.

Elvira must have had a love affair going with the color black because the vessel was all-black with a Mohican-style haircut. It was a sleek, high-performance superboat that looked like it was straight out of a James Bond movie – or something that Batman would come blazing out of his *Batcave* with. Although there was not much that she could tell anyone about it, she was certainly learning.

"Is it fast?" the twelve-year-old asked as they walked up the ramp and onto the yacht.

"It has four three-thousand-horsepower MTUs with Arneson drives," Elvira told them. "So you're talking a hundred knots at least."

Nina giggled at Elvira's playfulness with the cute boys.

Almara paid the youngsters $5 each and sent them on their way. Elvira met with Ally and Nina in the kitchen of the yacht and smelled the seafood gumbo the cook was preparing. The six-person crew Elvira had hired was from New York and all of them were females with the exception of the cook and captain. Elvira had her reasons for hiring mostly females ...

"Women have a lot of ice in them," Elvira had explained only a day earlier. "But they're easier to trust. Women are naturally loyal if treated well or in love. Like dogs. Most of all, women are relentless."

They walked out of the kitchen and out onto the yacht's aft deck, which had a sun lounge area with wraparound seats and dining tables. Within minutes they were being served bowls of the delicious gumbo with shredded cheese and sourdough soup crackers. For drinks they had iced herbal tea with lemon.

Once they were through with lunch, Elvira excused herself and went to the master stateroom. On the way past the double-level cockpit, the ship's captain greeted her. He was a tall, dark-haired Italian man in his early fifties and he had what looked like a permanent smile on his face.

"Captain Bovello." Elvira stopped and smiled. "Do you need anything?"

"No, ma'am," he told her. "Just good to see you."

"Does *anybody* need anything?" she asked.

"Everything's good," he assured her. "You've been very kind to us."

"Okay." She started off. "Carmine, the cook, made a great gumbo. We'll be gone for a day or two so be sure it's all eaten and not go to waste. It is really a lot of food."

"Will do."

The yacht had a front topside superstructure made almost entirely of tempered glass; thus, from where she stopped at in the living room, she could turn in a 360-degree angle and both light ingress and outward visibility were fantastic. She had yet to take *The Montana* out to sea but she had already seen how the calm Atlantic Ocean looked from the living room/day area when she'd been on a replica of this very same yacht with Tony in the summer of 1983.

The staterooms were accessed from the living room through a staircase which led down into the ship's lower level. The yacht's crew of six shared three of the five staterooms. Elvira had quickly designated Nina and Ally to share the fourth stateroom while she took the biggest room on the ship. Luxury was just not the word to describe the mastery put into the craftsmanship of the vessel. From the soft carpeting to the Corian countertops in the bathrooms, it was all so cheery and gave its passengers the feel of royalty and riches.

Elvira undressed, showered, put on sexy white undies, and studied Tony's financial files once again. This was something she'd been doing over and over for the past week. Before her eyes got too tired, she made several important overseas phone calls.

Nina appeared and sat next to her. "Can I help?"

"We need to charter a jet for about a week." Elvira pointed to a list. "We have to travel to these overseas banks – Spain, France, Italy, and Japan. I spoke to the managers at each bank and I'm *required* to appear in person so they could authenticate that I am the widow of the deceased. Mailing to them Tony's Death Certificate and a copy of his Will were not enough. Charter for us one of those big, heavy, luxury corporate jets with rooms in them so we can sleep and stretch and walk around."

"Make hotel reservations near the banks or … ?" she trailed off.

"Each bank," Elvira said. "You were thinking closest to the airports?"

Nina nodded yes. "Madrid first. Paris second. Rome third. And a very, very long trip to Tokyo last. This is such a friggin' dream job! My God, mon. Thank you so much."

"That won't be it either," Elvira said with a sigh. "We have a few other places to go. Get the private jet set up for Thursday, the hotel reservations made, and pack for a week.

Write out the itinerary and we'll do a detailed checklist so nothing's forgotten."

Later that night Almara got up out of her bed and walked over to Nina's bed. Almara slowly eased back the pink satiny covers and stared at the awesome beauty of Nina's perfect form. She only had on a sheer white top, which accentuated her firm perky breasts and erect nipples, and a very small pair of white silk panties. Almara wanted so badly to pull them off of the sweet Black China Doll but common sense told her that seduction takes time. Almara had to be careful.

"Ally?" Nina suddenly woke up.

"I saw the blankets had fallen off ..." Ally covered Nina but not before smelling her female scent. "You okay?"

Nina nodded and sat up. "We have to get up early. Get some sleep, Ally."

"I'm beside myself with lust for you, Nina." Ally looked down at the lovely angel. "I'm sorry ... I just am."

"I know." Nina grabbed Ally's hand. "And I'm flattered. Have patience with me. I don't know ... You're my friend. And this is a good thing we have. If we mess it up ..."

"We're not," Ally insisted. "Let's just tell her we know each other more than what we've let on. And that we've been attracted to each other, which is why we kept silent."

"That's the thing, Ally. I've never been with women. I certainly don't want to tell my *employer* that I'm attracted to her addiction therapist!" Nina sighed her frustration. "I took a huge gamble leaving my job – all the debt I owe, family in Jamaica I have to send money to ... I *need* this job, Ally. I don't wanna risk it cattin' around, mon."

"Okay." Ally patted Nina's shoulders, tucking her in. "I'll take care of it. Just know how badly I want you."

Ally went to her bed.

Nina jumped up and sat next to her. "What do you mean you'll 'take care' of it?"

"That I'll take care of it," Ally repeated.

"Ally," Nina said in a scolding tone. "If you do something stupid like steal from her, I'll turn on you."

"What do you mean?" Ally looked at her. "I never said I'll steal anything. I'm not a thief. I'm just in love. I'm stupid."

Nina was astonished. "No, you're not stupid. And you're *not* in love. You're fascinated and filled with lust. And, frankly, you're scaring me."

"I *scare* you?"

"*Yes*," she emphasized the word. "You're developing an obsession for me. At first I thought it was sort of flattering but now it's getting out of control. All we did was hang out and kiss. I shouldn't have done that. I don't want sex with a woman ... if that's what you'd even call it. I'm not a lesbian. I'm not a virgin; I love sex with a man. I want a baby with a man and I want to one day marry a man. I'm asking you, Almara, please stop."

"I'll stop." Almara was sounding sincere. "I promise."

Almara went back to bed thinking, *Sometimes the pieces just fall out of place ... but ... seduction takes time.*

CHAPTER TWENTY-THREE

La Hacienda de Sosa
Cochabamba, Bolivia
September 16, 1984

The entire Pentagon army had mobilized. Sosa had dressed in green army fatigues and he had also strapped an M-16 around his neck and carried a *Javelin Anti-tank Missile* made by master weapon engineers at the United States Army Advanced Weapons Department. The Javelin's features included the Single-Shot, Fire and Forget Command Launch Unit or CLU, with a 84mm HEAT (High Explosive Anti-Tank) rocket whose travel range is 3000m with a velocity of 300 meters per second.

Sosa's army of 950 men took up their positions in areas of the massive compound that could not be seen from above. The Pentagon did have its own landing strip and it also contained two hangars for his fleet of helicopters and jets. However, he rarely stored any of his smuggling jets at the Pentagon, and probably even more rarely did he ever permit random visitors to arrive unannounced or uninvited.

The incoming jet could be heard from a mile away. Before it was in sight, it finally came over the radio clearly that it was indeed Red Scorpion, the combat unit. The army of men roared and cheered because all of them had heard the radio transmission simultaneously.

It was Benito's voice. *"How we're still in the air, I don't know. We read empty on fuel ... and we have two more problems ... I have an engine with smoke billowing from it ..."*

"What color smoke?" a commander from the watchtower asked. *"Cambio."*

"It's not white if that's what you were hoping," Benny came back. "It's black. Black smoke. That means something is burning or about to burn."

"You said there were two problems," the commander probed. *"Red Scorpion, cambio."*

"I'm here," Benny stated. *"The landing gear is jammed. We're coming in with no legs. Cambio y afuera."*

The army was awaiting orders, nervous, tense now.

"You can do it," the commander coached. *"It'll work out best if you come in on the front lawns. Come on in. Buena suerte, soldados* (Good luck, soldiers). *Cambio y afuera."*

Moments later the army went to retrieve trucks, fire extinguishers, and other emergency equipment. Sosa stood on the front lawns of the compound and waited. Within moments they could all see the incoming jet. Yesenia, Rafa, his three girlfriends, the housekeeping staff, and Juan Carlos Sevilla Sosa – Alejandro and Yesenia's son – all stood near Sosa to watch either a miracle happen, or a disaster.

Sosa, and probably everyone else, stood and watched the big An-26 Russian-made Antonov fly straight in toward the Andean Mountain peak estate ... and continue on over it.

"What the hell is he doing?!" Yesenia shouted. "He pulled up!"

"He's scouting to take a look first," Rafa explained to her. *"Tranquilicese* (chill out)."

The Antonov flew past and veered to the right, then ascended about 2,500 feet as it did so. One-year-old Juan Carlos sucked his thumb as his father held onto him. Both Sosa men watched the big jet climb and then loop back around the mountain peak until it was almost back out of sight. Then, there it was once more.

"He's lining it up," Rafa was saying. "Come on, Benny baby." The emotion had tears brimming up in his green eyes.

The Antonov came in lower ... lower ... lower ... and lower still. This time there could be no fly-over. No more "one more time." This was it. The great lawns, at their longest stretch, were only 1,000 yards, far below the 3,800-foot standard required for a plane that size to takeoff or land safely at. However, this one had no landing gear. All it had was an underside, or a belly, and 1,000 feet of improvised runway.

"I can't watch!" Yesenia grabbed Juan Carlos and started to run into the house but her legs felt heavy, numb and frozen.

The jet came in, engines screaming, a giant bird angrily smashing through the top of the trees, then down onto the lawns in the distance. It looked like an enormous missile. Once it touched the ground, Benny had no more control! Now, it was up to God and gravity to slow its death-defying momentum as it slid, as if the lawn was a lake of frozen ice, bouncing and skipping like a rock over water.

"Oh, God!" Carmen, one of Sosa's cooks fearfully cried out, making the sign of the cross on her chest.

"Alejandro!" Yesenia shrieked out of sheer terror as the nose of the plane barreled up toward the mansion!

Sosa, teeth clenched, stood stock still!

Then, suddenly, the darn thing rocked to the left and the wing snagged into the soil and the fruit trees did the rest! It had come to a halt!

The army of men converged on the jet, spraying the right engine with fire extinguishers. By this time two of the large tanker trucks were also on the scene, spraying the entire jet with cold water, beginning with its engines. Prior to the door being opened to let the crew out, the transport helicopter carrying the support crew landed on the airfield on the other side of the property.

Sosa was there to welcome his combat unit as they exited the plane. Words could do nothing to describe the avalanche of emotions that Sosa and his crew felt, nor could any of them stop the rivers of tears. One by one Sosa hugged his men, his dear brothers, kissing them as a father would his sons and clutching their faces tightly, and them clutching his, to look at each other in the eyes with a look of pride and one of "*bravefear*," if even such a term could be meshed together into one word. One that simply means, "*We are all brave men but we each have that human side of us which causes us to love one another. And since we love one another, then we must also fear losing each other. Though one day it's inevitable, it has to happen. But since this is not the day, this look on my face says, 'I love you today. I'm proud of you today. I'm proud of your brave heart and – most of all of these – I'm proud of the love you have for me and your loyalty that comes with it.'*"

First there was Lucho, Buro, Bushwacker, La Gata Negra, Tatico, Nancho, and then, last, Benito. All looking like soldiers returning home from war.

"You did a truly great job landing that thing, Benny," Sosa said as his voice cracked with emotion. "There's no training for that, *hombre*."

"Yeah, boss, no problem." Benny looked around and saw Yesenia crying at what she was seeing. "Sorry about the lawns and gardens, *hermana*."

Yesenia hugged him. "I didn't know how good you guys really were until I witnessed this. I am absolutely blown away. Breathless."

The reunion turned to the support unit: Felipé, Edgar, Victor, Ivan, and Javier. The biggest hug probably came from Javier, who almost knocked the air out of Sosa when the two men embraced, laughing loudly.

"The hurricane hit the Pentagon?" Javi asked Sosa.

"Nothing more than wind and rain," Sosa scowled. "The country's been hit hard, mostly in the southwest lowlands. There's been heavy casualties, some places people can't even find shelter or medical care. We have to do something."

"Like what?" Yesenia asked as they all walked up closer to the house.

"Now's a good time to counter-attack those rumors about you, boss," Tato advised. "That dead *chivato* made us look very bad."

"The bomb," Sosa whispered. "That was him?"

"*Sí,*" Tato nodded. "*And* the wife and kids."

"Well, that's terrible." Sosa stopped for a minute. "It's his fault. It's not ours, eh? He attacked us first, right?"

"Right," his men all agreed.

"Okay, now that's all over with." Sosa sat down on the front steps. He gave an order to Lucho. "Tell the men to expedite fixing this plane. When it's fixed we'll sell it and all the others to our Colombian friends in Medellín."

The unit looked weary and tired.

"We have a lot to do," Sosa sighed as a medium-sized brown-skinned man stood about fifteen yards away from them. He was bald-headed and literally covered from head to toe with tattoos. He was powerfully built; he had piercings in his ears, nose, mouth, and nipples. He stood chewing on a piece of fruit as he observed the group out of the corner of his eye. Sosa told them, "One thing we still have to do is either kill him or use him."

"Who is he again?" Nancho asked.

"The African-American-Nicaraguan," Sosa stated. "But we also need to bury Alberto."

"*¡Coño!*" Tato exclaimed. "Don't tell me he's a pile of rot."

"Catalina." Sosa looked at her. "You didn't tell them."

"He was embalmed and wrapped up like a frickin' mummy," she told them. "They put him in a pinewood box and stacked him in a mass grave on Hart's Island, New York. It cost us thirty k, or five grand for every person secretly involved to exhume him. I had to unwrap seven bodies before I recognized him."

"He was unrecognizable?" Tato was visibly angry.

"He'd been shot once in the head," she revealed to the group. A silent moment. "On that island, the stench was just … *unbearable*. One of the groundsmen said that the state, to save money, has been using heavily-diluted formaldehyde to embalm those people, and kids, and babies that can't afford otherwise."

"Where is he?" Nancho asked. "Let's go see him."

"Upon my return, even before I presented the intelligence about Gutiérrez to Nino, I had Alberto transported to the best undertaker in La Paz," she assured them. "I gave them the go-ahead to fix him up and to store him until you all are ready to send him off the right way, with honor and dignity."

Tato took a deep breath and exhaled. "Boss."

"He's safe, not suffering," Sosa said, thinking it all over in his mind. "Tomorrow we'll coordinate efforts with Red Cross, the government, and all the people we can get to volunteer. Yesenia."

"Yeah, *Papi*."

"Spend a million dollars on national advertisement," Sosa ordered. "We need a television commercial of some kind with my face and the faces of at least a thousand *Andes Sugar/Imperio, Inc.* employees handing out aid to victims of Hurricane Isabel. You use my photos in the commercial. Tato!"

"*Señor*."

"Before you go to sleep you coordinate Alberto's funeral," Sosa told him. "However you do it is how it'll be done."

"*Muchisimas gracias, Señor*."

"Rafa." Sosa looked at him. "Start stuffing envelopes with a thousand dollars of cash in each. You and the army. On the envelope I want the '*ASC*' stamp with my name. Yesenia knows which stamp."

"How many?" Rafa need to know.

"You mean how much," Sosa corrected. "Just begin the process but follow every dime. Let's start with a hundred million in U.S. cash. If we need another hundred million, we'll do it. Bolivia is our home, our people. Everybody else pitch in. We need flyers made for mass circulation. Let everyone know that Andes Sugar/Alejandro Sosa and his partners are giving one thousand in cash to every family ravaged by the storm. We're also giving out food packages, water, batteries, flashlights, blankets, anything they need, including decent Christian burials for the dead."

"You mean use the helicopters to flood the departments and municipalities with flyers," Javier guessed.

"*Correcto*," Sosa nodded. "But first, everyone sleeps. We'll start tomorrow. It'll be a massive job that will take days, maybe weeks. No one is any good to anyone if you're not rested. Let's go in and break bread together in celebration of this day."

CHAPTER TWENTY-FOUR

Elvira Montana
International Cash Collection
September 27–October 8, 1984

Forty safety deposit box keys meant 40 different safety deposit boxes. Most of the banks, fortunately, were in South Florida; the others were in Mobile, Alabama; Biloxi, Mississippi; New Orleans, Louisiana; Corpus Christi, Texas; and Las Cruces, New Mexico. Elvira remembered each bank well because it had been her job to stuff the boxes with the yellow envelopes over the past few years. When she had complained about all of the exhaustive traveling distances and berated his thinking as a "miscibility," he had cursed her.

"You want Gucci, Bvlgari, Chloë, and all that expensive stuff, get off your sweet *culo* and earn it for once, baby," he'd commanded. In a softer tone he'd explained: "Those are the Gulf States; except Las Cruces. When Sosa's smugglers fly into the Gulf, we have crews in place who receive the merchandise. It's best to have the money available – close by – to pay Sosa's men off. That's why, when we get the call that a load is coming, I rush you to go take out the money. You are a sophisticated lady – the bankers will never suspect you."

It took her three days to complete but she did it. She'd also left Ally and Nina behind on the yacht without telling them of her decision to go to the banks on her own. She did call them to keep them from worrying but she was adamant that she would be okay.

She flew back to New York with $51M packed into six large trunks. The private business jet landed at Westchester Airport at 1 p.m. Nina and Almara met her there in the luxury van. Four men from the baggage claim helped load the six trunks into the van. Almara drove them up to Elvira's branch at Bank of New York in Nyack, where she had originally opened up her account. Obviously, the bank manager had been expecting her because as soon as she stepped out of the van, she was met by two-armed bank guards with a heavy-duty steel pushcart.

The trunks were taken into a rear area of the bank, where a group of bank personnel immediately began the long, tedious task of counting the money. Three hours later the bank manager came out and joined the three waiting women in his office.

"There was slightly more than fifty-one million dollars, Mrs. Montana," Mr. Mathias H. Ross informed her. "Fifty-one million, one hundred thousand even," he said as he sat behind his desk.

"I'm buying all of your staff dinner, Mr. Ross." Elvira laid ten one-hundred-dollar bills down on his desk. "And I'll pay the overtime I cost the bank."

"That's okay," he chuckled. "Truly it is."

She laid down another $1,000. "I insist. It's the least I can do. Especially since I heard counting my money broke a couple of your money-counting machines."

Almara and Nina joined in the laughter.

"Thank you, Mrs. Montana," he smiled and gave her the account receipt for the money. "Is there anything else I can do for you?"

She stood up. "Thank you but no."

Back outside, in the van, Elvira directed Almara to return them to the airport. "First to the Caymans, then Panama,

Zurich, then ... what was that order we said a few days ago, Nina?"

"Madrid, Paris, Rome, and Tokyo," Nina recalled them. "We're on the way."

$$$$$

Tony had either received great advice or he had been a very smart man for moving money down into the Cayman Islands. The Caymans have the fifth-largest banking center in the world with $1.5 trillion in banking liabilities. There are over 200 banks there, nineteen of which are licensed to conduct banking activities with Cayman-based as well as with international clients. The remaining banks are licensed to operate on an international basis with only limited domestic activity. The Caymans boast 40 branches of the world's 50 largest banks, including HSBC, Deutsche Bank, UBS, and Goldman Sachs.

Tony had more than $4M stashed in a safety deposit box at Deutsche Bank and an account with them that held nearly $700k. The wealth management services and private bank Rothschilds had been hired by Tony to invest $400k about two years ago, which was why he now had $700k at Deutsche. Elvira had the $4M deposited into a Deutsche account and then she made a total wire-withdrawal transfer of the money to her bank in Nyack.

Once the $4.7M wire-withdrawal was confirmed by Mr. Ross, the trio departed Georgetown and flew on to Panama, where Elvira had $3M more wired to New York. In Zurich she discovered what she described as "the jackpot" of stashes in one bank: $46M. Once that wire-withdrawal was completed and confirmed, they globe-trotted on to Madrid, Paris, Rome, Tokyo, and then finally on back to New York.

$$$$$

October 8, 1984

Following the advice of a local IRS tax accountant, Elvira simply filed income taxes on the $110,800,000 she had "discovered" of her husband's money. She did not have the energy nor the desire to pick a fight with the IRS. Especially when she knew what Tony had done to acquire the overwhelming bulk of his cash. She knew that the IRS would be ruthless with her when they examined her application and its numerous attachments.

However, they were surprisingly lenient with her case, taxing her $28.6M. Was she content with it? Not at all. But she would have to be because she knew that they were far from dumb. She stood out on the aft deck of the yacht and laughed out loud.

"What's so funny?" Almara said as she joined her outside in the cold, breezy moonlight.

"The U.S. Government wants their piece of the pie no matter what kind of action it is," Elvira grinned. "Whether it's whoring, gambling, dope, and so on. As long as the government gets a cut ..."

"You thought there'd be trouble, now there is none," Ally waved it off.

That's not exactly true, Elvira thought idly. Aside from the cash Tony had stashed away while he'd been alive, he had also been buying up a large amount of U.S. Treasury and Bearer Bonds. Elvira held those in a safety deposit box in Nyack. *Another $17M in security money in case it all goes sour,* she figured quietly.

"Penny for your thoughts." Almara put a warm shawl over her boss's shoulders.

"Let's go inside," Elvira said, grabbing hold of her hand. "I'm going to give you more than a penny ..."

Nina was inside of Elvira's stateroom, laid out flat on her back in the center of the soft queen-sized bed, chatting away on the ship's satellite phone to her mother. She was all ready for bed in warm pink wool pajamas, a head scarf, and big fluffy Mickey Mouse house shoes.

Elvira went straight to her closet and dragged out a huge Louis Vuitton suitcase. "First, I'd promised to give you each twenty-five thousand in twenty-four hours after quitting – to go with the ten I already gave you."

Nina had come over to help them bring the suitcase over to the bed where they all sat. Elvira opened the suitcase and removed a big manila envelope. Inside of it there were one-hundred-dollar bills, all in neat stacks marked $5,000. In addition to the money there were also three American Express Black Cards.

"This is a hundred grand each," Elvira told the two beautiful women. "The twenty-five is yours to burn. The additional seventy-five is for all your debts to be satisfied. I plan to let you each in on some business deals we'll need loans for, and you can't be loaned money if your credit is poor. Get it taken care of and take care of your families. Is it enough?"

"Lord God, it's more than enough!" Almara beamed happily.

Teary-eyed, unable to speak, Nina hugged Elvira and simply nodded.

"Hey," Elvira smiled at Nina. "Come on, Black China Doll. If you're going to cry every time I give you money, then you'll turn into a river. You were nice to me and even a little mean when I needed it. Both of you. I love youse for that. And I'm really in a giving mood because the IRS didn't bring down the hammer on me … So, enjoy."

Nina dried her tears, or at least she made an attempt to.

Almara helped her, kissed her cheek. "You okay?"

Elvira watched them curiously, patiently.

"These are Black Cards." Elvira held them up. "Or Black Centurions. American Express provides them to select customers. I've put both of you on my account. This way if I need something done, especially if it requires substantial cash, it's done without delay. Look ..."

Elvira pulled out several fashion portfolios. Inside of them were photographs of her and some of her favorite models.

"You're so pretty!" Almara squealed. "I forgot you said that you modeled."

"I'd *kill* for those shoes and that Fendi bag!" Nina swooned. "All of these clothes are high fashion designs."

"You see how I dress?" Elvira had a smoldering look in her blue eyes.

Almara and Nina nodded.

"You girls are scorching hot," Elvira commented. "Exploit it. Use it. Those drab clothes you wear – give them to the Goodwill. I know I hired you to take care of me. At least do it fashionably. I'm sending both of you to *Irma La Bella* in Manhattan. She's the biggest and best style expert in the Western hemisphere. Jewelry, handbags, clothes, accessories, hair, make-up, shoes, perfumes, cars. We will be dolled up together. Everything will go on the Black Cards."

"Why are you doing this?" Almara asked with a smile.

"Oh, there's a plan brewing in my head," Elvira told them. "Once you get a taste of real living ... You'll do everything in your power to keep it. So, if you ever think of betraying me, you'll only be betraying yourself. Makes sense, doesn't it?"

Almara and Nina glanced at each other quickly and agreed with Elvira. "Yeah," they chorused.

"We'd never – " Nina began but Elvira held up a hand, cutting her short.

"It was my father," Elvira said suddenly.

Almara looked confused.

Nina's mouth was frozen, slightly open.

"Your father ..." Almara looked intently at Elvira. "What do you mean?"

"I spoke of being molested as a kid, a baby, until I was a tenth-grader." Elvira let the words out slowly. "I wanted to tell Nina at the hospital ... and Almara at Aspen. Maybe I need to say it so I can try to heal up. I want a cigarette; a drink would be good. This yacht makes me think of parties. Almara said ... the root of my addiction is unresolved childhood issues."

"The worst of them ..." Almara took a deep breath. "The worst is the sexual molestation."

Almara thought that she was the type of person who could understand anything ... On the other hand, Nina's background had prepared her for just about every ghastly experience there was. But what Elvira said next left the psychologist and nurse completely flabbergasted.

"I've never told a soul what I'm telling you." Elvira squirmed, struggling to say what she wanted to say. "I've always been afraid to admit to anyone that my father began having sex with me – molesting me – when I was still a toddler. The actual intercourse began when I was six. We were married – well, what I thought was a marriage – before he took my virginity. It all went on for a very long time, until I was sixteen ..."

Elvira was in tears, her face and ears red from shame and embarrassment. Almara and Nina's mouths were ajar from the shock they felt at hearing this.

"I ..." She began to sob. "I was made crazy from all of it. What he did to me. I became addicted to it. I *liked* it ... I liked all of it ... Now [shrugging] I feel shameful and guilty. Every single friggin' day and night of my life. And there's more. A *whole* lot more. I, um ... just get yourselves ready to hear something very, very difficult to hear. That's all."

CHAPTER TWENTY-FIVE

La Hacienda de Sosa
Cochabamba, Bolivia
September 16, 1984

At 5:30 a.m. Sosa had a wholesome breakfast in his home dining room with Rafa, Benny, Tato, Nancho, and Javier. Right after breakfast they all walked out into the living room and stared at the gray canvas mail carts lined up near the far right eastern wall. There were twelve carts in all.
Sosa picked up one of the envelopes and nodded approvingly. Each one was stamped in black with:

From: Andes Sugar Corporation CEO Alejandro Sosa
and all of his family and friends.

"*Perfecto.*" Sosa patted Rafa on his shoulder. "A hundred million?"

"*Sí,*" Rafa concurred. "We worked through the night."

"No sleep?"

"Ah, boss," Rafa waved him off. "I'll get plenty of that when I'm with Alberto."

The men all chuckled.

"I've been on the telephone all night, too," Rafa continued. "The flyers will be ready by 8 a.m. Because of the short notice and the seven million copies we've ordered ... that took dozens of print shops. We'll need all of our helicopters to pick them up and distribute them over the hardest hit areas. We'll also need to have our cars out there, men going hand-to-hand."

"Sounds like a political campaign," Tato said.

"Yeah, Sosa for President," Yesenia stated as she came into the living room and kissed her husband's cheek.

"*Señora*," all the men greeted her simultaneously.

"I need a chopper in five minutes." She rushed off into the kitchen.

Sosa made the radio call himself for her helicopter. He spoke with her for several minutes before she left the house.

"The various printing shops are all located in La Paz, Sucre, and Cochabamba," Rafa said, producing a map which he laid out across the bar countertop. "The print shop owners will deliver directly to the designated areas where we've gotten approval to land, per Nino Cucombre."

"No coordination with them?" Sosa looked up at Rafa's face.

"Call it what you will, *jefe*," Rafa shrugged. "The general is able to deploy military units for purposes of security only … for now at least. The American government has pledged humanitarian aid, as have a few other governments such as Libya and Russia. The Americans, as usual, will drag their feet as the death toll rises. Our government … well, we're third on the list of poorest Latin American countries."

"Permission to speak, *Señor*?" Tato asked.

"Tatico," Sosa said.

"This is *our* mission," Tato began. "We can't let the government get involved. *Refuse* the military escorts. We have our own security forces. If we allow the military to escort, they will take credit due to the government's influence in media. They'll overshadow us and water down what we're doing. That will be counter-productive."

"Thank you, Tato." Sosa thought it over. "Tato's right. Rafa, get on the SAT-phone and cancel that escort."

"*Señor.*"

Minutes later Rafa was back, pointing at the map. "All of our ASC trucks, and several other fleets, will stage in Puerto Villarreal, Cochabamba. We have approval to land our helicopters here [indicating], in an abandoned used car lot."

"You said '*several other fleets*,'" Sosa stated curiously.

"Food companies, clothing companies, construction companies, et cetera," Rafa answered. "We need more trucks than the five hundred-plus in the Imperio/ASC fleet. Because of the state of emergency, many of these 'other' companies have stalled or staggered their fleets. I believe we needed all we could get so I've leased those trucks and their drivers for twenty-four to seventy-two hours, depending on their company. Those companies are putting together packages of their own goods for families in need and including a detailed list of each item, in each package – and our bill."

"How much is this bill?" Sosa wanted to know.

"So far, over three hundred million." Rafa watched Sosa closely.

Sosa took a deep breath. They'd all seen the devastation on the news and the news was not even the half of it. "*Hombre,*" Sosa mumbled as he scratched his chin. "*A lot ...*"

Rafa looked at Tato and they all shrugged as Sosa wandered away with his hands in his pockets.

"Did he tell you to pledge three hundred million?" Nancho whispered to Rafa, slapping him on the back of his head. "You idiot!"

"*Coño,* man!" Rafa whispered back.

"Tell me this," Sosa said as he came back to the map. "We all know Puerto Villarreal. We'll have our own ASC eighteen-wheelers ... five hundred-plus. How many others?"

"Two hundred fifty-six," Rafa replied, nervous.

"So, about eight hundred total." Sosa pointed at the map and said, "Good area for the first loads."

All the men looked at each other, surprised.

"'*First loads*,' boss?" Rafa looked at him quizzically.

"Reset the staging area in Andamarca," Sosa told him.

"Huh?" Rafa looked at the map. "Andamarca, *Oruro?*"

"*Sí*, Oruro." Sosa nodded, then explained why. "The Pan-American Highway runs directly through it. From Puerto Villarreal, Cochabamba, we have the railroad which stops in Andamarca. More aid will be needed so we will send more via the railway to be loaded into our empty trucks in Andamarca, Oruro. Our army will assist in the dispersal and the trucks won't block traffic. The Churches of Christ will help us. Make a note to call them."

"We'll need more men for security, *jefe*," Tato warned. "Bandits and Shining Path will eat the fleet for breakfast."

"That's why we have our Colombian and Nicaraguan consorts," Sosa told them. "Javi, can you handle giving a few of them a call? Tell them we need a few hundred extra men to help with security. Mention to them that I'm also selling off the entire fleet of jets and some old munitions I'm sure Pablo and José Gonzalo can use. They like dynamite ... add that we also have tons of dynamite. That'll get 'em here."

"I'll get right on it." Javier took the SAT-phone into the kitchen.

"Are you okay, boss?" Nancho inquired.

"What do you mean?" Sosa looked oblivious.

"You're giving away a *billion dollars* in aid." Nancho said it as if Sosa was hearing of it for the first time.

"I am," Sosa said. But then he corrected himself: "*We* are. *Tranquilo, monito*. We have other billions. What's one, when our people are out there cold, hungry, homeless ... dead? Babies, women, and tribe elders are sick? Don't worry, the American cokeheads will have it all back in no time. Right now it's just sitting in the vault, stashed in underground places, in businesses, and banks. Some of it is being eaten by rats who make nests from it."

"*Don and Doña Haché Sosa are landing, Señor,*" the radio command officer's voice cackled over the walkie-talkie on Rafa's waist. "*Cambio.*"

Rafa answered the call. "Ten-four. *Cambio y afuera.*"

"Did Haché call?" Tato inquired.

"No." Sosa went to let his mother and father in. All the men followed him. A few minutes later Sosa was hugging and kissing his mother and father. They all entered the living room.

"Hey, son." Don Haché, still a hard and vibrant white-haired man of 75, looked around at each man in the living room. "We came to see what the plans are."

Sosa sat across from his father. "They are what you think they are. You donating anything?"

Don Haché chuckled lightly. "Donating anything? Yeah. Our babysitting time. Where's Juan Carlos?"

Sosa glanced at his Rolex. "Readying himself for school upstairs."

"Me and Mama are going to Spain," Haché told him. "To Catalonia, Pamplona, Madrid, and then on to the Canary Islands."

"To Las Palmas?" Sosa guessed.

"No," Haché shook his head. "Not this time of year. We're going to Santa Cruz."

Sosa wanted to know more but his mother was there.

Getting the hint, she stood up. "You and your people here will be busy … and you men must talk. I'll be with Juan Carlos."

After her exit, Don Haché began to speak just as Javier returned to the room. "Javi," Don Haché greeted Tato.

"Papa." Javier warmly embraced Haché, kissing him on both cheeks. "*Mucho gusto.*"

"*Mucho gusto,*" Haché sat back down and looked at Rafa, Nancho, Javi, Tato, Benny, and Sosa. "*Muchachos. Cuidado.* The Gutiérrez thing is all in the news. The hurricane is saving you more hassles. How much are you pouring into this relief effort?"

"About a billion dollars," Sosa shrugged. "That's the earliest estimates."

"Have film crews on all of it," Haché wisely advised them.

"Yesenia's on it."

Haché looked at the men before him. "I've taught you all well. But remember that you'll still have enemies in our government, waiting. We've been the power behind the power for a very long time. We've been the alpha lion in the jungle. Me, Ariel Bleyer, Nino Cucombre, and a handful of other men in government office; senators, judges, and so on. Sooner or later other lions come to sniff and test the older lions. Those who are younger, faster, more agile, and more violent than the older ones. If our older friends get even an ankle sprain … or even a broken finger … any injury in the jungle can be fatal."

Haché looked at each man, dead serious.

"You are at the peak of power," Haché continued. "All of you are. Benny, Javi, Tato, Nancho, and Rafa … I'm sure if you wanted to retire you'd be given mansions, mega amounts of cash – so you can live like the kings you are for the rest of your lives … and have your women delivered to you by the dozens so youse all can eat *chocha* out of gold candy wrappers."

The group chuckled.

Haché sighed as he stood up. "The problem with money, such as what *La Corporación* has amassed, is this … there's no end to it. There's no end to what the Americans will use to get high. I never predicted this kind of money. Coke is like the invention of the wheel, sliced bread, or the car. Now I see … it'll only get bigger. *Imperio, Inc.* … all of its companies, especially ASC, will continue to grow because it'll never have a money problem. Like the name says … it is truly an empire. But remember the Ottoman, the Roman, the British, and so forth. They all fell. Yeah, I know the saying: '*The Roman Empire didn't fall, it just has a new address: USA.*' That's bullcrap. What I'm saying to you here is find an exit strategy. There's oil, gas, computers, satellite, and other lucrative businesses to get into. You have to plan a way out, wean yourselves off of the coke money. It is as addictive as the coke itself. Become dependent on billions per year from oil. You're smart enough to do it. Will you promise me to do that?"

Sosa thought about it. "Sure, Papa. I promise to work on a way out. I *have* already been thinking it."

"I'll take your word." Haché extended his hand out and his son took it. Then, looking at the other men, "And you all are my sons, too. You'll be with him on that?"

"To the death, Don Haché," Rafa swore.

The others all swore their allegiance to Sosa as well.

"So this trip won't be a waste," Haché said as he put on his coat, "I'm going to be looking for lands in Spain; places for you all to hide out at if it ever comes to that. You have to find shelter to go to *before* the storm hits, not *after* it hits. You have to pay off governments in places where there is no extradition treaty … for, you know, *extra protection.* You see, we made it a long time ago. Now, I didn't do you the best justice by giving this to you. I guess how I coached you *in* … I have to coach you *out.* I'll find those safe places in case the exit strategy stalls on you. At least you'll have a chance."

After Don Haché and Doña Rosalie exited with Juan Carlos, the men prepared to put their relief plans into immediate action.

"Did you get in touch with the Medellín Cartel?" Sosa asked Javier.

"I spoke with Pablo himself," Javier said. "He's on his way with an army."

"The Nicaraguan guy," Sosa stated as he watched the young man from the living room window. "I'll meet him now. Call him in."

Rafa went out to retrieve the man. He came back in with Rafa and stood before Sosa.

"Can you handle an M-16, *chico*?" Sosa questioned him.

"*Sí, patrón*," the brown-skinned, tattooed man answered quickly.

"What's your name?"

"Miguel Ibañez," he replied. "Please call me Cabayo."

"Cabayo." Sosa looked him in the eyes. "We'll speak when the time is right. We have a billion dollars to give out to the Bolivian people. That's a lot of work. You go on with my brothers. Show them how to use an M-16."

"*Sí, patrón*," Cabayo nodded as chuckles rippled around the room.

"Cabayo." Sosa stopped him, standing in his face.

He turned back to Sosa.

"We're finding out who you are, your relatives, birds, cats, dogs ... *everyone*. And we're also looking into your background. If you're here to betray me, I'll find out about it. If you're a rat, the streets will talk. If so, I have hungry friends in the jungles I'll feed your dead body to. Then I'll send a hit squad to slaughter everyone you care about. Got it?"

"*Sí, patrón*."

"Take his picture and fingerprints," Sosa ordered his men. "See if he can handle a machine gun, and put him into private army fatigues. Get the photo and prints to the General. If he checks out, we'll talk in three days. If not ... kill him and feed him to the Andean condors and the caracaras."

CHAPTER TWENTY-SIX

Elvira Montana
New Rochelle, New York
October 7, 1984

"She'll let it out," Ally whispered to Nina after they got into their beds. "She needs time," Almara commented as she switched off the lamp.

"God, Ally," Nina whispered back, looking over the small nightstand that separated the full-sized stateroom beds. "The earth shifted under my feet when I heard that. It's one thing for your father to touch you, but another to ..."

"To what?"

"To admit that it even happened."

"Not only that," Almara said.

"I know. I just don't want to be the one to bring it back up," Nina stated. "How awfully embarrassing to ..."

Almara looked over at Nina. "You mean that she became *addicted* to the sex. Damn ... can you imagine saying that to girlfriends?"

"Yeah," Nina nodded. "She said she was made crazy. That she *liked* it. What are we supposed to do with that? I mean ..."

"I really don't know. I'm still trying to process it."

"You're the psychic."

Almara laughed at her friend's wisecrack. "*Psychologist*, silly. There are no college credits available on the earth for

227

psychics, you only have to be a great flim-flammer. Elvee could only mean what she said. Whatever he was doing… made her derive so much pleasure from it that she couldn't get enough of it. He drove her into a sex maniac. He addicted her to his experience and skill. He used sex as a tool – to enslave her body and mind."

"I just can't see how it's possible to 'like' sex with my father." Nina tried to imagine it. "Eww."

"You have a healthy, loving relationship with him," Almara enlightened her. "Elvee did not have that. I guess when she was *freed* from her father's grip and she got a whiff at the normal world – out of isolation – she feels shame and utter disgust that she'd actually enjoyed sex with her father. She's probably still mentally isolated. Still a slave. And it's possible that she may even still yearn for and/or have sexual fantasies about her father. She feels alone in the world, as if … what she went through never happened to anyone else."

"Have you ever had a case like hers?" Nina propped herself up on one hand.

Ally shook her head. "Never have I heard a male or female admit to *liking* the sex with their abuser, let alone admitting addiction to it. No. I'll have to research this baffling issue."

"Please do that," Nina said, lying down. "Because I'm totally freaked out."

$$\$\$\$\$\$$

October 12, 1984

Elvira wanted to lease a fancy Victorian-style two-story black-and-white brick mansion in New Rochelle, on Coligni Street and North Avenue. She would retain the yacht across town in Davenport Park but she needed a place to really feel at home in. She operated quickly, too. At 9 a.m. she walked into a Century 21 real estate office in nearby Larchmont and by 9:30 a.m. she was being shown the 9,500-square-foot mansion.

"I want it. *Today*," she demanded.

"Mrs. Montana," the young Black male realtor started, "there's some work scheduled to be done inside of the house Monday and –"

"Forget it." She shook her head. "I'll use my own contractors. Cancel the work. I'll reimburse whatever losses that have been incurred. I don't have all day. Let's get the lease done for one year, I'll pay it in full, you give me the keys, and we're done. If not I'll find another Realtor."

By 11 a.m. she was visiting the White Plains architecture firm of *Epstein & Roache* on Post Road. She met with Josef Epstein and Timothy Roache about the creation of a mega-mansion paradise in ritzy Bronxville or Scarsdale. She ended up spending several hours with them.

"It'd be best if we went to take a look at each of these properties you've identified," Epstein, a quirky little Jewish man in his late forties, advised her as he adjusted his silver-rimmed glasses. "The ideas we've been discussing are very grand. Doable but very grand."

"He's concerned about the lake you want to create," Tim, a medium-sized blond man in his late thirties, informed her. "In Scarsdale they may say no. Bronxville could say yes. Or the other way around. Everything else we can do. And if there's no lake … ?"

"Then forget it," she said, shaking her head. "I want a lake. I like prime real estate. Westchester is prime real estate. But I think Scarsdale is bare and boring. My park and lake idea will give it pizzazz. Color. Excitement. So, please get it done for me."

From their offices she arranged for a moving service to pick up and deliver the items she had in storage to her new house. She also made a call to Hi-Tech International Security

Services (or HITISS) and made an appointment with its director, requesting armed bodyguards for her New Rochelle home, her yacht, her person, and the persons of Rachel Janine Lee and Almara Quijano.

"You'll likely have to come to my New Rochelle home to see me next time," she told Tim and Josef prior to making her exit. "Call me with the news on the town ordinance regarding the lake and we'll go from there. Get me the ordinance in writing."

$$$$$

No human being has so-called *human instinct*. Scientists all throughout the world have said that there is no such thing. They have proven that *animals* do indeed operate off of instinct, unlike humans, who operate off of their intellect. Migratory animals such as birds, sea turtles, and salmon all return to their places of birth due to *instinct*, not because their parents provided them with a written record. Instinct is pretty much all animals have as far as their survivals goes. Humans have the superior capability of common sense born of cognitive thought: that is, *intelligence*.

On her way home from a doctor's appointment to end her rounds of errands for the day, Elvira observed, in her rearview mirror, what she thought was a car she had noticed earlier in the day following her at a safe distance. She drove her Bentley into the *Pep Boys* parking lot on Sanford Avenue in Mt. Vernon. Out of her periphery she observed the silver sedan slow down and pull into the parking lot of *The Ice Cream Factory* across the street. She went inside of the *Pep Boys* store area and pretended to look at some tires on sale in the windows facing the strip mall across the street. The occupant (or occupants) of the silver sedan had not exited the vehicle.

She left the *Pep Boys* and drove up to the parking lot exit, hesitating as she eyed the silver sedan. If she had been in the offices of George Sheffield directly after the reading of Tony's Will, she would have known that the sheisty Miami mob lawyer was having her every move documented by private investigators at the behest of South Florida cocaine menaces Gaspar Gomez and Nacho "El Gordo" Contreras.

She drove out of the parking lot and headed for Pelham, the town which separated Mt. Vernon from New Rochelle. *They are following me*, she quietly affirmed. She sped through Pelham and, as she ran a red light on Main Street in New Rochelle, she was stopped by a New Rochelle police cruiser for the infraction. The sedan that had been following her passed on by.

"Ma'am, did you know you ran a red light back there?" The officer was enormous, bald-headed, big/thick mustache, no other facial hair – like *Magnum, P.I.* star Tom Selleck – minus the good looks. "*And* you were going forty-five in a thirty."

"Sure I know." She stepped out of the car. "I was afraid, and I'm pregnant."

The big man removed his Eric Estrada shades. "Okay. Afraid of *what*?"

"Look, Officer Gordon," she read aloud from his nametag. "You can give me a ticket if you want. I admitted it. But write this license plate down: *SN4-683*, New York plates, silver four-door sedan. A Crown Victoria, I think. It was following me all the way from Mt. Vernon."

He wrote it down. "License, registration, and proof of insurance ... following you, ma'am? Why?"

She dug into her purse and gave him what he asked for. "I'm not trying to pay my way out of a ticket but I need private security. Immediately. You and four of your pals. Do you do private security?"

By the looks of it she sounded serious. "That's affirmative, ma'am."

231

"I own the black yacht in Davenport," she informed him, "and I just leased a house on Coligni."

"The black yacht." He paused. "A beautiful vessel. Ma'am, I'm going to let you off with a warning. I have friends outside of the department who work private security, as do I. I'll escort you home and on the way I'll run this plate. To the yacht or Coligni?"

She looked very relieved. "The yacht."

The sun had just set when she stepped out of the gray Bentley and met with Officer Jack Gordon on the yacht. They sat inside of the living room and were immediately served a lobster and steak dinner by the ship's kitchen staff.

"You're being followed by a private investigation service," Jack stated as they ate. "The car's registered to the service, not a particular name. The service's name is simply *Security Inter-Continental, Inc.* An individual interested in you must have hired them to tail you."

That threw her for a loop. "How do I find out who hired them?"

"Oh, boy," he said as he chewed a mouthful of the delicious steak and lobster simultaneously. "Many of those P.I. guys are ex-cops, and FBI. They're pretty tight-lipped about naming a client. It's bad for business and there's also civil liability for doing so. You'd need somebody who knew somebody in the FBI to find that out. And it would be expensive. It's not exactly a national security issue."

Nina and Almara came in after spending an entire day with Irma La Bella, the style and fashion expert Elvira had sent them to. Elvira's eyes lit up when she beheld the dazzling transformation of the two women. They had already been beautiful, now they were both simply spectacular. With her exotic ethnic mixture, Nina was a devastating sight to take in. Her beauty caused pulse rates to increase.

"Girls, you look like a million bucks!" Elvira smiled ear to ear. "Meet Officer Jack Gordon of the New Rochelle Police Department."

"Hello," the women chorused.

Elvira turned back to him. "Nina, will you please bring me twenty thousand dollars from the cookie jar?"

"Excuse me." Nina left and returned several minutes later with four $5,000 stacks of cash.

"Thank you, Nina. Isn't she something, Mr. Gordon?" Elvira said, noticing his eyes struggling not to stare at Nina, who wore a sassy white leather designer dress.

"Have mercy on me," he said good-naturedly but he was not joking. "She's *gorgeous*. Both of you are."

Nina and Almara blushed like schoolgirls.

Elvira gave him the $20,000. "Fifteen for the information, the other five for the rush service."

He picked up the money, thumbed through it, and stood up. "In that case, I'll get right to it. How about the security detail, Mrs. Montana? My colleagues and I work for fifteen hundred dollars per week, we come heavily armed and will provide you with twenty-four-hour around-the-clock protection."

"I'll pay the one week for six men," she offered. "I need them to rotate on shifts so they're well-rested. They'll need to drive us and protect not only us but my property – such as this yacht and the house I leased. Let's see how it goes because I have also made an appointment with HITISS for their services. Have you heard of them?"

"Hi-Tech International. Certainly." He nodded. "I hope you find us up to par – like all of our previous clients have. I'll be sure to bring you a list of references for each man and woman –"

Elvira perked up. "*Women?* You mean female private security?"

"Of course." He sat back in his seat. "Military trained, cops, ex-cops ..."

"I like women," Elvira stated. "*Professionally*, that is. No offense, but I trust them more than men. Men are a distraction."

"I see," he smiled. "So, you'd rather six women?"

"Five," Elvira decided after a moment. "Including you. Do you have an eye for beautiful women?"

"Yes, ma'am." He glanced at Almara and Nina. "I like to think so." His comment caused Ally and Nina to chuckle.

"I want only the most beautiful girls working for me," Elvira said slowly. "See, it will be to my advantage to have beauties around. Their looks won't distract me but will distract others. Since it's a man's world ... what better weapon than a beautiful woman?"

Jack smiled, liking this demure, profound young blond. "You got it. You'll hear from me and your new security group in two hours."

He exited the ship.

"His muscles are like ... *umm!*" Nina held her hands up in a large round circle, demonstrating an imaginary bicep.

Elvira ignored the comment. "How was the day of pampering?"

The two women gushed for the next hour about their day at Tiffany & Company, Saks Fifth Avenue, and the Louis Vuitton, Hermés, Bvlgari, YSL, Gucci, and Prada stores. Then the pampering at the hair and nail salon, the full-body massages, total body hair removal and bikini waxing, and the purchases of their cars.

"You said to choose style so that's what we did," Nina slyly stated. "I bought a gold Mercedes SL and Almara a black Lamborghini Murcielago."

Elvira was happy for them. "I can see the transformation in both of you. Did someone say total body hair removal?"

"Yeah!" Nina laughed. "The only hair on our entire bodies is what you see on our heads, eyelashes, and eyebrows. It's a sweet musk and rose-scented cream the masseuse slaps *everywhere*. In every nook, crack, and cranny. Then they wipe it off with warm towels. They oil you and spread a fruity cream gel all over you, then bathe you. The hair – it's like it's never even been there."

"You feel sexy?" Elvira asked.

Almara giggled. "So sexy I need sex to stop the tingling."

"The treatment was just *insane*," Nina added with a smile. "Irma – my God – she is *truly* the real deal. How do you know her?"

"I met her years ago during a magazine photo shoot in Florida," Elvira said, leading the girls downstairs to her stateroom. "Moving on ... I leased a big mansion today. I need youse to meet them at the storage at 5 a.m. and I'll meet you all at the mansion when the trucks arrive. It's nearby on Coligni Street in New Rochelle."

"I thought you liked the yacht," Nina remarked.

"I *adore* the yacht," Elvira replied. "But it's not *home*. Speaking of which, I met with Epstein and Roache about the building of my dream home by the lake. They'll get back to me on the laws in Bronxville and Scarsdale about the lake. I hope it's Scarsdale – it's so cozy up there. It's like living in a town under a bunch of trees."

"There's always the Hudson," Almara quipped. "Ossining, Croton –"

"And have my baby born with three buttcheeks?" Elvira scoffed. "It's a toxic waste dump. Plus, I said I want a lake, not a river. A river has traffic, especially the Hudson River. The lands I want to buy are private havens, quiet. My children will want to fish, swim and throw rocks in the lake. I can't live on the Hudson and forbid them to stay away from water that's right in their faces. My lake will be big, clean, maintenanced, and I'll fill it with fish, frogs, insects, and all kinds of birds."

"You said children." Nina looked at her.

Elvira thought about that as she undressed. "I want more than one. After we get TMC established."

"TMC," Almara repeated.

"*The Montana Corporation.*" Elvira walked into her bathroom with the two women behind her. "A conglomerate – a multiple business enterprise. Starting with real estate, land development. I also want to get back into modeling."

Nina and Almara looked at each other as Elvira stepped into the shower.

"Modeling," Nina stated, sitting on the clothing hamper. "You're going to be a model again?"

"Maybe some," she spoke over the spattering noise of the shower. "But it's not about me. We're going to go big – national, international. Remember, TMC is a corporation with a very big cookie jar."

"I wouldn't even know where to start with the model business," Ally said.

"Me neither," Nina added.

Elvira finished up and came out of the shower with a huge peach-colored towel wrapped around her torso. They went into her bedroom and the two women stood behind Elvira as she blow-dried her hair in the mirror.

"Follow my lead," Elvira told them. "You can start by looking in the mirror. You are ethnic models. Almara, you have the gift of youth in your genes, although you are thirty. That's ancient in modeling years. Nina and I are twenty-five and even *that* is old in modeling years, but Nina ... you are so – you'll be the crown jewel of the company. The face of the company. That exotic mix you got going, your accent and voice, my goodness. You have me and Almara beat by miles! You'll be TMC's spokesmodel, our face, our biggest star. Can you handle it?"

"I'm flattered," Nina beamed. "You know you can count on me."

Elvira lay down and pulled the covers over her body. "Wake me when Jack comes."

Almara dimmed the lights and exited the master stateroom with Nina at her side.

CHAPTER TWENTY-SEVEN

Alejandro Sosa
Pan-American Highway, Bolivia
September 16, 1984

Sosa's four helicopters worked non-stop raining down hundreds of thousands of the flyers they'd picked up from the print shops. The fastest and easiest way to do it was to "bomb" as much of the hurricane-affected areas of Bolivia as possible from the air. There were seven million flyers to do the job with. *Six* million of which were dropped from above; another million were distributed by Sosa's army of volunteers on the ground.

Bolivia recognizes a total of nine "Departments" that cover its entire national territory. They are: Beni, Cochabamba, Chuquisaca, La Paz, Oruro, Pando, Potosi, Santa Cruz, and Tarija.

"Municipalities" in Bolivia are administrative divisions of the entire national territory governed by local elections. Municipalities are the third level of administrative divisions, below departments and provinces. Some of the provinces consist of only one municipality. In these cases the municipalities are identical to the provinces they belong to.

Rains from Hurricane Isabel reached as far east as Santa Cruz, Yapacani, and even as far north as Trinidad and San Borja, Beni. However, those areas were not as hard hit by the storm as those areas clearly defined by Sosa's top men. Their concerns were some areas south of Copacabana and Guanqui; and as far south into La Paz as Charaña; and as far east as the Pan-American Highway. The flooding there, in one word, was catastrophic.

"Boss." Tato, dressed in a waterproof rain suit, called Sosa over to where he was standing on a hill overlooking the Rio Desaguadero.

Sosa was standing inside of the trailer of one of the ASC 18-wheelers, handing out humanitarian aid packages to families. Hundreds of the big rigs were lined up on the shoulder of Pan-American Highway South near Exit 16 in Viacha. From where Sosa stood at in the back of the last truck in the line, he could see Tato and six heavily-armed soldiers who helped control the crowds of thousands who were lined up to receive the aid packages. Sosa saw Tato pointing out at the distance, holding a pair of binoculars in his hand.

"What is it?" Sosa said something to Nancho and two other private army men before he leaped out of the truck and over to Tato's side. "Yeah."

"*Hombre, mira,*" (Man, look out there) Tato sighed, handing Sosa the binocs. "We have to hold out on the rebuilding materials ... That's Rio Desaguadero. At least it *was,* or will be once those floods recede. Lake Titicaca's overflow is what powers this river. The rains have washed it out, I guess, from the swelling of Lake Titicaca."

"We'll stall the building materials." Sosa looked out over the flash flood with binoculars before handing them back to Tato. "Get Rafa to –"

"He's returned to the *Señora*'s security detail in Sucre," Tato informed him. "Once the Medellín Cartel and their army arrived, I told Rafa to meet her there at the television studio. She was not adequately protected with only five –"

"Put out the calls to withhold the building materials," Sosa ordered and returned to the truck. "You did good sending Rafa."

The private army soldiers and soldiers belonging to the Medellín Cartel were doing a prolific job in assisting with the distribution of aid. Families and individuals receiving the packages had to dip the tip of their index fingers in blue ink. This was done to prevent anyone from coming back twice. No matter how much scrubbing they'd use to clean the ink off with, it would be an exercise in futility because the ink was made to stain permanently and thus would not come off for several days or even weeks.

The convoy moved slowly down the Pan-American Highway to deliver the aid wherever it was needed. Obviously, the printed flyers they had bombed all throughout the affected regions of La Paz, Oruro, Potosi, Sucre, Chuquisaca, and Tarija had been effective in getting the word out. The commercials were apparently working their magic as well because national and international news crews were flocking in to take photographs, record footage, and report on the aftermath of Hurricane Isabel.

"We didn't count on this, *jefe*," Javier whispered to Sosa close to nightfall on the first day of the mission. They were still delivering aid on the Pan-American Highway but now they were in Oruro near the marshlands of Lago Poopó, home to several indigenous cultures such as the Quechua, Aymara, and Uru Uru peoples.

Wiping sweat from his forehead and neck with a burgundy bandana, Sosa looked at Javi. "Count on what?"

"International media cameras," Javier whispered.

"It crossed my mind," Sosa said as he affectionately palmed the cheek of a seven-year-old Uru Uru girl. "Who are you with, niña?"

In tears she explained, "They drowned! They all drowned!"

"Go get the cameras, Javi," Sosa ordered. "We can't make this stuff up."

Within minutes Javi returned with several reporters. Most were from neighboring countries but there were many there from the United States as well. Sosa recognized Diane Sawyer from *ABC* and Ed Bradley from *CBS* right away. There was also a man there with them who looked familiar. Sosa would recall his name later on as the night progressed: *Tom Brokaw*, from *NBC*. These were the very same U.S. networks that had been covering the Dr. Orlando Gutiérrez revelations about Sosa and his powerful friends. Javier led them all to the seven-year-old orphan girl.

Diane Sawyer, her cameraman catching it all on film, questioned the girl. "So you think your family never made it out of the water alive?"

"They didn't come out," the girl said tearfully. "They – they were in the river on a branch and they fell in! The water took them and I didn't see them come out!"

Even a hard-line reporter like Diane Sawyer could not help but to be moved by the girl's story, as were Tom and Ed.

"None of your family got out?" Tom asked her, giving the girl his handkerchief.

"No, *Señor*." She blew her nose.

Just then a water and mud-soaked mutt ran and jumped up onto the little girl, overjoyed to see her. The small seven-year-old squealed happily and wrapped her arms around the dog as she sobbed into its dirty coat.

"And who's this?" Diane inquired, the camera zooming in.

"This is my dog, Bonnie," the girl said, overcome with tears of joy. "She's a girl."

"Well, look at that." Diane had a tear in her eye. "Bonnie found you – out of all these people?"

"Yes." The child was choked up at seeing Bonnie.

"What's your name, *niña*?" Sosa interjected, knowing that the news correspondents had not recognized him yet.

"Yasca Angelica Cano Muños," she said.

Sosa spoke to his men. "Get the girl hot coca tea, a blanket, and a leash for the dog. Call the bus and tell them we have another orphan."

The reporters turned to him with Ed Bradley doing the questioning. "Your name, sir?"

"Alejandro Sosa," he stated.

"Alejandro Sosa?" Ed Bradley paused, recognizing him immediately. "Uh ... okay. Ed Bradley of *CBS*. Forgive me, Mr. Sosa, but we've been hearing about you and your organization in the States ... negative things. Suffice it to say, I'm confused. *There*, we hear of this ruthless drug overlord and *here* we see a giving man, laboring heartily to help humans who have been displaced by a devastating hurricane. Would you care to comment on the drug trafficking allegations and what we see here?"

"Obviously you cannot believe everything you hear," Sosa told the reporters who held microphones and tape recorders up to his face. He picked up the little girl. "I am a business executive with Imperio, Inc. We own Andes Sugar and a slew of other businesses. I *inherited* my shares of the business from my family. Naturally, I'll have enemies, most of whom I've never personally met. Namely, the late Dr. Gutiérrez."

"Did you have anything to do with the Buenos Aires bombing?" Diane asked him. "The assassination of Dr. Gutiérrez and his family?"

"*Absolutely* nothing," Sosa denied. "I'm insulted by that. I was in Cochabamba watching it on the news like anyone else. No, no, and no again."

"Do you own coca farms?" Tom Brokaw inquired.

"It's our number one gross domestic product," Sosa answered him. "Of course. But we make teas, sodas, candies, toys, and even medicines with coca. We do *not* process cocaine. However, your country's Coca-Cola Corporation has a plant in Pando that processes tons of coca every year.

Whether it's de-cocainized or not I do not know. We have a plant that de-cocainizes our coca leaves. I own lands that produce many other crops as well. But no, no, and no, again, that I nor anyone else in our business is a *narcotraficante.*"

"This little girl you hold," Diane switched the subject. "You said a few minutes ago, '*We have another orphan.*' You mean that there are other displaced children that you have found?"

Sosa affirmed that information. "All during the day we have been – by 'we' I mean Andes Sugar and its friends – have been putting stranded children onto our trucks but the trucks are either too hot or too cold. Our friends at the Churches of Christ have been sending in vans and buses but, as you may imagine … they fill up quickly. Some people need medical attention, others – like Yasca Muños here [indicating the child he was holding] – need to be *held*, given dry clothing and shelter."

"So, where will they be sent?" Diane Sawyer pressed. "Like Yasca Muños? I mean, my network has *personally* done stories on Bolivia's mortifying orphanages. What will you do with her?"

"You're right, Diane," Sosa agreed with her. "Red Cross has coordinated search and rescue ops with the military and I don't know the details of those cases … We're working alone, we have our own rescues and some recovery of the deceased. For the most part we're giving out aid and not interfering in what the government is doing. The only thing I can, and will, do with people and kids is respect the law. Yasca, and about one thousand others who need it ,will be housed in hospitals, schools, churches, and I'll even erect a tent city on my own lands and keep them safe. Yasca and her dog will likely come live with us. My wife will love that."

"*Really?* You'd do that?" Ed Bradley asked, surprised.

"Look, Ed," Sosa stated as though he and the African-American newsman were friends. "These are my neighbors, my peoples. There's an eight-hundred-truck fleet out here *tonight*, not in *three days* or *two weeks* while governments haggle over one dollar or hundreds of millions of dollars in aid. These peoples, my peoples, need help *now*."

"You mean the U.S. Congress," Tom suggested.

"Among others," Sosa shrugged.

"How much will all of this cost, Mr. Sosa?" Diane asked. "I've seen your aid packages. Blankets, bottled water, the one thousand dollars in cash stuffed into envelopes, coats, hats, shirts, gloves, tents, medical supplies, canned foods, diapers, fuel, generators. This is quality equipment. Eight hundred trucks. *Wow!* All from you and your company?"

"Imperio/Andes Sugar will survive," Sosa said. Then, adding with a smile, "We have pretty good credit with Bank of America and a few others on Chambers and Wall Streets. But let's not talk money, Diane. Let's talk *Yasca Muños*, who has lost everything, including her family."

"Except the dog," Diane stated warmly. "Bonnie."

"Yes, Bonnie … everybody likes dogs," Sosa smiled as one of his soldiers put a rope around the dog's neck. "Javi, let's get her and the dog on a chopper and to a hospital so there's a record made of her. Send one of the women with her. Once she's checked free of illness, she'll live with us until further notice."

"It's very kind of you to do what you're doing, Mr. Sosa," Tom Brokaw observed. "You are a very impressive and caring man. I hope you don't mind it much if we sort of tag along with the convoy."

"You are welcome to follow," Sosa offered. "And these security men will guarantee your safety."

"I'm very grateful. *We* are very grateful." Tom Brokaw and the others shook Sosa's hand, thanking him.

"Well, we could use some extra hands," Sosa told the news people. "We need all the hands we can get. You get the story, the security, and the people get the aid."

"Sure, Mr. Sosa," they all agreed. "We will help."
The mission continued.

CHAPTER TWENTY-EIGHT

Elvira Montana
New Rochelle, New York
October 16, 1984

Even with Elvira's increasing their responsibility to her each day, Almara never lost sight of what had placed her in Elvira's life to begin with: alcohol and drug addiction. Almara was deeply passionate about her own sobriety as well as Elvira's, so it was no surprise when Almara expressed her outrage toward Elvira when Almara discovered a half-empty bottle of wine in Elvira's Coligni Street bedroom nightstand.

Almara exploded on Elvira about it as the three women sat around the fireplace in the living room.

"It's only *wine*, Almara," Elvira insisted nonchalantly.

"Who're you fooling, Elvira?!" Ally scolded her. "That's how it starts!! The scotch, the vodka, the coke, the pills, the blackouts, the throwing up, the lies, the sleeping around with strange men!"

Elvira quickly became irate and defiant. "First off, you can stop yelling at me! And I *don't* sleep around! I've *never* slept around. I have myself under control, Ally, don't worry about it."

"You have it under control," Ally mocked her with scathing contempt.

"No one is in control of *anything*, Elvee!" Nina enlightened her. "I remember you choking on vomit and hospitalized after showing apparent signs of an overdose! You could have been dead."

"Now you too?" Elvira shot at her.

"Yeah." Nina decided to stay calm. "I signed on to take care of you *and* the baby. You need to own it and take what's coming."

Elvira got up and stormed out of the living room.

"Give her a few minutes," Nina instructed Ally, who got up to follow her.

"Forget that!" Almara went after Elvira, hearing a door slam upstairs. Almara reached the master bedroom door and entered. Elvira was sitting on the cushioned bench-chest at the end of the adorable king-sized canopy bed.

"Leave me alone," Elvira softly demanded.

"No." Ally shook her head. "It's time we face this. Tell me about your father."

"What??" Elvira was incredulous. "What does that – what does *he* have to do with anything?"

"Are you friggin' kidding me?! *Everything!*" Ally shot back emphatically. "He has *everything* to do with your addiction to booze, to drugs … and even to this asinine notion that you can control yourself once you get started. So, finish telling me about –"

"I'm not talking about that." Elvira crossed her legs and bopped her foot up and down in a rapid motion. "Forget about it."

"I'd *love* to forget about it but I can't." Ally turned up the pressure. "I can't because if I do it'll *napalm* everything in my life – including *you, Nina, me … everything.* So tell me. I quit my job to counsel you, so don't play with me, Elvira!"

"*The man's a MONSTER!! An evil beast!!*" Elvira got onto her feet, screaming the words as Nina came in. Elvira yelled loudly, painfully, and soulfully. "*Whaddaya want from me!!*" (shaking, crying; turning beet red).

"I want the *truth!*" Ally crossed her arms. "*Talk!*"

"I see," Elvira said coldly, fuming. "Whaddaya wanna hear, Ally? Nina? That my father *screwed* me? No … that he *made love* to me – as a man does a woman while I was five or six? You want to hear how I fellated him … that I masturbated *for* him, and together *with* him? You getting the picture in your heads now? [sobbing; sitting back down] I feel so deeply ashamed … Even when he'd tie me to the headboard and oral me into a frenzy as he spanked me, I thought it was normal. [tears flowing] The pain I felt when he took me anally … even the pain felt good because he'd put a vibrating toy inside of me. I was his sex slave – an open lab specimen. He kept me frazzled with body-bending and neck-breaking orgasms. He kept my mind enslaved, too. He'd whisper how much he loved me. He bought me everything and he was such a good-looking, strong, muscular man. He addicted me to sex … and to sex with pain. Did I like it? Oh, God, yes. Not a day goes by that I don't think of the powerful orgasms he gave to me. This is my sickness and my weakness. This is what I run from [sniffles]. As I grew older, watched TV, saw other people, couples, I – no one was *with* their father. It was no longer normal to me. It was weird. Gross. But I *needed* what he addicted me to … the pleasure and the pain. No one else could give me what he could."

"Choppy, Frank Lopez, Tony … ?" Almara questioned her. "Did you find pleasure with them?"

"Not with Frank," she admitted. "Choppy and Tony were wild. They loved it that I loved to be spanked, slapped around – *hard*; berated, bitten, choked … With Frank I got through the sex by fantasizing about the *pain-sex* I'd had with my father. I'd also masturbate with sex toys – I'd inflict my own pain. Plus I have tapes. I kept tapes."

Nina's mouth dropped. "*Video* tapes? You still have video tapes of the assaults?"

"I have many," Elvira told them as Almara gave her a box of Kleenex. "I also have his handwritten journals of his abuse, the sex, and the murders."

Nina almost choked, asking, "*Murders?* Plural? He killed some – ?"

"Hold on." Almara held a hand up toward Nina. "She finally opened up to us about the rapes. The man is clearly a monster. If any man can sexually abuse a child, then he can murder. Rape is worse than murder where I come from because when you rape someone, you kill what they *could have been*. This is serious enough. Let's deal with it first."

Nina was floored from it all but she contained her anxiousness and remained silent and patient.

"Thank you, Nina." Ally looked at the Black China Doll. "I have something I want to show the boss. Will you please bring me the LV file bag sitting on top of the dresser in my room?"

Nina left and returned a few minutes later with the bag. Ally opened it and removed several file folders from it.

"Is your father still alive?" Ally questioned Elvira.

Elvira nodded yes. "He's alive."

"How do you know?" Ally probed.

Elvira bit onto her bottom lip. "God ... this is so embarrassing."

"We're past worrying about shame and guilt, baby," Almara assured her in a relaxing tone. "None of this was your fault. You have me and China here because you trust us. Let the miracle happen so you can finally be freed from all of that madness congesting your soul. Trust me, you have no reason to feel embarrassed about anything. The process will take time, sweetie. We found the source of your addiction, now let's remove it. It's a malignant tumor – it needs to go."

"All right." Elvira explained, "I know he's alive because over the years I've called the house I grew up in. The number has never changed. I call to make ... God. [sighing] I call to *hear* him. It's weird but I still derive comfort at hearing his voice."

"Sexual fantasy?" Almara inquired. "The truth is best, Elvee."

"I can't help it." Her leg shook, nervous, afraid, shameful.

"I know, sweetie," Ally soothed her. "Get it out in the open."

"My ... I'm turned on by what I know only he can do for me ... I hate what he's made me into ... I hate him but I *need* him too. I know it's crazy but ... you demanded the truth. I'm telling it."

"After you left you've never returned to his bed?" Ally pressed on.

"He begs me to come but I never have," Elvira stated. "I resist because I'm afraid he'll kill me. The tapes I have ... he'll be convicted for murder. To tell you the truth, I'm still a child in his mind. I don't believe he wants Elvira the woman. He has a woman right now – one with a small daughter. I think the woman is a necessity in order for him to have access to the child."

"First of all, he is no longer interested in you, Elvira," Ally stated with some sadness. "Once you reached puberty he probably wanted to kill you and fill the void with another toddler – to repeat the cycle. That child is in danger and must be saved."

"The woman must be saved, too," Elvira added. "He's very capable of hurting her."

Ally gave her a concerned look. "What do you mean?"

"What do you mean what do I mean?" Elvira said more than she asked. "He's raving mad. He *intentionally* crashed a commercial airliner in a heartbroken murder-suicide attempt that killed everyone on board except for him."

Ally and Nina were both stunned by this revelation.

Elvira studied the shock on their faces. "Yeah. This is what youse wanted to know. Welcome to my *House of Terror*

... welcome to *me*. The woman he wanted murdered in the botched murder-suicide attempt was my mother. She died in the crash just like the other one hundred thirty-eight people. My father was the only survivor. He couldn't do a murder-suicide like a normal man with a bullet ... Don't believe me? Well, when I left home about eight or nine years ago, I stole his journals. Inside of them he *admits* what he did in lofty details. The molestation, the premeditated downing of the jet, his heartbreak. Everything."

"And you never told anybody? Did anyone see the journals or the tapes?" Ally asked, disbelief in her voice.

"Uh-uh." Elvira shook her head no.

"*Why??*"

Elvira shrugged, shy. "Y'all will never understand. That man is like a demon inside of me ... he has a hold on me – like a seal in the jaws of a killer whale."

CHAPTER TWENTY-NINE

La Hacienda de Sosa
Cochabamba, Bolivia
September 17, 1984

Sosa chose to pamper all of the international media who were covering the story. He gave them full access to several of his private jets and three transport helicopters. He also prompted General Cucombre to provide them with security as long as they were in the country. Sosa had his men see to it that they were moved to the more respectable *Ritz-Carlton de La Paz* and that they were driven around in his black fleet of armored Land Rovers and Mercedes Benzes. All bills were charged to Andes Sugar/Alejandro Sosa.

On day two of the Hurricane Isabel aftermath, Sosa and the Toros slept until 11 a.m. Upon rising they prepared to bury and say their final farewells to Alberto Jésus Hernán Molina. By noon Alberto's body was airlifted to the Pentagon via helicopter. The Toro men and Sosa were there on the front lawns to meet the private army pilots, Diego "Buro" Cortez and the slender, freckle-faced, redhead Alicia Anabella Camacho-Cucombre (the niece of General Cucombre).

The coffin was carried by Sosa, Tato, Benito, Nancho, Javier, and Buro, then sat atop a large white pegmatite pedestal. Sosa was quite content with how fast his mechanical engineers had fixed the landing gear on the Antonov and gotten it off of the lawns just in time for this event. Sosa knew how important it was to his family, his men, and even to all of his Pentagon staff to be able to say goodbye to Alberto. The men had all believed that they would not get this chance after word had reached them that Alberto had been killed in New York. For his body to be back home, in Bolivia, was a miracle.

"I'm sorry for having defied you, *Señor*," Tato said as he held back tears while they stood near the coffin. "Please forgive me."

Sosa looked at Tato for a moment before realizing, "You mean the other day when you thought we weren't trying to bring Alberto home."

"*Señor*." Tato nodded. "A man can be born anywhere but wherever he dies … I think a man should be brought home. To the place he loved, and to his people."

"You're *my brother*, Tato." Sosa hugged him. "And my friend. You did no wrong. You're forgiven."

Tato, the big strong Black Hulk that he was, finally weakened and the dam broke. Tato could not hold in the pain of losing his friend any longer. Seeing Tato break down caused Sosa to break down. Javier was next, then Nancho, Benito, Buro, and Alicia Anabella. Many others had begun coming down the lawn to attend the funeral, including Rafa and Yesenia, who joined in the crying and mourning of Alberto Molina. There were over 200 chairs set up but no one was sitting down yet. There was a sadness that had overwhelmed everyone, except for the members of the Medellín Cartel, though their mood was somber and respectful.

Sosa had called on the Medellín Cartel to help and they had brought along with them an army of 800 men and women. The cartel bosses (Pablo Escobar, Gonzalo Rodriguez Gacha, Carlos Lehder Rivas, Jorge and Fabio Ochoa, Felix Dixon Bates, Carlos "Carlito" Bustamante, and Griselda Blanco) had been persuaded by Sosa to not show their faces to the international news crews who had swooped into the country to cover Hurricane Isabel's destruction. Pablo and the others had been fine with that and Pablo had found a way to joke about it.

"Just admit it, Alex," Pablo had laughed. "You're embarrassed to be seen with your chubby friend in public."

There is nearly always a degree of truth in every joke and Sosa had wondered at the cartel leader's inner thoughts and feelings. "You have it wrong, Pablo. With all of the hell coming down on you in Colombia and the U.S., the last thing you need is to be seen with *me*, a man who is accused of funding the infamous Cocaine Coup and installing my cousin – Garcia Meza – as President-Dictator of Bolivia in 1980. Now I'm being accused of leading a drug syndicate and still controlling the Bolivian government. Last, this bombing of Gutiérrez in B.A."

"Ah, that was a beautiful explosion," Pablo had marveled. "Your men need to teach my men how to handle C-4. How about that? And, for compensation for the army, ten thousand sticks of dynamite and arms. Lots of arms."

"You got it," Sosa had agreed.

Sosa was now looking out over the crowd who had come to pay their last respects to Alberto "The Shadow" Molina. It was almost rare to see all of his most dear and loyal *La Corporación* members in one meeting, although they lived either on top of the mountain's vast grounds – in luxury Spanish-style guesthouses – or in the lower valleys and foothills that surrounded it. They were all dressed impressively for the occasion, especially the women. Sosa took note of each person there. First, there were the women:

Yesenia Dulce Sevilla-Sosa
Juca Belén Romero-Toro
Yulissa Nyelli Suárez-Espinosa
Acuzena Mina Fernández-Calderón

Yulianna Dimaris González-Sarmiento
Aracely Daniela López-Ramos
Noe Amanda Pérez-Álvarez
Mariana Cristela Díaz-Varela
Claudia Lovi Romero-Diazayas
Nelli Candice de Sousa-Solís
Emilia Villa Blanco-Vega
Gabriela Anisa Torres-Domínguez
Veronica Linda Ramirez-Martin
Antonia Moreno Ramos
Rebeca Rose Silva
Savana Madeline Espeja
Carinna Assisa Pereyra
Helena Lourdes Medina
Ximena Salomé Acosta
Amina Bello Aguirre-Burgos
Kimberly Roberta Cabrera
Felicia Louisa Molina-Rojas
Frederica Chanel Paz
Neftali Miranda Costa
Estefania Penélope Romano
Julia Sofia Serna
Catalina Lilli Romero-Toro
Raquel "Rock Candy" Garza
Maruja Selena Alonso-Sessa
Blanca Flori Rodriguez-Sanchez
Yurisa Arias Garcia-Feliciano
Lucia Nesi Martinez-Aroyo
Adriana del Sol Gómez-Sancha
Sasha Bonita Castro-Vásquez
Valentina Irís Suarez-Mayorga
Alicia Anabella Camacho-Cucombre
Marieli Bella de la Hoya-Ruiz
Ana Maria Giménez-Iglesias
Yana Teresa Ramos-Nuñez

Trinidad Chiasa Rossi
Dianna Camila Méndez
Jocely Rosa Hernández-Flores
Mariah Bernadina Ferrari-Ortiz
Monica Luna Benítez-Herrera
Liliana Endera Arias-Vidal
Dafina Fernanda Otero
Regina Korena Rey
Suzana India Sobija
Paulina Renata Russo
Marilyn Andrea Bruno
Angelica Aurilia Rios-Morales
"The Maza Sisters": Luciana, Victoria, Macarena, and Coca
And "The Jimenez Cousins": Gabriela and Renata

With the exception of Yesenia, Catalina, and Benny's sister (Juca Belén), all of the above women were either in Sosa's private army or they were "employees" of Imperio, Inc./Andes Sugar. As members of *La Corporación* they were also on a more sinister payroll. One that paid cash only. Juca Belén, who had been gang raped at age eleven, lived a quiet life with Benito. Their relationship was one of fierce love and protection of each other. Juca Belén was known mostly for her work with the horses owned by Sosa and the Toros. Benny had wanted to get her married off but the gang rape had seriously affected her desire to do so. Now 37, time was running short on her ability to reproduce. A fact that worried all those who loved her.

Thinking of this, Sosa's eyes went from Juca Belén to her brother Benito, whom she was seated next to. Sosa took note of all the men who were present. They were:

Vicenté León Romero-Toro
Javier Roberto Lugo-Toro

General Juan Gabriel Benino Cucombre
General Hugo Banzer Suárez
General Luis Garcia Meza-Tejada
Diego "Buro" Gonzalo Pineiro-Cortez
Felipé Mauricio Palacios-Borca
Nono "Bushwacker" Carbajal
Ivan Manuel Rendón
"Monstro"
"Lobo"
"Machete"
Nancho Sebastián Lugo-Toro
Tatico Arturo Lugo-Toro
Rafael "Rafa" Peluché Porras-Amayo
Colonel Luis Arce Gomez
General David Ariel Diaz-Bleyer
Carlos "Lucho" Rodriguez-Pantoja
Edgar Simón Galvis-Zerboni
Victor José Nava
"Blackout"
"Rock"
"Gallo"
"Chili"
"Chuletta"
"Mancha"
"Gatillero"
"Bongo"
"Chicky"
"Cuchillo"

And their immediate superior – a 39-year-old Barcel-onian everyone knew best as Pappy Meza, first cousin to the four Maza sisters.

The minister for the funeral was an old friend of the family, Juan Umala, from the Miraflores Church of Christ in La Paz. He gave a loud sermon on the salvation of Jesus

Christ and held everyone's attention when he stood in front of Sosa, the Toros, and the Medellín Cartel and spoke frankly to them.

"I watched you boys grow up," Mr. Umala said loud enough for everyone to hear. "Now, you are all men. Alex, Tato, Nancho, Javi, Benny, Hugo, Garcia Meza, Hugo, Arce Gomez, even you – Little Nino. [smiling] Now, some of you run the country ... very powerful men. Listen to me, [pointing at them] each of you. Even *you* [pointing at the Medellín Cartel members]. I see the news. Jesus Christ wants you too. It does not matter the sins you have committed. Remember John 3:16 ... *'For God so loved the world that he gave his only begotten Son, that WHOSOEVER believeth in him should not perish, but have everlasting life.'* Whosoever. That's *all* of mankind. Yesenia, Catalina, Juca Belén, all of you men and women here. But you have to change *now*; believing is not enough. Satan *believes*. You have to be baptized into Christ and live a life obedient to Christ's teachings. That's all I'll say. Let us all bow our heads and pray for Alberto."

However ... Minister Juan Umala knew that the prayer would be futile. Alberto had chosen doom over glory a long time ago.

CHAPTER THIRTY

Elvira Montana
New Rochelle, New York
October 16, 1984

Ally stood up and paced back and forth before coming back to face Elvira. "*What?!*"

"You heard it right," Elvira responded. "I know you wanted to stick with the sex abuse but you can't hear the one without the other."

"This thing just got deep," Nina murmured, astounded by what she'd just heard.

"So your father's a pilot with a U.S. airline company," Ally stated. "Is that right?"

"Yeah. Well, he was." She sounded uncertain. "He'd been injured, of course, and it was all a very huge thing. I believe he mixed his medicines and they found a substantial amount of the barbiturate *Seconal* in his blood. They held his doctor accountable in the end, saying that pilot error was due to involuntary intoxication or some bull like that. It's a very long story … if you want me to get into it I can."

"Hold that thought." Almara pulled out a printout from a file folder. "I've been doing some research on your case and I really want to take the time and go over this particular printout with you. It should at least give you some understanding about your own life and the issues you are faced with. Also, since it's us three here, I think we can all learn something from it. I have several copies so … let's just read it out loud. I guess we can each read a paragraph?"

"How about you read and if you get tired …?" Elvira suggested with a shrug. "Plus, I may have some questions."

The report was read in full as Nina and Elvira hung onto every word:

Sexual Abuse Survivors
By Kali Munro, Psychotherapist

Many sexual abuse survivors have trouble dealing with the fact that their body was sexually stimulated and felt aroused during the abuse. They may feel guilty and ashamed that they responded to the stimulation, and confused about why they did.

Feeling aroused during abuse is not an issue for every survivor. Some survivors never felt any kind of sexual arousal during the abuse. Others felt some sexual arousal, but readily accept that it didn't mean anything more than an automatic reflex response to touch. Still others experienced some pleasurable feelings in their bodies during the abuse, but because those feelings were overshadowed by the pain of the abuse, it isn't an issue for them either.

However, there are many survivors who are deeply affected by their bodies' natural responses. Some agonize over how their bodies responded to the stimulation; they experienced the sexual arousal as a humiliation, and believe it reflects negatively on them that their body responded at all. They perceive their body's response as a betrayal, with the abuser "winning," and they hate their bodies for it. This is compounded by the fact some abusers deliberately try to force a victim to have an orgasm so that the survivor will mistakenly believe that they wanted or enjoyed the abuse.

Anyone can be forced to have an orgasm. To be forced to have an orgasm does not imply consent nor pleasure.

Other survivors enjoyed some of the bodily sensations that came from the stimulation, but feel guilty, ashamed and/or secretive about that fact because they believe – or fear – that it means there is something wrong with them because they're "not supposed" to feel that way in the context of abuse. These survivors often keep their experience a secret for fear that no one will understand how they could have liked some parts of it. But what they liked was their body's own natural responses; not the abuse.

Elvira was very tearful during the session and repeatedly stopped Ally from reading to ask a question or make a comment.

"This is so me," Elvira cried, blowing her nose and wiping her tears. "I never would have thought that anyone could understand this trap I've been in. A confused slave is what I've been. I don't or would never seek an incestuous relationship out of my father but … my body responded naturally to what he did. The abuse was wrong and I hate him. I hate that I'm *still* his slave … he has a hold on me. I never thought somebody in the world would understand. This is *right on*, Ally. I thought – I felt so alone, isolated, and afraid."

"You're making me cry." Ally hugged Elvira as Nina wiped tears from her own face. "Should I keep reading?" Ally asked her.

"We're having a breakthrough here," Elvira nodded eagerly. "Go ahead."

Ally continued:

For boys, achieving an erection does not mean that they were even aroused; boys can have erections even when they are afraid. The impact of having been sexually stimulated or

261

aroused during abuse is rarely addressed, and when it is, it is given minimal attention. One reason why this is such a neglected subject is that we live in a culture that likes to think that children are asexual, and believe that those who suggest otherwise are sexual perverts.

Just as it is shocking for many people to think that sexual abuse could lead a child to feel aroused or to feel pleasure in their body, it is equally, or perhaps more shocking to survivors themselves to acknowledge this. By acknowledging that some children feel aroused reduces the emotional charge, or stigma, associated with it, and helps survivors to heal.

Feeling sexual arousal in the context of abuse does not mean that the abuse was okay, nor that the abuse did not negatively affect the victim. A parallel argument can be made that if the love of your life suddenly dies, and you receive tens of thousands of dollars from life insurance, money that you desperately need, this doesn't mean that you like the fact that your partner died or that you're not suffering from that loss. Liking that you have money to support you, or needing that money, does not change the basic fact of what happened, or how devastated you feel at the loss of your lover.

Children Can Feel Sexual Feelings

Given that children can feel sexual feelings and can be sexually stimulated during abuse, it's understandable that some children like the feelings of sexual arousal that can happen during abuse, however, that does not mean that they enjoy the abuse nor want to be abused or stimulated in that manner; they enjoyed their body's natural reactions and sensations, and perhaps some aspects of how the perpetrator treated them. If the abuser gave them attention or was kind to them, that may have felt enjoyable, too. It's also understandable if that child, later as an adult, feels upset if someone tells them that they couldn't have enjoyed any part of it because it was abuse. How does the adult survivor reconcile the reality that her/his body did feel sexual when they "weren't supposed" to? They feel guilty and ashamed. On the other hand, it's also understandable if that adult survivor feels upset about her/his body having felt aroused since it occurred in the context of abuse.

"Kali Munro goes on to explain *how to deal with* these issues." Almara looked up at Elvira.

The first step is to acknowledge to yourself how your body felt, and later to a supportive and understanding person. Try to do this without judgement, but if you can't, simply telling yourself and someone else (who is non-judgemental) how you felt will help reduce some of the guilt, shame, isolation, and secrecy. If you feel judgemental about yourself, remember that feelings are simply feelings, nothing more. They are not facts or statements; they do not say anything about you or anyone else, other than you are a fully feeling human being. It's normal to experience a range of feelings during abuse, and one of those feelings may be sexual. It might help to remember the other feelings you felt during or after the abuse because you did not simply feel sexual feelings, but you also probably felt betrayal, sadness, fear, confusion, and hurt even if you did not realize that until you were much older.

"Thank you, Ally." Elvira smiled at the beautiful Puerto Rican. "This knowledge is … it's amazing."

"I can finish reading if you like," Ally offered. "There's more."

Elvira yawned and stretched. "I'm getting tired – and very hungry. But we can read from it each time we pow-wow. It's monumentally helpful to hear – to know that your field didn't forget me. I'm not alone."

"The most important thing is to speak about it," Ally told her. "The more you talk about it, the easier it is to cope with. We'll see if we can locate this *Kali Munro* and perhaps find a group for us to join. It's not like we'll go run out and yell from a mountaintop or publish a book on it or anything. We'll Just –"

"Wait a minute," Nina said out loud from the kitchen as she checked on the chickens she'd been slow-roasting. She stood at the mouth of the kitchen to make her point. "Publishing a book might just be the best thing for baby girl … from a therapeutic standpoint as well as for the Montana Corporation," Nina suggested to Ally.

There was only silence for several long seconds.

"You're considering it," Ally stated accusatorily to Elvira.

"You gotta remember, Ally," Nina started, sitting back down in front of the two women, "she has video of the abuse … and she also has his journals which she says documents the intentional downing of a commercial airliner. A book like hers – think about it … It's a *New York Times* and *Essence Magazine* bestseller. Her story can correct one of this country's biggest lies – while everyone involved is still alive. We may not ever know who shot JFK but we know who the living monster is that brought down that airliner."

Nina had Ally and Elvira thinking.

"What better way to bring success to TMC than with a major book?" Nina stood back. "One hundred thirty-nine people dead – murdered – and their families were lied to. Fed some crock of bull mess about involuntary intoxication? Elvira … you will sell *millions* of books, grab tremendous headlines worldwide for free advertising, fame, recognition, justice for those poor families, justice for society, and justice for you."

Ally held up the Kali Munro printout. "This issue you suffer from – being aroused during abuse, sexual feelings from your abuser – can be thrust into the national spotlight instead of it being swept and kept under the rug."

Nina and Ally looked at Elvira.

"Elvira?" Nina had a hand on her hip.

"Whaddaya want from me?"

"I think it's time we took a good long look at the evidence," Ally stated. "The journals and the videotapes."

Elvira stood up. "I really need to think on it some more. I'm not saying no. I'm just … jittery. I'm also so hungry that I can eat a horse."

"We don't have a horse," Nina told her as they all went into the dining area to eat. "But we do have chicken."

CHAPTER THIRTY-ONE

La Hacienda de Sosa
Cochabamba, Bolivia
September 17, 1984

Gunshots rang out over the mountaintop paradise and echoed for miles throughout the valleys, streams, and rivers below. Alberto's casket had been lowered into the ground and the men each took a turn tossing a shovel full of the thick cement mixture in on top. The cement was added protection from any wild animals, or even people, attempting to disturb the grave. By this time the men, and many of the women, had several swigs of the potent whiskey and tequila being passed around. Hundreds of bullets were being pumped into the sky, in classic Latin American tradition, to send Alberto off.

"Hey, Sosa," Gonzalo Rodriguez Gacha called over to Sosa as people continued to empty clips into the air.

"José Gonzalo Rodriguez-Gacha," Sosa said to the straw-hat-wearing rancher. *"Alias 'El Mexicano.' ¿Que pasó?"*

"You have a beautiful home here," Gonzalo complimented him as Pablo Escobar waddled over to them. "It's a palace."

"Thank you." Sosa shared shots of whiskey with the men.

"The women you have outnumber the men," Pablo stated mischievously. "All due respect, Alex, but they are all yours?"

"Actually, the men outnumber the women," Sosa corrected him. "Most of my men are still with your men, participating in the hurricane aid. But these women are mine, yes. Intimately, no. You interested?"

"Well ..." Pablo trailed off. "Our wives are safely away in Panama. We want *girls*, you have *women*. Most are very sexy but ..."

"How old should they be?"

"Fifteen," Pablo answered. "They're never a problem."

"Rafa!" Sosa called over to Rafa, who was reloading an M-16. "Stop wasting bullets and come over here!"

Rafa slung the rifle over his shoulder and walked up to the three men, facing Sosa. "*¿Señor?*"

"Make a call and have about a dozen fifteen-year-olds transported here," Sosa ordered. "Be sure they're no younger than that because they'll lie for the money. Our friends here are bored and want a party with them. You know who to call. Don't haggle over the costs. *¿Está claro?* (Is that clear)"

"Sure, boss," Rafa said, looking at Pablo and Gonzalo. "China girls, Spanish, Argentine, Black?"

"All of those," Pablo said as he produced a large roll of *pesos*.

"Guests do not pay, Pablo," Sosa declined the gesture.

"*Permiso*," Rafa excused himself.

The crowd took the party to the center swimming pool area of the Pentagon and the house staff served delicious food and drinks to everyone. Sosa used the opportunity to meet privately with the men that he did not always have the luxury of meeting with at one sitting. When they were all seated inside of his basement study, he even said as much.

"This is a sad occasion but a rare one as well," Sosa started as the men each accepted small glasses of whiskey and cigars from their host. Some declined cigars, opting to smoke cigarettes instead.

Nancho, Tato, Benny, and Javier stood around on the outskirts, so to say, while the rest of the men sat in a circle around a table during the meeting. Clockwise, starting on Sosa's left, sat General Cucombre, General Banzer, General Garcia Meza, General Ariel Bleyer, and Colonel Arce Gomez.

"It is indeed a sad occasion when we lose one of us," Cucombre agreed as he lit his cigar with a wooden match. "But let's hope that we can prevent anything like this from ever happening again."

"Let's," said Ariel Bleyer, Bolivian Minister of the Interior. "Did we see this coming?"

General Cucombre shifted in his seat. "You mean Gutiérrez?"

Ariel nodded once.

"I have to admit, we had him in our sights," the dour, ruthless-looking Bolivian Minster of Defense answered. "He was on our radar and he was being looked at by DOD Intelligence Division. He'd always been an outspoken reporter on the human rights issues, the 1980 '*Cocaine Coup*' and various military crackdowns on protestors. What we didn't realize was his political alliances in Washington and at the UN in New York had gained some momentum. He'd been ranting and raving – intelligently so, I must add – to Washington congressmen and senators about what we, the Bolivian government, had been doing with the cocaine. He told them how the U.S. ignore their own laws and how, if they enforced those laws, it would stem the cocaine flow into the U.S."

"What do you mean '*laws*'?" Arce Gomez inquired. "He pointed to specific laws?"

"You know," Cucombre spoke quickly. "He read to them, on the House of Congress floor, the '*Single Convention on Narcotic Drugs.*' That's one. In the UN he was claiming violation of the '*United Nations Convention Against Illicit*

Traffic in Narcotic Drugs and Psychotropic Substances.' His big one was at that damned speech he gave before the UN General Assembly where he claimed that the U.S. was violating the 1970 Controlled Substances Act by turning a blind eye to CIA activity in Central and South America ... pointing to Bolivian cocaine exports."

A brief pause swept through the room. Sosa looked at the Toros, who knew what he was thinking.

"What I've been wondering is how did he come to know about that?" Sosa wondered aloud. "How did he get that type of information?"

"There's quite a few people involved," said Cucombre, "including the Medellín and Cali Cartels. They're both sophisticated in many ways but they're wild cowboys. Pablo ran for Congress. They talk a lot. *He* talks a lot."

Sosa took a deep breath and chugged back the rest of his whiskey. "The point of this meeting is to prevent this type of embarrassment from ever reoccurring. I won't get into each detail of what we are doing in Nicaragua other than we are playing both sides of the fence up there, which is inherently dangerous ... There's the Contras we use to guard our airstrip in Managua and the Sandinistas we use to facilitate shipments on the Mosquito Coast. Managua is critical for our western U.S. loads and the Mosquito Coast is critical for our Gulf State loads. In other words, we're talking about thirty thousand pounds of merch per month if we lose the route."

"Do you think we should intervene in the war?" Bleyer suggested with the question.

"The U.S. would like to see the Sandinistas fall," Sosa explained, lighting his cigar. "But Reagan is sending mixed messages. He stands for the Contras but he can't quite get Congress to fund them. In fact, I was reading *The New York Times* and saw that Congress passed that *Boland Amendment* we've been hearing about."

"Which prohibits direct Contra funding," Cucombre added. "We heard that, too. Let's talk about this."

"This isn't our fight," Sosa told them. "However, it will work for us in a variety of ways. While Nicaragua is at war with itself, we win. Why? *Primero*, there are Reagan's public displays of affection for the Contra rebels. *Segundo*, word has reached us that the CIA are still inside of the country at either the behest of those inside of the Reagan Administration, those congressional leaders who voted against the Boland Amendment, or Reagan himself."

"That helps how?" Garcia Meza asked.

Sosa scratched his left cheekbone area. "The only reason the CIA could have for being in Nicaragua is to help the Contra rebels with what? Logistics, weapons, air raids – maybe even a few men on the ground. Snipers. Reconnaissance aircraft, I'm certain. You're talking *millions* in funding needed. If the U.S. is involved, you're getting the best they have in tech and weapon support. It's a war the U.S. wants to see the Contra rebels win. So where's the money coming from since the Boland Amendment prohibited funding? From the CIA's take-home pay? From their children's piggy banks?"

The men all chuckled as they looked around at each other. They knew what Sosa was implying.

"Are you saying that the CIA will assist in illegal drug trafficking?" Ariel Bleyer inquired incredulously.

"You're the Bolivian Minister of the Interior," Sosa reminded him. "The CIA killed Kennedy and have committed more crimes than *Hitler* and *Bubonic Plague* combined. They're people, Ariel, and you know what I think about people."

Ariel waited for him to elaborate.

Sosa said simply, "We're all corrupt ... Leave it up to me. We'll adjourn for now and I'll get back to you shortly."

The meeting was adjourned.

"Tato," Sosa said in a low voice. "Where's the Nicaraguan at? Cabayo?"

A smile spread across Tato's face. "The '*Gang Plan,*' *jefe?*"

"Ah, Tatico," Sosa said, walking Tato to the door with an arm around his shoulder. "It's bigger than that now."

Tato exited the study wondering what was going on in that wizard's mind of Sosa's.

CHAPTER THIRTY-TWO

Elvira Montana
New Rochelle, New York
October 23, 1984

"Scarsdale is yours, Mrs. Montana." Epstein reported the great news to Elvira in an early morning telephone call. "There's no city or county ordinance preventing you from creating your own private lake. Bronxville is quite another matter. Their town ordinance *limits* homeowners to a five-hundred-foot-long lake. You want a fifteen-hundred-foot-long lake, which is the length of five NFL football fields."

"We need to meet as soon as possible." Elvira was looking at her ladies Longines watch. "While the day is young you should make your way on over to discuss architecture and development with me."

"First things first," he stated, cautious. "You should be heading to your real estate agent's office to get that property purchased and loan secured."

"You're behind the times, Mr. Epstein, I already own them," Elvira said, sounding insouciant.

"'*Them*,'" he repeated. "What do you mean, '*them*'?"

"The Bronxville estate *and* the Scarsdale property," she stated. When a moment passed without comment, she spoke again. "One of my assistants, Ally, read a *New York Times* report on how Westchester County was one of America's richest counties and a sound prediction about real estate prices rising. The Montana Corporation is officially open and we want in. Get down here, Epstein. Time is something I don't have a lot of before the birth of my baby."

"I'll be there in an hour."

$$$$$

Around the same time Epstein and Elvira were completing the architecture and design plans for her Scarsdale estate, the butterfly doors of Almara's black Murcielago were popping open in front of the new office headquarters of The Montana Corporation located in the prestigious but obscure Greenlee Executive Office Park on Main Street in New Rochelle. Pulling up and parking next to her in her sporty gold Mercedes SL was Nina. Three white female administrative office assistants walked out of the four-story building which housed TMC to help Ally and Nina haul boxes of office supplies inside.

"Good thinking, Tabitha," Ally mentioned to the blond assistant who donned a stylish burgundy leather knee-length dress by *Dior*, white stockings, and high black leather boots. "Glad you brought that pushcart down because these boxes are heavy!"

Nina and Ally stood by as the three young office workers removed various bags and boxes from the trunk, floor, and seats of the Mercedes and from the front seat of the Lamborghini.

"A hundred forty-five grand and that *thing* can only carry two banker's boxes," Nina teased Ally for buying the Lamborghini.

"You wanna race me?" Ally shot back. "For your next paycheck?"

"Yeah, right." Nina turned her eyes back to the assistants. "Tabby, Savanna, Krystal … y'all look *nice*. Let us see you."

The three women blushed and showed off their new clothes to their supervisors.

"Krystal," Ally said to the thin girl with black hair, "just because you're thin doesn't mean you can't sashay like curvier women. When men look at us walk, it's not the curves he's always thinking of. He's thinking of what we *have* that makes us sashay as if we have what's best for him. Pop that little booty out, move that little thing with confidence. You were hired because of your office skills but also because you're hot."

Krystal grinned at the comments. "Thank you, Ms. Quijano."

They all walked up the handicap accessible ramp and into the front entrance in lieu of taking the concrete stairs. Elvira, Nina, and Ally had, thus far, already hired 79 employees to help run the company. All of whom already had substantial experience in administrative office management, business administration, publishing, accounting, sales, legal services, advertising, quality assurance, short-term planning, long-term planning, investigative services, real estate, land development, investment banking, the stock market, fashion and design, and more. Elvira was not naïve. She knew that in order to be the best, she had to hire the best team. Nina and Ally were professionals in their fields but not skilled enough to be given corporate titles such as CEO or CFO.

"No disrespect, girls," Elvira had told them weeks earlier. "Not even Elvira Montana would call herself *Chief Executive Officer* or *Chief Financial Officer*. Those titles come with great risk and responsibility. Would I purchase the Yankees from George Steinbrenner and play first base? No, I'd leave that to Don Mattingly. I could *own* the Yankees but I couldn't *manage* them. I'd go out and hire a manager – like Billy Martin. Same with TMC. All I can do is *own* the team. You two will assist me in that ownership and for your services you will each be given a five-percent stake in the team and paid an executive's salary once we get TMC HQ fully staffed: two hundred fifty thousand dollars per year for your salaries … but you won't have titles."

They were nowhere close to completing the short-term plan for TMC's headquarters. Office space in the building would allow them a minimum of 260 employees so they were almost at one-third capacity. Nina and Ally moved aggressively forward to fill the vacant positions in the company by running full-page ads in *The New York Times*, *USA Today*, television and radio slots. Nina and Ally allowed the managers in the company's human resources department to conduct the interviews of personnel hired for the non-executive positions without any interference. They merely acted as observers during the interview but behind closed doors Nina and Ally had all the say …

"Elvira wants highly skilled, educated, and experienced, Ally, not just good looks," Nina reminded her a time or two.

"The boss says a hot *frontline* will determine the company's *bottom line*," Ally would come back. "If a chick is hot and educated at Columbia University's School of Business, then we can train her. We're operating off of the concept of sex sells without actually selling sex."

"We need *experienced* frontline people," Nina would insist. "I think you're making your judgments based on the type of girl you'd make it with."

"Is that jealousy I hear?"

"No, dummy," Nina had to laugh. "Let me choose the chicks. I want bigger dividend checks each quarter with the bonuses."

As the two women walked into the 4th-floor office of the company CEO – Natalia Navickova – they respectfully paused at the lip of the open office while the sultry, well-dressed CEO finished up a conference call she was having on speakerphone. Natalia quietly waved Nina and Ally to sit down in two black leather cushioned chairs situated in front of the enormous desk.

At 42 years old Natalia was still a very beautiful woman. Born in Crimea, Ukraine, to well-to-do parents, she had been educated in France and later at Princeton, where she'd obtained her master's degree in Microeconomics. She had begun her illustrious career at Rutgers University as a financial aid officer but that had been way below her speed. She had had her sights set on Wall Street and that's where she'd ended up: at JPMorgan Chase, where she had started out as an assistant and moved on up to various management positions, overseeing a great number of foreign and domestic corporate investment accounts. However, just like the majority of women in the American workforce, no matter how hard she worked, she made less than a man with the same qualification level as she. As a result of that gender discrimination, there were many instances where she'd been bypassed for a promotion to an executive position. The glass ceiling was there to haunt her without ceasing until the day she'd seen the *New York Times* ad seeking "female executives only" for TMC. Elvira was the only one with the power to hire and fire executives.

"I want the Crimean chick," Elvira had told the girls after the interview. "She's edgy, bossy, very experienced, sexy, and angry. Get 'Investigations' on her immediately because I told her to come back in three days. She's been scorned and has everything to prove if given the right chance."

In three days Natalia Navickova was CEO and President of The Montana Corporation.

"Ladies," Natalia smiled at the two co-owners of TMC. "What can I do for you?"

"Elvira's shopping around for helicopters and jets." Ally laid out several brochures on the desk in front of the blue-eyed executive with the long, black, wavy hair that seemed to flow forever down her back. "TMC will get a helicopter and a jet. She said you all should be the ones to select what aircraft best fits the needs of TMC now and for the foreseeable future."

"Goody." Natalia took the brochures, looked briefly at them, and dropped them into a desk drawer. "One moment, please."

She used two of the three computers she had on her desk, typing in some information on both keyboards. Natalia could be heard cursing in her accented English, which caused Ally and Nina to laugh.

"What's so fonny?" Natalia shot at them.

Nina laughed. "The way you talk and say the word 'funny.' You say *fonny*."

"Have you heard your words lately, Miss China and *Jamekka*?" Natalia teased Nina back. "Come, I show you the set-*op*."

Nina and Ally stood behind her.

"I am hired to run company," she began. "TMC wants to stay in the big money so I *mosst* keep my eyes on where we *are* investing ... and where we *should* be investing. These three computers are okay for me but not enough for me to do *best* job. I need to have *big* monitors so I can watch ... *major indexes:* Dow Jones, NASDAQ, S&P 500, and Russell 2000. I'm watching S&P's top 500 biggest gainers and losers on one *small* screen. On the second screen: Top 10 Mutual Funds; Top 10 Exchange Traded Funds; Interest Rates and Mortgage Rates; Commodities; Foreign Currencies; Foreign Markets. The third computer is for office use. I'm not satisfied this."

Ally took a deep breath. "I don't get it."

"I do," Nina stated as the beautiful CEO turned to face them. "She needs an entire room dedicated to the stock market. She has to see these major indexes, company ticker symbols and such, as she did at JPMorgan. She needs a state-of-the-art setup."

"Boss *geev* us green light to invest so we're going for the bank," Natalia elaborated. "To get the bank Ms. Navickova *mosst* see *everything on wall* and state-of-the-art monitors. *Beeg.*"

"Bigger than life," Ally nodded and picked up the phone. "We get it. Let me call the boss."

Ally called Elvira and explained the problem.

"Do it," Elvira ordered. "There's an entire building for lease across the parking lot from TMC. We need it anyway for our modeling agency, studios, et cetera. Set her up there – anything she needs. She's the one who put it in my head to create our own brokerage firm. Do it."

Ally hung up the telephone. "You get a second office and an entire floor across the street. Get that equipment ordered and set up yesterday. Come on, Nina. We need to get that building leased. Satisfied *now*, Natalia?"

The bossy Crimean woman looked at Ally. "Never have I been satisfied. Not even after hot bath, orgasm, cigarette, and vodka."

Nina and Ally left the office laughing.

CHAPTER THIRTY-THREE

La Hacienda de Sosa
Cochabamba, Bolivia
September 17, 1984

"Can you fight?" Sosa challenged the Nicaraguan gangster from inside of the boxing ring in the basement level sports complex.

"*Sí, patrón*," the brown-skinned, tattooed man replied as he observed Sosa working out with Tato, whose chiseled, hulk-like body resembled a Grecian statue of the war god Mars. Sosa, although smaller than Tato, was fit and powerfully built, too. Both men were wearing black boxing shorts and boxing gloves, perspiration pouring from their bodies.

"Good," Sosa said as Tato gave the young man a pair of boxing gloves and clean boxing shorts, gold in color. "Every person in my organization is highly-skilled and fit. Let's fight. I'll use Thai boxing. You?"

"Fighting." That was all the man said as Tato assisted him in securing the boxing gloves.

Yesenia, Rafa, Nancho, Javier, and Benny came in and sat on the bleachers to watch the duel.

The two men squared off and the match began. Sosa held up both arms, fists clenched high, and advanced. Cabayo, who was left-handed, threw two jabs at Sosa, which Sosa easily defended by smacking them both away. Thai boxing is

50% feet and 50% hands. Sosa's feet were dangerous, which was proven when he jumped and landed the ball of his left foot into the upper lip and nose of an unexpecting Cabayo, who stumbled backwards but did not fall.

"Alejandro," his wife whined, not wanting him to take advantage of the African-American-Nicaraguan. "Go easy, *Papi*."

Sosa had heard her but he did not heed her. Cabayo, regrouping, got into a southpaw boxing stance – right hand and right foot leading – and stalked Sosa, trying to set Sosa up with right-handed jabs. Cabayo threw a flurry of punches, hitting Sosa in the abdomen and right cheekbone. Sosa came back with a right hammer punch to the top of Cabayo's head and a left knee to Cabayo's rib cage, knocking the air out of him. Sosa noticed the injury and landed another knee to the left side of Cabayo's face, knocking him out on the mat. Yesenia winced.

"Hey, boy." Sosa kneeled down, shaking Cabayo awake.

Tato helped Cabayo sit up.

"You okay?" Sosa asked him.

Cabayo nodded. "Yeah. I was down there thinking."

"Thinking." Sosa and Tato chuckled.

Yesenia shook her head.

"You smoke cigarettes," Sosa said to him. "I smell them in your sweat. You're out of shape. I beat you easily."

"Weed, cigarettes, stress, beer …" Cabayo stood up. "A lot of women."

"I found out about you," Sosa said as he removed his and Cabayo's gloves. "In my organization you have to be ready, *chico*. Come."

The men sat in the Jacuzzi and had a discussion over cold drinks and fruit. Sosa spoke frankly to Cabayo.

"This cop you killed – was he dirty?" Sosa asked him.

"More than that," Cabayo replied. "He was a rogue; gone all the way bad. Six shootings in five months; four people died out of the six."

"Can you prove the dirt?"

Tato, Nancho, Javier, Benny, and Rafa sat on benches and chairs in the room, listening.

"Nothing solid." Cabayo shook his head in exasperation.

"I know you have friends and family in Nicaragua," Sosa told him. "You informed my associates at ASC headquarters that you were my family and you had an emergency."

"Lying was the only way," Cabayo admitted. "I went through hell getting through Mexico … shaking the FBI off my tail. It took me two weeks to get to La Paz. I have no documents."

He explained his long trek through Central America and how he had been assisted by his MS-13 associates in Guatemala to get to Panama. He had run out of cash and had to trade off pieces of his jewelry to stow away on a ship that carried pigs and cattle from Panama to Colombia. From Colombia he'd hitched rides all the way from Medellín to Bogotá, and from there to Loja, Ecuador. He had stolen a horse in Loja and it had taken him all the way to Pucallpa, Peru, where he had met a beautiful farm girl. The two had lain together all night in a barn, and in the morning she had disappeared. So had the horse.

Sosa and his men burst out laughing.

"Let me get this right, *hombre*," Javi said as he stood by the Jacuzzi. "She rode you around in the hay and then she rode off with your horse?"

"*Sí*," Cabayo nodded. "But I stole another one. He was smaller, with big ears."

"You mean a donkey?" Sosa was laughing so hard he was in tears at the story.

"Yeah, a really slow one."

"So you eventually make it to La Paz," Sosa stated once he and his men finally got their laughter under control. "Who told you to come to me? And what made you think I could or would help you?"

"The streets talk." Cabayo looked him in the eyes. "A Mexican woman with cartel links supplied my people with Colombian coke that was flown into a flight school strip in Las Cruces, New Mexico."

Sosa looked at his men, then back at Cabayo. "Las Cruces. Go on."

"We did the deal; thirty kilos," Cabayo explained. "Fat girl, not that pretty, not that bad either. I met with her in L.A. about a week later. We screw, party a bit, and she said that Tony Montana was your partner and the Colombians didn't like it. Neither did the Mexican cartels."

"This woman," Sosa said, thinking it over. "She mentions me and when you get into all this trouble ... you travel thousands of miles of jungles and wetlands ... to me?"

"Let me explain," Cabayo stated, squirming in the hot bubbling water. "She also said that it was Bolivia ... probably *you*, who supplies the Colombian and Mexicans with merch. They don't have the lands nor the ability to grow coca crops. Mr. Sosa, the way I see it, your organization can monopolize the coke flow in America and cut the Colombians and the Mexicans out."

Sosa got out of the Jacuzzi. "Cabayo ... you speak faster than you think. First, whoever this woman is, she won't last. The Colombians and Mexicans are on the front line, facing a high-tech foe with an economy in the double-digit *trillions*. That country loves wars; we don't. I won't cut out the Colombians nor the Mexicans because then we'll have a war with them. They are a relentless force who pays us hundreds of millions every time we do business. Now, I'm all for making more money and I know for a fact that those cokeheads up there want more. Sure, about eighty percent of the merch flowing north comes from Bolivia and we're cornering the market here. We sell cocaine paste to the Colombians, Mexicans, and many of the smaller groups and individuals who we deal with. Now ... you."

Sosa accepted the towel Nancho gave to him.

"Yes, Mr. Sosa?"

"I've heard of your leadership position in the MS-13," Sosa said as he left the area with all of the men following him up into his bedroom, where he disappeared into the bathroom. The shower came on for several minutes.

"What's he going to do with me?" Cabayo asked Tato.

Tato shrugged and answered, "Do I look like I read minds?"

Sosa returned fully dressed in white Armani linen slacks and a white shirt. "I have heard of the MS-13 ... Tato, the file. Will you please bring it to me?"

Tato excused himself and returned minutes later with a thick file in his hand. Sosa opened it and read it. Miguel "Cabayo" Ibañez was certainly the real deal. He was born a bastard, never having known his father – and the worst part was probably that his Nicaraguan mother had not known him either. All she'd known was that Cabayo's father had been the man she'd slept with before he had returned to the U.S. Navy. He had been an African-American, which was what had made Cabayo a U.S. citizen, having been born in East Los Angeles. His mother had returned to Nicaragua, where Cabayo had grown up until he was seventeen, and he had chosen to run cocaine into the U.S. for MS-13 gang leaders from El Salvador who had set up shop in Managua, Nicaragua. Hence, his status now as MS-13.

Cabayo had never been caught smuggling drugs and, subsequently, he'd became a full-fledged member of the gang. Because of his ruthlessness and violent ways, he'd earned the respect of the most feared gangs in L.A., Guatemala, El Salvador, and his own native Nicaragua. He had been jailed 32 times but charges had never stuck. The witnesses had always been murdered or intimidated into not testifying. Now, 29 years old, he was on the run for a cop killing.

"The FBI wrote this report." Sosa showed everyone a sheet of paper with Cabayo's photo on it. "They write: '*MS-13 is the gang that has the FBI most worried. Mara Salvatrucha is the most dangerous gang in the country at this point. Originating in El Salvador, the gang has gone transnational, with members across the United States and in countries like Nicaragua, Guatemala, and Mexico. MS-13 has worked with Mexican drug cartels and communicates frequently with incarcerated members despite no official leadership structure. The gang is notoriously violent, relentlessly cruel and merciless, with plenty of well-documented public crimes, such as a San Francisco member who killed a family for briefly blocking his car. Though the gang is in the FBI's 1984 Gang Assessment, the FBI has a separate section and an MS-13 Task Force dedicated to stopping the group and alerting the public to the threat it poses.*'" Sosa paused to look at Cabayo. "You, my African-American-Nicaraguan friend, are *Number Ten* on the FBI's Top Ten *Most Wanted Fugitives List.*"

Cabayo nodded nonchalantly. "That cop had it comin'."

"Maybe so," Sosa said, walking up to Cabayo. "Even with your legal problems, we have work for you. How well do you know Nicaragua?"

"Like I know me."

"Okay. I have much to do," Sosa told him. "Prepare yourself mentally for plastic surgery and tattoo removal. You need to change identities."

Cabayo took a deep, nervous breath as Sosa left him there to think about the mystery of what was to come.

CHAPTER THIRTY-FOUR

Elvira Montana
New Rochelle, New York
October 25, 1984

Almara and Nina followed the red carpet into the popular *Latin Quarters* nightclub in Manhattan. Tonight entry was by invite-only due to the club being reserved as one of the after-parties of the *MTV Music Video Awards*, which had been held at Madison Square Garden. All that the L.Q. security needed to see out of Almara and Nina was their top-of-the-line Lamborghini pull up behind Madonna's white Mercedes stretch limo with Almara waving and saying hello to Madonna. Almara took the ticket from the valet and held Nina's hand as they went on inside.

The upstairs sections were as tightly packed as the downstairs sections. People were everywhere, standing around, dancing to the latest Michael Jackson hit, expensive champagne was flowing nonstop, the bars were inaccessible due to all of the partygoers crowding them, and all of the club's tables, booths, and sitting areas were at full capacity.

Nina drank Dom Perignon. Each time her glass looked empty, it would be refilled by the club's floor waiters almost instantly. Almara danced with her and several others she met. For a short time they had even gotten separated and Nina had gone into a bit of a panic because men kept approaching her, touching her, and being rude. She frantically searched for the exit when locating Almara seemed impossible. As she walked up a few stairs, away from one of the dance floor areas, she saw Almara and a really good-looking Black male kissing and pawing all over each other in a corner booth. His left arm was around her shoulder and his right hand was up her dress.

"Ally!" Nina yelled over the loud music, pulling on her. "Let's go!"

Ally looked up at her, as did the muscular model type she was latched on to. "Why?" Ally wanted to know.

"I just want to go!" Nina said irritatedly.

Ally was obviously into the sweet man she was with. "Duke, don't move! Let me speak to my friend!"

"I'll just take a cab, mon!" Nina spun around and started making her way through the crowd.

"Nina!" Ally called out to her. She caught up to Nina, grabbing her hand and stopping her. "What's your problem?"

"Can we please leave?!" Nina cried. "I just want to go!"

"I *needed* that man tonight!" Ally complained as they walked out of the club. The valet brought them their vehicle and Almara drove off. "Man!" she lamented frustratedly.

$$$$$

New Rochelle Police Department Officer Jack Gordon was now also head of security for Elvira. He knocked on her bedroom door and she invited him in.

"Ma'am," he said as he shut the door behind him. "We finally gathered the information on not only who was surveilling you but who had hired them. Initially, it proved difficult to uncover who the client was so what we ended up doing was placing a phone tap on his home and office telephones. We came up with the name of an attorney named Sheffield. George Sheffield of Miami Beach. Ring a bell, ma'am?"

"That'll be all, Mr. Gordon," she dismissed him. "Thank you."

$$$$$

It was 1 a.m. by the time the low rumble of the Lamborghini engine was heard pulling into the silent, well-lit Davenport Marina parking lot. Nina was feeling a whole lot better after explaining how rude the drunken men were acting at the Latin Quarter. They parked and made their way to the super-yacht, where they took showers and called it a night. The champagne had gotten to Nina and she fell asleep in Elvira's master stateroom bed at nearly the same moment her head hit the pillow.

Nina was startled awake when Almara climbed into the bed with her, saying, "I hope you don't mind ... it's cold in our room."

"Go to sleep," Nina whispered tiredly.

Ally had other plans. She watched the beautiful angelic-faced Nina as she re-closed her chinky eyes. Ally gently ran her fingers through Nina's cute reddish-brown hair and, after softly tracing love lines across the contours of Nina's face, kissed her full pink lips. Almara placed slow, soft pecks on Nina's cheeks, across her ear, and down her warm, slender neck.

"You smell so warm and sweet, China," Ally whispered as she continued to lay lazy lover's kisses to her friend's neck. "I need you tonight. You need me?"

"I told you no ..." Nina protested weakly. "We can be friends, but not this."

Almara smoothly moved her hands underneath the flimsy pink silk nightgown and massaged the Chinese-Jamaican beauty in an area every woman would appreciate: the lower back. Almara had Nina moaning blissfully for several

287

minutes. Almara managed to pull the entire nightgown off of Nina. Then, her moist $500 silk panties.

"Ally, we can't!" Nina turned to her, clutching onto the sheets to cover her nudity. "You're taking advantage of me because I was drinking ... and I'm tired. Stop, Ally. I said *no!*"

Ally had removed her own clothes, revealing her own awesome beauty. She pulled at the covers that Nina was holding onto for dear life. "Your panties ... they tell a different story, *mamita*."

"Ally, don't!" Her hands covered her round perky breasts. "Stop!"

Ally laid more sweet kisses onto Nina's lips, face, and neck, snatching away the covers. "Hey! *You* stop!"

Nina looked confused as Ally climbed on top of her, their warm bodies fused, skin to skin. "Stop what? Ally, I said no! *Get off me!*"

"Nina!" Ally grabbed her hands, stopping Nina from pushing and hitting her. "Okay, okay, *okay!!* Look at me! Look me in the eyes!"

"What?" Nina looked at Ally.

Ally was tearful. "You clearly said no. You can tell the world you said no. I heard you. But I love you. Okay? You won't like it. Just stay put. I know you won't like it."

Nina stayed frozen. "Ally ... *don't* ... *please* ..."

Despite her resistance Nina quickly became a helpless mass of something she no longer had control of. The flame was lit and, soon, the fire spread. Some fires could burn themselves out; others could not.

$$$$$

Nina was the first to awake. When she did, she came very close to having a heart attack at what she was seeing. Almara was tied up, nude, with her hands behind her back; her ankles were tied to the front legs of a cushioned non-movable chair next to the stateroom door, and her mouth was gagged with duct tape. On the sofa nearest to the bed was a man: Latino, ugly, mean scowl, pockmarked face with a burn scar along the left side that had melted off his ear. He wore dark shades, all black clothing, black Stetson cowboy hat, black leather knuckle gloves, black leather biker boots, and a long leather trench coat.

Pointing a nicotine-stained finger at Nina, he said, "Shut up or I'll cut your throat. Go to your lover there and take your panties out of her mouth."

Shaking and crying, Nina got up with the bedsheet wrapped around her.

"Drop the sheet," he commanded her.

She did as he commanded, revealing her cocoa butter-colored body. She peeled the tape off of Almara's face and pulled the silk panties out of her mouth, imagining how he'd forced them there.

"Who the hell – ?" Almara gasped for fresh air.

"Be quiet," he ordered in what Almara thought was a Cuban accent. "Chinese girl, put your panties on."

Nina hurriedly did as she was told, not caring that the panties were soaked with Almara's saliva.

"Untie her," he ordered, throwing her the knife.

Nina cut through the ropes, freeing Almara.

"Both of you, get dressed." He pulled out a silenced .32 semi-automatic. "Toss the knife back to me, Chinese girl. When you're done sit here on the bed and face me."

Moments later they both sat, hands idle, facing him.

"Stop crying, Chinese girl, I'm not here to hurt you or rape you." He scratched his melted-off ear with the barrel end of the silenced weapon. "You're probably wondering how I got the burn scar, huh?"

"If you're not here to hurt us …" Almara stared at him. "Then why are you here?"

"*No questions!!*" he boomed at them. "The scar first. Okay?"

Almara nodded and held Nina's hand.

"I fought in the war," he growled. "In Cuba, against Castro. The Castro army used phosphorus shells on us. Do you know what Phosphorus is?"

The girls shook their heads, frightened to speak to the assassin.

"A highly reactive, poisonous, non-metallic element mostly used in safety matches, pyrotechnics, and fertilizers." He sat forward. "And incendiary bombs and shells ... We were riding on horses in the forests of Las Tunas, Cuba, when the dark skies suddenly lit up so bright we were blinded instantly. The phosphorus came down like rain but it was fire that rained. See, phosphorus – the fifteenth element – is what God will use to destroy us ... and the earth, when Christ returns. The phosphorus is not earthly fire. It touches the skin and burns straight through to the bone. It killed all of us except sixteen. That is sixteen out of seventy-five men on horses. All the horses died. For a year after the fire-rain I felt lava flow on my face. Now what I feel are fingers of a baby touching me there. Very strange, hm?"

He stood up and holstered his weapon. He walked toward the door and paced back and forth with one hand in the trench coat pocket, the other rubbing the scraggly black beard on his face.

"I've been watching Elvira for weeks," he went on as he continued to pace. "Trying to figure out the best way to deliver to her this message from Miami. I was glad to see the security guards and all the holes in their ... strategy. Even the men guarding this magnificent vessel were easy to bypass once I saw you come in last night. The ship's crew ... loud radios, noise ... they never heard anything. Watching you two 69'ing was a sight to behold ... You should feel lucky that I'm not a rapist. Only a killer."

Nina squirmed as he approached her and held her chin up. "Yeah," he gave her a wicked grin. "I saw her tongue slide … right … inside … of … your … hairless … little … anus. And yours into hers. I never did understand how two men could want each other … but two women? It's very obvious. Look at youse. Do you both like men?"

Almara and Nina nodded, both uncomfortable.

"Over women?"

They nodded yes again.

"My point exactly." He lit up a smoke, a Pall Mall. "Cigarette?"

"We don't smoke," Almara nervously declined.

"*Chica*," he said to her, "if I were ever asked what was more dangerous, cigarettes or *chocha*, I'd say *chocha*. More fights have been started, more wars have begun, and more men have died over women than all deaths from tobacco combined. *Chocha* … it's just soooo gooood, right?"

Almara and Nina, frightened, quickly nodded.

"I was hired by some very powerful men." He finally got to the point. "*Gaspar Gomez, Nacho Contreras, The Diaz Brothers – Nolo and Vito*. They have a copy of Mrs. Montana's tax settlement. They know all about the hundred million dollars-plus left behind by the late Scarface. Well, my two little *chocha*-lickers, they are willing to settle, too. With *fifty million dollars*. There will be no negotiations. She has seventy-two hours … then I'll start killing."

He dropped an envelope and exited the room. And just like that it was all over. The creepy man had exited the stateroom.

CHAPTER THIRTY-FIVE

La Hacienda de Sosa
Cochabamba, Bolivia
September 18, 1984

At 4 a.m. the following morning, after a small breakfast, Sosa was filled in (via the SAT-phone) about all the developments on the ground by one of his paramilitary commanders. The commander gave Sosa a synopsis of what was taking place in lieu of a point-by-point accounting. Sosa learned that the distribution of aid was going well and that more and more assistance was arriving, particularly by Bolivia's regional allies: Suriname, Ecuador, Paraguay, Brazil, and Venezuela.

"The Americans there yet?" Sosa demanded to know.

"No, *Señor*," the commander replied. "The UN are here and Red Cross, along with a handful of Bolivian allies. I have been hearing that the U.S. is trying to get clearance for seven hundred fifty aid workers to be allowed into Tarija but they're haggling with the President over something. The body-count, from our estimate so far, is three hundred eighty-nine; half of them are children. Our refrigerated trucks will be left with the stench, boss."

"Bleach and pine will fix that. Any other problems?"

"Pablo's men exchanged gunfire with Shining Path," the paramilitary commander informed him. "They killed one SP guerrilla and they're holding another wounded SP."

"Have him executed. Is that it?"

"*Sí, Señor.*"

Sosa, dressed in a black hooded sweatshirt, exited the mansion and jogged all the way to the far western end of the massive property to the barns and horse stables. His determined eyes scanned the pig pen to see if he could find a medium-sized pig – one that was under 200 pounds. There were several dozen of them but they were all much too large. He moved past the llamas, guanacos, and vicuñas to the goats. They sauntered right up to him, wanting to be fed and petted like house cats. He picked up a young male goat that was approximately 110 pounds and carried him away.

"*Bueno, jefe,*" stated one of his closest soldiers.

"Buro," Sosa nodded his way. With Buro were eight other soldiers and six of Sosa's prized Presa Canarios, including his favorite. Noses was the alpha beast who'd fought with a wild Andean jaguar and lived to tell about it. Sosa looked at his men. "Leave the dogs behind, they'll frighten the birds."

Sosa broke the neck of the young goat and slung its lifeless body over his shoulder. He began to run as fast as he could northwards, down the mountain. The head of the goat bobbled behind him as he picked up speed along a narrow trail that curved left into the dense forest and, after a half mile or so, led him back up the mountain. A dense forest fog had crawled over the El Chaparé mountain region but it did not have any effect on Sosa's sense of direction. He stayed on the trail until it ended and where it turned into an undisturbed rocky terrain.

He was careful as he navigated his way through the rocks and back up the mountain. The day had dawned, the dark skies now becoming an eerie glow of purple and gray. Sosa could hear the animals and birds coming alive at the sound and scent of a familiar stranger intruding upon their territory. But he was something ... someone ... they either knew or "somehow" remembered. Knowledge of Sosa had been passed down to the birds from their parents. Instinctively, those that did not know Sosa knew automatically that his appearance, his sudden encroachment, was a safe one.

Sosa finally edged his way up through the dew-covered terra firma and back to the very rear of his own estate. Where he now stood at was in a vast cathedral of ancient forest which was a thousand years in the making. He could literally smell the nine million acres of the massive Andean region; the moss, the hemlock and spruce, the cold and soggy smells wafting up from the Rio Chaparé and valley below.

He trudged slowly up the trail until he walked out onto an enormous clearing. He knew that this was the place. He laid the goat down and drew a knife. Next, he cut the dead animal open from its throat down through its belly and left it open, exposed. Sosa stepped away and walked back to the end of the clearing – about 80 feet away. By this time his men had caught up to him, out of breath.

"Quiet." Sosa spoke in a low voice as he took a seat on a fallen tree. The seven heavily-armed men sat down on either side of him and waited.

By now the purplish-gray skies had disappeared and the coming sun had added a pink blush to it. High in the trees a band of spider monkeys were screaming at the top of their lungs. The men all wondered why when the monkeys had been silent moments ago. The spider monkeys had a number of enemies; namely, the harpy eagle, South America's greatest aerial predator. However, the spider monkeys had a long list of enemies to worry about. There was also the short-eared dog, Azara's fox, the Andean fox, the maned wolf, the jaguar, and others, but none were as spider monkey-hungry than the harpy eagle. These magnificent, enormous gray eagles were the true kings of the Andes …

The Amazon covers 40% of South America and the scarlet and green-winged macaws (such as those Sosa had living at the Pentagon) inhabit all 40%. The same for the rose-crowned parakeet, and the meat-eating menaces such as the giant petrel, caracaras, and Bolivia's national bird: the Andean condor. The harpy eagle is a living nightmare for all of them.

"*Mira* [Look]." Sosa pointed to the sky. "They smell the blood."

The giant petrels came in first, briefly eyed the eight men who were eyeing them, then their ravenous feast began. At first there were only two of the brown petrels, and then a dozen more were there, tearing at the soft entrails of the goat, Sosa's blood sacrifice to the Andes. Before long, the petrels were bombarded with company: caracaras. The petrels, seriously out-numbered, conceded the loss of the tasty prize and stood aside. As it is known, the aggressive caracaras are nothing more than feathered food tasters for who came next: the black vultures. They came in and bullied the entire table.

However, as is the case with any bully, one punch in the nose and he's not a bully anymore. That was the case when the great Andean condor arrived on the scene squawking, mouth open wide, ready for a fight. Sosa and his men observed what was probably the largest mass-gathering of Andean condors in the world on the cliffs of El Chaparé. The goat got devoured by the birds until an enormous adult male patriarch arrived. All he had to do was show up and all the others, out of respect, moved out of his way. He took his time eating while the juveniles fought over the scraps.

"Look at them," Sosa whispered. "They live to be about fifty years or more. I remember him from when I was a kid. He has to be close to fifty. You see twenty, thirty generations there."

When the patriarch was done he hopped over in Sosa's direction and stared at him. The 30-pound patriarch had eaten straight out of Sosa's hand in the past but only while he was alone. Sosa stepped forward and slowly approached the old condor. The huge male spread his wings and stood still. Sosa crouched down and the bird looked around at the other men

30 feet away, not trusting them. Sosa reached out to touch him and the bird allowed it but only for a moment.

"You remind me of me," Sosa whispered to him.

The bird used the clearing for its runway and soared off into the distance. It was also time for Sosa to leave.

"Come on, *muchachos*."

$$$$$

It was a horrible thing to have to do but Sosa had allowed the seven-year-old Uru Uru girl – Yasca Angelica Cano-Muños – to view the 400 dead bodies recovered by his men. From the outset they had all been refrigerated inside of his tractor trailers. He had been conducting some very important business in Villa Tunari with Tato, Nancho, Benny, and Javier as little Yasca tagged along with them. They had been made aware that the dead were being made available for public viewing by the government in La Paz prior to being turned over to the Coroner's Office. By 3:30 p.m. the men had made the 360-mile trip from Villa Tunari to La Paz in Sosa's private jet.

Yasca was brave as she walked around the bodies laid out on display in the grassy center of Bolivar Park. The bodies were inside of body bags and there were hundreds of people and news cameras there capturing it all. Fortunately, the bodies were in good enough condition for Yasca to positively identify her missing family members. Seeing her small finger point each of them out was heartbreaking. She was very sad but she stayed composed.

"My mom," she pointed, looking up at Sosa and his men, Yasca's guardian angels. "My papa … my brother … my baby brother … my sister …" One by one she continued.

In all, she was able to point out seven people but she said there were others.

"We'll try to find them for you, *mamita*," Sosa swore to her. "The others, we'll bury them in a place you can always go see them. And, *I swear* to you, you'll have *us* as your family now. You're a princess and you'll live in a castle."

"Me and Bonnie?" she asked in her small voice.

Sosa held in his tears. "You and Bonnie."

Sosa picked her up and kissed her cheek.

CHAPTER THIRTY-SIX

Elvira Montana
New Rochelle, New York
October 26, 1984

Elvira's blue eyes perused the faces of the two closest people in her life until they were all done telling their story. The envelope that the death messenger had left behind was simply a routing number for UBS Bank in Switzerland, and the nine-digit PIN to a numbered account.

"Those men he named," Nina broke through Elvira's thoughts as the three women sat in front of the living room fireplace catching the warmth from the fire as it burned. "Gaspar ... Nacho ... the Diaz Brothers. You know them?"

Elvira was still numb and processing what had taken place. "Yeah. Gaspar Gomez, Nacho Contreras, aka El Gordo, and Nolo and Vito Diaz. Cuban Mafia, Miami drug kingpins, strip club owners, they run high-stakes gambling outfits, prostitution, porno films, loan-sharks, underaged girls, international sex slavery, et cetera. Real dirtbags, worse than V.D. on a petri dish. Keep in mind that I was just the wife ... I mean sometimes these guys stopped at our table to say hi. That's it. I couldn't help but to know who was who."

"Tony owed them all this money?" Nina asked hysterically.

"No!" Elvira snapped angrily. "You just saw a filthy, maniac psycho, waving a knife and a gun in your faces and you don't see what this is?!" Elvira was clearly shaken up about it.

Nina, feeling sheepish, looked down at her lap.

"It's a stick-up!" Elvira yelled at her. "A robbery! *Pressure* by these gangsters and killers! Extortion. You need me to spell it out for you?! It's extortion! A Mafia shakedown!"

"She's just a *nurse*, Elvira," Ally reasoned, her voice soft, as Nina ran out of the living room in tears. "She's a nurse. She knows nothing about the streets. *Nada.*"

Elvira heard her run all the way up the stairs. Sighing, her hands shaking, Elvira looked at Ally. "Classic Mafia stuff seen in Scorsese, DePalma, Oliver Stone movies, Mario Puzo books … [pausing] How are you holding up?"

"I'm a little tougher than her," Ally shrugged, recalling how the assassin had pulled her out of bed and threatened to kill her before binding her to the chair. Almara began to shudder and cry at what had happened to her. "I was naked, he felt me up some … gagged me with her panties and put a knife to my throat."

"Did he … ?" Elvira couldn't get the dreaded word "rape" word out.

"No, he didn't rape us," Ally answered knowingly. "Thank God."

"You and Nina," Elvira said slowly. "Why were you on the boat?"

Almara shrugged, shy in front of Elvira's piercing stare.

"I've known that there was *something*, Ally." Elvira was blunt. "Stop skipping around on what I'm asking! If you two humped, you humped. So what! *Why* were you on the boat?"

"To sleep together," Ally admitted. "But it was our first time, for what it's worth. I'm not lesbian but I desire a woman sometimes."

"No one else was hurt or killed on the ship?" Elvira probed.

"No." Ally shook her head and ran her fingers through her cute, black, pixie-cut hair. "I checked the staterooms ... I even saw the sleeping security in his car."

Elvira used the edge of the nearby sofa to rise to her feet. "Security? *What* security? Process termination notices for all members of our security through the Human Resources Manager. Effective immediately."

"*All* of them?"

"Are you a parrot or something? All means all."

"The cop can be useful is what I'm saying." Almara stood up and grabbed the cordless telephone.

"Depending on what you need done," Elvira countered. "I'm not paying security to sleep on the job. Y'all could have been killed."

Almara paused and looked at Elvira. "What kind of protection will we have then? At the docks, our employees at TMC, us, your properties?"

"Don't trust me to handle it?" Elvira asked, walking up to Ally and toying with one of her expensively-done hair locks.

Almara rapidly answered, "There's no question of trust. Just a thought."

Elvira slowly leaned in toward Almara's pretty face, looked her in the eyes, and heard her breathing pattern change. "If I kissed you ... would you want to do to me what you did to her?"

A smile broke out on Ally's face. "*Elvee!*"

Elvira waited.

"Well ... I've had fantasies," Ally admitted. "But ... it would be unethical. You're my client. I could lose my license."

"There's going to be a lot of women." Elvira stared at the Latin beauty. "Will they distract you? I don't want a rooster in my henhouse."

"They're *chicas*," Ally said back, indignant. "Playthings. I have fun with them. Nina ,,, I've been after her for a couple of years. She's young, innocent, beautiful, straight ... I just had to have her. I'm sorry for not telling you sooner. She hasn't distracted me. No one will."

"Maybe you can even keep them in line for me, huh?" Elvira was thinking. "You know, control them?"

"Perhaps," Almara chuckled lightly. "Anyone in particular you had in mind?"

"Natalia Navickova," Elvira stated. "Our company's Queen of Crimea."

"*Ooo!*" Ally squealed with delight. "Hmm. I could be wrong but I caught her eyeing Nina's butt. She's a boss. An alpha female. I'd love to have her in the palm of my hand. Let's see if it becomes necessary."

"Yeah. You do that." Elvira walked away but stopped. "Is there anything else?"

"I don't do girls, Ally," Elvira smiled. "The kind of sex I love is way out of the universe, as you know. But look ... there's a few things I want to say before I go handle our security situation. Don't ever withhold anything else from me again."

Almara put her head down. "I'm very sorry."

"I want *you* to approve each model our scouting crew recommends for a contract with TMC Models," Elvira went on. "We will scout locally but only for ethnic talent. The world is tiring of the same old thin white chicks. We'll use white girls but only European ones with unique looks. We'll fly the globe to hunt for the world's most beautiful girls – Asia, Mexico, Central America, South America, Africa. All different shades, uniquely beautiful young girls. We'll open up a modeling-acting-dance-vocational-educational academy and we'll provide housing only for those girls we award contracts to. Ages seven to eighteen primarily. I'll need you and Nina to help get the project off the ground because it's not as simple as it sounds. Focus first in New York – USA. Because going abroad to scout ethnic talent gets so time-consuming and complex. Those girls'll need passports, student visas, et cetera. Try not to focus on orphans or street kids because without parental consent to travel, we'll look like human traffickers. We need to be extremely careful with this. Try to avoid the girls with illnesses and emotional problems. It's an all-girls school so there'll be drama enough. I do want a *second* school for girls *and* boys who have been victims of sex-trafficking and molestation but first things first. Your job is to write us up the plan for both. You have eight weeks from today to have both plans on my desk."

"Okay." Almara looked at her boss, expectant.

"You, Nina, me," Elvira said. "Let's apply for our gun carrier's permits. It's time we get armed."

Nina came back downstairs carrying two Fendi suitcases. "I'm going to stay with my mom and dad for a few days. I hope I have your blessing."

Elvira took a deep breath. "After what you went through … yeah, sure. But I'd rather you didn't leave. This is your home."

Nina nodded, but remained quiet.

"Are you leaving because I yelled at you?" Elvira inquired. "I'm sorry."

"It's okay," Nina told her. "I'm just sad. And scared."

Elvira walked up to Nina and slowly removed the suitcases from her hands. "You're gonna leave us and we love you? *I* love you and need you here. With me. *And* I know about you and Ally. I don't care. Okay?"

Nina looked over at Ally. "Okay."

"Still, if you really want to leave …" Elvira gave a reluctant shrug. "I won't stop you. Just don't leave like *this*. It isn't right. It's wrong. I can always send you and your parents to an all-expenses-paid trip at a later time," Elvira offered. "Plus, I've made a decision on your proposal to publish a book about my story."

Now Nina was all ears. "What? What'd you decide?"

"To write the book," Elvira stated.

Nina looked at Ally and then back at Elvira. "All-expenses-paid trip later – for me, my mom *and* my dad?"

Elvira held up her right hand. "All-expenses for the three of you but *after* my baby is born."

"Okay," Nina agreed. "Now … the book."

CHAPTER THIRTY-SEVEN

La Hacienda de Sosa
Cochabamba, Bolivia
October 25, 1984

Coming back from a catastrophic storm was not something that a country could do overnight. Bolivia, Sosa knew, would survive it just as it had survived *El Niño* some few years back. After spending in excess of one billion in U.S. currency on the efforts to help out his fellow countrymen, it was now time to turn his attention to other critically important matters on the agenda.

"Look, boss," Tato said as he carried a large stack of newspapers and magazines into the money vault on the lower level of the Pentagon. Tato spread the newspapers and magazines out onto the long table where Sosa had been reviewing the money ledgers. "They have suspicious undertones about you but they still talk okay. *New York Times, Los Angeles Times, USA Today,* and all of the Latin-American papers … and Diane Sawyer has an article in *Time* about you."

"Yeah, they made you look like Satan five weeks ago," Javi scoffed as he, Nancho, Benny, and Rafa picked up the reviews. "Now they have you looking like Mother Teresa."

"The power of the media," Rafa commented dryly. "It influences the world."

"No, Rafa," Sosa rebutted, picking up a handful of U.S. currency. "*Money* does. Mission accomplished."

"That taking in the girl and the dog," Nancho reminded them. "That was *genius*, boss."

"How you mean, Chito?" Sosa inquired.

"Because in the United States," Nancho began, "they think of a dog's rights before they think of a man's rights. Look at their movies, *chico*. Old Yeller, Benji, and Lassie. That Bonnie and Yasca did it."

"Rafa," Sosa changed the subject. "You have your hands full with what the *Señora* has regarding her plans with *Dulce*. She's been selfless over the past several weeks so I have to show her my appreciation. I'll let you in on what that will be but you have to go. I'm having a big corporate jet customized for *Dulce*. Keep that secret. And I'm also retiring all the airplanes and bringing in a brand new fleet."

Sosa passed out to each one of his top men a hefty bonus. "You've *all* been selfless. Here's something to have fun with. I don't want to see any of you for twenty-four hours. Go."

The Toros accepted the big stacks of cash and eyed Sosa strangely.

"Rafa, you leave with Yesenia for the States tomorrow so have your fun however you can have it ..." Sosa looked at the others. "Twenty-four hours. Go."

$$\$\$\$\$\$$

Later in the morning Sosa held a meeting with General Cucombre, General Bleyer, and General Meza inside of his lower-level office-study. The four men were in a highly secretive talk about Nicaragua and the Nicaraguan-Sandinistan War.

"I can't sleep thinking about this," Sosa was telling them. "For years we've known Nicaragua to be a hotbed of political unrest ... but Bolivia has had its own. After our last meeting I realized that we *must* explore this thing before it's too late."

"There were 'whispers' about it even back in '83 sometime. Maybe even in '82." Cucombre shrugged. "You knew that."

"But I wasn't hard-pressed in '82," Sosa responded. "This year has been chaotic. Four big seizures in the Caribbean, we lost Tony Montana, this Gutiérrez emerges, my jet fleet is showing signs of the millions of miles put on them, and I had to spend a billion dollars on this hurricane disaster. *Forget* '83. Fill me in on what I need to do to get in tight with the CIA so we can get free passes on our merch up the Pacific/Gulf waters and into the United States."

"That's the wrong route," Garcia Meza stated. "You don't get 'in with the CIA' *through* the CIA. You get to the CIA via CIA assets: the Contras. We've dealt with the CIA so ... I know."

"That was 1980," Sosa said. "This is different. I want to deal face to face."

"True," Meza nodded, thinking it over.

Sosa clasped his hands together and looked at Garcia Meza. "So, do I read your mind or ... ?"

"How do you think we got to power in 1980, Sosa?" General Meza probed.

"We financed the junta," Sosa stated. "Many of our own men lost their lives in the fighting. However, it wasn't me at the table with the CIA. What I want now is direct contact. *Cara a cara.*"

"If it was that simple I'd pick up the phone and make an appointment," General Meza dryly joked. "Believe me, I can use the cash after what I've been through."

"You're broke, General Meza?" Sosa asked, not believing it.

"Not yet," he replied. "I'm very embarrassed ... but after I left office I tried to stay low-key. I ... I messed up."

"What about the fifty-one million dollars you're into *La Corporación* for?" Sosa kept a straight face. "We all agreed as partners to loan you that cash with no interest because of the relationships you had over the years with Mujahideen leader Gulbuddin Hekmatyar in the Soviet-backed Afghan conflict, and the arms/opium deals you had going with the Iranians. What happened?"

"Things have been going wrong," Garcia Meza told him. "We lost the support of the CIA."

"The CIA," Sosa repeated. "Okay. We won't make this sit-down about your debt. You obviously have the way I need in order to establish something workable with the CIA. Let me ask you ... [pausing briefly to think] Without the CIA support in the 1980 coup d'état, would we have failed? Even though we spent two hundred fifty million dollars to get it done?"

"I think we would have failed," Meza nodded. "The U.S. could have chosen to intervene and stop us but they did not. They selected to help us because it benefitted their war efforts in El Salvador at the time."

"*Muy bien,*" Sosa nodded. "You need our help with the fifty-one million dollars ... we need your political contacts within the CIA ..."

"Actually, I believe that I can raise the fifty-one mil by selling off my boat and seafood companies in Costa Rica," Garcia Meza said confidently. "However, I'd rather keep them. In light of what you are seeking to do ... I am in position to help you establish invaluable air routes into the U.S. – and to help you to the table to establish a relationship with the CIA."

Sosa excused himself to the bathroom and while he did so, he felt a growing distrust for General Meza. Sosa thought about Meza's proposal carefully ...

$$$$$

Luis Garcia Meza Tejada, born August 8, 1932, in La Paz, Bolivia, was a career military officer who rose to the rank of general during the reign of dictator Hugo Banzer in 1971 through 1978. Meza became dictator in 1980. Prior to that, Meza had graduated from the military academy in 1952 and served as its commander from 1963 to 1964. He then rose to division commander in the late 1970s.

Garcia Meza became leader of the right-wing faction of the military of Bolivia, which was most disenchanted with the return to civilian rule. Many of the officers involved had been part of the Banzer dictatorship and disliked the investigation of economic and human rights abuses by the new Bolivian Congress. Moreover, they tended to regard the decline in popularity of the Carter administration in the United States as an indicator that soon a Republican administration would replace it – one that was more amenable to the kind of *pro*-U.S., more hardline, anti-communist dictatorship they wanted to reinstall in Bolivia. Ominously, many allegedly had ties to cocaine traffickers, namely Sosa, and made sure that portions of the military acted as their enforcers/protectors in exchange for extensive bribes which, in turn, were used to fund the 1980 'Cocaine Coup.' In other words, there had been a *conspiracy* to purchase the Bolivian government for themselves.

Backed with Sosa's cash, it was this military group that had pressured Bolivian President Lidia Gueiler (Meza's cousin) to install General Garcia Meza as Commander of the Army. Within months, the Junta of Commanders, headed by Garcia Meza, had forced a violent coup d'état – better known as the Cocaine Coup of July 17, 1980 – when several Bolivian intellectuals such as Marcelo Quiroga Santa Cruz were killed. When portions of the citizenry had resisted, as they had done in the failed putsch of November 1979, it had resulted in dozens of deaths. Many had been tortured. It was also known that the Argentine Army unit *Batallón de Inteligencia 601* had participated in the coup. Former Drug Enforcement Administration (DEA) agent Michael Levine had arrested two men with ties to Sosa and what the DEA had called the "Bolivian Cartel" (the primary cartel linked to the coup). Michael Levine had claimed that the CIA had intervened to drop charges against the two men (Diego "Buro" Gonzalo Pineiro-Cortez and Carlos "Lucho" Rodriguez-Pantoja), allowing them to escape their U.S. trial in 1979. Both men had returned to Bolivia and participated in the coup along with the aid of former Nazi war criminal Klaus Barbie. Levine had publicly alleged CIA cooperation with the coup.

An extremely conservative anti-communist, Garcia Meza had endeavored to bring a *Pinochet*-style dictatorship that had been intended to last twenty years. He had immediately outlawed all political parties, exiled opposition leaders, repressed the unions, and muzzled the press. He was backed by *La Corporación* associates such as Italian neofascist Stefano Delle Chiaie, continued help from Gestapo Nazi officer Klaus Barbie, and the most notorious of all was European neofascist Ernesto Milá Rodriguez, who had been accused of the 1980 Paris synagogue bombing. Among other foreign collaborators were professional torturers who had been imported in from the infamously repressive Argentine dictatorship of General Jorge Videla.

The Garcia Meza regime had become internationally known for its extreme brutality. The population had been repressed in the same ways as under the Banzer dictatorship. In January 1981, the Council on Hemispheric Affairs had named the Garcia Meza regime "*Latin America's most errant violator of human rights after Guatemala and El Salvador.*" Some 1,000 people had been killed by the regime's army and security forces in only 13 months of its reign. The regime's chief repressor had been the Minister of the Interior, Colonel Luis Arce Gomez, who had cautioned that all Bolivians who may be opposed to the new order should *"Walk around with their written Will under their arms."*

$$$$$

"When you say that you are 'in position' you mean what?" Sosa questioned him.

"The CIA is *definitely* training and arming Contra rebels," Meza replied. "At a CIA airbase in Costa Rica."

"And you know this how?"

"We own some old cargo planes at my company," Meza explained. "One of my pilots was approached by the Contras and asked if he would fly in and out of the U.S. and Nicaragua for their cause, and he was guaranteed one hundred percent safety if he ran into any legal problems."

"All right," Sosa said after a second. "I'm interested. But, first, let's have lunch and we'll figure this out on a full stomach."

CHAPTER THIRTY-EIGHT

Elvira Montana
New Rochelle, New York
October 27, 1984

"How sure are we that she has no one to turn to?" Gaspar Gomez asked. It was a general question directed to any of the other men who sat in the all-white decorated living room of Gaspar Gomez's multi-million-dollar Miami Beach estate.

Present in the room with him was Nacho "El Gordo" Contreras, Nolo and Vito Diaz, and Cuban Mafia attorney George Sheffield.

Gazing out of the panoramic view windows at the crashing waves of the Atlantic Ocean, it was Nolo who answered, "I'd say as sure as the hurricane moving toward that coastline out there."

"How will we know about the fifty-million-dollar transfer?" El Gordo wanted to hear precise details.

"The bank will call *that* phone right there." Gaspar pointed at the telephone sitting on the countertop of the bar.

Vito Diaz looked around at the others. "Okay, *compañeros*, in case she fails to meet the deadline ... who dies first?"

"That's easy," Gaspar lightly chuckled. "The Ukrainian woman. The business mind behind this conglomerate Elvira has created. My reasoning, of course, is to hit her where the finances are rather than where her home is. If we kill one of her two assistant-friends, she'll lose all rationale. They are all she has as far as family and friends go. So, we must be very, very careful. The situation is delicate. However, we will threaten to kill the two assistants next if she fails to pay."

$$$$$

New Rochelle, NY 10 a.m.

Elvira was at her New Rochelle home, wrapped up in a robe, fresh out of the shower, pondering what she knew for certain was a credible and dangerous threat. Many questions lingered … such as who was on the top of their kill list. She wondered if she should take Nina and Ally's advice and go to the cops. That suggestion did not sit well with Elvira. She could not trust cops, which was why it was so easy to fire Jack and all the others. *I'm not even living in that criminal underworld and they're threatening to kill me, and those closest to me, if I don't pay fifty million of my husband's fortune.*

Tears of anger quietly rolled down her pretty face as she sat curled up in the bedroom armchair, staring out the window. She already knew that she was not going to pay a *dime* to those cockroaches. She was not by any means a confrontational person who would pick up weapons and stand ready to fight. She *felt* like being violent – like a man – but she was practical. Practical *and* pregnant. El Gordo, Gaspar, and the Diaz Brothers all were aware that she could not fight them, and they also had to know that she had no killers to protect her. They were all dead.

Killers, she suddenly thought to herself.

She put her bare feet down on the carpet in reaction to what she had begun to think. She went into her walk-in closet and looked for a suitcase which had belonged to Tony. She found it and dragged it out to the enormous castle-sized bed she'd had customized by a former NASA employee. That employee had been in charge of the design and creation of the seat padding and bedding inside of NASA space shuttles. He now owned a mattress company.

After pulling the suitcase up onto the bed, she opened it and pulled from it bottles of Tony's cologne that she'd bought for him, several of his passports, and a distinctive, white photo album. She flipped open the U.S. passport and studied the official time and date stamps by various foreign customs personnel: Bolivia, Peru, Colombia, Venezuela, et cetera.

"Venezuela," she said aloud. "One of Tony and Manny's pick-up places was at a Venezuela shipping port," she whispered to herself.

She flipped through the wedding photo album until she found the photo she was looking for ... Elvira, Manny, Chi Chi, Gina, Tony, and many beautiful women in bikinis. She could see the women tanning themselves on the front upper deck of the super-yacht in 1983 (the yacht she had been so impressed with that she'd bought her own replica of it: *The Montana*). In the background of the photo she saw him standing there dressed in all-white linen, solid gold Rolex, a drink in hand, conversing with Tony.

"*Alejandro Sosa.*" She said it at the same time she felt her belly expand with fear and squeamishness. His name had been mentioned by the Federal agents and police as a possible suspect with the reach and capability of masterminding the massacre. "*Did you kill my Tony?*" she whispered to the photograph as she stared at the sinister crime figure.

She scratched her head and kept looking at Sosa's photo. *He's the only one I know who has the power to help me. To protect me and my child ... Nina, Ally, Mama, TMC. But at what cost? A man like Sosa will demand a price higher than cash. Men like him desire more than a person's word or money – he wants to own their soul. Tony spoke of Sosa as if he was a man who possessed Deity, something immortal.* Suddenly, she realized that she was attracted to Sosa.

"Elvira!" Almara suddenly was standing before her with a tray of delicious home-cooked food on it. "Snap out of it, girl. You have to eat and take these vitamins."

"Leave it and let me be alone for a while." Elvira clutched her white satin YSL robe closed around her and rushed into the bathroom. She used several paper towels to stem the flow of moisture streaming from between her legs. She whispered, *"What the hell is wrong with you, Elvee?* It's probably just the baby."

"Are you okay?" Ally asked from outside the closed door.

Elvira came out a few minutes later. "I'm fine ... What just happened to me is just ... too crazy to repeat. Trust me. I'm fine though."

Ally looked at her strangely. "Okay. You're acting really weird, boss."

"Go," Elvira kicked her out. "Find something to do."

Elvira searched through the suitcase again and located Tony's "little black book." Inside of it she searched for "Sosa." Tony had no one written down in the book by the name of Alejandro Sosa but there was the name "Alex" scrawled on the last page.

"Ally!" Elvira yelled. A few moments later she had to yell once more. *"Almara!"*

"What?!" Ally came rushing into the room only wearing a towel. "The beauty team is here. They were doing me."

"That sounds nasty." Elvira quickly took her vitamins when she noticed Ally examining the food tray. "Is the name Alex short for Alejandro?"

"That's why you called me?" Ally put her hand on her hip. "Yeah. Alejo or Alex. Why?"

"Bye, Ally." Elvira ate the food on the tray and stared at the phone numbers next to Alejandro's name. She looked at the picture once more and this time she was better able to control herself. "Alejandro Sosa ... you made me *cream* myself. God! What. Am, I. About. To. Get. Myself. Into."

She picked up the cordless telephone and dialed the U.S. exit code, which must be used when making any international calls. Then she dialed Bolivia's country code, *591*, followed by the Cochabamba city code, *4*, and then she dialed Sosa's seven-digit private eleven-line number.

"Sosa here," came the deep accented voice moments later.

In that instant ... she knew that she had stepped completely out of her lane and crossed over into something more evil and more sinister than ever before. But in a strange way, she desired it. Ordinary men, even rich men, did nothing to ignite Elvira's fire. This was her level.

"Mr. Sosa," she finally managed to squeak out.

"Yes," he stated, the connection exceptionally clear. "Who am I speaking to?" he wondered. Everyone who had his eleven line number he was familiar with their voice, but hers was strange.

"You may not know who I am," she told him. "My name is Elvira. I'm –"

"Elvira? Tony's wife?" he said almost immediately.

"Well, yes. His widow," she corrected him.

"I remember you very well," he reminded her. "The yacht party out in the ocean. Summer 1983. I saw you briefly but who could forget such a beautiful woman?"

"Thank you, Mr. Sosa," she said with sincerity. "I'm sorry to call you out of nowhere."

"I only wonder where you got this number," he stated.

"Tony's things," she informed him.

"How have you been?" he inquired. "Is everything well?"

"To be honest, no."

"No," he repeated. "Okay. What can I do to help? That's why you call, no?"

"That's why I called, yes." She took a deep breath. "I feel silly calling you. You ever hear the phrase people say: '*You only call me when you need something*'?"

"I have heard of that saying."

315

"I need something," she said. "From you. I need help. *Fast* help."

"Okay ..." He waited. When she hesitated, he convinced her to spit it out. "You are the widow of a man whom I considered to be a dear friend and brother. What do you need?"

She went ahead and explained everything. *"George Sheffield ... Nacho 'El Gordo' Contreras ... Gaspar Gomez ... The Diaz Brothers, Nolo and Vito of the Miami Cuban Mafia ..."*

She began the story from the reading of the Will by Sheffield, and how she'd felt as if he'd been pressing her to sell Montana Realty at the behest of someone, or something, bigger than him.

"So he's a mob lawyer," Sosa stated more than asked. "He represents a high-end criminal clientele only, yes?"

"Right," she replied and then went on. "I sold because I just wanted to leave Florida and put it all behind me. I moved to New York. Sheffield had me put under surveillance. He wanted to know, for the MCM, if I had my hands on Tony's *true* fortune. He had asked me straight up and I'd refused to give him details. I *did* have it. It was over a hundred million."

Sosa whistled. "Money that even God would kill for. Go on."

"I said screw it and claimed the money to the IRS," she revealed. "I settled what they offered me and now the rest of the money is legit. I've created The Montana Corporation which has cost me thirty million dollars of my own money and thirty million more in loans. Several big banks are betting on us. Yesterday my two closest assistants were tied up and terrorized and told to deliver me a message: Pay fifty million to a numbered Swiss account within seventy-two hours or they'll start killing."

"You have no security?" Sosa hit it head on.

"Guns do not mean we are secure," Elvira told him. "My properties and businesses are all vulnerable. I am in need of the type of security your *mom* has. Or, if you have a wife, that your *wife* has. I had cops who do *private* work as security. I had a bucket with no bottom in it. How can I water the horses with that? I fired them."

"I get it," Sosa assured her. "These mobsters ... I have knowledge of them from an associate of mine in Miami – Griselda Blanco. The lawyer I know of him through Tony. I'm not going to start a war with them. I don't believe that it's necessary. They think that you are alone now. That you have no muscle. I'm going to show them that you do. Just keep it in mind that you will have to return a favor for a favor."

"You want money."

He laughed at that. "No."

She hesitated. "Me?"

"I'd never disrespect you like that," he told her. "Although I'm certain you'd be paradise to have."

"I can't be who Tony was."

"Oh no!" he exclaimed. "You're reading me all wrong. I'm a businessman. I simply want to invest with you, make a lot of money with you. You need protection. I'll go one step more. I'll give you power. I'll *guarantee* to you that you'll never be threatened by them again. In return, you will be my business partner in the States."

"Agreed."

"Do you still own the Coral Gables mansion?"

"Yeah."

"Eight hours," he instructed her. "Be there."

The line went dead in her ear.

"Dear God ..." she sighed.

Elvira put a French-tipped pinky nail into her mouth and stared at the telephone. She sat and wondered if she'd done the right thing. She went back and forth in her mind, second-guessing herself.

317

She was accustomed to playing dangerous games with dangerous men. Hadn't she done the same sort of thing back when she'd been with Frank? *Well*, she thought, *desperate times call for desperate measures.*

Sosa was a powerful man. Just the thought of him, saying his name even, evoked fear, but that's what Elvira was betting on. Using Sosa's power and the "fear factor" he had to destroy her enemies. She stood up and looked at her beautiful form in the full-length mirror on the closet doors. She clasped her hands over her baby bump.

"I'll burn the world down to protect you," she whispered to her unborn. "I don't care who else has to die or be hurt, but we will survive ..."

To be continued ...

CAST

I. Mr. Sosa's crime syndicate and family:

- Alejandro César Dalmacci Sosa. Boss and drug overlord of an empire that stretches across the Andes, La Corporación Mafia Cruzena.

- Yesenia "Yessi" Dulce Sevilla Sosa. Miss Bolivia 1983, wife of Sosa, creator and owner of fashion empire Dulce Fashion & Design Co.

- Vicenté León Ramero Toro (AKA "Benny the Skull"). Arguably Sosa's dearest, most loyal and closest comrade. Benny delivered the killshot to "SCARFACE"/Tony Montana.

- Nancho Sebastián Lugo Toro. Top henchman of Sosa's and first cousin to Benny.

- Tatico Arturo Lugo Toro ("The Black Hulk"). Top henchman of Sosa's, first cousin to Benny, brother of Nancho.

- Javier Roberto Lugo Toro. Top henchman of Sosa's, first cousin to Benny, brother of Nancho and Tatico.

- Simona Mira Lugo Toro. Aunt to Benny and Benny's only sibling, Juca Belén. Simona is also mother of Nancho, Tatico, and Javier.

- Juca Belén Ayllón Toro. Mother of Catalina Lilli and Benny's older sister.

- Catalina Lilli Romero Toro (AKA "La Gata Negra"). The young mistress to Bolivia's most ruthless Army General and Minister of Defense (General Cucombre). She is Juca Belén's daughter and Sosa's hitter.

- Juan Gabriel Benino Cucombre ("General Cucombre"). Minister of Defense and the syndicate's high-level enforcer.

- Silvestre Haché Chabán Sosa ("Don Haché"). Father and "retired" Mafia Cruzena boss.

- Anabianca Rosalie Dalmacci Sosa ("Doña Rosalie"). Mother to Sosa and daughter of Italy's most infamous Mafia boss, Don Vittorio Dalmacci.

- Rafael "Rafa" Peluché Porras Amayo. Former child prisoner of the Shining Path (guerrillas) freed by Sosa, who adopted him into the family. Rafa is trusted enough to become Head of Security for Sosa's wife, Yesenia.

- Juan Carlos Sevilla Sosa. The son of Mr. and Mrs. Sosa.

- Yasca Angelica Cano Muñoz-Sosa. Adopted Uru Uru girl orphaned by a devastating hurricane which killed her entire family.

- Alberto Jésus Hernán Molina ("The Shadow"). The Sosa henchman killed by Tony Montana during the failed assassination of Dr. Orlando Gutiérrez in Manhattan (NY).

II. Mr. Sosa's private army (men)
and coca crops protectors:

- Sgt. Pappy Meza
- Diego "Buro" Gonzalo Pineiro-Cortez
- Felipe Mauricio Palacios-Borça

- Nono "Bushwacker" Carbajal
- Ivan Manuel Rendón
- "Monstro"
- "Machete"
- "Chili"
- "Mancha"
- "Bongo"
- "Cuchillo"
- Carlos "Lucho" Rodriguez Pantoja
- Edgar Simón Galvis-Zerboni
- Victor José Nava
- "Blackout"
- "Rock"
- "Lobo"
- "Gallo"
- "Chuletta"
- "Gatillero"
- "Chicky"

III. Mr. Sosa's private army (women):

- Alicia Anabella Camacho-Cucombre (General Cucombre's niece)
- Raquel "Rock Candy" Garza
- Yulissa Nyelli Suárez-Espinosa
- Blanca Flori Rodriquez-Sanchez
- Yulianna Dimaris González-Sarmiento
- Lucia Nesi Martinez-Aroyo
- Adriana del Sol Gómez-Sancha

- Maruja Selena Alonso-Sessa
- Acuzena Mina Fernandez-Calderón
- Yurisa Arias Garcia-Feliciano
- Aracely Daniela Lopez-Ramos
- Noe Amanda Pérez-Alvarez
- Mariana Cristela Diaz-Varela
- Sasha Bonita Castro Vásquez
- Claudia Lovi Romero-Diazayas
- Valentina Iris Suárez Mayorga
- Nelli Candice de Sousa-Solis
- Emilia Villa Blanco-Vega
- Marieli Bella de la Hoya-Ruiz
- Gabriela Anisa Torres-Dominguez
- Veronica Linda Ramirez-Martin
- Ana Maria Giménez-Iglesias
- Helena Lourdes Medina
- Ximena Salomé Acosta
- Amina Bello Aguirre-Burgos
- Kimberly Roberta Cabrera
- Felicia Louisa Molina-Rojas
- Frederica Chanel Paz
- Marilyn Andrea Bruno
- Estefania Penélope Romano
- Julia Sofia Serna
- Gabriela Jimenez ("The Jimenez Cousins")
- Renata Jimenez ("The Jimenez Cousins")
- Yana Teresa Romos-Nuñez
- Trinidad Chiasa Rossi

- Antonia Moreno Ramos
- Rebeca Rose Silva
- Dianna Camila Méndez
- Savana Madeline Espeja
- Jocely Rosa Hernández-Flores
- Carinna Assisa Pereyra
- Mariah Bernadina Ferrari-Ortiz
- Monica Luna Benitez-Herrera
- Liliana Endera Arias-Vidal
- Dafina Fernanda Otero
- Regina Korena Rey
- Suzena India Sobija
- Paulina Renata Russo
- Neftali Miranda Costa
- Angelica Aurilia Rios-Morales
- Luciana Maza ("The Maza Sisters")
- Victoria Maza ("The Maza Sisters")
- Macarena Maza ("The Maza Sisters")
- Coca Maza ("The Maza Sisters")

IV. Mr. Sosa's associates/partners in business:

- General Luis Garcia Meza-Tejada
(Former President/"Cocaine Dictatorship")
- General Hugo Banzer Suárez (Former Dictator)
- Colonel Luis Arce Gómez
- General David Ariel Diaz-Bleyer
- Klaus Barbie ("The Butcher of Lyon")
(Former Nazi Gestapo). Hired by Sosa to

train his armies.

V. Mr. Sosa's CIA/Nicaraguan Contra associates:

- CIA Agent David MacMichael
(His men: "Grant," "Colson," "Brooks," "Sal," "Wilcox," and "Calabrese")
- U.S. Marine Lieutenant Colonel Oliver North
- National Security Advisor Robert McFarlane
- The Contra Leaders: Eden Pastora
Hugo Spadafora
Alfonso Rebelo
Carlos Cabezas
Arturo Cruz
Julio Zavala
Sebastián Gonzalez-Mendiola

- Fuerza Democratica Nicaraguense (FDN):
Adolfo Calero, Colonel Enrique Bermudez

- CIA Operatives: Oscar Danilo Blandon Reyes,
Juan Norwin Meneses, Luis Enrique Meneses

VI. Mr. Sosa's drug cartel associates:

A.   The Medellín Cartel
- Pablo Escobar
- Gonzalo Rodriguez Gacha
- Carlos Lehder Rivas
- Griselda Blanco ("La Viuda Negra" or "The Black Widow")
- Fabio, Juan David, and Jorge Ochoa
- Felix Dixon Bates (U.S.)
- Carlos "Carlito" Bustamonte (U.S.)

B. The Cali Cartel

- Jonathan Almanza-Orejuela
- Jose Santacruz-Londono
- Gilberto Rodriguez-Orejuela

C. The Juarez Cartel

- Amado Carillo Fuentes ("El Señor de los Cielos" or "The Lord of the Skies")
- Vicente Carillo Fuentes ("El Viceroy")

VII. Mr. Sosa's friends/other staff/and associates:

- Alessandra Dominguez. Juan Carlos' nanny.

- Miguel "Cabayo" Ibañez. The African-American-Nicaraguan MS-13 gang capo who came to Sosa/Bolivia for refuge subsequent to killing a Los Angeles police officer.

- Juan Umala. Minister of the Miraflores Church of Christ in La Paz, Bolivia.

- Silas Ramirez Cruz. A Bolivian Army man sent by DOD to infiltrate the security detail of syndicate enemy Dr. Orlando Gutiérrez.

- Cassandra Acero Rossi. The Copacabana woman who presented her two young daughters and two young nieces to Sosa in the desperate hope of marrying them off to Sosa's men before her possible death from breast cancer.

- Ana Sophia Acero Rossi. The 15-year-old daughter of Señora Rossi.

- Alanna Romea Acero Rossi. The 16-year-old daughter of Señora Rossi.

- Sandra Ruth Rossi Cartegena. The 16-year-old niece of Señora Rossi.

- Milagro Maximma Rossi Cartegena. The 15-year-old niece of Señora Rossi and sister to Sandra Ruth.

VIII. Mr. Sosa's enemies:

- Dr. Orlando Gutiérrez. Bolivian human rights attorney-reporter who Sosa wanted dead for blowing the whistle on him and his crime syndicate. When Tony Montana fails to deliver on his promise to kill Gutiérrez, it leaves Sosa & friends vulnerable to international backlash. Now, it is critical to silence their high-profile threat so that La Corporación Mafia Cruzena can move forward.

- Martín Cassillas Vasquez. Bodyguard for Gutiérrez.

- Cespédes Villanueva. Commander for the Shining Path Guerrillas in Peru. After slaughtering Rafa's entire family, Rafa had been imprisoned by the group until, by happenstance, Sosa negotiated Rafa's release.

- Miska Hinski. A Russian model "hastily" killed by Yesenia and Rafa, who acted swiftly to cover up the crime. However, there are some very powerful people asking some questions about her death.

IX. Mrs. Montana's organization:

- Elvira Denise Hancock-Montana. The widow of slain kingpin Tony "Scarface" Montana.

- Rachel Janine Lee ("Nina" or "Black China Doll"). Nurse and personal assistant of Elvira's.

- Almara Daniela Belarios Quijano. A sassy Nuyorican clinical psychologist who's hired to be a personal drug counselor and assistant to Elvira.

- George Sheffield, Esq. Mafia attorney for the Miami Cuban Mafia, former attorney of Tony Montana's and he's hired briefly to represent Elvira in settling Tony's "Montana Realty Company."

• Georgina Montana ("Mama Montana"). Mother of Gina and Tony Montana.

• Viola Johnise Hancock. Elvira's mother.

• David Hancock. Elvira's pedophile father.

X. Mrs. Montana's other associates:

• Natalia Navickova. The sultry 42-year-old Crimean CEO of Elvira's company, "The Montana Corporation" ("TMC").

• Josef Epstein. Master architect from Epstein & Roache in White Plains, NY.

• Timothy Roache. Partner and second half of Epstein & Roache.

• Captain Bovello. Captain and operator of Elvira's 200-foot Riva superyacht.

• Jack Gordon. New Rochelle police officer hired by Elvira for private security.

XI. Miami Cuban Mafia ("MCM"):

• The Diaz Brothers (Nolo & Vito)
• Gaspar Gomez
• Nacho Contreras ("El Gordo")
• Lugo
• Ronnie and Miguel Echeverria

XII. Deceased "SCARFACE" cast:

• Tony Montana (Hit by Sosa)
• Frank Lopez (Hit by Tony Montana)

- Chi Chi (Hit by Sosa)
- Nick the Pig (Hit by Sosa)
- Omar Suárez (Hit by Sosa)
- Manolo "Manny" Ribera (Hit by Tony Montana)
- Angel Fernandez (Hit during the Sun Ray Motel shootout)
- Gina Montana (Hit by Sosa)
- Ernie (Hit by Sosa)

ACKNOWLEDGMENTS

Thank you, Lord God.

Next, my appreciation goes to Mike Enemigo and The Cell Block.

To the whole Scarface Nation, we got you with a whole series. Tony Montana forever, baby! "Who put this together!? Me! That's who!" Fuck whoever don't like it. Take it however.

Selena, my greatest friend since we met that fateful day in 1996 during a car crash of all things! Love you, mama.

My kids: LeAndre Christine ("LC"), Xiana, Little Lou, Mykela, and Xiaa (R.I.P.). I love you all for eternity. Hey Layanna, Grandad ain't forget you!

Shout out to my Urban Ain't Dead, LLC Fam – especially Elijah R. Freeman, CEO/Author/Publisher. And everyone at U.A.D. for all you've done to push, market and promote my *Hittaz: Get it Back in Blood; Hittaz 2: Real Killaz Don't Miss*, and all you're doing to get the rest of the series out to the public.

Thank you.

To all my readers. I appreciate you whether you buy the book or not. Y'all hearing my voice and showing support is key to everything.

Chad, Prissy (the best sister ever), Lashanna, Carlton, Max, Dad, and Tammy Price, I love each of you.

Universal Pictures, y'all see what's going on. The whole Scarface Nation wants that "Sosa" movie deal signed, sealed and delivered! All y'all gotta do is keep bangin' on Uni-versal Pictures' social media pages. They're reading every word.

Last, shout out to all my guys at James T. Vaughn who never switched up. Eric Rosa ("ER"), Claude LaCombe, Blood Nimrod, Trap, Page (Bronx NY), Heyward Evans, Randy Madric, Champ (Garvey), Lav, Mr. Pope (Baltimore) and Gotti (Mike Jones / Brooklyn NY), Sinba, E.S., Pete.

Lou Garden Price, Sr.
Paralegal.LouPrice1@Gmail.com

REFERENCES

1. *"Sexual Abuse Survivors"* by Kali Munro. ©All Rights Reserved.

2. *"The Eighties Club"* by Jason Manning. ©All Rights Reserved.

3. *"The Politics of Heroin: CIA Complicity in the Global Drug Trade"* by Alfred W. McCoy with Cathleen B. Read and Leonard P. Adams, III

4. *The Scarface Scriptbook* by Oliver Stone (pp. 193-196, IDW Publishing) (2007)

5. *The Scarface Scriptbook* by Oliver Stone (pp. 184-187, IDW Publishing) (2007)

ABOUT THE AUTHOR

LOU GARDEN PRICE, SR., always dreamed of being a writer like his early literary heroes: Donald Goines, Iceberg Slim and the late great Maya Angelou. In 1987 he read Sidney Sheldon's *Master of the Game* and from then on he was hooked. Between his time of growing up in the Bronx (NYC), graduating from Canisius College (NY), and traveling, he wrote a dozen street novels, short stories, heartbreaking poetry, including *Latin Heat* – under the sobriquet BP Love. It was during this juncture of his literary journey that he realized how much was missing in the street fiction genre he had confined himself to. He knew exactly what his writing lacked: risk, rogues, and epic characters as cold and ruthlessly unforgiving as the world we have all come to know. Currently Lou is working on his *HITTAZ* (Book Six) series.

THE CELL BLOCK
BOOK SUMMARIES

MIKE ENEMIGO is the new prison/street art sensation who has written and published several books. He is inspired by emotion; hope; pain; dreams and nightmares. He physically lives somewhere in a California prison cell where he works relentlessly creating his next piece. His mind and soul are elsewhere; seeing, studying, learning, and drawing inspiration to tear down suppressive walls and inspire the culture by pushing artistic boundaries.

THE CELL BLOCK is an independent multimedia company with the objective of accurately conveying the prison/street experience with the credibility and honesty that only one who has lived it can deliver, through literature and other arts, and to entertain and enlighten while doing so. Everything published by The Cell Block has been created by a prisoner, while in a prison cell.

THE BEST RESOURCE DIRECTORY FOR PRISONERS, $19.99 & $7.00 S/H: This book has over 1,450 resources for prisoners! Includes: Pen-Pal Companies! Non-Nude Photo Sellers! Free Books and Other Publications! Legal Assistance! Prisoner Advocates! Prisoner Assistants! Correspondence Education! Money-Making Opportunities! Resources for Prison Writers, Poets, Artists! And much, much more! Anything you can think of doing from your prison cell, this book contains the resources to do it!

A GUIDE TO RELAPSE PREVENTION FOR PRISONERS, $15.00 & $5.00 S/H: This book provides the information and guidance that can make a real difference in the preparation of a comprehensive relapse prevention plan. Discover how to meet the parole board's expectation using these proven and practical principles. Included is a blank template and sample relapse prevention plan to assist in your preparation.

THEE ENEMY OF THE STATE (SPECIAL EDITION), $9.99 & $4.00 S/H: Experience the inspirational journey of a kid who was introduced to the art of rapping in 1993, struggled between his dream of becoming a professional rapper and the reality of the streets, and was finally offered a recording deal in 1999, only to be arrested minutes later and eventually sentenced to life in prison for murder... However, despite his harsh reality, he dedicated himself to hip-hop once again, and with resilience and determination, he sets out to prove he may just be one of the dopest rhyme writers/spitters ever .... At this point, it becomes deeper than rap .... Welcome to a preview of the greatest story you never heard.

LOST ANGELS: $15.00 & $5.00: David Rodrigo was a child who belonged to no world; rejected for his mixed heritage by most of his family and raised by an outcast uncle in the mean streets of East L.A. Chance cast him into a far darker and more devious pit of intrigue that stretched from the barest gutters to the halls of power in the great city. Now, to survive the clash of lethal forces arrayed about him, and to protect those he loves, he has only two allies; his quick wits, and the flashing blade that earned young David the street name, Viper.

LOYALTY AND BETRAYAL DELUXE EDITION, $19.99 & $7.00 S/H: Chunky was an associate of and soldier for the notorious Mexican Mafia – La Eme. That is, of course, until he was betrayed by those, he was most loyal to. Then he vowed to become their worst enemy. And though they've attempted to kill him numerous times, he still to this day is running around making a mockery of their organization .... This is the story of how it all began.

MONEY IZ THE MOTIVE: SPECIAL 2-IN-1 EDITION, $19.99 & $7.00 S/H: Like most kids growing up in the hood, Kano has a dream of going from rags to riches. But when his plan to get fast money by robbing the local "mom and pop" shop goes wrong, he quickly finds himself sentenced to serious prison time. Follow   Kano as he is schooled to the ways of the game by some of the most respected OGs whoever did it; then is set free and given the resources to put his schooling into action and build the ultimate hood empire...

DEVILS & DEMONS: PART 1, $15.00 & $5.00 S/H: When Talton leaves the West Coast to set up shop in Florida he meets the female version of himself: A drug dealing murderess with psychological issues. A whirlwind of sex, money and murder inevitably ensues and Talton finds himself on the run from the law with nowhere to turn to. When his team from home finds out he's in trouble, they get on a plane heading south...

DEVILS & DEMONS: PART 2, $15.00 & $5.00 S/H: The Game is bitter-sweet for Talton, aka Gangsta. The same West Coast Clique who came to his aid ended up putting bullets into the chest of the woman he had fallen in love with. After leaving his ride or die in a puddle of her own blood, Talton finds himself on a flight back to Oak Park, the neighborhood where it all started...

DEVILS & DEMONS: PART 3, $15.00 & $5.00 S/H: Talton is on the road to retribution for the murder of the love of his life. Dante and his crew of killers are on a path of no return. This urban classic is based on real-life West Coast underworld politics. See what happens when a group of YG's find themselves in the midst of real underworld demons...

DEVILS & DEMONS: PART 4, $15.00 & $5.00 S/H: After waking up from a coma, Alize has locked herself away from the rest of the world. When her sister Brittany and their friend finally take her on a girl's night out, she meets Luck – a drug dealing womanizer.

FREAKY TALES, $15.00 & $5.00 S/H: *Freaky Tales* is the first book in a brand-new erotic series. King Guru, author of the *Devils & Demons* books, has put together a collection of sexy short stories and memoirs. In true TCB fashion, all of the erotic tales included in this book have been loosely based on true accounts told to, or experienced by the author.

THE ART & POWER OF LETTER WRITING FOR PRISONERS: DELUXE EDITION $19.99 & $7.00 S/H: When locked inside a prison cell, being able to write well is the most powerful skill you can have! Learn how to increase your power by writing high-quality personal and formal letters! Includes letter templates, pen-pal website strategies, punctuation guide and more!

THE PRISON MANUAL: $19.99 & $7.00 S/H: *The Prison Manual* is your all-in-one book on how to not only survive the rough terrain of the American prison system, but use it to your advantage so you can THRIVE from it! How to Use Your Prison Time to YOUR Advantage; How to Write Letters that Will Give You Maximum Effectiveness; Workout and Physical Health Secrets that Will Keep You as FIT as Possible; The Psychological impact of incarceration and How to Maintain Your MAXIMUM Level of Mental Health; Prison Art Techniques; Fulfilling Food Recipes; Parole Preparation Strategies and much, MUCH more!

GET OUT, STAY OUT!, $16.95 & $5.00 S/H: This book should be in the hands of everyone in a prison cell. It reveals a challenging but clear course for overcoming the obstacles that stand between prisoners and their freedom. For those behind bars, one goal outshines all others: GETTING OUT! After being released, that goal then shifts to STAYING OUT! This book will help prisoners do both. It has been masterfully constructed into five parts that will help prisoners maximize focus while they strive to accomplish whichever goal is at hand.

MOB$TAR MONEY, $12.00 & $4.00 S/H: After Trey's mother is sent to prison for 75 years to life, he and his little brother are moved from their home in Sacramento, California, to his grandmother's house in Stockton, California where he is forced to find his way in life and become a man on his own in the city's grimy streets. One day, on his way home from the local corner store, Trey has a rough encounter with the neighborhood bully. Luckily, that's when Tyson, a member of the MOBTAR, a local "get money" gang comes to his aid. The two kids quickly become friends, and it doesn't take long before Trey is embraced into the notorious MOB$TAR money gang, which opens the door to an adventure full of sex, money, murder and mayhem that will change his life forever... You will never guess how this story ends!

BLOCK MONEY, $12.00 & $4.00 S/H: Beast, a young thug from the grimy streets of central Stockton, California lives The Block; breathes The Block; and has committed himself to bleed The Block for all it's worth until his very last breath. Then, one day, he meets Nadia; a stripper at the local club who piques his curiosity with her beauty, quick-witted intellect and rider qualities. The problem? She has a man – Esco – a local kingpin with money and power. It doesn't take long, however, before a devious plot is hatched to pull off a heist worth an indeterminable amount of money. Following the acts of treachery, deception and betrayal are twists and turns and a bloody war that will leave you speechless!

HOW TO HUSTLE AND WIN: SEX, MONEY, MURDER EDITION $15.00 & $5.00 S/H: *How To Hu$tle and Win: Sex, Money, Murder Edition* is the grittiest, underground self-help manual for the 21st century street entrepreneur in print. Never has there been such a book written for today's gangsters, goons and go-getters. This self-help handbook is an absolute must-have for anyone who is actively connected to the streets.

RAW LAW: YOUR RIGHTS, & HOW TO SUE WHEN THEY ARE VIOLATED! $15.00 & $5.00 S/H: *Raw Law For Prisoners* is a clear and concise guide for prisoners and their advocates to understanding civil rights laws guaranteed to prisoners under the US Constitution, and how to successfully file a lawsuit when those rights have been violated! From initial complaint to trial, this book will take you through the entire process, step by step, in simple, easy-to-understand terms. Also included are several examples where prisoners have sued prison officials successfully, resulting in changes of unjust rules and regulations and recourse for rights violations, oftentimes resulting in rewards of thousands, even millions of dollars in damages! If you feel your rights have been violated, don't lash out at guards, which is usually ineffective and only makes matters worse. Instead, defend yourself successfully by using the legal system, and getting the power of the courts on your side!

HOW TO WRITE URBAN BOOKS FOR MONEY & FAME: $16.95 & $5.00 S/H: Inside this book you will learn the true story of how Mike Enemigo and King Guru have received money and fame from inside their prison cells by writing urban books; the secrets to writing hood classics so you, too, can be caked up and famous; proper punctuation using hood examples; and resources you can use to achieve your money motivated ambitions! If you're a prisoner who want to write urban novels for money and fame, this must-have manual will give you all the game!

PRETTY GIRLS LOVE BAD BOYS: AN INMATE'S GUIDE TO GETTING GIRLS: $15.00 & $5.00 S/H: Tired of the same, boring, cliché pen pal books that don't tell you what you really need to know? If so, this book is for you! Anything you need to know on the art of long and short distance seduction is included within these pages! Not only does it give you the science of attracting pen pals from websites, it also includes psychological profiles and instructions on how to seduce any woman you set your sights on! Includes interviews of women who have fallen in love with prisoners, bios for pen pal ads, pre-written love letters, romantic poems, love-song lyrics, jokes and much, much more! This book is the ultimate guide – a must-have for any prisoner who refuses to let prison walls affect their MAC'n.

THE LADIES WHO LOVE PRISONERS, $15.00 & $5.00 S/H: New Special Report reveals the secrets of real women who have fallen in love with prisoners, regardless of crime, sentence, or location. This info will give you a HUGE advantage in getting girls from prison.

THE MILLIONAIRE PRISONER: PART 1, $16.95 & $5.00 S/H

THE MILLIONAIRE PRISONER: PART 2, $16.95 & $5.00 S/H

THE MILLIONAIRE PRISONER: SPECIAL 2-IN-1 EDITION, $24.99 & $7.00 S/H: Why wait until you get out of prison to achieve your dreams? Here's a blueprint that you can use to become successful! *The Millionaire Prisoner* is your complete reference to overcoming any obstacle in prison. You won't be able to put it down! With this book you will discover the secrets to: Making money from your cell!

Obtain FREE money for correspondence courses! Become an expert on any topic! Develop the habits of the rich! Network with celebrities! Set up your own website! Market your products, ideas and services! Successfully use prison pen pal websites! All of this and much, much more! This book has enabled thousands of prisoners to succeed and it will show you the way also!

THE MILLIONAIRE PRISONER 3: SUCCESS UNIVERSITY, $16.95 & $5.00 S/H: Why wait until you get out of prison to achieve your dreams? Here's a new-look blueprint that you can use to be successful! *The Millionaire Prisoner 3* contains advanced strategies to overcoming any obstacle in prison. You won't be able to put it down!

THE MILLIONAIRE PRISONER 4: PEN PAL MASTERY, $16.95 & $5.00 S/H: Tired of subpar results? Here's a master blueprint that you can use to get tons of pen pals! *TMP 4: Pen Pal Mastery* is your complete roadmap to finding your one true love. You won't be able to put it down! With this book you'll DISCOVER the SECRETS to: Get FREE pen pals & which sites are best to use; successful tactics female prisoners can win with; use astrology to find love, friendship & more, build a winning social media presence. All of this and much more!

THE MILLIONAIRE PRISONER 5: FREE MONEY, $24.95 & $7.00 S/H: Wish you could find more FREE MONEY like your stimulus? Seeking an end to your money problems? Look no further! Here's a master blueprint that reveals all that's available! *Tmp 5: Free Money* is your complete roadmap to finding all the FREE MONEY options out there for convicts. You won't be able to put it down!

GET OUT, GET RICH: HOW TO GET PAID LEGALLY WHEN YOU GET OUT OF PRISON!, $16.95 & $5.00 S/H: Many of you are incarcerated for a money-motivated crime. But w/ today's tech & opportunities, not only is the crime-for-money risk/reward ratio not strategically wise, it's not even necessary. You can earn much more money by partaking in any one of the easy, legal hustles explained in this book, regardless of your record. Help yourself earn an honest income so you can not only make a lot of money, but say good-bye to penitentiary chances and prison forever! (Note: Many things in this book can even he done from inside prison.) (ALSO PUBLISHED AS *HOOD MILLIONAIRE: HOW TO HUSTLE AND WIN LEGALLY!*)

THE CEO MANUAL: HOW TO START A BUSINESS WHEN YOU GET OUT OF PRISON, $16.95 & $5.00 S/H: $16.95 & $5.00 S/H: This new book will teach you the simplest way to start your own business when you get out of prison. Includes: Start-up Steps! The Secrets to Pulling Money from Investors! How to Manage People Effectively! How To Legally Protect Your Assets from "them"! Hundreds of resources to get you started, including a list of "loan friendly" banks! (ALSO PUBLISHED AS *CEO MANUAL: START A BUSINESS, BE A BOSS!*)

THE MONEY MANUAL: UNDERGROUND CASH SECRETS EXPOSED! 16.95 & $5.00 S/H: Becoming a millionaire is equal parts what you make, and what you don't spend – AKA save. All Millionaires and Billionaires have mastered the art of not only making money, but keeping the money they make (remember Donald Trump's tax maneuvers?), as well as establishing credit so that they are loaned money by banks and trusted with money from investors: AKA OPM – other people's money. And did you know there are millionaires and billionaires just waiting to GIVE money away? It's true! These are all very-little known secrets "they" don't want YOU to know about, but that I'm exposing in my new book!

HOOD MILLIONAIRE; HOW TO HUSTLE & WIN LEGALLY, $16.95 & $5.00 S/H: Hustlin' is a way of life in the hood. We all have money motivated ambitions, not only because we gotta eat, but because status is oftentimes determined by one's own salary. To achieve what we consider financial success, we often invest our efforts into illicit activities – we take penitentiary chances. This leads to a life in and out of prison, sometimes death – both of which are counterproductive to gettin' money. But there's a solution to this, and I have it...

CEO MANUAL: START A BUSINESS BE A BOSS, $16.95 & $5.00 S/H: After the success of the urban-entrepreneur classic *Hood Millionaire: How To Hustle & Win Legally!*, self-made millionaires Mike Enemigo and Sav Hustle team back up to bring you the latest edition of the Hood Millionaire series – *CEO Manual: Start A Business, Be A Boss!* In this latest collection of game laying down the art of "hoodpreneurship", you will learn such things as: 5 Core Steps to Starting Your Own Business! 5 Common Launch Errors You Must Avoid! How To Write a Business Plan! How To Legally Protect Your Assets From "Them"! How To Make Your Business Fundable, Where to Get Money for Your Start-up Business, and even How to Start a Business With No Money! You will learn How to Drive Customers to Your Website, How to Maximize Marketing Dollars, Contract Secrets for the savvy boss, and much, much more! And as an added bonus, we have included over 200 Business Resources, from government agencies and small business development centers, to a secret list of small-business friendly banks that will help you get started!

PAID IN FULL: WELCOME TO DA GAME, $15.00 & $5.00 S/H. In 1983, the movie *Scarface* inspired many kids growing up in America's inner cities to turn their rags into riches by becoming cocaine kingpins. Harlem's Azie Faison was one of them. Faison would ultimately connect with Harlem's Rich Porter and Alpo Martinez, and the trio would go on to become certified street legends of the '80s and early '90s. Years later, Dame Dash and Roc-A-Fella Films would tell their story in the based-on-actual-events movie, *Paid in Full.*

But now, we are telling the story our way – The Cell Block way – where you will get a perspective of the story that the movie did not show, ultimately learning an outcome that you did not expect.

Book one of our series, *Paid in Full: Welcome to da Game,* will give you an inside look at a key player in this story, one that is not often talked about – Lulu, the Columbian cocaine kingpin with direct ties to Pablo Escobar, who plugged Azie in with an unlimited amount of top-tier cocaine at dirt-cheap prices that helped boost the trio to neighborhood superstars and certified kingpin status... until greed, betrayal, and murder destroyed everything....(ALSO PUBLISHED AS *CITY OF GODS.*)

OJ'S LIFE BEHIND BARS, $15.00 & $5 S/H: In 1994, Heisman Trophy winner and NFL superstar OJ Simpson was arrested for the brutal murder of his ex-wife Nicole Brown-Simpson and her friend Ron Goldman. In 1995, after the "trial of the century," he was acquitted of both murders, though most of the world believes he did it. In 2007 OJ was again arrested, but this time in Las Vegas, for armed robbery and kidnapping. On October 3, 2008 he was found guilty sentenced to 33 years and was sent to Lovelock Correctional Facility, in Lovelock, Nevada. There he met inmate-author Vernon Nelson. Vernon was granted a true, insider's perspective into the mind and life of one of the country's most notorious men; one that has never been provided...until now.

THE MOB, $16.99 & $5.00 S/H: PaperBoy is a Bay Area boss who has invested blood, sweat, and years into building

The Mob – a network of Bay Area Street legends, block bleeders, and underground rappers who collaborate nationwide in the interest of pushing a multi-million-dollar criminal enterprise of sex, drugs, and murder.

Based on actual events, little has been known about PaperBoy, the mastermind behind The Mob, and intricate details of its operation, until now.

Follow this story to learn about some of the Bay Area underworld's most glamorous figures and famous events...

MOB TALES, $16.95 & $5.00 S/H. In 1992, Suge 'The Mobfather' Knight launched Death Row Records with a rumored 1.5-million-dollar investment from then-incarcerated drug kingpin Michael 'Harry O' Harris. Under Suge Knight's leadership, Death Row would go on to boast a roster consisting of some of the greatest names in hip-hop history, such as Dr. Dre, Snoop Dogg, and Tupac Shakur. Suge ultimately generated well over 200 million dollars selling records that detailed life in the streets.

Now, from his prison cell, Suge Knight has partnered up with incarcerated publishing boss Mike Enemigo, and longtime Mob affiliate O.G. Silk, to create Death Row Publishing, and drop a new series, *Mob Tales*, as a platform to shed light on some of the hottest incarcerated street-lit authors in the game today. Each book in this series will be a collection of stories written by those who have lived that of which they write, and who are surely to be among the next generation of street-lit legends.

SOSA: THE PRICE OF POWER (BOOK ONE), $16.95 & $5.00 S/H: The 1983 classic gangster film *Scarface* wooed over a billion fans worldwide, but it ended in the abrupt, violent massacre of Tony and his squad at the behest of ruthless Bolivian crime boss, Alejandro Sosa.

Since then, *Scarface* has birthed a nation of diehards who have been waiting decades for a Hollywood response. The wait is now over. Tony is dead, but his legacy lives inside of Elvira, who has resurfaced in the riveting masterpiece saga entitled: *Sosa; The Price of Power*. First, Sosa must scramble to pick up the pieces which were left shattered by the betrayal of Tony.

The true *Scarface* fan will be glued to the coldblooded cunning, the bigger-than-life characters who Sosa surrounds himself with, and the skilled moves he makes on an international scale. For the blonde bombshell, the game becomes life or death. Who can't remember Tony's enemies: Gaspar Gomez, the Diaz brothers and others? They are the Miami Cuban Mafia and are hunting Elvira down for the huge nine-figure fortune her husband left behind....

AOB, $15.00 & $5.00 S/H. Growing up in the Bay Area, Manny Fresh the Best had a front-row seat to some of the coldest players to ever do it. And you already know, A.O.B. is the name of the Game! So, When Manny Fresh slides through Stockton one day and sees Rosa, a stupid-bad Mexican chick with a whole lotta 'talent' behind her walking down the street tryna get some money, he knew immediately what he had to do: Put it In My Pocket!

AOB 2, $15.00 & $5.00 S/H.

AOB 3, $15.00 & $5.00 S/H.

PIMPOLOGY: THE 7 ISMS OF THE GAME, $15.00 & $5.00 S/H: It's been said that if you knew better, you'd do better. So, in the spirit of dropping jewels upon the rare few who truly want to know how to win, this collection of exclusive Game has been compiled. And though a lot of so-called players claim to know how the Pimp Game is supposed to go, none have revealed the real. . . Until now!

JAILHOUSE PUBLISHING FOR MONEY, POWER & FAME: $24.99 & $7.00 S/H: In 2010, after flirting with the idea for two years, Mike Enemigo started writing his first book. In 2014, he officially launched his publishing company, The Cell Block, with the release of five books. Of course, with no mentor(s), how-to guides, or any real resources, he was met with failure after failure as he tried to navigate the treacherous goal of publishing books from his prison cell. However, he was determined to make it. He was determined to figure it out and he refused to quit. In Mike's new book, *Jailhouse Publishing for Money, Power, and Fame*, he breaks down all his jailhouse publishing secrets and strategies, so you can do all he's done, but without the trials and tribulations he's had to go through...

KITTY KAT, ADULT ENTERTAINMENT RESOURCE BOOK, $24.99 & $7.00 S/H: This book is jam packed with hundreds of sexy non nude photos including photo spreads. The book contains the complete info on sexy photo sellers, hot magazines, page turning bookstore, sections on strip clubs, porn stars, alluring models, thought provoking stories and must-see movies.

PRISON LEGAL GUIDE, $24.99 & $7.00 S/H: The laws of the U.S. Judicial system are complex, complicated, and always growing and changing. Many prisoners spend days on end digging through its intricacies. Pile on top of the legal code the rules and regulations of a correctional facility, and you can see how high the deck is being stacked against you. Correct legal information is the key to your survival when you have run afoul of the system (or it is running afoul of you). Whether you are an accomplished jailhouse lawyer helping newbies learn the ropes, an old head fighting bare-knuckle for your rights in the courts, or a hustler just looking to beat the latest write-up – this book has something for you!

PRISON HEALTH HANDBOOK, $19.99 & $7.00 S/H: The *Prison Health Handbook* is your one-stop go-to source for information on how to maintain your best health while inside the American prison system. Filled with information, tips, and secrets from doctors, gurus, and other experts, this book will educate you on such things as proper workout and exercise regimens; yoga benefits for prisoners; how to meditate effectively; pain management tips; sensible dieting solutions; nutritional knowledge; an understanding of various cancers, diabetes, hepatitis, and other diseases all too common in prison; how to effectively deal with mental health issues such as stress, PTSD, anxiety, and depression; a list of things your doctors DON'T want YOU to know; and much, much more!

All books are available on thecellblock.net website.

You can also order by sending a money order or institutional check to:

The Cell Block
PO Box 1025
Rancho Cordova, CA 95741